PRAISE FOR THE OTHERWORLD NOVELS

"Yasmine Galenorn creates a world I never want to leave."
—Sherrilyn Kenyon, #1 *New York Times* bestselling author

"Erotic and darkly bewitching . . . a mix of magic and passion."
—Jeaniene Frost, *New York Times* bestselling author

"Yasmine Galenorn is a hot new star in the world of urban fantasy."
—Jayne Ann Krentz, *New York Times* bestselling author

"Yasmine Galenorn is a powerhouse author; a master of the craft who is taking the industry by storm, and for good reason!"
—Maggie Shayne, *New York Times* bestselling author

"Spectacularly hot and supernaturally breathtaking."
—Alyssa Day, *New York Times* bestselling author

"Simmers with fun and magic."
—Mary Jo Putney, *New York Times* bestselling author

"Yasmine Galenorn's imagination is a beautiful thing."
—*Fresh Fiction*

"Galenorn's gallery of rogues is an imaginative delight."
—*Publishers Weekly*

"Pulls no punches . . . [and] leaves you begging for more."
—*Bitten by Books*

"Her books are always enchanting, full of life and emotion as well as twists and turns that keep you reading long into the night."
—*Romance Reviews Today*

"Explore this fascinating world." —*TwoLips Reviews*

"As always, [Galenorn] delivers intriguing characters, intricate plot layers, and kick-butt action." —*RT Book Reviews* (★★★★)

Berkley titles by Yasmine Galenorn

The Otherworld Series

WITCHLING
CHANGELING
DARKLING
DRAGON WYTCH
NIGHT HUNTRESS
DEMON MISTRESS
BONE MAGIC
HARVEST HUNTING
BLOOD WYNE
COURTING DARKNESS
SHADED VISION
SHADOW RISING
HAUNTED MOON
AUTUMN WHISPERS
CRIMSON VEIL
PRIESTESS DREAMING
PANTHER PROWLING
DARKNESS RAGING

The Indigo Court Series

NIGHT MYST
NIGHT VEIL
NIGHT SEEKER
NIGHT VISION
NIGHT'S END

The Fly by Night Series

FLIGHT FROM DEATH

The Whisper Hollow Series

AUTUMN THORNS

Anthologies

INKED
NEVER AFTER
HEXED

Specials

ICE SHARDS
ETCHED IN SILVER
THE SHADOW OF MIST
FLIGHT FROM HELL

Berkley Prime Crime titles by Yasmine Galenorn

GHOST OF A CHANCE
LEGEND OF THE JADE DRAGON
MURDER UNDER A MYSTIC MOON
A HARVEST OF BONES
ONE HEX OF A WEDDING

Yasmine Galenorn writing as India Ink

SCENT TO HER GRAVE
A BLUSH WITH DEATH
GLOSSED AND FOUND

Darkness Raging

An Otherworld Novel

YASMINE GALENORN

BERKLEY BOOKS, NEW YORK

BERKLEY

An imprint of Penguin Random House LLC
375 Hudson Street, New York, New York 10014

DARKNESS RAGING

A Berkley Book / published by arrangement with the author

ISBN: 978-0-515-15477-1

PUBLISHING HISTORY
Berkley mass-market edition / February 2016

PRINTED IN THE UNITED STATES OF AMERICA

10 9 8 7 6 5 4 3 2 1

Cover art by Tony Mauro.
Cover design by Danielle Abbiate.
Map by Andrew Marshall, copyright © 2012 by Yasmine Galenorn.
Interior text design by Laura K. Corless.

Penguin
Random
House

Dedicated to

Samantha Tennant, whose contribution to the Pixel Project in exchange for this dedication helped make the world safer for women.

As a survivor of abuse, I thank you.

ACKNOWLEDGMENTS

Thank you to everyone who has helped me get to this point:

Samwise: My husband and consort.

Meredith Bernstein: My agent.

Kate Seaver: My editor.

Tony Mauro: My cover artist.

Andria Holley and Jenn Price: My assistants.

My furry "Galenorn Gurlz": My feline brigade.

Ukko, Rauni, Mielikki, and Tapio: My spiritual guardians, and Brighid, my muse.

To my readers: Your support by buying my books helps keep my work continuing on. You can find me on the net on my site: Galenorn.com. You can also find an Otherworld wiki on my website. If you write to me snail mail (see my website for the address or write via my publisher), please enclose a stamped, self-addressed envelope with your letter if you would like a reply.

The Painted Panther
Yasmine Galenorn

Hell is empty and all the devils are here.

—SHAKESPEARE

True love is selfless. It is prepared to sacrifice.

—J. P. VASWANI

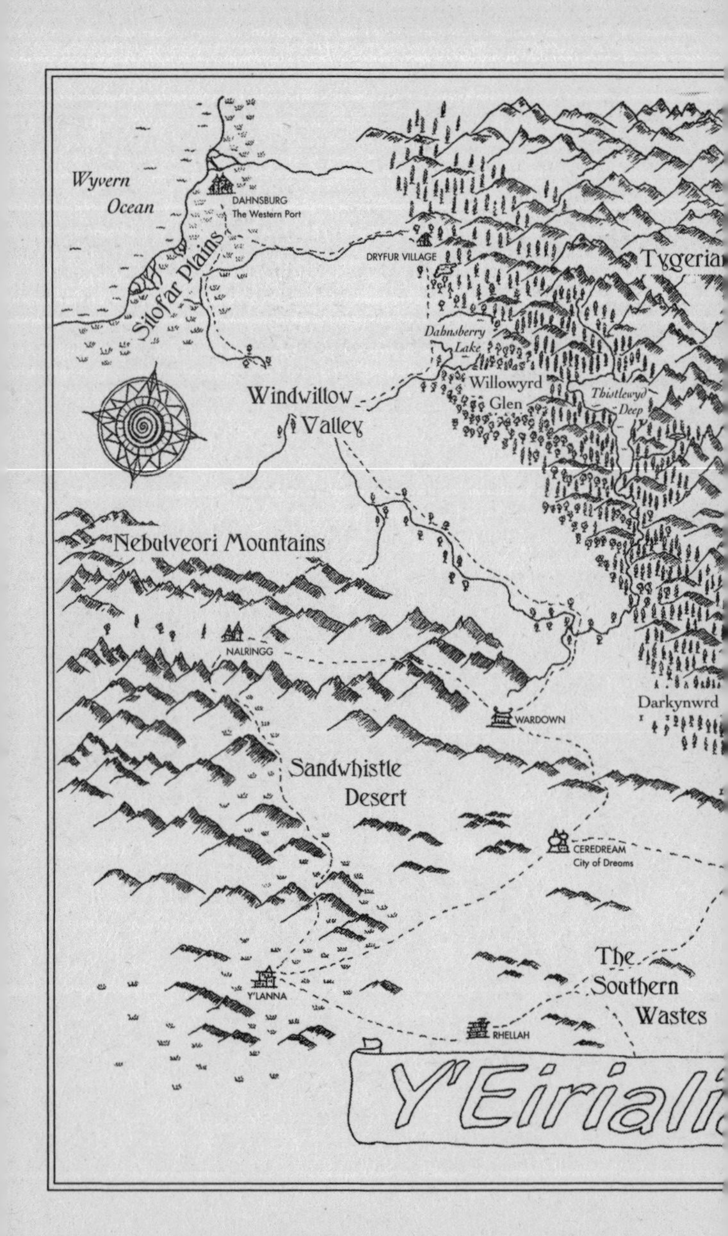
Wyvern Ocean
DAHNSBURG
The Western Port
Silofar Plains
DRYFUR VILLAGE
Tygeria
Dahnsberry Lake
Willowyrd Glen
Thistlewyd Deep
Windwillow Valley
Nebulveori Mountains
NALRINGG
WARDOWN
Darkynwrd
Sandwhistle Desert
CEREDREAM
City of Dreams
The Southern Wastes
Y'LANNA
RHELLAH
Y'Eiriali

The Golden Wood
SILVER FALLS
Mountains
SVARTALFEIM
Kelvashan
The Elvan Lands
Arvanal Lake
GYLDYN
City of the Goldensun
ELQANEVE
SANDSTONE FALLS
Sandstone Flats
GUILYOTON
The Shadow Lands
ALADRIL
City of Seers
Ranakwa Fens
Y'ELESTRIAL
Lake Y'Leveshan
Erunzi Falls
Starsbyl Lake
Shalebnar River
TERIAL
The Eastern Port
Y'SHAYSAR
Mirami Ocean
astar

Chapter 1

"Any activity so far?" Nerissa hustled through the kitchen door and made for the table, where Camille, Delilah, and I were sitting. We were listlessly toying with whatever we could find to keep our minds occupied. All our phones were on the table, waiting. The minute one of them rang, we'd spring into action—and we knew there *would* be a call. Until then, Camille was reading, Delilah was working a crossword puzzle, and I was trying to unknot a jumble of thin gold chains that had gotten tangled up when I tossed them in the jewelry box without thinking.

Dropping into the chair next to me, Nerissa used the towel hanging around her neck to wipe the sweat off her brow. She had just returned from her workout with Jason Binds, a mechanic-cum-martial-arts-instructor. He was attempting to turn her into a lean, mean shredding machine. Her face was clear of makeup, her workout top was soaked through with perspiration, and her tawny mane of hair was pulled back in a tight ponytail, although a few wisps had escaped to straggle out. But to me, my wife was the most beautiful sight in the world.

"No, but it's only a matter of time. We haven't had a quiet night in several weeks." I pushed the chains aside. I had doused them in oil and was trying to use a straight pin to separate the tangle. I wiped my oily fingers on a napkin and reached for her hand.

Camille and Delilah had been awake since around five P.M. I, of course, rose at sunset, which was—in early May—running closer to eight thirty. I longed for autumn and winter, when the nights were longer and I could rise earlier and stay up longer. Sometimes I thought I should move to Alaska for half the year, when the darkness held sway over the land. My sisters had switched over to a nocturnal schedule because, so far, all of the attacks had come during the night—usually around two or three A.M.

Everything had snowballed so quickly that we gave up waiting around, and now—instead of simply responding to the danger, we had gone on the offensive. At the first sign of dusk, the guys headed out, hunting for any signs of trouble as they scoured the city. My sisters and I waited at home for their call.

If they found a problem before someone reported a skirmish to the Faerie-Human Crime Scene Investigation Unit, the men called us and we headed out to put out the fire. If the FH-CSI got the call first, they transferred it over to us. Either way, we were front on the line. So far, we had managed to keep this nightmare under wraps, but we were barely holding on. All it would take would be one misstep or overlooked incursion and everything would blow sky high. Once news of what had been going on hit the papers, the ensuing panic would take over from there. We were trying to prevent that panic from happening in the first place.

Earlier, the three of us had pored over a map of the city, trying to figure out if there was some pattern to the attacks. Never mind that we'd already gone over it a dozen times—the activity kept us busy, and right now, busy was good because waiting around like this was getting on all of our nerves.

"I need to shower and change." Nerissa pushed back her chair and stood.

"Hurry up and I'll have your dinner waiting." Iris set a

plate of grilled cheese sandwiches on the table in front of Camille and Delilah. She handed them mugs of hot tomato soup. "I'm not cooking anything extravagant because right now, fancy takes too much time. I want to make certain you all get good, solid food into you."

Nerissa nodded. "I won't be long. I'm so sweaty from working out, and I need to rinse off, but I'll be quick. Thank gods there's been a lull tonight."

I glanced up at her. "So, how did it go at Jason's?"

"Good. He says that I'm learning extremely fast." She shrugged. "I wish I could make more progress, but he seems satisfied so I guess I should take what I can get." With a glance at the clock, she added, "I'd better get moving. We really don't have the luxury of just hanging out anymore, I guess." Sounding sad, she leaned down to meet my lips.

The proximity to her body and her hot breath on my cheek made me ache. I wanted nothing more than to curl up with her in the living room. I wanted to cuddle with her and Maggie while we watched the Demon Twins play video games and listened to Iris and Hanna argue over who made the best pie. Basically, I wanted to just go about my daily routine and forget that all of this was happening. But reality was biting us on the ass, hard and fast and with sharp teeth. As Chase was fond of saying, *If wishes were pennies, we'd all be rich.*

"Don't be too long. We haven't had a call yet tonight and you know it's going to come."

As she headed toward the bath near the laundry room, a high-pitched note sounded from a ring of crystals sitting on an end table in the kitchen. Nerissa froze as Camille ran over to the wards. Delilah and I immediately shifted into prep-for-battle mode. Nobody had broken through to our land lately, but with everything going on, we didn't dare ignore the rogue portal out in the backyard. Even though it had been tuned to the realm of the Elder Fae, the very fact that it *was* a portal still made our home a dangerous target. And not five miles away was Grandmother Coyote's portal to Otherworld. Though, I thought with a silent grin, I would hate to see what she would do to anybody who tried to mess with her.

Camille ran her hands over the crystals, which had calmed down. "Nothing to worry about. I think it's just some ghost or something passing through. But, Delilah, can you run and ask the guards to make a sweep around the land? Just to be on the safe side."

"On it." Kitten was up and out the door before Camille could say another word.

"Okay, I'm getting my shower in." Nerissa planted another kiss on my lips. I lingered in her embrace, wanting to stay there forever. I loved her more than I thought I ever could love anybody.

I slapped her on the ass. "Get moving, wife."

As she darted into the bathroom, I thought about how close I had come to losing her. Only a few months back, we were having serious problems. But I had finally listened to my sisters, and I had quit being so pigheaded. Especially after Vanzir dragged me off to one side to inform me of what an ass I had become. When he wanted to be, he could be extremely blunt and unflattering. But I appreciated his warning because he was right.

I finally started talking *to* Nerissa instead of talking *over* her. But mostly, I started listening to her worries and complaints, and taking them seriously. Turns out, shutting up and paying attention? Actually works. Now, though we weren't perfect and never would be, it felt like we were finally on the same page. And honesty and clarity were a whole lot better than the illusion of perfection.

As the sound of the shower started up, I went back to the chains, my thoughts still lingering over the dangers. We'd done our best to mitigate the hazards. Hanna and Maggie were sleeping in my lair during the night because we never knew when we'd be called out, and we didn't want them in any sort of danger.

Because of their proximity to the rogue portal out back, Iris's husband Bruce had taken the babies—including Chase's daughter, Astrid—and moved into Nerissa's old condo. His mother had come to help out, along with a nanny and a guard. We needed Iris here with us, so she spent her days with her family and her nights with us. And Tanne Baum, the Woodland Fae from the Black Forest, was on twenty-four-hour call, only a speed dial away.

The doorbell rang. I answered it, surprised to see Chase there, a tray of drinks in his hand.

"I stopped at Starbucks before I came over. I thought it might make a buffer for what I have to say." He forced a pale smile, looking as stretched thin as we all felt.

"Uh-oh, that sounds bad." I took the tray from him and led him into the kitchen.

Camille put her marker in her book. Chase had brought a grande chai latte for Delilah. Camille got the iced venti quad shot mocha. And Chase, the venti black coffee with cream. I foraged in the refrigerator for a bottle of blood, enchanted to a chocolate flavor. Thanks to Morio, I had a wide variety of choices.

Chase settled down at the table beside me, but before the detective could say a word, Camille's phone rang. She stared at it, a dark wave steeling her gaze, then answered.

"Yes? How many? Okay, we're on the way. Text us the directions." She punched the Off button and texted Delilah to get her ass around front ASAP, then yanked the top off her iced mocha to gulp down as much as she could. "We have to book. That was Morio. A raiding party's breaking through a rogue portal in Vanderson Park. At least a dozen goblins and twice that many bone-walkers. There may be more—they just started coming through the portal when Morio called me. He and Vanzir will hold them off as best as they can until everybody gets there."

"We'll have to talk later, Chase. Wait here for us? When Nerissa gets out of the shower, tell her where we went, if you would." I grabbed my keys, then jammed my wallet in the pocket of my jeans.

He nodded. "I'll call the Supe militia and put them on standby. One word from you and they'll be on the way." He pulled out his phone. "Text me directions the minute you get them. I'll have Frank and the boys ready to roll if need be."

Without another word, we grabbed our jackets and headed

into the cool, clear evening. I glanced up at the stars that hung over us like an icy canopy, wondering how long we could keep this up. But we couldn't falter. If we did, Telazhar would win, and Earthside would turn into a vast battleground.

Vanderson Park was about fifteen minutes out from our house in the Belles-Faire district of Seattle. Thank the gods, traffic was scarce, so we made good time. I reached the parking lot first, but Camille and Delilah were close on my heels, and they swerved into the parking lot behind me. As we slipped out of our cars, we could hear shouts coming from beyond a nearby copse of trees.

"Fuck, let's hope that there aren't any joggers out here braving the chill for a late-night run. And speaking of weather, the calendar says it's May, but it feels like March tonight. Where are the temps in the seventies that the weather guys promised us?" Camille neatly slid her dagger into the sheath strapped to her thigh, over the leg of her catsuit. She started jogging toward the shouts.

"News report said the warm front is stalled off the coast but should move in by tomorrow afternoon." Delilah joined her.

I caught up to them. We followed the curve of the sidewalk, twisting around the bend to see Morio and Vanzir in the middle of a copse of maple trees, caught in midbattle.

A host of bone-walkers swarmed around them, magically animated skeletons that were dangerous and hard to kill. Hack them to pieces and the bones would still skitter until the spell wore itself out. The goblins hung back, shouting encouragement to the bone-walkers. They were using the skeletons as cannon fodder to take the brunt of the damage, which made total sense. Wearing out the enemy before you have to face them was never a losing proposition. Just then, a shout from the other direction told us Shade and Trillian had arrived. Smoky and Rozurial would be on the way.

"We have to prevent the goblins from getting out of the park." I moved toward a pair of the ugly brutes, but they dodged behind a big boulder.

Camille headed toward Morio. The two of them could do far more damage working together than separately—their death magic was growing stronger every day, it seemed. Delilah unsheathed Lysanthra—her sentient dagger. The blade hummed with a shrill growl of hunger as it smelled goblin blood. As she jockeyed into position with a bone-walker, I sped into a run, then, using the boulder that was standing between us as a springboard, launched myself into the fight, landing square in front of two of the goblins. Their eyes lit up until I smiled, my fangs descending. A sudden lack of enthusiasm flashed across their faces and I smiled, satisfied.

"The *oh-shit-it's-a-vampire* look works for you, boys." I darted in, ignoring their blades. Unless they clipped me in the heart or cut off my head, they couldn't do anything to me that couldn't be repaired.

One of them managed to dance out of my way, but the other was within easy reach. I barreled into him, knocking him down and landing on his chest. Throwing my head back, I bared my fangs and lunged at his throat, savagely tearing into the flesh. As muscle was severed from muscle, veins ripping, the blood stained my lips, sending me into a frenzy. I'd been doing a lot of this lately, and each time, it seemed to get easier. I caught a mouthful of the fountaining liquid, hot and coppery and fresh on my tongue and gulped it down. Ignoring the aftertaste—goblin blood was nasty at best—I staved off the desire to stay and drink deep. I rolled to the side and came to my feet. The goblin gurgled with one last burbling noise and collapsed.

His buddy took one look at his dead comrade and raised his sword. I recognized the look in his eye. Vengeance mixed with stupidity did not for sanity or safety make. He tossed the sword from hand to hand, showing off, a shit-eating grin on his face.

"Oh, sugar, you really don't want to waste your last minutes trying to impress me." I sauntered toward him. "I've taken down creatures far bigger and badder than you. And maybe you should remember what just happened to your buddy. After all, a vampire's gotta do what a vampire's gotta do."

I bent my knees slightly and launched myself into the air, flipping over his head to land in back of him, very Bruce Lee. As the goblin let out a surprised grunt and struggled to turn around, I slammed against his back, knocking him forward onto his own sword. He shouted "Oh crap!" in Calouk—the common tongue of Otherworld—but I cut him off. I grabbed his head and wrenched his neck to the side, the resounding *crack* putting a stop to anything else he might have to say.

On my feet again, I turned, staring at the host of creatures surrounding us.

Camille and Morio had joined hands and were taking down a circle of bone-walkers with their death magic. The purple lightning from the circle of power surrounding them crackled, destroying every skeleton it touched as they walked forward, driving the magic in front of them. Delilah was slashing her way through the goblins, her blade singing every time it bit deep into the flesh of one of the creatures.

A glance toward the parking lot announced the arrival of Smoky and Roz. They asked no questions, merely joined Shade and Trillian, who were knee deep in battle, driving their swords through the chaos that spilled out from the portal.

Vanzir was guarding the vortex, attacking as more goblins poured through the opening. He couldn't prevent them from coming through, but he was making a dent in the incoming tide. And, thank the gods, only a handful of goblins could come through at a time. We were lucky in that regard.

The energy vortex spread between two of the tallest trees like a spider's web, overshadowing the brilliant green of early-summer leaves. The energy fluctuated enough to signify that it was a rogue portal—not one that had been opened and stabilized when Otherworld decided to reconnect with Earthside. That alone was cause for concern. There were too many rogue portals showing up lately, and we knew why, even if we couldn't do anything about it right now. And their numbers would only increase until we found a way to stabilize the time-space continuum through which they worked.

I grabbed out my phone and put in a conference call to Iris and Tanne Baum. The Woodland Fae from the Black Forest had been working hand in hand with us over the past few weeks. In December, we had discovered that—if they worked in tandem—Iris and Tanne could shut down rogue portals.

"We've got another one." I gave them directions. Tanne said he would swing by and pick up Iris, and they'd be here in fifteen minutes.

As I returned to the battle, the others were just finishing up the last of the bone-walkers. The goblins were all dead. And Smoky had taken Vanzir's place, guarding against anything else that might take a notion to emerge from the portal.

"Iris and Tanne are on the way." I stared at the blood saturating the ground and the field of broken bones. "Anybody call the FH-CSI to send out a cleanup crew?"

"I did." Delilah shook her head. "How many this time?" She pulled out a notebook and pen.

"Twenty-four goblins and forty-two bone-walkers. The raiding parties are getting bigger." Camille cast a dark look at the portal. "Either Telazhar has managed to figure out how to find rogue portals or he's creating new ones. I have no idea how he might be able to do that, but we have to take him out. Eventually, he's going to figure out how to rip open the portals from the Sub-Realms even without the spirit seals, and then we're going to have demons coming through instead of goblins."

Delilah let out a long sigh. "That makes . . ." She stopped to calculate for a moment. "Over two hundred goblins, three hundred bone-walkers, forty-five ogres, and two trolls since this started. A drop in the bucket compared to the thousands under Telazhar's command, according to Trenyth. And do we even know if he's opened up rogue portals to other countries over here? Are there goblins overrunning small towns in Norway or Russia that we haven't heard about, simply because they're cut off? Camille's right. We have to kill him."

Trillian stared somberly at the carnage. "Last we talked to Trenyth, he said Telazhar is bearing down heavily on Ceredream. His armies are pounding at the gates. The City of the East is beleaguered, but luckily they've managed to stave off the assault, but you know that's not going to last unless somebody intervenes. But for now, that gives us an advantage because with most of Telazhar's resources tied up trying to invade Ceredream, he can't focus too much on Earthside."

"Maybe. But I wouldn't bet on that lasting for long." I stared at the bleak remains of the goblins and the twitching parts of the bone-walkers. A hand skittered past me on the ground—finger bones clutching at the grass to pull itself along. Without thinking, I stomped on it, hard, crushing the bones. "Why do you think he only sends his recruits during the night?"

"Perhaps he thinks it's the best way to get one up on us. Who knows?" Shade wiped his blade on the grass. The half-dragon had adjusted to the lack of his Stradolan powers remarkably well, but then none of us had been given much of a choice in how we reacted to changes in our lives. It had become adapt or die, and we were all feeling the strain of too much change, too much chaos, lately. The fact that his shadow-walker self had vanished due to a freak show energy-sucker was harsh, but right now it wasn't our biggest problem. Luckily, Shade seemed to understand that.

Camille sucked in a deep breath. "I wanted to save this card for when Shadow Wing made his big move, but I think we have to use it now. It's time for me to call on the dragons for help. They've pledged to me they would work on our side during the war. We can set them after Telazhar, over in Otherworld. That might be enough to give us a respite." Her expression grew dark, sweeping across her face like a thundercloud. She had paid dearly for the promise of help from the Dragonkin. Their offer had been given as reparations for a wound that she would never fully be able to leave behind her.

"I think you're right, my wife. It's time." Smoky smiled faintly. "We need help in Otherworld, and so does every free country over there. We'll talk to my people in the morning."

As Morio and Vanzir poked among the dead, searching for any information that might help us, my sisters and I headed over to a nearby bench to wait. We were all covered with blood—except for Smoky, who was his usual pristine self. It occurred to me that Shade didn't share the same trait. Maybe it was because he was only half dragon. But the good news was, we had managed to avoid any damage to ourselves except for a few bruises here and there.

"You really think it's time to summon the dragons?" Delilah's eyes were wide. She had lost her naïveté over the past years, but she still could look the part of the little Kitten.

"You're marrying a half-dragon and I'm married to a prince of the realm. Don't sound so surprised." Camille laughed, breaking the tension. "It's not like we don't know any."

I chimed in. "Cut her some slack." But I was smiling. "After all, we are talking about *dragons*, and anybody in their right mind knows better than to be blasé about Dragonkin."

Delilah wrinkled her nose. "I just meant . . . are we at that point? Has it really come to this?"

"Yeah, I think we're really all in." Camille smiled grimly. "It came sooner than I expected, but right now, I'd say we're beyond the point of no return. There will be no more demon generals . . . no more Mr. Nice Guy. Shadow Wing is on the move, and Telazhar is his angel of death, leading the brigade. I feel it in my bones." She shivered, crossing her arms. Then, softly, she added, "Let's face it—life is changing all around us. We can't avoid the future."

"Destiny's a bitch." I let out a short grunt.

Camille entwined her fingers, staring at her hands. "Destiny will out. We can't stop the future from coming. Once I move out to Talamh Lonrach Oll after my coronation on Samhain, nothing will ever be the same. Unless you two come with me, this will be the first time in our lives we've lived apart." Her eyes were misty, her voice quivering just enough to reveal a hint of fear. "I'm going to be a queen . . . and I'm not sure I know how."

And none of us could give her advice. We sat silent for a moment, and then Delilah let out a long sigh.

She straightened her shoulders. "We were waiting to tell you, but I think we need some good news now. Shade and I have decided that we want to get married this year. We don't want to wait any longer. *I* don't want to wait any longer."

Camille forced a smile and kissed her on the cheek. "Yay, another wedding to plan! I love weddings."

I wrapped an arm around Delilah's shoulder. "Whenever you want, love. Tell us and we'll make it happen. You want a white gown and a Cinderella wedding, you've got it. You want a quiet garden wedding—you've got that, too. Just promise me you'll marry at night so I can be there."

"Oh, there's no doubt about that. A nighttime wedding for sure."

As I stared at the darkening sky, I thought about everything that was happening. Finally, after a few minutes of silence, I said, "Will you and Smoky go to the Dragon Reaches tomorrow?"

Camille stared up at the stars, then slowly nodded. "Yeah. We will."

I pursed my lips. "War has sneaked in to land on our doorstep and there's no way to turn back the clock. It would be a good idea if we could establish whether Telazhar is filtering his recruits through other portals around the world. Delilah, can you ask the Supe Community Council to put out feelers, to see if there's been an increase in activity? And I'll ask Roman to check through the Vampire Nation."

Camille let out a long sigh. "And I'll ask Aeval and Titania to check with the Earthside Fae. Maybe we can figure out just how wide a swath Telazhar is managing to cut."

And with that, we saw Chase's cleanup crew coming up the walkway. They headed over to the carnage. They would clear up all signs of what had happened here. And behind them, Iris and Tanne Baum came striding up the sidewalk. Shelving further discussion, we wearily met the pair and led them to the portal.

"We're getting all too much practice at this." Iris stared at the shimmering energy. "It's so beautiful, and so deadly."

Tanne said nothing, simply waited for Iris to ready herself. She cast a spell and a layer of ice began to form across the surface of the crackling vortex. As soon as it had frozen solid, Tanne began to sing, his voice resonating deeply through the air. He placed his hands on one side of the ice and Iris placed her hands on the other, joining him in song, weaving a contrabeat with her voice as they drove their magic through the portal, fracturing it from within its core.

We knew enough to stand clear as cracks began to race through the ice covering the opening. Iris and Tanne held their song steady. It undulated through the portal like an earthquake rippling through the ground. Nearby trees began to shake as a shrill hum filled the air. The cracks widened, light pouring between them. Iris dropped the beat, then found a single alto note and held it—her voice trilling with a rich wave of power. Tanne followed suit, and the vibrations of their voices blended together to force their way through the fractures. Another moment, and the vortex began to blink in and out of phase, rapidly rotating through a whirl of colors. Then, with one last groan, the frozen web of lightning shattered—splintering into a shower of hailstones, destroying the magic as it did so. Fragments of ice pelted everything in the area, including us, the rock-hard pellets striking like sharp pebbles.

Iris glanced at Tanne, a tight smile on her pretty face. Together, they had destroyed five new portals over the past two weeks, and each one was a strain. The magic required to rip apart a vortex that joined two worlds was immense, and it was taking a toll on both of them.

"You okay?" She held her hand out to Tanne, who allowed her to lead him over to another bench. They both looked bone-weary.

"Yeah, but this is getting old. I've got the clan looking out for more activity, by the way. We've taken out three groups of psy-demons lately. They are Earthside-based, but rare, so I figure something must be riling them up." He paused. "Would you like to meet the Hunters Glen clan? I'd be happy to introduce you." Demon hunters from the Black Forest, they were a group of Woodland Fae who had sent a select faction of their members to establish a new colony over here in the United States.

I glanced at Delilah and Camille, then nodded. "We should, at some point. We need as many allies as we can get. We'll call you and set up a time. Meanwhile, we had better get back home and clean up before another call comes through. You want to come with us, Tanne?"

He shook his head. "I'm all right. I'll go hunting with the guys—they can always use another hand."

And so after a brief discussion, we split up again, the men heading back out on reconnaissance, and the four of us women back to the house. As I sped through the silent night, my jeans covered with goblin blood, I wondered just how long we could hold out under this schedule.

Chase was still there when we got home. He had fixed a plate of sandwiches and a potato salad with Hanna's help. As we trailed in, he began serving up plates for Camille, Delilah, and Iris. They all looked tired, and so was I. The continual fighting from the past couple of weeks felt like it was seeping into my bones, like a chill that would not go away. As Chase carried the tray into the living room, complete with another bottle of blood for me, he seemed even more sober than when we had left.

"Nerissa went downstairs to sleep. She's going to need it for tomorrow. A situation has cropped up and I'm afraid the ramifications aren't going to be good. Maybe we'll luck out and nothing will come of it, but I'm not hedging any bets on that outcome."

"What's going on?" Kitten settled onto the sofa with her plate.

Chase let out a long breath. "This afternoon, I got a call from a friend of mine. John's an investigator with Scotland Yard, over in England. He told me that early morning, there was some unauthorized activity within Stonehenge. He was sent out to check on it. He said a great host of creatures was pouring out of the center of the ring. Now, he's well aware of what the Fae are, and he said they looked like no Fae he'd ever encountered. Instead, they were *large, burly men with massive weapons*, along with a group of creatures that, when he described them, I can pretty much guarantee are bloatworgles."

Delilah paled. "*Tregarts*. The men. You know they have to be Tregarts."

Tregarts were humanlike demons who were incredibly strong and brutish. They often paired with other lower-level demons as the brawn—in this case, the bloatworgles, demons who could breathe fire. We had fought both types far more than we cared to remember. Chase had nearly lost his life to them. Only the Nectar of Life had saved him, extending his life to well over a thousand years if he wasn't murdered or didn't meet with an accident before then.

"Demons at Stonehenge? But are they coming from the Sub-Realms? Or were they sent from Otherworld? And if so, how did they get over into Otherworld to begin with? The vortex at Stonehenge hasn't been opened in hundreds of years." Camille frowned. "You're right, this is a serious problem."

"Yes, and possibly worse than you think. The papers caught wind of it. London—all of the U.K.—is buzzing with rumors. And thanks to the Internet, that news has reached our shores. You can't do anything anymore without it being instantly broadcast worldwide." Chase looked a little green around the gills. "If the governments find out about this and actually give it credibility?"

"That would be bad. Very bad." I shuddered to think about what could all too easily happen.

The governments of the world liked their nuclear bombs. What they did *not* realize—because they didn't know about the demons yet—was that uranium and radioactivity only made Demonkin stronger. If the president got it into his head to go on the attack, chances were he was going to plunge us into a dark hole so deep that you'd have to look up to see bottom.

"*Bad* doesn't begin to encompass the danger." Chase shifted in his chair. "I've got a call in to a few of the guys I know. They're higher up in the Department of Defense. In fact, I worked directly with them when we were creating the FH-CSI. I'll try to explain it to them. How they'll take it, I can't even begin to guess. But I'll do my best to make them understand that we absolutely have to keep this under wraps, that we cannot let the politicians take control of this situation, and above all—no nukes."

He let out a long sigh. "The day we feared was coming has arrived, girls. The world is about to find out that the demons exist. Given the hate groups that sprang up against you, I dread to think what's going to happen."

I closed my eyes, envisioning the potential for disaster. Human supremacist groups were already on the rampage. And we all knew they wouldn't differentiate between the demons and any other Supe. This was just the extra fuel they needed to blow their campaigns sky high, turning the sparks of a wildfire into a massive conflagration.

"What can we do?" Delilah's voice was hushed, almost reverently afraid.

"Stop Telazhar. That's the only way. Take him down, wipe him out, drink his blood. I don't care what method you choose, but he has to be destroyed. Then we worry about Shadow Wing." And with that, Chase stood. "I need to get back to the office. I've been working eighteen-hour days the past few weeks." He turned to Iris. "Thank you for watching Astrid while I'm there. I haven't heard from Sharah in a few weeks. Sometimes I feel like taking my daughter and heading over to Otherworld to be with her mother, and leaving all of this behind."

Iris nodded, her eyes wet with tears. "I understand. Bruce was talking about heading back to Ireland, but as I told him—it doesn't matter where we go. Shadow Wing is determined to burn everything to the ground and it won't matter what country we're in. Or even what world. We're all in danger until he's destroyed."

With that, we saw Chase to the door.

Camille turned to us as we returned to the living room. "I'll head out to Talamh Lonrach Oll tonight. I'm tired, but I think we should ask Merlin to go to the U.K. He might be able to quash the mess over there."

Delilah nodded, her expression fading from worried to dark and beautiful. She had changed a lot since her last round of training with the Death Maidens. Now she routinely saw ghosts and spirits, but they couldn't touch her unless she chose to allow it. And she was transforming even still.

"I'll talk to the Supe Community Council." She stretched, yawning. "We have the militia here, but it's time to call up reinforcements everywhere."

I let out a long sigh. "I've got time before sunrise to go talk to Roman. We can marshal the vampires. It's time we all pulled together and walked into the fires of war united."

And with that, we were off, doing what needed to be done even as the clock seemed to tick away all too fast.

Chapter 2

Sunrise was clocking in at five forty-five, so I headed out as soon as it seemed we were good for the night, in order to talk to Roman. We'd been lucky—no other calls, though the guys had taken down a few muggers and freaks out to cause trouble. It was three thirty when I climbed in my Mustang. The car still felt odd—I missed my Jag but then again, I missed a lot of things.

As I sped through the silent streets, I thought over the past couple of years. My sisters and I had come Earthside expecting the equivalent of a sabbatical. We weren't that great at our jobs, and because Camille wouldn't give a blowjob to her boss, he managed to get us assigned Earthside. We had crossed between the worlds, our main worry being—would we be able to manage life in what was essentially an alien culture? Our mother was human, but our father was full-blooded Fae. And the three of us? Half-breeds, each with an odd mix of powers due to our mixed heritages.

Our mother, Maria D'Artigo, had fallen for Sephreh ob Tanu during the later days of World War II, when she had moved to Spain to go to college. With no roots to tie her to

Earthside, she chose love, crossing worlds to be with him. They married, to the chagrin of the Court and Crown, and a few years later, along came the three of us.

First Camille—the oldest. She's a Moon Witch and Priestess, and far more to come—she's slated to take over as the Fae Queen of Dusk and Twilight. But her natural powers fritz out when she least expects it, though that happens less now that she's taken to death magic. It seems she plays well in the dark, which is a good thing given the destiny waiting for her. She's married to three men: Smoky, a prince among the Dragonkin; Morio, a youkai-kitsune from Japan; and Trillian, a Svartan, one of the Dark and Charming Fae.

Second born were our sisters Delilah and her twin, Arial, but Arial died at birth and we only found out about her a few years ago. Delilah's natural form is that of a werecat. She's a beautiful, silken long-haired golden tabby. But when the Autumn Lord—one of the Harvestmen and an Elemental Lord—claimed her as his only living Death Maiden, a second Were form emerged, that of a black panther. Delilah's come a long way from the naïve young woman she started out as. She now walks with one foot in the world of ghosts and spirits, and she's engaged to Shade and is destined to one day bear the child of the Autumn Lord.

And then there's me. I'm Menolly. And I'm a vampire. I was a *jian-tu* by trade and birth, which simply means that I've got incredible acrobatic abilities, and therefore I made a pretty good spy. But when the Y'Elestrial Intelligence Agency assigned me to spy on a nest of dangerous vampires, my half-human heritage kicked in. I fell—literally—into their midst. Dredge, the biggest, baddest vamp around, caught hold of me. What he did to me still haunts my dreams, but a few years ago I got my revenge and staked him dead. But I will forever walk in the world of the living dead, my soul trapped in an ageless body until either I choose to walk into the sun or someone manages to stake me. I constantly struggle to keep a leash on my inner predator, forever watchful that my nature doesn't turn into the monster I'm fully capable of being. Nerissa, a werepuma, is my gorgeous Amazon of a wife. And I'm also the official consort to Roman, son of Blood Wyne, Queen of the Vampire Nation.

Together the three of us and our lovers and friends watch over Seattle and the surrounding area. Because when we came Earthside, little did we realize we were walking into a minefield. We stepped one foot over the line and found ourselves at the front of a demonic war.

Shadow Wing, Demon Lord of the Subterranean Realms, has been trying to break through the portals that separate the worlds. He aims to turn both Earthside and Otherworld into his private playgrounds, razing the beauty that exists as he blights everything alive with his fiery hell. Telazhar, an ancient necromancer from Otherworld, has become his right-hand man. The leader of an army of upstarts in Otherworld, they've nearly destroyed the Elfin lands and race, razed several other cities, and now . . . and now, Telazhar is setting his sights Earthside.

Camille's right. It's time to call in the dragons, and anybody else we can get to help. Because it's only a matter of time before Shadow Wing breaks through from the Sub-Realms. And between Telazhar's armies and Shadow Wing's demons, we haven't got a prayer of a chance.

Roman wasn't at home, but I knew where to find him. He was at the Seattle Vampire Nexus. My daughter was there, as well. I had never meant to sire another vampire, but Erin had been our friend, and she ended up collateral damage when Dredge hunted me down. He left her for me, nearly dead, and the only choices we had were either to let her die, or I could turn her. So I offered her the chance to become a vampire. I didn't want to do it, but it was her choice, and I capitulated. And now she worked for Roman in the security division. She was good at her job and I was proud of her for integrating so seamlessly into the vampire community. It hadn't been an easy road, but she had managed it.

I hustled through the doors and over to the receptionist's desk. The building was actually a mansion that had belonged to Sassy Branson, a vampire who had been a friend of mine until her inner predator took over and I had to make good on a promise to destroy her. Doing so had been one of the hardest tasks I'd ever faced, and even now I hated thinking about it.

The secretary glanced up and immediately recognized me. I was consort to the Regent. It stood the vamps in the area good fortune to know who I was.

"Lord Roman is in his office. I'll buzz ahead that you're on the way in, Lady Menolly."

I still wasn't used to the "Lady" business, but that was okay. I swung around behind the desk and headed for the office. As I entered the room, once again, Roman's sense of style overwhelmed me. He loved *lavish*. Opulent for him was over the top for me. Antique letter openers and original Monets and one-of-a-kind porcelain sculptures were scattered around like a cloud of beautiful clutter. When I was at his place, or in his office, I often felt like I was in the middle of a treasure chest filled with disparate but exquisite items. I wouldn't call him a hoarder, but he was definitely on the road to starring in a bad reality TV show.

Roman, son of Blood Wyne, the Queen of the Vampire Nation, was behind his desk. His long brown hair hung in a neat ponytail, not a wisp out of place, and he was so old that his eyes were almost entirely white. He had a long, regal nose, and I knew from experience that beneath the black turtleneck and neat black trousers were a number of long scars—legacies of his life as a warrior prince from thousands of years back. Roman was an ancient vampire, and how he had managed to keep his inner predator in check eluded me. It was a rare feat for someone his age.

He had re-sired me to break another bond that was proving dangerous, and I felt the tug of allegiance pull on me. As I entered the room, shutting the door behind me, he rose and was at my side in a whisper of movement. He pulled me to him and lightly pressed a kiss to my forehead.

"My darling Menolly, I returned not an hour ago from visiting Mother. I'm so glad you decided to come welcome me home." He glanced at the very large, ornate grandfather clock sitting in the corner. "But it's so late. Shouldn't you be home, just in case? What's going on?" Every time he visited Blood Wyne, he came home sounding like Prince Charming.

I gave him a light peck on the cheek. "We have a problem. I need your help."

He stepped back, glanced at my face, and shook his head. The pretense of graciousness dropped and the prince was gone. He was just Roman again. "What's going on? What happened since I left?"

I started to explain, a rush of words forming on my lips, and then I just collapsed in one of the nearby chairs, leaning my elbows on my knees, staring at the floor. "We're at war." I mumbled the words, not wanting to hear myself say them aloud.

"What?" He sat beside me, not touching me, not offering any comfort or care. His voice was measured, but clear. His behavior was precisely what I needed. He knew me well enough by now to know that if he tried to comfort me, I might not be able to keep it together.

I paused to collect myself, then straightened my shoulders. "We're at war. Telazhar has figured out how to get his army over here. So far, his incursions are on the smaller side, but we think it's only a matter of time before he is able to send larger contingents, and then we'll be screwed. Once he's over here with his armies, he can work on breaking open the portals to the Sub-Realms so Shadow Wing can come through. We've been fighting nonstop every night for the past two weeks. The insurgents are growing in number each time."

"So it has finally come to this." Roman eased back in his seat, crossing his legs. He examined his nails, but I knew it wasn't a stalling technique or a brush-off. When Roman thought things over, he often engaged in behavior that seemed dismissive, but it was just him allowing his brain time to process and plan. While he was thinking, I stood and headed for the door.

"I'm going to see Erin. I'll be back in a few minutes." I paused, my hand on the doorknob. "Roman, I need you to align the vampires with the Supes. We need backup out there. I would have asked for it before you got back, but this . . . this is big. I must know if you're behind us in this."

And with that, I slipped out the door. Giving Roman the space to plan would be a better use of my energy than sitting there wheedling. And I wasn't the begging kind.

Erin was part of Roman's security team now, working her way up the ranks. He had her in mind for one of the leads in the operations room, I knew that, but she started out at the bottom like everybody else. Security was found in the basement—it made for the best protection—and so I headed for the stairs, passing several other vamps hurrying around. A familiar voice stopped me.

"Menolly? Hey, it's been a while." Wade was standing there, a sheaf of papers in his hands. He had a Bluetooth headset in one ear, and he was dressed in tight-fitting leather jeans and a simple button-down shirt. His tousled curly hair was its usual jumble, and he had long lost the glasses that he had relied on as a crutch even after he was turned.

Wade and I had dated briefly, before I met his mother—Belinda Stevens—who was also a vampire. Whoever had turned Wade had a nasty sense of humor. It took a real sadist to turn your overprotective, annoying, intrusive mother into a vampire after they turned you into one. As long as Belinda walked this earth, she would be breathing down his neck, chasing off his girlfriends, and embarrassing him at social gatherings. It was a wonder that he hadn't staked her himself.

"Long time no see." I paused, feeling a fleeting sadness drift by. We had been good friends, then dated, then had been enemies, and now . . . it felt like we were back to acquaintances with a lot of water under the bridge. "How are you doing?"

"Not bad. I do have exciting news. I don't know if Roman told you, but my idea for Vampires Anonymous? Apparently the Queen loved the concept and she has put me in charge of a nationwide program. I'm setting up new groups all up and down the coast."

He beamed, a sparkle of excitement in his eyes. Wade had been a psychologist when he was alive, and after he had been turned, force of habit led him to attempt to ease the way for vampires new to the undead life. He had set up a support group to keep newly minted vamps from running off and turning everybody in sight. Once Roman instituted the Seattle Vampire Nexus, Vampires Anonymous was sucked in under the umbrella organization.

I smiled for real, for the first time that night. "Good news is welcome right now. I'm so happy for you. I think it's a wonderful idea. How are you otherwise?"

He shrugged. "Dating a woman I met a few months ago. Life is good, overall. And you?" Wade didn't know everything about what was going on, but he knew enough.

"We're in a rough spot, in terms of fighting the bad guys. But my sisters and I are well, and so are our loved ones. I guess that's all that counts."

Wade's face clouded. "I heard about your father. I'm sorry."

"Yes, well . . . war doesn't play favorites and life isn't fair. That's why we're fighting. I have to go, but we need to catch up soon. I'll give you a call." And with that, I waved and moved on. The fact that he was dating made me happy, but I wondered if his girlfriend had met his mother yet.

Erin was in the main room of Security Ops, clipboard in hand. While Roman was training her for combat—as he did all his security personnel—he also was fast-tracking her through a computer course. Erin was a middle-aged, short, stocky woman who preferred jeans and a flannel shirt, but dress codes ruled in Roman's employ. She was wearing a neatly tailored black pantsuit with a pale blue sweater peeking out beneath the jacket. She had a short butch cut and looked smart and chic. The vampire glamour that emerged at the moment of turning and increased throughout the years worked for all body types and all ages.

"Menolly!" She lit up. The siring effect would hold for a long, long time—for some vamps forever. At least she had quit kneeling when I came into the room, but she still gave me a low bow. But I knew she did it partially for show, because I was Roman's consort, and it was a sign of respect in front of the others.

I held out my hand and she took it, briefly and lightly. Vampires didn't generally touch much. A light handshake was as good as a hug among the majority of our kind.

"Erin, I thought I'd drop down to say hello and see how you are getting on while Roman is thinking over a situation I need his advice on." I glanced around. "How do you like the new job?"

She, like Wade, was sparkling with excitement. "I love it. At last, I feel useful. In fact, I have to tell you—I never thought I'd be interested in computer work, but I love it. Roman told me he thought I'd have a knack for it, and he was right. I don't know how he knew, but I'm glad he enlisted me. Thank you for giving me permission."

As a relatively new sireling, Erin still technically needed my permission to change jobs, residences, or any other number of things, though as the decades had gone on, the rules of the Vampire Nation had evolved and changed. But with Blood Wyne's reemergence into mainstream vampire society, I had a feeling we were headed back into a more regimented manner of decorum.

"I'm just glad it agrees with you. Listen, Erin—I have to cancel our plans next week. I can't tell you exactly why, but trust me, I'd rather *not* have to bail on you. But right now, my sisters and I are into something pretty deep and we need all our focus." I had recently begun instituting a weekly get-together with Erin. I didn't want her to feel like I had just left her to fend for herself, and since she had moved to the Seattle Vampire Nexus to work, chances were I was going to run into her more and more.

She nodded. "No problem. We have exams coming up next week, anyway. It will give me more time to study. I want to make you proud." Simply put, but plain and poignant, nonetheless.

I smiled. "You already do. But yes, study hard. If you're going to rise through the ranks here, you'll want every advantage you can get. I'll call you later on and we'll reschedule." As I turned to go, another one of the security officers dashed up.

"Lord Roman is asking for you, Lady."

"I'm on my way." I nodded as he bowed. Glancing at the clock, I took the stairs two at a time. It was already close to four thirty and I had less than an hour before I needed to be home. I could always sleep here, no problem, but I preferred my home base. Though I was probably safer here than at home, if I was honest about it.

Roman was behind his desk when I entered the room. He glanced up at me. "You talked to Erin?"

"Yes, she seems happy and I'm grateful you took her under your wing." I meant it. Roman liked overseeing people. I didn't mind at the Wayfarer—after all, it was *my* bar—but that was about the extent of my desire to be any sort of a leader.

"She's going to go far here. I'm assigning you twenty of my elite guards. They can patrol the streets for you and fight with you. They're all trustworthy—they've been through *loyalty tests*." His emphasis on the last gave me an involuntary shudder. From the little I had seen, Roman's "loyalty tests" were brutal and harsh. They were far better than a lie detector and only one step down from a truth serum. "Be here as soon as you can after sunset tonight in order to explain their duties and your expectations of them. I have given explicit orders that your voice is my voice in matters of authority on this subject."

I nodded, grateful for the extra help. "We need all the help we can get."

"I agree. Which is why I am going to make a trip to visit my mother again. She needs to know about this development. I'll go as soon as I wake up this evening, and I'll be back as soon as I can. We may be able to reach some of the vamps over in Otherworld to go up against Telazhar, but to be honest, I have my doubts about that. They do not kneel to my mother."

"No, they don't, and they're far more loners than team players." I shook my head. Once they had kicked Dracula over Earthside, it was every vamp for himself, and while certain city-states and lands had rules regarding vamps, truth was, they were hard to enforce. In fact, vampires got along with general society over here much better than they did in Otherworld. Yet one more odd disparity. I glanced at the clock. "I'd better get home or they'll be worrying."

Roman stood then and held out his arms. "Menolly . . ."

I slid into his embrace, the cool chill of his skin mirroring my own. When he stood still, he reminded me of an alabaster or porcelain statue, he was so pale. How he had managed to keep his mind from careening into madness over the centuries, I wasn't sure. And I wondered about his mother, as well. Blood Wyne was formidable and—in so many ways—terrifying, but she was as sane as I was.

"Thank you. Thank you for wanting to help." I leaned my head against his shoulder, wishing I had time to stay and play. I could let go fully with Roman, in a way I never could with Nerissa without fear of hurting her. Roman was my fail-safe. We could get rough and dirty and feed on one another when the hunger overwhelmed us. But there was one little problem. Roman had fallen in love with me. And I didn't love him. Oh, I did, in a way. At least, as a friend. And we had incredible sexual chemistry together. But I would never love him the way I loved Nerissa.

Nerissa and I had agreed, when we realized we were serious, that our hearts belonged to each other. Other women were off-limits, but we could play with the boys as long as it didn't get emotionally serious. I knew she had a male partner, too—a Were of some sort, though I hadn't met him yet. We had a real go-round about that one, because apparently my inner idiot believed in double standards. But we had come to a truce, though at some point we were going to have to figure out better rules for coping with the issue.

Roman sensed my need and pressed closer. "If you can carve out an hour or two when I get back . . ." And then, reluctantly, he let me go and returned to his desk. "I'd better get a few of these things out of the way so I can be ready to leave when I wake up tonight. Menolly, fear not. There's absolutely no question of the Vampire Nation doing its part. This is our world, too. And we have no desire to be under Shadow Wing's rule." And with that, he blew me a kiss and went back to work.

On the way home, I thought about his words. *This is our world, too.* Vampires and Supes and Fae and humans. We all had to work together to keep it from the demons. But there was no way we could enlist the majority of humans, who were too busy fighting their own wars among themselves. And even if they did listen to us, there was no way the majority would trust us to lead the battle.

I reached the house and hurried inside. It was five ten. I was cutting it close. Delilah was dozing in the living room—asleep on the sofa. I wasn't sure where Camille was. Hanna was awake, and she had covered them both with afghans. She motioned for me to join her in the kitchen.

"There was a call for you in the Whispering Mirror. I tried to wake up your sister, but she's dead to the world. You girls have been pushing yourselves too hard. Fae or not, none of you can go on like this."

"Who was it?"

"I have no idea. I'm not authorized to activate the mirror. But I thought you should know."

I nodded. "Thank you, Hanna. I'll check the call log and see if I can figure out who it was before I head downstairs." I bustled into the parlor where we had stowed the Whispering Mirror so it would be out of the way and yet easily accessible. Another glance at the clock told me I had twenty minutes at best before I needed to be downstairs and in my bed.

I slid in front of the mirror, settling on the bench. I couldn't see my reflection—and whoever was on the other end wouldn't be able to, either—but that didn't mean my voice wouldn't carry through the miles and worlds. I said my name. The mirror was voice activated, keyed to Camille, Delilah, Nerissa, Iris, and me. After a moment, the mist in the silver-framed mirror cleared. Most likely, it had been Trenyth on the other side. The mirror was tuned to Elqaneve.

A moment later, a harried elf appeared in the mirror. He looked confused. "Yes? Who's calling? Identify yourself."

"This is Menolly D'Artigo. I'm a vampire; you aren't going to be able to see me. My sisters aren't available right now. I needed to find out if Trenyth called us before I head down into sleep for the day, so if you could hurry, I would appreciate it."

Another moment passed, the elf still looking confused, but then he stood and trundled off out of sight. I waited, tapping my foot on the floor. If he didn't get his ass back, I was going to have to end the call. But just as I was gearing up to shut the mirror down, Trenyth appeared.

"I was worried—I seldom call this early and don't get an answer."

"Delilah's asleep and Camille's out. And I was over at Roman's. So you were the one who called?"

He nodded. "Yes, it was me."

I rushed on. "You need to hurry. It's near sunrise and I have to get my ass down to bed."

"I have some sobering news, Menolly. Can you wake your sisters? I'd rather tell you all at the same time. And what about the men?" He glanced beyond me—Trenyth was fully aware of why I wasn't showing up in the mirror—straining as he looked to see who all was here.

"I'm alone right now and only have a few minutes before I have to get down in my lair. Can it keep till sunset tonight?"

He frowned, then shrugged. "I suppose it will have to. But first thing, contact me. I'll be waiting. We have some new information from the Subterranean Realms, and it's not good." And with that, the chief advisor to the Elfin throne signed off, looking all too weary.

I scribbled a note for the others and then headed downstairs, praying for dreams free of fire and demons and pain. And for once, I got my wish.

Chapter 3

By the time I woke up, showered, dressed, and hauled ass upstairs, it was quarter to nine. The summer months sucked; the increased length of the days severely curtailed my time spent awake. Besides being an inconvenience, during times like this—when every minute counted—it felt like I put everybody I cared about at risk because I wasn't there to help them out as much.

"Any activity so far?" I glanced around. Everyone in the household was gathered around the huge oak table Smoky had bought when we built the extension onto the kitchen, including Iris. Everyone except Chase, Bruce, and the babies.

The kitchen counters overflowed with food. Apparently, Iris and Hanna had gone on a mad cooking spree. I spotted just about every favorite dish that every single person in the household loved. I suspected that cooking served as stress relief for the pair of them. The smells made my mouth water, but I ignored the food—there was nothing else I could do.

Camille shook her head, but she looked pale. In fact,

everyone seemed subdued. "No. Not here." But the edge to her voice told me that wasn't the whole of the story.

I dropped into the chair next to Nerissa and planted a kiss on her lips. "Hey, love. You look tired." She actually looked exhausted.

"That's because I just got home from work."

"Rough day?" At her quiet nod, I began to worry. Nerissa worked with victims of crimes and disasters at the FH-CSI. That she had been at work this long told me something big had gone down. Glancing around at the dour demeanor on everybody, I finally just planted my elbows on the table and said, "Okay, I know something happened. Will someone tell me what? And where's Chase?"

"Chase is still at work." Nerissa motioned to Delilah. "Show her the papers, Kitten. A lot of people have been busy little bees today. Or should I say, wasps. Nasty wasps and hornets."

Delilah tossed a newspaper in front of me. Several of them, in fact. The first—the *Seattle Tattler*, a rag that had been the bane of our life since Day One when we arrived Earthside—sported a big, bold headline splashed across the top: DEMONIC CREATURES TAKING OVER SEATTLE! CAN OUR INTREPID FAE FRIENDS SAVE THE DAY OR ARE THEY IN LEAGUE? Of course it was hyperbole, but the trouble was, they had caught several bone-walkers and a bloatworgle on film. I winced. Not only had they caught the enemy on camera, but Smoky was there, too, right in the middle of destroying one of the bloatworgles. It wasn't a pretty picture, either.

I quietly set the paper aside without reading the story and picked up the next one. This was out of the U.K. Another yellow rag, it had pictures of Tregarts and bloatworgles emerging from a shimmering portal in the middle of Stonehenge. The headline there was: DEMONS POURING FORTH FROM THE GATES OF HELL! Two more papers—one from Scotland, one from Oregon—showed the problem as having spread farther than Seattle and Stonehenge.

I knew that the minute I started reading any one of these

stories, I'd blow my stack. Shoving them to the side, I leaned back and folded my arms. "All right, before I read these and go apoplectic, somebody tell me just how bad this is. And why is Chase still at work?"

"The incident at Stonehenge was bad." Morio's eyes were shimmering topaz, which meant his youkai side was close to the surface. And that meant he was upset. "There were fatalities. A group of Fae from over in Sherwood Forest managed to take them out, but four humans and ten Fae died during the fight. Up in Scotland—somewhere near Loch Ness—another batch poured through. Again, the Fae took them down. This time without loss, but they were seen."

Trillian took over. "Down in Portland several creatures were spotted that we think are demons, but they vanished into the crowds near the Columbia River. We have no idea what they are up to or where they are, but Chase is working with the up-and-coming FH-CSI they have been creating there to contain the issue. Frank Willows, from the Supe Community Council, sent a small contingent down there to help mobilize the Supes in that area."

This was bad. Very bad. We'd worked so hard to keep news of the demons away from the general populace, but events were slipping out of our control. Fae were a novelty. Weres? A little more problematic. Vampires scared the hell out of humans, but they also held a certain mystique. But demons? No, demons would push people over the edge.

Camille cleared her throat. "I went out to Talamh Lonrach Oll before bed this morning. You were downstairs by the time I got back. I spoke to Aeval and she's sending warriors over to England now, to fast-track the Fae there into the fighting force they once were. Merlin is going, too, and Áine went with him." She shook her head. "This came too soon. We've been planning for this but they still caught us off guard."

I tried to take in all the information at once. Turning to Nerissa, I said, "What about you? Why were you at work so late?"

She shifted uncomfortably in her seat. "You need to

know something, but I'm not sure how to tell you. There was an incident today . . . It's bad."

The way she said it chilled me to the bone. Her voice was flat, resigned. Even during disasters, Nerissa was right on top of things, but tonight? She looked harried and out of it.

Bad could mean a number of things. "Tell me."

She gave a helpless look at the others. "Okay, here's the thing. The Fellowship of the Earthborn Brethren staged an attack—using the Freedom's Angels as their front men—on one of the vampire apartment complexes today." At my reaction, she hurried to add, "Not the Shrouded Grove Suites, where Wade lives. It's a new complex. One called DarkTower Gardens."

I waited. Whatever happened, it had obviously affected her. Sometimes Nerissa's job could be rough. She was a victim's aid counselor, and she dealt with more than her share of grief and despair. Considering the Fellowship of the Earthborn Brethren were involved, it meant something bad had gone down. They were a hate group and they actively campaigned for violence against anyone other than human. They used the Freedom's Angels—a militant activist group—as their primary weapon.

After a pause, she continued. "They tried to burn the building down, and when they couldn't, they used C-4 to blow up the bottom two floors. We know there were at least twenty-three vampires living on those floors, but there might be others who were killed. Chase is still at work because they couldn't take a head count of who survived until after sunset. Then we start sorting through the labyrinth that always happens when vampires disappear."

I nodded very slowly, trying to maintain my temper, which was usually the first thing to go when I received really bad news. I had friends and acquaintances who lived in that complex, but right now, I needed to keep my cool.

Nerissa was right. It would be a labyrinth. It was never easy to tell if a vampire had merely moved on or been killed. The only thing that remained when a vamp died the final death was a pile of dust—and it didn't sparkle, shimmer, or anything else to indicate it was anything other than regular dirt or ash. Their clothes would be caught in the destruction, as well.

So if somebody dropped out of sight for a while and nobody knew about it, we did our best to track them down and count them among those who survived.

"Did they catch the people who did it?" I tried to keep my voice from cracking. Even if the cops caught them in the act, it still wasn't illegal to destroy a vampire. Property? Yes. Vampires? Had no standing or protection under the law, even though the government expected them to pay taxes. Vampire rights were caught in a quagmire of legislation hell. The laws were deep-sixed time and again by a flood of terrified voters. Given our predator nature, I kind of understood. But truth was, anybody who went out and bought a gun was actually more dangerous than we were. Hell, because of the current legal situation, any freak could come along and dust me and the courts wouldn't blink an eye. Anybody could kidnap me and lock me in a room for a hundred years, leaving me to starve and go mad, and not one jury in the land would convict them.

She shrugged. "A couple. Two of them managed to catch themselves in the blast. They're hurt but alive. The rest vanished. The men will be charged with destruction of property and domestic terrorism. The group came prepared, I'll tell you that. The security cameras caught the action on film—at least until one of the guys shot the camera down. They left a scattering of pamphlets, which directly ties their actions to the *Seattle Tattler* headline."

Twenty-three dead. At least, twenty-three that we *knew* of. "What happened to the rest of the vampires living in the complex?"

Nerissa shook her head. "Don't know yet. Their apartments escaped damage, we think. The building is still standing, thanks to the earthquake retrofitting—it was the one thing that held up the structure after the explosion. But it won't be for long. Nobody can get in there. It's too dangerous because the metal is so twisted that a structural engineer says it could come down at any time. So any rescue workers have been held up."

Wearily reaching for another cookie, she rubbed her temples, squinting. "Man, I need the sugar. I am so tired, and so stressed. But I have to go back in an hour or so, now that sunset's here. We've been waiting for the vamps to wake up and manage to find a way out. We figure that most can escape out of the building via the hallway windows. The majority of apartments don't have windows because of the sunlight—which is why it's a vampire-only complex. It wouldn't be legal for anyone still living to rent there due to the lack of egress."

I stared at the table, a bleak mood washing through me. "What did Governor Sarkness say about this?"

Camille snorted. "His usual spiel. *Such a tragedy, we will find who did it*, blah blah blah . . . You know that this isn't going to bode well for the Vamp Rights bill. Sarkness fought against the Supe Rights bill as well, but that one managed to pass even with his opposition. You know he's going to find a way to make these attacks bounce back on the victims and claim it's their own fault. *They were asking for it*, and *if they didn't want to be attacked, why did they come out of the coffin* sort of crap."

Nerissa shrugged. "I spent today setting up a task force. Once we know who the victims are, we can immediately reach out to their families, if any of them have living kin. I also had to hold a press conference about the incident. Sarkness was there. He was walking a thin line, but Camille's right. He looked about as sorry as somebody who just won the lottery."

I sat, mute, for a moment. Then—"Do we have a list of known dead yet?"

Nobody bothered to point out to me that all the victims were already dead. Vernacular was tricky when coping with vampire deaths, but right now, the fact was twenty-three lives had been wiped out by hatred.

Nerissa was about to say something when the phone rang. Camille answered.

Chase, she mouthed, and handed the phone to Nerissa,

who motioned to Delilah for a notepad and pen. She began taking down what looked like names.

"Roman's promised a vampire contingent to guard the city, then?" Camille leaned forward, keeping her voice low so she wouldn't bother Nerissa.

"Yeah, I need to go over there after we talk to Trenyth. He's going to introduce me to the squad before he leaves to meet with Blood Wyne." I stretched, feeling too bound up.

Delilah cocked her head. "His mother's getting involved?"

"I think she has to, don't you? We have to bring the vampires in against Shadow Wing. It's time we joined together—banded as a unified force. But attacks like this one are going to make things that much more dicey, though."

In fact, it was likely to make human-vampire relations pretty damned nasty for a while, and I hoped to hell all the work Wade, Roman, and I had done to establish an acceptable truce between the two factions hadn't just blown out the window along with the first two floors of the DarkTower Gardens. Vamps were testy creatures—I knew that from personal experience. We were easy to ire, and given the fact that we had a rung or two up the ladder on humans meant that some vamps found it more than acceptable to take advantage of humans as juice boxes, rather than as equals.

Nerissa handed the phone back to Camille. "He gave me the names." She handed the list to me. I scanned over it. I recognized them all, though none of them were close friends. But they had all been members of the Seattle Vampire Nexus, and at least one of them had been in Roman's employ as a security guard.

"Fucking wingnuts. Can I have a copy of this for Roman? Or is Chase going to e-mail it over to him?"

"I'll have him e-mail it. Meanwhile, you guys need to call Trenyth." Nerissa pulled out her phone as we headed to the living room. The parlor was too small for us to all comfortably fit, so Smoky and Shade carried the Whispering Mirror out to the living room and set it up. Camille, Delilah, and I gathered around it, and the others in back of us. Times used to be, when we'd call, there would be a chance of talking to our father. Now that was gone, along with so much else.

Elqaneve was still clearing out the rubble from the disaster Telazhar had sicced on their doorstep. A good share of the Elfin race was dead, but they were doing their best to pick up the pieces and as much as I didn't like the basic concept, I understood why the government was putting an emphasis on the fertile women to get pregnant and breed. Even if their husbands had died during the war, they were being encouraged to pick a partner—preferably full-Elfin blood—and get knocked up. Meanwhile, Sharah was doing her best to make being half-elf acceptable, especially since she had a daughter with Chase, but the sentiment of the basic populace wasn't behind her on that. Especially not now.

As we stood there, waiting while Camille activated the mirror, I said, "It still seems so weird to think of Sharah as a queen."

"That may be, but she'll be a good one." Camille glanced over her shoulder. It suddenly hit me—even though I had known it was going to happen, it really hadn't registered that Camille was slated to ascend to a throne, as well.

"She's certainly stepped up. She hasn't seen Astrid since birth. It has to be tearing her up." Delilah frowned. "I still think the elves were cruel to make her leave her child hours after the birth."

Of all people to defend the elves' actions, I didn't expect it to be Iris, but she cleared her throat.

"They needed their queen. With Asteria dead, if the Elfin race has any hope of survival, they absolutely have to have someone to flock behind, and she must be someone with royal blood. With the other heirs dead in the carnage, Sharah was the next in line. It's her duty. As grave as the choice was, she made the right one. Chase is raising little Astrid with love and care. Sharah will be there when she can. When you live that close to the throne, you grow up knowing that you might be forced one day to make the choice between duty to throne and duty to family."

Camille hushed us as the mist in the mirror cleared. Trenyth's image flickered in. We were ready to rock and roll. "You said we should all be here to hear what you had to say?"

My sister wasn't wasting any time, I'd say that for her.

Trenyth nodded. "I have been watching your reports come in. Based on Telazhar's moves, we sent spies into the Sub-Realms. It's a fool's mission, but we have some loyal men who can pass—Svartans willing to return and seek out information. I'll just come flat out with the news. Shadow Wing found a fourth spirit seal. We don't know how or where, but he found one. He now has four, to our four, and there's one left on the loose. And worse, rumors have it that he's setting up his own sinister version of the Keraastar Knights, using demons as the hosts."

Dead silence, and then we all started talking at once. After a moment, Vanzir let out a loud whistle and we quieted down.

He looked particularly pale. "What do we do?"

"What can we do? If we could find that other seal we could combat this more easily. But Camille, according to the legend, now that you are taking the throne as a Fae Queen, you will be in charge of uniting the Knights and training them. You need to find the last spirit seal and also the Keraastar Diamond and do what you can with what we have."

She bit her lip. "I'll do what I can, but we are fighting nonstop over here against Telazhar's insurgents. Can you find out anything about how he's managing to find the rogue portals?"

Trenyth had only looked this defeated once before—when Queen Asteria had been killed. He sat back. "Elqaneve . . . we are a makeshift city now, in a land that has been devastated. We can do nothing about him except ferret out what information we can."

Camille glanced over at Smoky, who nodded. "Smoky and I will be going to the Dragon Reaches tonight. We were going to head there before dawn, but I had to go out to talk to Aeval and Titania. But we will go after we finish talking to you. Trenyth, I've decided it's time to call in my marker.

We're going to ask the dragons to help fight Telazhar. They are bound by a promise to help me when I call, so they will come. When they appear, it's going to be up to you to let the other lands know not to attack them or impede them. The dragons will be coming to war."

For a moment I thought Trenyth was about to laugh, but then tears began to trickle down his face. "You may just have saved thousands of lives. Go and the gods speed you. Let me know what happens. And tell Chase the Queen fares well and she misses him and their daughter." And with that, the screen went black.

For a moment, the room was silent, then Camille pushed back her chair and stood.

"I guess we should get ready to leave." She turned to the rest of us. "We'll try to be home by morning. At least the vampires will be out patrolling." And with that, she kissed Delilah and me and walked over to Smoky. "Let me dress for traveling, first."

He nodded, silent and brooding. As she headed up the stairs, he turned to us. "My mother and the Wing Liege will honor their promise. Telazhar may be a mighty necromancer, but he will not stand against dragonfire. That I will tell you."

Delilah glanced at me. "I suppose you better get going too. The Nexus must be up in arms after today's attack. I'm going to call an emergency meeting of the Supe Action Council, so I'm manning the phone trees tonight."

Vanzir, Rozurial, and Trillian headed out to patrol. Shade opted to stay and guard the house until Hanna and Maggie were also downstairs, safely locked away. Nerissa was dead tired. As I kissed her, I hated that she had to head back out again. Pocketing my keys, I could only wonder what hell life would be like in a week . . . two weeks . . . by the end of the year if we made it that far.

I decided to swing past the DarkTower Gardens on the way. The area had been roped off and a crowd was still milling around. After debating whether to stop, I decided to just get my ass over to the Seattle Vampire Nexus. I stepped on the gas and sped past, gripping the wheel as I struggled to settle my anger.

The Nexus was busy—the moment I walked into the building, I could tell that the explosion had hit home and everybody was up in arms, probably trying to pinpoint exactly who had been destroyed. The receptionist motioned to me.

"Lord Roman's waiting for you—he asked me to send you right in."

I nodded, heading toward his office. As I entered the room, he was leaning against his desk, reading through some e-mail on his tablet. He glanced up, his eyes pale as moonlight. I didn't wait for him to acknowledge me, I just slid in beside him and he wrapped one arm around my waist and gave me a light kiss on the forehead.

"What's the damage?" There was no use going over what had happened—we both knew the story.

"We're up to twenty-nine missing and presumed dead. We're following up on the names now, but I think it safe to say that most of the vamps were in their beds. The entire complex is still off-limits due to the zone still being so hazardous, so we're setting up emergency sleeping quarters in the basement here for the rest of the residents. I've called in extra security for the day from the Supe Militia to guard the Nexus during the light, when we cannot." Roman seldom raised his voice, but at his most calm, he could be his most deadly. "We will find the culprits and they will be punished . . . *our way.*"

I nodded. The courts wouldn't dole out justice on our behalf, and I wasn't going to argue him on this point, or mention it to anybody else. "Where are my troops for the city?"

"In Training Room Two. But, before you go, a kiss. I'm leaving in an hour or so to visit Mother to discuss the situation—well, your situation, and this situation. I'm not sure what she'll say, but I'll bring home the point that Shadow Wing won't stop at destroying humans, that he's going after anyone who opposes him."

I wrapped my arms around his neck and leaned up to

kiss him. As he set the tablet down and pressed his lips to mine, the weight of the world seemed to settle around our shoulders. But his lips were cool and passionate, pulling me deep into the darkness that surrounded our lives. I let out a soft moan, wanting him—wanting to reaffirm the dark hunger that rose whenever we were together. He shifted slightly, and I could feel his erection pressing hard against my thigh.

"Do we have time?" My voice was barely a whisper, but he nodded.

"We will make the time. In this world, you have to take what you want and fight for what you have. And at times, you grasp hold of the joys when and where you have the chance, because the Hags of Fate like to fuck with us all. They're all too willing to shovel us up on a sacrificial platter." He swung me around, grabbing my wrist. We headed out the French doors to the gardens beyond. With a gesture to one of his security officers, he motioned for her to fall back. She gave him a curt nod in return and disappeared into the shadows.

We were in a secluded and gated area, heavily wooded. The moon was up, still round enough to shed silver beams down through the foliage. I pulled away from him and a slow smile filtered across my face. Time to hunt, to play, to tear through the forest and give in to the bloodlust. I tagged him on the arm—*"You're it!"* And then I was off.

I scaled the tall fir next to me, swinging from branch to branch with ease, paying no attention to the limbs and needles sweeping across my face. As I reached twenty feet up, I leaped for the next tree. Roman—true to our rules—gave me a sixty-second head start. But then he was on the move, heading up the other trunk. We had developed an odd set of rules for our game of chase, but they worked for us. No shortcuts allowed—at least not for the first few minutes. No turning into bats or anything else. Simply, we took parkour to a level no breather ever could.

I flipped through the air to land on a branch, steadying myself as the soles of my boots found purchase. I was sixty feet up now, still scaling toward the sky as I went. Douglas fir trees—which were actually false hemlocks and not true firs—were common through the Pacific Northwest and easily soared up to several hundred feet.

I scurried up, using the branches as a ladder, until I found one sturdy enough to tightrope out on. The next tree was about fifteen feet over, and I crouched, coiling my muscles to spring. As I went flying through the air, I missed the branch I was aiming for and went freefalling down, but only about ten feet before I caught hold of another. I swung my feet up to catch the limb and within seconds was crouching in the new tree. Roman let out a laugh from a few feet lower down on the tree from which I had just jumped.

"Catch me if you can!" I taunted him, tossing him a kiss.

"Oh, I will catch you, my darkling, and the things I will do to you . . ." His voice was growly and made me shiver from head to toe.

I turned back toward the tree trunk and began climbing again. Sixty feet. Seventy. Eighty . . . at ninety I managed another leap into the next fir over. Up at this height, the trees swayed heavily in the wind and even though I had long ago stopped breathing, the power of the gusts filled me with energy, recharging me with their sweeping force that went galloping past.

Sneaking around to the other side of the trunk, I began to look for a hiding place. There, another thirty feet up, a thick pair of branches offered a comfortable place to sit. I quietly skittered up to them and crouched in my hidey-hole, waiting.

A moment passed, and another. I felt the tree shudder and knew that Roman had landed in it. Now to see if he would go on to the next or figure out that I had stayed in this one. I kept perfectly silent, holding on to the trunk as I waited. The moon was riding the sky, and I gazed up at her beauty. Camille and Delilah were both bound to her in a way I would never understand, but the moonlight was my sun, and the night was my life. Suddenly exhilarated, I stood and edged out on the branch, spreading my arms wide to greet the sky. I was a daughter of the night, a creature of the darkness, and my inner predator rose with joyful glee as I let out a long shriek.

Roman paused, and then I heard the branches rustle as he scaled the tree. As he came to where I was standing, a feral smile replaced the silent smirk and he let out a low laugh.

"My beautiful consort—you revel under the moon?"

"I revel in my nature tonight." And then, as he moved toward me, I stripped off my shirt and let it fall over the side. "Fuck me. Tear into me. I need to play."

That was all it took. One moment he was Blood Wyne's son, the next he was my wild, primal mate, grabbing my wrist. He glanced around. "We will play hard, but not here. There are too many broken branches that could inadvertently stake us." And with that, he wrapped his arm around my waist and leaped over the side. We sped toward the ground, but Roman was an ancient vampire, quite capable of flight—and of controlling his descents. At the last moment, he pulled out of freefall and we landed, laughing, on the soil beneath the tree.

He pushed me down on a bed of moss. The ground was prickly but nothing sharp threatened my back, and so I leaned back and let him strip my jeans off me. I was going commando, so no underwear or bra hindered the moment. The next moment he was naked, standing above me as his body shone with an inner luminosity, gleaming beneath the moonlight.

Roman moved in, his eyes glittering in the night. "Kneel before me, sireling."

A shudder raced through me. My gaze fastened to his, I slowly brought myself to my knees. He knew how much I both hated and craved this, and he was playing the glamour for all it was worth. I sat back on my knees in front of him.

"My Liege, what is your will?" My voice was steady, firm as the ground beneath our feet.

"Suck me. Taste me." He made no move to force my head; he did not even touch me. But his words were the only impetus I needed—I could no more ignore them than I could the imperative from the sunrise to sleep.

I leaned forward, my mouth seeking his erection, the icy smoothness of his cock sliding deep into my mouth as I began to work my tongue around him, tickling the tip, stroking the vein below it that pulsed slowly, faintly, mirroring no heartbeat. I sucked, hard, sliding along his length to draw him into my throat, and then pulling back only to drive forward again, my lips creating a tight suction that held him fiercely and wantonly.

Roman shuddered. After a moment he let out a long groan and leaned down to suddenly catch me by my arms as he lifted me to face him. "Feed from me. Feed deep and drink your fill."

As he exposed his throat, I leaned back and, fangs fully descended, plunged them into his glorious flesh, piercing deep into the jugular. Vampires had blood, but it flowed ever so slowly and without the need for our hearts to pump it. The viscous liquid began to stream into my mouth and I shivered at the taste. Roman was ancient—and the older the vampire, the more intoxicating the taste. It was sweeter than wine, sweeter than honey, sweeter than the most magical nectar in the world. As the crimson drops trickled across my tongue and down my throat, a ripple of power began to race through me. Roman was strong, and his blood took on a power and life of its own. The energy began to trace its way through my body and I coaxed the blood faster, my lips fastened against his neck as the coppery liquid bubbled up to the surface. I made it hurt, I made it delicious, I drove pain and pleasure with my bite until the force rippled through his body.

Roman let out a long cry, echoing through the night, and then—with a sharp bark—"Enough. *My* turn."

His gaze blazing, he shoved me back onto the ground, a cruel smile playing across his lips. He was hungry. My drinking from him had spurred on his desire, and he came at me, fangs bared, cock rigid and hard. I let the need to please my sire take over—it was a new feeling for me, and that I could actually enjoy the desire to please was both astounding and heady.

There was a power in submission that I had never before

understood. Camille understood it—we had talked at length about the need to balance strength to the outside world with vulnerability in the one place it was safe to express it. But with my background, with the torture and degradation Dredge had put me through, I never thought I would ever be able to open the door to that side of myself. And yet . . . here I was, hungry to please Roman, aching and willing to obey his commands.

He loomed over me, cupping my chin in his hands. As if reading my mind, he whispered, "You know that I will never abuse my place in your life. You know this, don't you? It's important to me that you understand I will never betray you."

I nodded. "I know how you feel about me, and I know you understand why I can't return the same feelings. But we have something together that is powerful and untouchable. Something I share with no one else. Feed on me, Roman. Drink from me. Take me deep into your darkness."

His lips touched my throat and as smooth as silk, his fangs pierced my vein, driving deep. I let out a throaty cry as the weight of his body pressed against me. He lapped at my throat, and in a tidal wave of hunger and desire, I shifted—spreading my legs so that he could drive his cock deep inside me, plunging into the core of my sex haze.

He was thick, and hard, and as he shifted, angling so that he slid in to the hilt, the motion sent a ripple through my entire body. He began to pump against me, and I rose to meet him, encouraging him to ride me hard. He freed one hand, bringing it down to caress my clit, circling it—demanding that I not ignore his presence. He filled me full, and the smell of him was everywhere—heady and musky and overwhelming. He was my world at this moment—inside me, touching me, drinking from my blood—Roman was the only reality and everything else faded into white noise.

And still he drank deep, the blood flowing from my body into his mouth in slow, exquisite droplets. His tongue lapped in a rhythmic motion, the sound of it grazing my skin became my only focus—and then the haze became a dance, a swirling mist of sensuality that flowed around us like a cloud of tendrils, and every inch of my body felt caressed by the motions carrying me into the depths of the night. All my scars—all of the marks that Dredge had claimed me with—faded in my mind. They would always adorn my body but now they were merely war wounds, scars of survival rather than of subjugation. Nerissa had helped me reclaim my soul from Dredge's torture, and Roman had helped me reclaim my ability to revel in my power.

With one last cry, I let go, coming hard, as Roman met my lips—my blood on his tongue—and kissed me deep under the early-summer moon.

Chapter 4

By the time we reached Training Room Two, forty vampires were waiting for me, all clad in Roman's signature black turtlenecks, black jeans, and black sunglasses. They were standing at attention, hands clasped behind their backs, legs slightly spread, staring straight ahead as we walked into the room. Both Roman and I had taken some time to freshen up after our tryst in the woods, and we looked entirely presentable.

I glanced over at Roman. "I thought you said twenty."

"The attack on the apartment complex changed my mind. I'm giving you double. We're facing threats from both outside this world and inside, so we might as well put more manpower on the streets." He moved to the front of the room, motioning for me to join him. As I did, he saluted the contingent and they came to full attention, saluting him back. In unison and with precise form, they reminded me of robots.

Two words echoed as a single voice from forty throats. "Lord Roman!"

Roman nodded. "Stand down."

They returned to their former position, but this time a little more relaxed.

"I'm appointing my consort, Menolly, in charge of you. Soldiers, you will obey her commands as if they came from me. She has full authority in this mission, and you will neither question her methods or her choices nor disobey her. Any man or woman who refuses to carry out her orders will be staked. We are at war, and you are my warriors. I expect you to behave the part. Do you understand?"

"Yes. Sir!" They came to quick attention again, saluting both of us.

It was odd to see vampires working in unison. Mostly we were solitary creatures. But with the reemergence of Blood Wyne into the public eye—at least as far as the undead brigade was concerned—the Earthside vamps were falling into a far more regimented nature. Like the Supe *Community*, the Vampire *Nation* was truly becoming a reality.

I took my place in front as Roman backed away. "I appreciate your cooperation. As you know, my sisters and I work for the Otherworld Intelligence Agency. Normally, what I'm about to tell you would remain under wraps, but a situation has risen that we need help with. Before I go into detail, I want to make this clear: Under *no* circumstances are you to discuss what I'm about to tell you with *anyone*. That is an *order*. This mission calls for diplomacy and stealth, and unless you are given permission, this is top-secret status. Do you understand?"

"Yes, ma'am!" echoed through the room.

"Break the rule and you will be staked," Roman interjected.

I wanted to hop on a stool and have them circle around me, but I knew that wouldn't command the respect I needed to earn. So I straightened my shoulders, wiped expression from my face, and stood as formally as I could.

"Seattle is facing an incursion of goblins and various creatures from Otherworld. They are troops sent from an army over there, an army that is doing its best to raze the land and destroy everyone who will not knuckle under to them."

I paused, then decided—in for a penny, in for a pound. "Telazhar—a necromancer—is in charge of this army. He is leading it on behalf of Shadow Wing, Demon Lord of the Subterranean Realms. Shadow Wing is planning to invade Earthside and Otherworld and turn both into his private little playground. My sisters and I have been fighting against him for a long time now, but the tide is turning against us. We've reached a tipping point in the war. Either he gains an upper hand and we pray for a miracle, or we manage to drive him back. These incursions are paving the way to help him gain that advantage."

I paused. There were no changes of expression or shifting, though the energy changed in the room. The temperature felt like it was dropping, though I was pretty sure it was just their mood as they realized what I was saying.

"Telazhar is trying to infiltrate Earthside from Otherworld. This is where you come in. We need you to patrol the streets, to keep an eye out for incursions of goblins and their ilk. They will most likely be coming through rogue portals. You are to notify us of any troops you find, then keep them penned away from any bystanders until we can get there. You are free to destroy any goblins, bone-walkers, or other creatures of that sort. But we want numbers. We're keeping track of how many come through, so we need an accurate count. Do you understand?"

A rousing "Yes, ma'am!" rang through the room.

"As I said, you will most likely find rogue portals in the areas where these attacks take place. We need to know their location and we need you to guard them until we can get our forces there to seal them off. So far, the attacks have been coming solely at night, so go out there expecting to find action. This is not a drill, and there have been two to three attacks a night for weeks now."

Roman cleared his throat. "Any and all attacks will be reported to three places: Arleth Mendez of the Seattle Vampire Nexus, Menolly and her sisters, and Chase Johnson at the Faerie-Human Crime Scene Investigation Unit. All phone numbers are in the handout you have been given. Program them into your cell phones before you leave this room." He glanced at me. "Anything else they should know?"

I thought for a moment. "We want to maintain absolutely no collateral damage if at all possible. If a hostage situation arises, contact us before you make a move. Try to minimize property damage. Let's handle this in a way that the hate groups can't bitch about, should they discover what's going on."

"Speaking of the Fellowship of the Earthborn Brethren . . . keep your eye out for human terrorists as well. The home boys are out to play rough, and they don't give a flying fuck if they take out innocent human lives along with the vamps and Supes they are targeting." Roman's voice was gruff. "If you happen to catch sight of a hate group in participation of a crime, you are *not* authorized to kill them. I repeat: You are only authorized to use force if your lives depend on it."

One of the vamps raised his hand. "What do we do in that situation?"

"The proper procedure is to contain them until such time that you can turn them over to the FH-CSI. We want no martyrs rising out of this."

And with that, we dismissed them, and the vampires moved into the streets under the cover of night.

I turned to Roman. "I should get home now. This is one hell of a situation. We're all having a hard time dealing with it. And after today . . . I'm afraid I'm beginning to lose some of my hope."

"I have feelers out on the missing and presumed dead. We'll see what we can find out. But I'm pretty sure nobody on that list was away on vacation. Let's just hope some were caught at friends' houses and had to sleep there through the day instead of returning to their apartments." He leaned in and placed a gentle kiss on my lips. "Go now, my love. I am going to talk to Mother, and I'll be back in a night or so. Give Nerissa my best."

And with that, he turned away and headed back to his

office. I gathered my coat and checked out at the front desk. It was close to eleven thirty and I had a lot to do.

I had no sooner started my Mustang when my cell phone rang. A glance at the Caller ID told me it was Derrick, the bartender in charge of the Wayfarer. The bar had first been my cover when I came over from Otherworld, and now I owned it outright. I punched the speaker.

"Go ahead."

Derrick was a brusque man—werebadger, really—and he was never offended with my lack of chitchat. "Boss, you need to get down here now. We have a situation."

"What the hell does that mean?" I hated it when people pussyfooted around.

"We've got a group of the Earthborn Brethren in here stirring up trouble. I've asked them to leave, but they have a few bikers from the Freedom's Angels with them and I'm afraid things are at a standoff right now." Derrick was whispering, so I knew that it had to be bad.

"I'm on my way. Hold them at bay as long as you can and please, please don't let them tear up the joint. But if it looks like they're going to start tossing things or people around, clear the place—that's top priority. People's safety. *Capiche?*"

"*Capiche*, boss." He hung up and I gunned the engine and headed toward the bar. Along the way, I put in a call to Delilah. "I just talked to Derrick. Big bad going down at the bar. Hate group there, looking for trouble. Can you and the guys meet me there?"

"Camille and Smoky left for the Dragon Reaches, but the rest of us will be there as soon as we can." The line went dead and I focused on driving.

By the time I reached the Wayfarer, I could see that there was, indeed, a problem. Outside the bar, a large group of people were picketing. They were dressed in long, navy robes, hoods pulled over their faces, and they were carrying signs that ranged from mild insults to inciting hate crimes.

FAGGOT VAMPS DIE.
NO SUPE RIGHTS!
GO HOME, FAE FUCKERS!
THE ONLY GOOD VAMP IS A DEAD VAMP!
BLOODSUCKERS, ROT IN HELL!

I screeched into a parking spot that contained several motorcycles I recognized as belonging to the the Freedom's Angels, knocking them over like a stack of dominoes with my car. Smiling grimly, I leaped out of the car and headed toward the door. Two of the picketers tried to stop me and I bared my fangs, my eyes turning crimson with bloodlust. I hissed at them, deciding to let them know just who they were dealing with. Reaching out, I placed a hand on each of their shoulders and shoved as hard as I could. The two men let out shouts as they went flying back, knocking down several of their buddies as they slammed into the brick wall of my bar.

"You *really* want to make trouble in *my* bar, boys?" I headed for the door as the rest of them backed away from me. "That's right, let Mama through or you're going to fucking wish to hell you'd stayed home watching reruns of *What Not to Wear*. Because, dudes, you have some serious fashion faux pas going on." As I finished my little speech, I slammed through the door, almost knocking it off the hinges.

As I entered the bar, I took in the situation with a single glance. Derrick was standing in front of the bar, holding one of the two sawed-off shotguns we kept behind the counter. Digger—a vampire and one of my bartenders—was standing on the bar behind him, holding the other shotgun. Around the room, the customers were backed up into the booths and corners, while a group of about fifteen of the Brethren and FAs had spread out, some of them carrying crowbars and baseball bats. The bikers were dressed in leathers, the Brethren in their hoodie robes.

I moved to stand between Derrick and the front of the group. "Whatcha doing, boys? You might want to put down those batons of yours before somebody—and by *somebody*,

I am referring to *you*—gets hurt. And by *hurt*, I am referring to being beaten to a bloody pulp."

The leader of the group, or at least he seemed to be the leader, stepped forward a half step. I hissed, showing him my fangs, and he retreated again. "We don't want your kind in our city."

"Seems like you don't want *my kind* anywhere, do you now?" I sneered at him. "Seems to me that you are going to be a long time hoping for days long gone. Get with the program, boys—the world is more diverse than you will ever hope to understand and either you change and accept it, or you're going to end up drop-kicked to some desert island."

"Cunt. You're an abomination. A demon. You have no feelings, no conscience. Be gone in the name of the Almighty!" He thrust out a cross made of wood.

I stared at it, then at him. "Nobody calls me that in my own bar." With a deliberate nonchalance, I reached out and grabbed the cross out of his hands, stared at it, shrugged, and tossed it back to Digger, who caught it and stuck it in his pocket. "Sorry, but that's going to do as much good as a feather. And it's an insult to those of your belief who have more foresight than you do."

"There is only one true race—and it's the human race."

I had to give it to him, he had more guts—or, most likely, stupidity—than most.

"Fine, you want to play, boy? I'm game; when I go for blood, trust me, I get it. I gave you a chance to leave my bar without incident. I'm going to give you one last opportunity to turn around and head for the door with your cronies." I was usually less in-your-face with pathetic, desperate men, but after the destruction of the DarkTower Gardens, I wasn't feeling charitable.

He wavered, and for a moment, I thought he was going to turn around and head out, but then one of his buddies murmured something and it seemed to spur him on. He leaped forward at me, and I caught him by the wrist, squeezing till the bones broke with an audible crack. I might as well have let loose the hordes, because that was all it took for the brawl to break. At that moment, Shade, Roz, Morio, and Delilah entered the bar and immediately moved in on the freaks.

"Subdue only, unless they make a move to kill you!" I raised my voice so it echoed through the room. And we were into it. I had to hold myself back. I was so used to going for broke with the enemy that fighting to restrain and not to kill was a challenge.

Morio had just shifted into his youkai form—an eight-foot-tall fox demon that would send terror into any sane human—when three prowl cars pulled up and several officers raced in. I recognized them as being from the FH-CSI and mentally sent a huge hug to Chase. Within ten minutes, the cops had rounded up ten men and two women between the gang in the bar and the picketers outside. A number of them had scrammed when the law arrived. Yugi—second in command to Chase, and a Swedish empath—was in charge. He waved me over.

"You want to press charges?" He glanced around and I followed his gaze. There had been some damage, but thankfully it was superficial.

"Yes. I do. They threatened my bar patrons and my staff, and me, and damaged my bar. Anything you can throw at them, Yugi." What I wanted to do was to pound them into the ground, but now that the cops had them out in a wagon—they'd had to bring in a bigger vehicle to transport them all—it wouldn't be good form to drag them out and rub their faces into the concrete.

"A couple of the guys out there are pretty beat up. They said you did it."

"I did. They were harassing me and I was afraid one of them might have a stake." I was lying, but then again, when I thought about it, the possibility had been all too real.

As if reading my mind, Yugi jerked his head toward the wagon of prisoners. "We found five stakes on them, two guns with silver bullets, and a variety of switchblades. We also found one flare gun and two Tasers, several pairs of silver handcuffs, and two pairs of iron handcuffs."

"Those freaks came prepared." A chill ran through my

heart. They were out for trouble, and out to harm. That much was clear. "It could have been so much worse."

"It probably would have been if we hadn't arrived when we did. Derrick called us earlier but damn, the town is jumping tonight and there were quite a few calls. We got here as soon as we could." The way he said it told me that something was up.

"What kind of calls?" I held his eyes.

Yugi's gaze flickered to the ground. "Apparently the Brethren were holding synchronized events tonight. They also tried to hit the Supe-Urban Café, the Supe Community Council, and a major wedding tonight—two Weres from notable families were getting married. We've been fielding one crisis after another. By the way—your vamps? They've jumped in and helped us a couple of times already. Tell Lord Roman we appreciate the muscle."

I nodded, feeling a little overwhelmed. That we were being attacked on two fronts, even though we were helping to save the butts of those who were attacking us, left a bitter taste in my mouth. I slumped back against a wall. "Tell me the truth. Will those guys get any time?"

"We'll make sure. One way or another, they get some sort of jail time. I don't care how we have to write up the charges. And remember: all of us at the FH-CSI fully believe they committed twenty-three . . . if not more . . . murders today, regardless of what the courts say about vampire rights. So . . . we'll jump through every hoop we have to." He paused.

Then, smiling at me through those gentle blue eyes, he reached out and gently laid a hand on my shoulder. "We're here to stop this stuff from happening. And when we can't, we're here to clean up the mess. Not everything at the station goes on in plain sight. Remember that." And with that cryptic but oddly comforting remark, he left.

We closed early, paying for all drinks because of the trauma my customers went through. After picking up the bar, I slumped down at one of the tables. Delilah and the guys had gone home, and Roman was sending over a couple of guards to watch over the bar till daybreak, when three of the Supe Militia would come down to stand guard.

Derrick, clutching a club soda, slipped into the chair next to me. He shoved a bottle of blood across the table. "You should drink something."

I stared at it, then moodily pulled it toward me, drinking deep. It wasn't as good as fresh, nor as tasty as the flavored blood Morio enchanted for me, but it was nourishment, and right now I needed it to take the edge off.

"Is it worth it, Derrick? First my bar gets torched and burned to the ground, killing eight people, including a friend. Now, we're being attacked by hate groups. Should I fold up? Say *screw it*, and sell the joint?" I cocked my head, gazing steadily at the werebadger.

He was a sturdy man, not tall—not short, with a streak of white through his dark hair, and a few scars that marred his face. He shrugged, his T-shirt rising and falling with his shoulders. "That is only something you can answer. But let me ask you this, boss. Have you ever run away from anything in your life? And what about the portal in the basement? You can't really let that fall into somebody else's hands."

I mulled over the question. "Once . . . yes. I ran away from my old sire, Dredge. I ran all the way here to Earthside."

"And he found you."

"Yeah, he did."

"So you had to face him, even though you tried your best to get away?" The corners of his lips tilted up just a little.

I wrinkled my nose. "I hate it when you're right."

Exasperated, yet knowing he was only pointing out the obvious, I leaned back in my chair and slowly slid my bottle back and forth on the table.

"I know you're right. If I sold the Wayfarer, I'd never forgive myself. For one thing, I love this place. I don't care if it's just one bar in the middle of a city full of them—it's *my* bar. I built it into what it is today. When I first arrived here, I was undercover as bartender. The OIA still owned this joint and they didn't give a damn about it, as long as they could control the portal in the basement. But now it's mine. I didn't buy it because of the portal. I didn't buy it to get rich. I bought the place because . . ." I paused, not quite sure what I was trying to say.

"Because it spoke to you." Derrick's voice was soft. "Because when you thought of walking away, it felt like you'd be leaving an old friend behind."

Nodding, I took a swig of the blood. It raced down my throat, warm and comforting. Derrick had warmed it to just the right temperature.

"I had no clue what we were in for when we came over here. None of us did. But now . . . we're all in. That's the thing—we're all in and we can't turn away. And I can't turn my back on the Wayfarer. This place owns a piece of my heart."

Derrick finished his club soda. "I know what you mean. In the time I've worked here, I've come to care about the bar in a way I didn't expect to. I've worked in a lot of places, Menolly. I've done a good job most times . . . sometimes had a few problems. But I've never looked forward to coming to work like I do here. I've got your back, you know? I'm here to watch over the bar when you can't. I'll do my best to make sure you don't feel I ever let you down."

With that, he pushed himself to his feet. "Go home, boss. Take the night off. Try to relax. I'll stay till the guards get here—in fact, I think they're at the door now." He nodded to two shadowy figures standing outside the door. Sure enough, even from here I could tell they were vamps. "Go on. Rest easy. I'll see you tomorrow night, if all goes well. If not, just drop me a note and I'll watch over your baby."

I swung out of my chair and, taking the werebadger by surprise, gave him a firm hug. "You be careful. We need you here. I need you here." And with that, I headed for home.

I arrived home just in time to find Trenyth speaking to the others through the Whispering Mirror. Delilah motioned me over.

"We got home just as he called. Trenyth has news . . ." She looked mildly alarmed.

"Please, let it be good. Or at least something easily dealt with." I cocked my head to the side. "I really don't want to hear anything else bad going on." But, with a sigh, I turned to the mirror. Trenyth couldn't see me, but he could hear me so I simply said, "Hey, Trenyth. I'm here."

Delilah cleared her throat. "Hold on, I need a drink of water." She jumped up and ran into the kitchen.

I frowned. Vanzir offered to bring me a chair, but I shook my head. I wasn't tired. In fact, the adrenaline was still coursing through my veins from the incident at the bar. It hit me that none of us could withstand more bad news. Morio, Roz, Vanzir, and Shade all looked beat. The war was bearing down on us now. We needed a break—something to reenergize us and give us hope.

By the time we were all gathered again, the tension in the room had built to a point where I could almost rip into it with my fangs. "Sorry, Trenyth. I think we're all a little antsy. It's been a rough past couple of weeks. Tell us what's going on, please."

The confused expression on his face fell away. "I can understand that. It seems like something's always coming. There's always a horror on the horizon, or behind the cliff, or in the cave, or riding the sky. But this time, it's good news."

The collective sigh in the room was audible.

"I got a call from Camille about an hour ago. The dragons are coming. She and Smoky asked me to tell you that we need you over here. The dragons are on the way, and they are going to war against Telazhar, but they need you with them." The joy in his eyes was impossible to ignore. "We've finally caught a break. They'll be here within the hour and they want you all to go with them."

Even though we knew that they had promised, there had been a little part of me—at least—that had expected them to renege at the last minute. Roz let out a huge cheer, thrusting his fist into the air. Vanzir and Morio followed suit, and then we all joined in.

But a thought occurred to me. If I went over there, what would I do come daylight? "What about me? I'm a vamp—"

"Camille and Smoky have rigged something up for you, just in case. You'll be safe, she promised. I know you hate to leave the house empty, but they said for you to send Maggie and Hanna to a safe location." Trenyth looked like he was about to cry.

"We've needed a break . . . ever since Kelvashan was besieged and Elqaneve fell, my people have been a mass of walking wounded." His voice was clouded and he wiped his hand across his eyes. "Even those who were unhurt by the destruction . . . everybody lost someone dear. Everybody lost their roots. Elves are grounded to their homeland, you know. The very land gives us strength and it shores us up. The land itself was wounded, and is still bleeding, and as long as it bleeds, so shall we. Now, the dragons will give us hope. Just the *news* gives me hope."

I nodded, slowly, even though he couldn't see me. "We'll come. We'll make arrangements and go to Grandmother Coyote's portal. We'll be there within the hour. Daylight is still a ways off."

And with that, the mirror fell silent.

Delilah pulled out her phone. "I'm texting Tanne. We need him with us to work with Iris."

Iris said nothing, and I realized that she meant to go with us. I turned to the others. "Hanna, take Maggie and stay with Bruce and the babies at the condo. When Nerissa gets home—well, I'll call her. Her place is big enough for all of you for now. I don't want her staying here, and we can't take her with us."

"Speaking of . . ." Morio nodded to the front door as it opened and Nerissa hustled through.

"I'll tell her. The rest of you get ready. Hanna, can you pack a small bag for me—you know what I wear. I'll need boots without heels." I unbuckled my stiletto knee-highs and slid them off as everybody else jumped to get ready.

Nerissa looked confused as I drew her into the parlor and shut the door.

"We're heading to Otherworld. Camille and Smoky are on their way to Elqaneve with the dragons, and they want us there. We're about to go to war against Telazhar. I have to go." I caught her gaze, holding it steady. "And you can't come with us. Chase needs you here."

She hesitated, her tawny hair flowing down her shoulders. I could sense her frustration, probably because I was paying a lot more attention these days. But I also saw the understanding that crept into her eyes.

"I don't want you to go, you know that."

"I know, but I have no choice."

"I love you. Do you know how much I love you?" She pulled me to her. Nerissa was far taller than I, and when I gazed up into her face, I saw only love shining back.

"Yes, I do. And I'm sorry. I'd rather stay here. I'd rather take you with us. But . . ." I sought for the words, which weren't coming that easily.

Unlike Delilah and Camille, I knew I couldn't take Nerissa with me. She would distract me—worrying about her safety would take my attention away from where it needed to be. I knew it was unreasonable; after all, she was a werepuma and was learning quickly how to defend herself against all sorts of beasties, but the fact was she was still extremely vulnerable. More importantly, she hadn't yet learned how to *think* like a warrior. And that, perhaps, was the biggest danger.

Nerissa was a healer at heart. She knew how to take in pain and transform it. But she still didn't think in terms of enemies and opponents and sizing up strengths and weaknesses in order to best attack. She thought like a healer, which was wonderful. Beautiful. But not during a battle, when the focus had to be on survival and *us versus them.*

I rested my head against her and she pressed her lips to my hair, then trailed them down my face, to reach my lips, where she gently—passionately—slid her tongue between them. We kissed, long and lazily, and I pushed the thoughts of the impending battle out of my mind, focusing on her touch, on her smell, on the pulse of her heart against my silent one. I cherished her warmth and every single rise and fall of her chest that meant she was alive, and well, and still my wife.

We stayed like that, frozen, holding each other, until she finally pushed me back to hold me at arm's length. "I know you have to go."

"Thank you." My voice was barely above a whisper. "I will do everything in my power to come back to you alive. I can't imagine life without you. And Nerissa, I'm so sorry about the past months. I'm sorry I haven't been able to understand . . ."

"Stop." She gently pressed her finger against my lips. "Just stop. You've made mistakes. I've made mistakes. We learn and go on. I'll be here, waiting, doing my best to keep things moving on this side of the portal. I'll help Chase. I'll help Bruce and Hanna watch over the babies. You and your sisters go stop Telazhar." Pausing, she let a faint smile creep through. "I do wish . . . I wish I could go see the dragons. To see a grandeur of dragons sweeping through the air, to see them going to war? I wish you could take pictures!"

I laughed, then. "You're like Samwise in *The Lord of the Rings*. Only instead of wanting to see the elves . . ."

"Yes!" She clapped her hands. "I'd love to see so many dragons filling the sky." Then the smile faded again. "I wish we had time to spend together before you go. I want to taste you."

I glanced at the clock. "I know, me, too. But I think . . . I think . . ." But she silenced me, pulling me to her and quickly unzipping my jeans. As her hand slid inside them, her fingers feeling their way down to the thatch between my legs, I slipped my hands under her blouse and unfastened her bra, cupping her breast, pressing my thumb against the erect nipple. She gasped, working me, her mouth crushing mine, in a haste brought on by the desperate fear that we might never see each other again.

We tumbled to the sofa, and with my other hand, I reached beneath her skirt, sliding my fingers inside the thin slip of material that masqueraded as her panties. I quickly found her clit and began to work it, gently, then harder as she moaned.

Her pussy was wet, and I plunged my fingers inside her, smearing the juice up to lubricate her clit, swirling it harder and harder as she began to thrash. Her fingers were deep in my pussy, but she was losing focus as I brought her higher, pressing my breasts against hers, kneading away at the ripe globes. I managed to rip open her blouse and lowered my lips to suck on her nipple, biting just hard enough to elicit a sharp cry.

Then I pushed away from her, pulling away from her touch as I lowered myself to the floor and—holding the material away from her crotch—pressed my lips against her sex, licking and sucking hard. She let out another cry and then—before I could do more—she came, hard, tears pouring down her face. I kissed her inner lips gently, then sat back and watched as she curled on the sofa, weeping.

"I'm so scared you'll die." She had climaxed out of fear and need and passion, and her orgasm had released her so that now the tears were able to flow.

"I know. So am I." I leaned in, gathering her close as she held out her arms to me. "I'll do my best . . . we all will. I love you."

She sat up then, trying to wipe her eyes. "I guess . . . you'd better go."

I nodded. "Yeah. I need to get a move on. Promise me you'll take Hanna and Maggie with you as soon as we leave?"

"I promise. I'll watch over them." She hung her head. "I guess Iris has it worse, leaving her babies and Bruce. She is going with you, isn't she?"

"We need her and she understands. And we're taking Tanne. Delilah said something about texting him to come with." I zipped up my pants and tucked my shirt in again. "Nerissa, if something happens to me . . ."

"Nothing will. Don't you dare say another word." She rearranged her skirt and stared at the ripped shirt. "I think this one is for the rag barrel."

"But if something does happen—" I wanted to tell her to go to her Were friend, to let him make her happy, but she pressed her lips together firmly and shook her head.

"I don't want to hear it. I'll tell Roman you had to go. Now get moving before I have another meltdown." And with that, she kissed me one last time and pushed me out the door, staying in the parlor. I realized she needed to stay there, to not watch me walk out the door.

The others were waiting. If they knew what had gone on behind the closed door, nobody said anything.

Delilah cleared her throat. "I texted Tanne. He'll meet us at the edge of Grandmother Coyote's woods. We'll run there—it won't take us long and it will save leaving a car out for somebody to come along and strip." She tossed me a bag. "Hanna packed for you."

"Then I guess we're ready." I turned to the door. "Let's go meet the dragons . . . and go to war."

Chapter 5

The portal to Otherworld from Grandmother Coyote's lair led to a cave near the great Barrow Mounds outside Elqaneve. The cave, at least, looked like it had taken no damage, and there were seven portals in the giant cavern, all heavily guarded. In fact, I had never seen such a great military force in this area before. Elfin guards, Fae, even a few Goldunsan—the desert Fae—watched over the interdimensional vortexes. They were heavily armed and I had the feeling that some of their weapons weren't visible—like magic.

As we stepped away from the portal with Delilah and me leading the way, I saw someone who looked suspiciously familiar. Turned out, I was right. He was one of the guards we often saw in the background when we were talking to Trenyth through the mirror.

"I've come to escort you into headquarters." He motioned to the entrance of the cave. "We have carriages waiting, and an escort."

As we emerged from the cave, I glanced up at the sky. We were near midnight. There were three carriages waiting by the Barrow Mounds. Instead of the noblas stedas of

Otherworld—a gorgeous, six-legged horse—they were being pulled by *gorts*. Gorts were usually found in barren wastelands and were like giant lizards, though a great deal larger, much like a squat Komodo dragon in looks. They were reptilian in nature, like lizards, and they were fast and vicious.

"That's new." I nodded to the creatures.

"We don't like to chance the steeds we have left to raiding parties. The gorts are fast and mean. And they're a lot quicker to breed." The guard motioned for us to proceed.

The Barrow Mounds were remnants of days long past. A thousand years before, they had once sheltered the heart and soul of the Elfin nation. An oracle, she had been half Svartan and half elf. Worshiped almost as a goddess, she had read the future for all who passed by. But bandits had overwhelmed the Mounds and killed her. Since that day, the area had been haunted and barren, a stark contrast to the lushness that was Kelvashan.

I glanced over at Delilah, who was staring at the mounds. "What do you see?"

"Women and warriors . . . wounded men. Ghosts of the past, all whispering by me. They know I see them—I'm letting them know. There are so many elves here who died during the storm, too. I see them everywhere I turn. The rites of the dead haven't been performed for most. At some point, Sharah needs to preside over one mass ritual for all who were taken by Telazhar's fury." She turned back to me, her face drawn. "So many died. The entire world—both here and over Earthside—will be a walking graveyard if we don't come through this."

Her voice broke, catching on the words, and she hung her head. Beside her, Shade wrapped his arm around her waist and she rested her head on his shoulder for a moment.

I reached out to take her hand, holding tight. She was right. If we could take down Telazhar, then we would make a wonderful, blessed impact on Shadow Wing's efforts. "Then we win. Regardless of what it takes or the price we pay, we win. We won't let that happen."

Delilah squeezed my hand. "Oh, this is too funny."

"What is?"

"You, cheering me up. Usually I'm the eternal optimist and you're the realist. Though I can't say that I've felt much like an optimist lately. The bright-eyed young woman that I was when we first set eyes on the portals and went Earthside . . . she's long gone." She said it almost wistfully, but when I started to ask if she missed that side of herself, she held up her hand. "What's gone is gone. As Camille would say, *It is what it is*. And that's okay. Say, do you think she'll come in riding on Smoky's back?"

I laughed. "That's a lovely sight. She knows how, for sure."

Our sister and her dragon husband often went out for a flight, him in dragon form and her on his back, holding on with gleeful delight. He had helped her with her fear of heights, though she still didn't like standing on the edge of a cliff. But somehow, being astride her husband's back with his giant wings seemed to take the fear of flying right out of her.

The carriages were comfortable, though we cautiously avoided the gorts as we climbed in. Iris sat next to me, and Rozurial sat opposite. Morio, Trillian, and Vanzir went in the second carriage. Shade, Delilah, and Tanne rode in the third.

Iris leaned back against the seat. She looked as tired as the rest of us. "I really don't want to be here, but I know I had to come." She frowned. "I received a note from the Temple of Undutar not long ago."

I cocked my head. She hadn't told us about *this*. "Oh, and what did it say?"

"They would like it if I would bring my children to them for an official blessing. They can take their note and shove it up their . . . iceholes." Iris shook her head. "I know what they want. They want to punish me for what happened by claiming one of my children for the temple. But Undutar herself made me her Earthside High Priestess. They don't dare go against her wishes, so I'm pretty sure they were going to do their best to be *inclusive* . . . in other words, use guilt to talk me into claiming one of my children."

"Can they do that? Doesn't the fact that you are the

Goddess's Earthside agent give you the right to set your own rules?"

I had no clue how the Priestesshood worked. It was different for every temple, every deity. Iris was the priestess of Undutar, the Finnish goddess of mist and ice and fog. She had been cast out of her temple for a terrible crime, long ago, and had managed to extricate herself from the charges, but it hadn't healed the breach caused by their violence against her when they had exiled her. Iris was quick to forgive small slights, but when it came to holding a grudge for an egregious act, she was one of the best.

"I operate under that assumption, but I'm thinking they aren't betting on my lack of cooperation. I have no clue why they're being so asinine about it. Perhaps the High Priestess of the order has gone dotty or something." She shrugged. "Whatever the case, they better not be waiting by the mailbox for an answer from me."

Roz was leaning back against the seat, his eyes closed. But I knew he wasn't asleep. He was listening to every word we said. The incubus had started out a bounty hunter; he was after the same vampire who had turned me. Dredge had destroyed Roz's entire family. But Rozurial had ended up joining forces with us and had been part of our extended tribe for years now. He had also developed a mad crush on Iris, though it went unrequited, and he did his best to remain on a friends-only basis. Even if she had not married Bruce, nothing would have come of it. Incubi and succubi couldn't have normal relationships—not and remain true to their nature.

The Barrow Mounds were located right outside Elqaneve, the capital city of Kelvashan. Unfortunately, Elqaneve was a pale shadow of its former glory. My sisters and I had been at the palace the night the storm came thundering down from the sky, and by morning, the city and most of the Elfin countryside lay in charred, smoking ruins. The Queen was dead, and the storm had rolled on to attack a new target. Telazhar and his band of sorcerers had created the sentient mass out of rogue magic and anger—and it had rained death and destruction from the sky over several of the cities before being destroyed.

As we rode through the outskirts of the city, fires lit the sides of the roads. Some were in houses that had been hastily cobbled back together. Others were out in the open, where we could just make out the shadows of tents and makeshift camps. It had been about six months—almost seven—since the sorcerers marched on the city, but even now, I could still smell the heavy scent of charcoal and dust in the air. Luckily, I didn't have to breathe.

Iris coughed, shaking her head. "So much madness in the world. So much destruction. I knew it was bad, but I haven't been back to Otherworld since then—at least not to Elqaneve. There used to be row after row of brightly lit houses lining this road. Now everything is gone."

I followed her gaze out the window of the carriage. We were being escorted by twenty guards, all on alert, all with weapons drawn. Was it really still so dangerous here? Were the goblins still overrunning the lands? The thought of Camille and Smoky leading the dragons down through Elqaneve made me smile, because when they came in, the elves would rally. They would have something to gather behind and support. Sharah would be able to whip them into a frenzy. And right now, hope was our greatest ally. Hope for the future, hope for the present.

As we wound our way into the city proper—or what was left of it—my mood perked up a little. I didn't realize how much the fall of the Elfin city had hit me, but now, staring at the remains of the toppled buildings, I could only wish that the storm had hit anywhere but here. The city had been graceful, beautiful in its simplicity, yet as majestic as they came. But as I gazed at the flickering fires that lined the city streets, I realized that here and there, new life was springing from the rubble. Where a row of apartments had stood, a new building was slowly being erected. A devastated fountain was flowing again—next to the ruins of the first. Slowly, but surely, the elves were taking back their city, reclaiming Elqaneve from the damage done.

Iris followed my gaze. "They're rebuilding. Even in the midst of such total destruction, they are rebuilding."

"Life will go on. Survival isn't enough. They're doing as

best they can to recover. We need to make Otherworld safe for them to start over. If Telazhar is eliminated and his armies destroyed, then the elves—and everyone over here—stands a chance." I found my hopes beginning to rise.

"Aren't you forgetting about Shadow Wing? He will still be pressing."

"Ah, yes. But how demoralizing will it be if we destroy his host here in Otherworld? If we grind his army down to the ground? And if we can defeat Telazhar, maybe . . ."

"Maybe we can defeat the Demon Lord himself?" She smiled softly. "Optimism and hope—we are in dire need of it. I'm glad to see you find your way through the mire. I will follow you in that hope. Because the world has to survive if my children are to grow and thrive in it."

She was right. And I suddenly understood something about caring for others. I might not have children, but I had Nerissa. And I had my sisters and Iris and all my friends. And the thought of them walking into a future built on the fires and destruction of Shadow Wing was too much to handle. I had to keep hope in order to make it possible to even try.

"You're right." I glanced over at Roz. "Quit pretending you're asleep, dude. I know you aren't."

He grinned and opened his eyes. "Right. I'm not."

"Will you hold hope with us, Roz?" I caught his gaze, challenging him.

He let out a soft breath, looking out the windows. "If I didn't hold hope for the future, I would have let Dredge kill me when I was young. I would have thrown myself on my sword when Zeus and Hera destroyed my marriage. If I didn't have any hope for the future, I'd be long gone, leaving all of you in the dust. It's because of you that I believe we can make it through this. Without the three of you . . . without Iris and all the others, there is no defense. So we *have* to believe we can defeat him."

When put like that, it was even simpler. I smiled softly and leaned back as the carriage wound through the streets. It wasn't far to the palace, but there had been so much destruction that we were taking detours right and left.

"Sing something for us, Menolly." Iris leaned close to me. "Sing us a song . . . you have such a beautiful voice."

I was about to say no, but then decided what the hell. Why not? After thinking for a moment, I remembered a song that Sephreh—our father—had sung to us when we were children. It had been called "Courage, My Child," and Father had always sung it to us the night before he had to leave for a mission, the nights when we were so afraid he wouldn't come back.

"There are times in the world when you must raise
your sword,
When peace is lying in tatters.
There are times in this world when you must go
to war,
Before all hope is shattered.
So listen to me, my child, my love,
Courage—in your heart must be burning.
The gods will watch from the heavens above,
And the world will go right on turning.

"In the heart of the wood, an oracle speaks,
She tells you of death and destruction,
But in the heart of the world, a single drum beats,
And the light finds a pathway to shine in.
So listen to me my child, my love,
Hope—in your heart must be burning.
The gods will watch from heavens above,
And the world will go right on turning."

I let the words drift away as we pulled into what had been the courtyard of the palace. Every wall had been shattered, so much marble into dust, but the bodies had been moved and buried, and the moonlight shimmered down on the scene, a melancholy and eerie sentinel from above.

"Why are we meeting here? I thought they moved headquarters to a secret area."

As we hopped out of the carriage—with Roz helping Iris down—I couldn't help but wonder. After all, this was an easy target and if Sharah had taken up residence in the ruins again, then it wouldn't be that hard to find her.

But Iris had the answer, or at least one that made sense until we talked to Trenyth. "Dragons. There's a lot of open space here and it will be the easiest place for the dragons to gather before heading out. Once they get here, they probably won't stay long—while the word will likely pass ahead, if they can travel through the Ionyc Seas, then they won't have to worry about Telazhar being prepared for their arrival."

That made total sense. "I think you're probably right. So where are—" I stopped as Delilah and the others joined us. As we stood there, a contingent of white-robed figures rose from behind the giant stones that had been tossed around like gumballs falling out of a machine. Trenyth, and with him Sharah, as well as a number of guards behind them.

"Sharah!" I started to run forward but then stopped. She was the Queen of Kelvashan now, and she deserved our respect, especially in front of her comrades. Nudging Delilah in the side, I did a half curtsey, half bow. Delilah followed suit. Iris had swept into a low curtsey, and the men bowed, paying their respects. We rose, waiting for her to speak.

"I'm so grateful to see you all again!" Sharah hurried forward, Trenyth by her side. She didn't hug us—that wouldn't be appropriate—but in the light of the torches, her eyes were glimmering. "How are Chase and my Astrid?" The hunger in her voice spoke volumes.

"They're fine, Your Highness. They are both well and both are being watched over." Delilah looked delighted at being able to give some good news for a change. "We're so happy to see you again. And . . . at least these are better circumstances . . . more or less."

Trenyth was about to speak when one of the guards shaded his eyes and looked past the moon. "There they are! They're coming. The dragons!"

Like kids in a candy shop, we all crowded forward, staring up into the sky. The dark shadows of massive wings came flying toward us—and then the glimmer of their scales began to show. I hadn't realized that dragons in their natural form had a faint luminosity, but they did, like bioluminescent plankton or deep sea jellies. And then, the next moment, they lit up the sky. The entire horizon was glowing with the great winged beasts, magnificent in their flight. The dragons had, indeed, arrived.

"A grandeur of dragons," I whispered. "Have you ever seen anything more beautiful and terrifying? I'm so glad they're on our side."

"You and me both." Trenyth was standing near me, and he glanced over at me with a brilliant smile on his face. "I can't believe I'm actually seeing this. I never in the world thought they would actually keep their promise."

"My sister would have their heads if they didn't." But I was thinking the same thing, to be honest. Some dragons played fair, but I wasn't really sure if I had believed they would come to help us out. Yet here they were, at least a thousand strong.

The front beast circled overhead—a great dragon with shades of white and silver mingling throughout his body, and massive wings that stretched out to steer his way. He slowly settled down onto what had once been the plaza of the Court. I suddenly realized it was Smoky—with Camille riding on his back. She slipped off as he lowered his head to the ground, using the silky mane to balance herself. Once her footing was secure, she stepped to the side and within seconds, Smoky stood there in his human form. He wrapped his arm around her waist and lifted her up for a kiss.

Other dragons began to land, setting up a significant wind as they circled in for landing. One by one, they began to shift and move aside for others to land until there was a host of extremely tall, brilliantly beautiful men and women standing in front of us. Next to Smoky, I recognized Vishana—Smoky's mother. There were others, all kinds—reds, golds, blues, whites, silvers, even shadow dragons.

Camille and Smoky escorted his mother forward to Sharah first. "Your Majesty, Queen of the Elfin lands, may we present Lady Vishana, Countess of Silver, and Most Valued Friend to the Throne of the Dragon Reaches."

In dragon-speak, that meant Smoky's mother wasn't a

princess but she might as well be. Smoky had been referred to more than once as a prince of the realm. Vishana was tall—seven feet if she was an inch. Her skin was as pale as Smoky's, her eyes gunmetal gray. Her hair was pure spun silver, flowing to her knees. The strands twisted and wound themselves to curl around her as she adjusted her ice blue gown. Diaphanous, it looked as though it could tear at the simplest breeze, but I had a feeling it was stronger than spider silk.

She inclined her head, then slowly curtsied to Sharah. An incoming monarch always bowed to the one with home court advantage. At least, that was how it worked in Otherworld.

"Your Majesty, I am pleased to meet you." Vishana glanced around at the destruction. "Let's dispense with small talk. There is so much damage here that I cannot imagine prattling on about nonsensical things. We are here to go to war. I have given my promise to my daughter-in-law, and the Dragon Reaches owe her more than we can ever return to her. Therefore, we are ready to take up arms against your foes. I declare that your enemy is our enemy."

And that sealed it—a strong, firm bond created in a promise.

Sharah's pale demeanor brightened. "I cannot thank you enough. I declare the elves allies of the Dragonkin, and may our bond hold." And then—it was all down to business. She motioned for Vishana, Smoky, Camille, Delilah, and me to follow her, leaving the rest of our crew to make certain the dragons didn't go ballistic on the elves for any wayward reason.

As we approached what had once been the grand ballroom of the palace, it was clear the elves had been busy. The rubble had been cleared away to show a cracked and shattered foundation. But in the parts that were still stable, long tables had been set up, with rough benches. Another table held loaves of bread stacked high, and what looked like a couple of roast pigs. A mound of apples and a massive bowl of spring greens sat beside them. Simple fare, but filling.

Torches ringed the area, but I still had the feeling the makeshift headquarters had been hastily assembled. Then it hit me that the elves didn't want the Dragonkin to know where they were hiding their throne room. That made sense, but I wasn't going to draw attention to the fact, because any slights now might be taken the wrong way.

We gathered around the table, where Trenyth began marking several massive maps with wooden figures. "Here's where we are. This"—he motioned to a border on the map—"is what's left of our city and Kelvashan in general. Most of our lands have been destroyed, but as you probably noticed on your way over from the portals, we've attempted to start the rebuilding process. It will take years, and who knows if the Elfin race will ever be what it was before the attack. Unfortunately, we're still besieged by contingents of goblins and other miscreants. They seem more scattered now, though—probably those who broke off from Telazhar's armies to loot on their own, but they see our city and lands as easy picking, so half our efforts are used up on keeping them at bay."

Vishana frowned. "We can help you with that. The Elfin race is a noble, ancient one. You should not have to put up with lowbrow cretins." She turned to the man—a gold dragon by the looks of him—next to her. "Appoint a small garrison to guard over the borders of Kelvashan. And summon the Builders. They can help to restructure Elqaneve."

The Builders? I glanced at Camille, but she shrugged. Apparently she had no clue what Vishana was talking about either.

"Where is Telazhar right now?" I leaned over the maps, squinting in the dim light.

"Here—surrounding Ceredream, the City of the East."

Ceredream was a beautiful city, but a dangerous one. And it lay south of the Sandwhistle Desert, north of the Southern Wastes where the rogue magic played havoc with anyone or thing crossing its path. To the east of Ceredream were the Ranakwa Fens—a massive swamp land dangerous to pass through, filled with deadly armies of ghosts. To the west lay vast grasslands and prairies that led to the forests surrounding the base of the Nebelvuouri Mountains, where the dwarven king ruled. I suddenly realized how much I missed my home world, and how torn between here and Earthside I was at my core.

"Didn't he already attack Ceredream?" Delilah frowned, leaning closer to study the map. "Are these big red Xs places that Telazhar has conquered?"

Sharah nodded. "More to the effect, places he has destroyed. Telazhar made a play for Ceredream once before, but they managed to beat him back. Now his armies are laying siege to the walls of the City of the East again. I think he's worn them down. While we could not help them—obviously—and Y'Elestrial was strapped from helping us, Aladril came to their aid the first time. So did King Gwyfn of Nebelvuouri. Svartalfheim was heavily damaged but not fully destroyed. The Goldunsan city of Gylden was attacked, but they were able to raise help from the Tygerian monks. The monks cloaked their city till it became impossible to find, so Telazhar gave up on them."

The Goldunsan were a reclusive, peaceful offshoot of the Fae race. They were golden skinned and incredibly beautiful people, and kept to themselves for the most part. That the monks came to their defense said a lot for them. The Tygerian monks were aloof and seldom spoke to anyone outside their order, though they were gracious to visitors and never turned away an honest request as long as the intent behind it was for good.

Vishana frowned. "How did you manage to stop the storm?"

"Eventually, through a combined effort. Sorcerers from Svartalfheim, a few of our remaining mages, and the Seers from Aladril managed to destroy the storm."

"Why is he hammering back at Ceredream?" It didn't make sense to me. Why go back to a place you've already beaten down?

"We believe he's managed to take over the portals on the outskirts of the city, and that's why he's been able to break through to Earthside. If he can take the city, he will have full access to any portal in it. And Ceredream has many portals, not just leading Earthside, but elsewhere in Otherworld."

That answered that. "We think he's managed to figure out how to create portals, too—unstable, rogue ones." I explained how we had been finding them all throughout the city.

"Not quite accurate." Trenyth motioned to one of the elves standing near him. "This is Quith. He's the strongest techno-mage who survived the storm. Quith, will you explain to them what Telazhar is actually doing?"

Quith launched into a smatter of magical jargon that only Camille and Morio seemed to understand before Trenyth put a hand on his shoulder. "For the unenlightened, boy."

"Oh, yes sir."

It was then that I realized Quith was quite young, in Elfin terms, and he suddenly looked like a quiet, scared rabbit to me. He was probably terrified of letting his people down. And if he was the most seasoned techno-mage to survive the onslaught, I wondered how the elves would ever rebuild the magic inherent within their race.

He cleared his throat and straightened his shoulders like a schoolboy. "Telazhar has found a way to pinpoint where the rogue portals are forming. As you know, the spatial fabric keeping the realms separate is breaking down, and as a result, rogue portals have been appearing. Telazhar has developed a way to track where they are going to happen. But he can only work within a dozen or so leagues of the area in order to make it there while the portal is active before it shifts its position. It takes an immense amount of energy to focus on this. Several sorcerers have to combine forces. So it's requiring a great deal of his resources to track and use these portals."

"In other words, his attention is divided." Smoky grinned, and the dragon within was suddenly glaringly apparent, toothy and dangerous and making me cringe.

"Yes, exactly. Which puts him at a disadvantage right now." Quith grinned back at him.

Vishana, who had been listening closely, smiled, too—like a cat at the sight of a mouse. "Time to play then. We must go. We can shift through the Ionyc Seas and be there in minutes. I don't think they've had time to hear about us—we came here the same way."

I glanced at the sky. "I don't know if I can go—I'm a vampire. It's not anywhere near morning yet, but . . ."

"Don't worry, little fanged one." A tall, dark-skinned dragon stepped forward, reminding me a lot of Shade. "I will fly you, and keep you safe. If worse comes to worst, we can shift into the Netherworld."

I was right. He was a shadow dragon. "The Netherworld?" I cocked my head. "I can't go to the Netherworld because I'm a vampire—I'm technically undead and there's some weird mismatch of energy."

"Then I can keep you safe by taking you out into the Ionyc Seas until daylight passes."

That would work. "All right, but I can't be in the sun—at all. Sunrise comes, I'm toast unless I'm protected from it. And even then, if I'm in a place that sees sunrise, I'll fall asleep."

"Do not fear. Ride my back and I'll protect you." He bowed, a solemn expression crossing his face. "You may call me Vapor."

"I'm Menolly." I shook his hand as the others paired off.

Camille was with Smoky, of course, and Delilah would ride on Shade's back. Iris and Tanne went together on the back of a blue dragon shifter—a tall, gorgeous man with long dark hair that was streaked with blue and purple. Morio and Trillian were paired with a lanky Amazon of a woman. Even as far as dragons went, she was incredibly tall, at least eight feet or more, and by the wheat-colored hair and emerald eyes, I had the feeling she was a green dragon. Vanzir and Rozurial were matched with a red dragon shifter.

"The elves should stay here." Vishana shook her head when Trenyth offered to send some of his warriors. "You have lost too many already. While we will no doubt lose a few of our own, I don't want to chance your numbers diminishing even further."

Sharah looked visibly relieved. "Thank you—we need every man, woman, and child we still have standing."

"I imagine repopulating your race will be a priority." Vishana's lips crinkled into a smile, and Sharah laughed.

"Yes, actually." She sobered then. "And I'm expected to

produce an heir as soon as possible. Unfortunately, my sweet little Astrid won't be eligible to take the throne."

Camille, Delilah, and I all gave a sharp turn of the head at that. While we had suspected this might happen, we also knew that Chase hadn't said a word if the thought had crossed his mind. I hoped, for his sake, that the idea had already occurred to him and that he was working on accepting it. It wouldn't be an easy thing for him—watching the woman he loved get pregnant by another man. But Sharah owed it to the throne and when dealing with royalty, duty almost always won out over the heart. Delilah opened her mouth but stopped when I shook my head.

"Then let us waste no more time. To the sky." Vishana strode forward. Apparently she was at the helm of this operation. "Warn the officials in Ceredream that we are coming, if you can."

I turned to Vapor, who motioned for me to step back. "If the sun begins to rise while we are there, I will instantly transport you into the Ionyc Seas, Mistress Menolly." He grinned—a very engaging grin—and then shifted and a massive, skeletal dragon stood before me. I gazed up at him in awe. Shadow dragons were bonelike in their natural form, and unlike the rest of the dragons who lived primarily in the Dragon Reaches, the shadow dragons inhabited the Netherworlds.

I scrambled astride the massive, bony neck as Vapor lowered his head to the ground beside me, and managed to fit myself in between two vertebrae. It was time to rock and roll. As soon as I was settled, he launched into the sky and we hovered there, circling as the other dragons began to shift form and take wing. I glanced through the night sky to see Camille and Smoky nearby, and Delilah astride Shade. The others were soon near us and—led by Vishana—one by one they winked out of sight into the Ionyc Seas. I wondered how they all knew where to go, but then a current raced through the air, an undertow in the wind, and I had the strangest feeling they were talking without saying a word. Another moment and Vapor shot forward, and we—too—shimmered out of the skies over Elqaneve—and into the roiling mists of the Ionyc Seas.

Chapter 6

The Ionyc Seas were a brilliant swirl of sparkling mist—an ocean of icy energy currents. I had always seen it from being encircled with someone's arms before, but now the bubble of protection that barricaded me allowed me full sight out into the roiling mists. The channels of energy running between the realms separated them so the energies wouldn't go colliding into one another, which would be a bad thing, apparently. *Very bad*, though I wasn't entirely sure exactly what would happen. Something about *implosions* and *ripping through reality*, neither of which sounded appealing.

I had ridden on the back of a dragon once, on Smoky's back through the astral plane as Camille raced on ahead after a demon who was threatening Delilah. But this? This was different. This dragon was made of bone, and the energy of death swirled around him. I could feel it, being a creature from beyond the veils myself.

I seldom talked about it, especially not with my sisters or my wife, but there were times when I was exhilarated by the realization that I had passed through the veils of death and returned, when I reveled in my power and strength caused by denying death. During those times I watched myself carefully because the predator within would rise, feeling invulnerable and aching to exert her power. At other times, the thought of what I had gone through was a hellish memory, and I wanted to just walk outside during the next sunrise and cleanse my tainted body. But most of the time . . . I tried to focus on what I could do now. On the good I could do. The life I could live. The love I could accept, and the love I could offer.

Vapor was huge, about twice as big as Shade was in dragon form. I wondered if that was because Shade was half dragon or if there was some other reason, but it would never be a question I'd ask aloud. For one thing, men had a thing when it came to size comparisons, and for another, it wasn't any of my business.

Going through the Ionyc Seas didn't actually feel like we were traveling. In fact, it felt very much like rocking in a hammock or floating in the middle of a gentle lake where the waves sloshed you gently from side to side. Though I had heard of great storms that rolled through the currents, tornadoes with massive lightning storms thundering through them.

Time vanished the moment you entered the Seas. I still had no clue of how the dragons and ice serpents and various other creatures who could venture here navigated between spaces, but there was a rhythm here—an ebb and flow, just like the ocean. If I hadn't been a vampire, I would have succumbed to the tides, falling into a waking/sleeping pattern that was, in reality, actually energy draining and then recharging. The pattern mimicked a circadian rhythm. But with my nature and no sunrise or sunset to contend with, I stayed awake, my personal energy relatively immune. It was then that I realized this must be why certain creatures could enter the Ionyc Seas and travel through them—they didn't follow the natural patterns of humans and the like.

The massive skeletal dragon beneath me swayed and dipped through the currents of mist. The Ionyc Seas' currents weren't actual liquid like water, but liquid energy, like flowing lightning and fog. I had wedged myself between two of the giant vertebrae at the base of the dragon's neck, and the bone felt comfortingly steady.

And then, just as I was getting used to the ride, we emerged from the sea into the night sky. Below us stretched the city of Ceredream—pronounced with a hard *c*. The lights from a hundred thousand houses and the fires lining the city walls blinded me momentarily—I had grown used to the darkness here. Then a grim specter rose up to greet us. Even from overhead, we could see the massive armies gathered on all sides of the city. They were like a seething colony of ants, swarming against the gates. Goblins, mostly, but also sorcerers and mercenaries and ogres, and probably trolls. Their shouts filled the night, spiraling up to assault my ears.

I glanced over to the other dragons appearing in the sky—I could see Camille on Smoky, and Delilah on Shade, and the others. Vishana was leading the pack. As the dragons blurred into view, I suddenly realized how massive our force was. A thousand dragons strong, we blotted out the stars. We could level the city from here. Surely we could take on the armies below.

The goblins and other common creatures would be no problem—they would fall under the dragonfire, but we had to be wary of the sorcerers. I figured they were our main targets—and they would be farthest back from the front gates. Cannon fodder always went first unless you had a martyr at the helm. And somehow, I didn't think Telazhar was the martyring kind.

There was a sudden outcry from the battalions below. They had spotted us. At that moment, Vishana surged forward, her sleek, massive form dive-bombing toward the ground. She leveled out, keeping just out of arrow-shot, and with a massive stream of fire blazing out from her mouth, she strafed the forces below her as she made a screaming run toward the back of the armies. Within seconds, the others followed suit, circling the city.

Vapor rumbled something that I thought was, "Hold on, Lady Vampire," and then we were plunging toward the ground. I grabbed the vertebrae in front of me and held on for dear life as the ground rose to meet our spiraling descent. The wind whistled around me, streaming my cornrows back, and I suddenly realized I wished I could fly like this. Just as quickly, I brought my attention back to what we were doing. I couldn't afford to make any mistakes. One wrong move and I'd fall off into the middle of a thousand soldiers clamoring to kill us.

I braced myself as the ground came closer. Then—at the last moment—Vapor pulled out of his freefall and we were flying on a level line, above arrow-reach, but low enough that Vapor could blast them with his fire. He opened his mouth and a massive jet of flames licked down to torch the troops below. Screams rose, along with a plume of smoke, as he struck barrels of oil they were dragging with them. I watched in silence as figures began to run and scream, flames flickering as their bodies turned into living torches. One whiff made me very grateful that I didn't have to breathe. The char of burning flesh was beginning to fill the air, billowing in massive clouds as anything combustible around the area went up in flames.

All through the site, fires began to rage out of control as the screaming armies fell into chaos, trying to get away from the dragons, but there was nowhere to run. The dragons were everywhere. I began to realize we were just along for the ride. Vishana had this planned out and we were coming along on her terms.

And then we were near the back of the armies, and the goblins gave way to a group of men—Fae and dark crossbreeds. I realized we had found a group of sorcerers. Telazhar had conscripted just about every sorcerer he could find to be part of his plan, and a good share of Otherworld's malevolent mages were here. Vapor made a run at them and let out a long blast of flame. One of the men raised his staff and the flames licked to the side, repelled by some sort of force field. Without further ado, the dragon headed toward the ground and I realized we were going to land right on top of the men. I braced myself for the impact.

Don't get off my back unless you have no other alternative.

The thought intruded in my mind and I realized Vapor had managed some sort of link to me.

I won't. I closed my eyes as we landed. The jolt was as good as an earthquake as the skeletal dragon slammed into the ground as hard as he could without hurting himself. We landed on at least seven of the men who had been trying to keep away the flames, and I knew they couldn't have survived the impact.

It was then that I found myself staring down at a robed figure who looked all too familiar. Oh fuck, we were right in front of Telazhar. I screamed his name so Vapor would hear, but I needn't have bothered. Apparently, dragons were good at figuring things out. Vishana landed in back of Telazhar. And to either side, Shade and Delilah, and Smoky with Camille on his back, landed.

I froze. It couldn't be this easy, could it? We had been fighting Telazhar, a necromancer, for over a year now, and in that year he had managed to terrorize Otherworld once again. Long ago—thousands of years—he had led the Scorching Wars in Otherworld. He had been responsible for creating the Southern Wastes—vast areas of desert that had, at one time, been unending forest. Like Mt. St. Helens when she blew back over in Earthside, his forces had taken down millions of trees and turned a massive swath of vibrant forest into wasteland. The magic had flown so strong and fierce that it had seeped into the very soil and sand itself, creating pockets where rogue magic flourished—shifting and changing everything that passed through it. Telazhar had annihilated cities and countries back then, before he was caught and sentenced. Queen Asteria had fought for his death, but the Great Fae Lords sent him to the Subterranean Realms.

And now he had returned, with a Demon Lord standing behind him.

I glanced over at Camille and Delilah. In the flickering lights from the fires that now raged around us, I could see their expressions. They were staring at the necromancer with blended fear and hatred. We had found our quarry. It was time to end it.

If we flame him, he will use it against us. Vapor's whisper crept into my mind. *We can rip him from limb to limb, but we have to get that staff away from him. And he wears one of your spirit seals. If you want it, you're going to have to take it back.*

I slowly slung my leg over his neck. *We've got this.*

I noticed that Camille and Delilah were doing the same. We managed to time it right and landed to surround the necromancer at the same time. Just what we were going to do, I had no clue, but then Morio came racing into the fray along with Roz, Vanzir, and Trillian. Smoky and Shade stayed in dragon form.

Morio and Camille joined hands and a brilliant pentacle of glowing purple flame surrounded them. Vanzir held out his hands and long, neon-colored tubes began to shoot forth, heading toward the necromancer's head. Rozurial swept open his duster and the next moment I saw the magical stun gun in his hand that we'd been carrying around for months now. And Trillian, a glint in his eye, pulled out a thin, long curved silver blade.

We didn't bother trying to bargain with him. He knew we were out for his blood, so why waste our breath? Instead, we began crowding in toward him, surrounding him on all sides. And now—on the ground, this close to him—I could see it. Around his neck, the spirit seal. The gleaming sapphire pendant rested against his robe, gleaming with life and power. He reached up to lightly stroke it and the next moment, with a quick flash of his fingers in the air, a vortex began to appear.

"Demon Gate! He's creating a Demon Gate!" We had been down this road before with Telazhar and I didn't want to go there again.

Morio and Camille lurched forward, his left palm and her right one facing out as they kept their other hands clasped. *"Mordente, destavano, del gattius."*

Their voices thundered through the air and a massive cloud began to sweep up around them, black and shadowed and *thick*. I hadn't seen this spell before, but instinct told me I wouldn't want to be on the receiving end of whatever they had summoned up.

Delilah raised her head and stared up at the sky for a single moment before a shimmer flickered around her, and when it died down, she stood there, in her panther form, massive and muscled and furious. To one side of her, I caught a glimpse of a shadowed, translucent form. Arial—Delilah's twin—a wereleopard—who had died at birth. We only managed to see her in leopard form—Camille and I, that is. But Delilah had met her in the temple at Haseofon where the Death Maidens congregated in their service to the Autumn Lord. They had talked, at length, and eventually Delilah had come to understand how they both ended up with the Autumn Lord.

We were a poised tableau, including Telazhar, who cagily scanned each of us, only his eyes moving as he looked from face to face. The Demon Gate was forming, and the sly smile on his face told me he was planning on bringing something terrible and big and bad through it.

Camille and Morio pressed their shadow cloud closer. It hovered around the gate now, waiting. I debated on whether to attack the necromancer, but even as I was about ready to move forward, Vanzir's soul-sucking tentacles reached the old man. With a blinding flash, Telazhar flicked one hand toward them and Vanzir went flying back a good twenty feet to land inches from his dragon. He rolled to his feet and raised his hands again.

At that moment, the ground began to shake around the Demon Gate, and I quickly returned my attention to whatever the hell was about to come through. And then—the gate was suddenly full of mist and shadow as a figure stepped through. He was twenty feet tall if he was an inch, a skeleton warrior dressed in ancient armor, wielding a massive sword of bone and crystal. What the hell? A wave of fear spread out from the creature, as tangible as Morio and Camille's shadow cloud that immediately descended on him.

"Lychkonneg . . ." Roz whispered, pronouncing it "Lihk-kohn-negg."

Holy fuck, I knew what that was. A lychkonneg was a skeletal king, and his touch could freeze the flesh and instill instant hypothermia. He could suck the magic out of the soul, as easily as a kid sucked soda out of a straw. And I knew something else, something I wasn't sure if Morio and Camille knew.

"Don't send your cloud over to him—death magic will only strengthen him!" My voice wasn't all that loud but when I wanted to, I could make myself heard and right now? I needed them to hear me.

"Wuucan—attack!" Telazhar's voice was harsh.

The skeletal figure turned toward us, a garish grin on his face. He raised his sword and swung it into the shadow cloud, which clung to the blade. Wuucan—the lychkonneg—spread his arms wide, laughing as the energy spun around the blade and up to his mouth, where he sucked it in. It strengthened him—his energy flared as he drank it in.

Energy vampire, I thought.

Immediately, Morio and Camille broke off their attack and Morio shifted into his youkai-kitsune demon form, growing eight feet tall, his face lengthening into a muzzle, his nails growing into sharp talons. He let out a roar and lunged forward. Roz focused the stun gun on Telazhar and let loose with it, hitting the old sorcerer in the back. Camille raised her hands, calling on the power of the Moon Mother. As clouds began to pack in over the city and lightning flashed, her eyes grew wide and flecked with silver. The Moon Mother was listening tonight.

Arial had been sneaking around, and now she attacked the necromancer from the back. As Telazhar lurched forward from the force of the stun gun, the bolt hitting him hard, Arial pounced. I wasn't sure what she was doing, but she seemed to have done something because Telazhar turned sharply, his eyes wide with the first flicker of worry I had seen.

A goblin wielding an ax ran in front of him, trying to protect him. That, I could do something about, I thought. I flipped through the air, landing in back of the goblin, though trying to keep my distance from Telazhar. I had no doubt he had plenty of kill-the-vamp spells in his repertoire. The goblin jerked as I caught hold of his head. This was no time for subtlety. I twisted, hard, and the crunch of bones told me that I had done my job.

As he fell, I grabbed the ax—which was quite a pretty thing—out of his hand and hoisted it over my shoulder. I turned to see Telazhar, with his back to me, fighting Morio, who was bearing down on him.

I didn't waste any time but brought the ax back and swept it around as hard as I could in a semicircle. I managed to connect with his back, driving it hard into his flesh. As Telazhar sputtered and dropped his staff, Morio let loose with a long sweep of his talons, raking Telazhar's torso.

"Stand back!" Camille's voice echoed through the fray, and we all obeyed immediately. Any time Camille was dealing with magic and yelled for a duck-and-cover, we had learned to duck and cover. It was bad enough when her spells worked, but if they backfired?

She held out her hands and a flash of silver raced from her palms—the Moon Mother's magic. And the Moon Mother was a direct enemy of Telazhar and all his revolt stood for.

The bolt hit the necromancer in the head, and for once, her magic didn't backfire. She drove all her force into it, building it to a high-pitched shriek. As she let go of the silver fire, the ray snaked around his body, squeezing hard. A rumble sounded overhead and then a bolt of lightning raced from the sky to hit him square on. Like water dropped on a hot stove, Telazhar turned to vapor, the spirit seal falling to the ground where he had been standing.

At that moment, the lychkonneg roared and charged toward us. Just because his summoner had vaporized didn't mean that we were out of hot water yet.

Smoky turned toward the towering warrior and, wings back, slammed against him. The warrior was strong, but dragons? Stronger. The skeletal king went down in a shower of bones and sparks.

"We have to destroy that gate—" Camille looked utterly spent.

Vapor shimmered into his human form. He walked silently over to the Demon Gate and whispered in a low, guttural voice. A moment later, the gate imploded. He turned back, smiling cagily at me. "I don't live in the Netherworld for nothing."

I stumbled back, realizing I still had the ax in my hands. The sounds of battle roared around us. The dragons were tearing the armies to pieces, and fires blazed everywhere. The air was so thick with the smoke from the dead that it blotted out the sky. As the full impact of the dragons' carnage soaked into my thoughts, a deep, obliterating numbness crept over me. The blood was running so thick and free that it overwhelmed my senses, and I wanted nothing more than to tear through the crowd, drinking deep.

Vanzir was standing near me. "Go," he said. "Feed. You have to or the predator will take over. Go now. I'll tell the others."

Grateful that he understood, I pressed the ax into his hands. "Save that for me, would you?"

And then I was off, driving forward into the mob. I grabbed the first goblin who came my way and savagely drove my fangs into his neck. When I was done feeding, the blood flowing down my throat, I took another—and another, until the world was a haze of red. Goblins, Fae, it didn't matter. As long as they were the enemy, I tore into them.

The memory of what they had done to Elqaneve, to Queen Asteria, to our father . . . the thousands of elves dying . . . it all ran together in one crimson haze. As soon as I drained one, I was on to the next, until they became mere numbers, forgotten as soon as I was done with them. Until I found myself holding one very young boy by the collar. All the others had been seasoned soldiers—goblins mostly, but the boy was Svartan, and he stared at me, terrified. He couldn't have been into puberty yet—and he began to shake.

Suddenly coming to my wits, I stopped, fangs an inch

from his neck. As I pulled back, I shook my head and dropped him. "Go home. Go home and never take part in anything like this again. The next time, you might not get a second chance."

He pressed his lips together and then turned, scrambling away. I looked down at myself. I was streaked with blood; my shirt, my pants, my face was a smear of it. Satiated, able to focus again, I looked around at the rabble that was left.

Most of the enemy who could stand were fleeing, but the dragons chased them down. Flames lit up the sky and the ground was soaked crimson.

As I turned toward the city, I reminded myself that we had done this to save lives. If we hadn't come in, the gates would be overcome and everyone inside would be fodder for Telazhar's demonic zeal. We were agents of death, agents of chaos, agents of life. Feeling numb and battle weary, I turned and walked quietly back through the last throngs who were doing their best to escape. Along the way, I grabbed goblin after goblin, breaking their necks, feeling nothing as I watched them fall. They were soldiers for the dark, soldiers for the demons. Unlike the boy, they would never look for redemption, or take the chance if it were offered.

By the time I reached the others, the area was fairly clear. I looked over at Camille as Vanzir handed me the ax. She looked as blood-spattered as I did. We all were, except for Smoky's infernal ability to keep clean. Nix that. The other dragons who were standing around in human form—Vishana, Vapor, and a couple of others—were also spotless.

"He's dead. We have the spirit seal." Delilah held it up, gazing at the pendant. "One more for our side."

Vishana reached for it. "I will take it with me back to the Dragon Reaches and entrust it to the Keraastar Knights." She paused, then flashed a keen look at Camille. "You must take over their training soon enough. You know this."

She nodded, looking as weary as I felt. "I know. I have no clue how, but I imagine I'll find out the hard way." She bit her lip. "May I hold that for a moment?" Vishana handed the spirit seal to her, and Camille silently clutched it in her hand. After a few minutes, she handed it back. "I know what I need to know."

We waited for her to explain, but she just shook her head and turned away. "It will come in time."

Vishana signaled to Vapor. "Take them back to the elves. We will finish the job here. We won't rest until we've hunted down every single soldier and sorcerer that we can find."

As we gazed over the thousands of fallen bodies, it crossed my mind that the goblin race had just taken a huge dent, as well. Maybe not as much as they had dealt out to the elves, but big enough. Payback? Their deaths couldn't begin to atone for what had happened to Elqaneve, but it was a start.

"Do you think this will put a stop to the incursions over Earthside?" Delilah frowned. "Telazhar probably has off-shoot regiments out scouting down rogue portals."

"Yes, but the necromancer's dead, and so are most of his reserves. We can take care of the few who might come through before they find out what happened to their glorious leader. Once word gets out that the dragons destroyed most of his armies, my bet is that the remaining forces won't be so keen to get involved." I leaned down and picked up Telazhar's staff. "What about this? We shouldn't just leave it lying about."

Smoky took it and—with one swift motion—broke it in half. I thought I could hear a faint scream, and then a whiff of shadow spiraled out of the broken ends and the staff lost the inner light that had set it agleam.

Morio reached out and stroked the wood. After a moment, he smiled grimly. "It's dead. And he's dead. I think a bit of his essence remained in the staff, but breaking it did the trick."

"Are you sure?" Delilah worried her lip. "We didn't actually see him *die*."

"The lightning finished him. He's dead. I felt his spirit vanish into the Netherworld." Vapor grumbled lightly. "I would have liked to have a bite of him. He was a scourge and he wrought more damage than perhaps any other mortal on this world."

I thought about what he said. The Scorching Wars had swept across Otherworld. Tens of thousands and more had died in the wake of Telazhar's armies. And still more had died with his return. There was no punishment that could have ever been equal to his misdeeds. But he was gone now, and hopefully the Hags of Fate would judge his soul and send him to the abyss rather than let him go around on the circle again. As a blaze nearby flared up from one of the dragons finishing off yet another party of goblins, I suddenly wanted to go home. I wanted out of the muck and the blood and the smoke.

Camille voiced my very thoughts. "Too much. It's all too much. Delilah and I fought our way through the fall of Elqaneve. The screams still ring in my head. I stole the shoes off a dead woman so that I could run." She paused, looking up, her eyes filled with the mist of memory. "I want to go home."

"Come, my love. We'll go." Smoky moved back and the air around him shimmered as he shifted back into his dragon form. Camille mutely hoisted herself up on his back. Just as silently, Delilah climbed aboard Shade's back, and when I turned, Vapor was back in dragon form. I accepted a lift up from Morio and settled myself between the vertebrae. One by one, the dragons we had come in on shifted, and when we were all seated on our mounts, we took to the sky, leaving the carnage behind. As we entered the Ionyc Seas, all I could think about was how much I wanted to see my wife, and how all I wanted to do was hold her in my arms and forget about the rest of the world.

Chapter 7

Back at Elqaneve, I checked the time and saw that it was getting close to sunrise. After a quick thank-you to the dragons, I left Camille and Delilah to talk to Trenyth. Roz, Vanzir, and I crossed back over to Grandmother Coyote's portal. We arrived home with ninety minutes to spare. The moment I got home, I called Nerissa and she insisted on coming over. She sounded like she had been sitting up all night.

I slung my jacket over a chair and then headed downstairs. I was determined to wash the blood off before Nerissa got home. I peeled off my clothing, piece by piece, dropping it in my tracks, until I reached the shower. I flipped on the water, hot as my skin could take it without blistering. I would heal up from any burns, but I didn't need to look as rough as I felt. Stepping under the spray, I lathered up my cornrows with a vanilla-scented shampoo that was Nerissa's favorite. The water streaked down me, turning crimson as it pooled at the drain, then washed away.

And then everything hit me. I seldom went to pieces—I had learned too hard that you couldn't let yourself falter or you would die. Dredge had taught me that. He had taught me what pain really was, taking me beyond the limits of what I thought I could endure to the brink of death, then dragging me back to experience more. Every scar on my body, every intricate piece of scrollwork he had carved into my flesh, reminded me of what I was capable of surviving. Even after he had killed me and turned me, after a long night's torture, and sent me home to feast on my family, I had somehow managed to hold on long enough for Camille to lock me in the safe room. I had gone insane, yes, and it had taken all the resources the Y'Elestrial Intelligence Agency could muster to bring me back to myself. But I had endured. I had survived.

I had seen so many people die that I cared about. I had turned Erin when I swore I'd never sire another vamp. I had destroyed Sassy Branson, who was my friend, at her request. I had taken my friend Chrysandra out of the world of pain in which she was immersed, which she would never be able to heal from. Right now, I was feeling very much an angel of death.

No, that's Delilah's department, a small voice inside whispered. *She's the Death Maiden. And Camille runs death magic under the Dark Moon. All of us have suffered. All of us have caused suffering. It's the nature of being alive. It's what being human . . . what being Fae . . . means. We live. We die. We kill. We save. We burn brightly and then are gone to the ancestors. What matters is which side we fight on. Which side we pledge ourselves to.*

Tired of thinking, tired of worrying over my thoughts, I turned off the water when it finally ran clear and clean and wrapped myself in a towel. As I padded into the bedroom, I passed the mirror. It was just as well I couldn't see my own reflection. I didn't want to face myself right now because it felt like the ghosts of the past would be staring back at me.

Nerissa was sitting on the bed, my bloody clothes piled in a laundry basket at her feet. She pushed it aside when she saw me and silently held out her arms. Her welcoming eyes, the bow of her lips, the soft rise and fall of her breasts beneath the V-neck sweater she was wearing, the nimbus of tawny hair tumbling down to her shoulders . . . the sight of my wife waiting for me in silence broke the numbness. Stumbling forward, I landed on the bed and she wrapped me in her embrace, holding me as I began to shiver. I wasn't cold—vampires didn't feel the cold or heat unless it was extreme, but a bone-chilling weariness spread through me to the point of where I felt barely coherent.

"Ssh . . . don't speak. Just be. Just let me hold you." The empathy in her voice, the love, filtered through and I found myself starting to cry. I tried to push away the tears—vampire tears are a bloody affair and I didn't want to ruin her sweater—but she simply grabbed my towel and slid it over her shoulder and tucked me into that wonderful nook again. I struggled against my emotions, not wanting to feel, not wanting to admit how exhausted I was by this war, but the face of the young boy flashed through my mind again. The fear in his eyes, the realization that he was very young but had joined an army to destroy a city and had probably done his share of killing . . . it all hit me, and I began to sob in earnest.

"So much death. There were so many screams. The fires . . . we were a thousand dragons strong, and the night was on fire." Pausing, I admitted what I really *didn't* want to tell her. "I lost control. My inner predator came out and I gave her free rein. I went on my own rampage."

Fearing to see her expression, I slowly sat back and used the towel to wipe my face, then raised my eyes to meet hers. But she merely shrugged and gave me a sad smile.

"This is war. This is what war does to you. It breaks you, and you pull yourself back together. You go back in and fight, and you do it as many times as necessary. Rozurial told me that you won the night?"

I nodded slowly, once again amazed by her ability to accept stark reality. "We destroyed Telazhar. His armies . . . there aren't that many troops left and I doubt if there's anybody alive to lead the cause now. Vishana led the attack. She drove them into the ground. *Never, ever* get on the bad side of a dragon."

I paused, remembering that Camille had unfortunately

been on the receiving end of a dragon's hatred—Hyto, Smoky's father. She had learned just how vicious they could be. "We lit up the sky like a thousand aerial flamethrowers." And then I was able to tell her about the battle.

When I finished, she was sitting back, her arms wrapped around her knees, shaking her head. "The dragons just saved our butt, you know. What happened sounds horrible, but think about it: Those same armies were the ones who destroyed the elves. They would have gone on to tear through Otherworld and take down every city and country that stood against them. Telazhar was paving the way for Shadow Wing."

I pressed my lips together and lay back on the bed. "Yeah, I know that. There was nothing else that we could do. You can't reason with a war machine, and that's what Telazhar had created. I still can't believe we destroyed him. I know the Moon Mother had something to do with it—Camille's magic is strong but not *that* strong, and that lightning bolt came out of the heavens."

"Telazhar would have razed her grove. He tried it once before, thousands of years ago, didn't he? Of course she had something to do with it. Camille's her Earthside high priestess." Nerissa leaned over me, on her hands and knees. "And to the victors, the spoils of war," she said softly, her breath rippling over my breasts.

I gazed up at her, my numbness slowly vanishing as she trailed her fingers along my side, her flesh warm against the chill of my own.

"Are you sure?" I asked softly. "You must be tired."

She shook her head. "Adrenaline. I waited up for you, to make sure you were coming home to me." And then she leaned in, pressing her lips against mine, petal-soft and delicate.

I tugged on her sweater, pulling it free from where it was tucked into her jeans, and she slowly backed off the bed, stripping it off with one quick movement. Her jeans landed on top of the sweater, and she shrugged off bra and panties. I watched, making no move, just soaking in the vision that stood before me. My beauty, she could have been Helen of Troy, she could have been a Playboy bunny. Five ten, voluptuous, with full breasts and hips, she glowed with an inner light that soaked through every pore in her body.

A new fire took hold of me, but this time it wasn't my inner predator. No, this lit a different hunger, and I pushed myself to a sitting position. And then, in a blur, I was on my feet and in front of her, staring up into her face. She leaned down and cupped my chin.

"I want you. Menolly D'Artigo, I claim you as my wife. I claim you as my clan. My pride. My chosen one." Her words were cloaked in a sultry arrogance, a possessive demand that I instantly responded to.

Pressing against her breasts, I felt the feral need rise up. "I can hear your heartbeat."

"You're going to feel more than that." She pushed me back on the bed and I let her take control. I might be a vampire, but she was a werepuma and no slouch in the strength department. I fell back and she landed on me in a pounce, straddling my hips. Her eyes lit up as she very slowly and deliberately lowered her mouth to my breast. As her lips pressed against my flesh, I gasped, fire shooting a straight line from my nipple to my cunt. I let out a moan as she took hold, nipping me lightly.

"What do you want? What do you need?" Her eyes were glittering and hard as she brought her face up to meet mine. "Who do you want me to be tonight?"

The rush of blood and fire raced through my mind again, and I began to shake. "Just make me forget the blood and the death."

She gazed down at me for a minute, then stood up and went over to the chest we had designated for our toy box. As she opened the lid, I shivered. I had just given her carte blanche, and sweet or not, my wife could be downright ruthless at times. She had trained under Venus the Moon Child, the shaman of her Pride, and he had taught her how to take pain and transform it into pleasure.

And then she was back, pushing my arms over my head, tying my wrists firmly with a velvet rope and looping it over the hook at the top of our bed.

"Don't speak. Do as I say." Her cheeks were flushed as she slid the blindfold over my eyes.

In the darkness, I felt her spread my legs and, with my knees slightly bent, she bound my ankles to a spreader bar. The music started up—Rob Zombie blasting out of the speakers. As the driving beat raced through my body, overwhelming me, I could only wait for what she chose to do next.

A faint tickle began to run up my leg. I twitched, unable to move. I could have broken my restraints, but Nerissa and I had worked together to create a psychological bondage that was stronger than the body. When either of us needed it, we were able to slip into the submissive part, regardless of our strength. So I gave in, allowed her to take the helm.

The feather—I thought it was a feather—brushed lightly up my leg, irritating my skin. My muscles began to twitch as the tickling continued, and then the light touch brushed between my legs. Startled as the teasing hit my clit, I tensed, but there was no relenting as the sensation continued. Then, just as suddenly, it was gone. I waited, tensed, but nothing. Feeling exposed, I wanted to ask if Nerissa was still there, but she had ordered me to remain silent.

I waited, but there was only the sound of the music. Another minute and my stomach began to knot. And another and I was starting to shake, in the darkness, unable to move.

Just as my nerves were beginning to fray, she began to stroke my calves. The scent of jasmine wafted up and I realized she was oiling me—lightly kneading my muscles with her light touch. Her fingers slid up to my thighs, still massaging the fragrant oil into my body.

The warmth of her flesh, the soft circular motion of her touch acted like an instant sedative and I relaxed, letting her work her magic. The next moment, a gentle kiss touched the one scar I would give anything to be rid of—Dredge had carved his name on my pubic mound, claiming me as his. The scar was the last one he gave me before killing me.

But Nerissa's lips had long ago taken away the shame. She had taught me how to reclaim myself from the memories, to believe that I was lovable, to believe that I was beautiful.

I shivered as her lips moved from the scar to between my legs, her tongue swirling around my clit, teasing me lightly, coaxing a moan from my throat as the fire between my legs blazed to life. I stiffened against my bonds. In the darkness, unable to move, I could only focus on the sensation of her touch, the drive of the music.

Spiraling into the flow of her rhythm as she bathed me with her love, I tensed. The knot in my stomach grew, but now it was anticipation and desire. I wanted to whisper *Don't stop*, but that would break the rules, and we were strict on our rules. Instead, I let out a low moan as she became more insistent, laving my clit, working me hard. I twisted, but her hands held my hips firm.

Then one hand let go of my side and the next moment, she spread my pussy wide and drove a thick dildo deep inside me, working hard as she penetrated my folds.

"You like this?" Nerissa's voice was low, husky with desire. "Answer me." And then again—the pressure against my clit as she drove the dildo into me with an increasingly frantic rhythm.

"Yes . . . more, please more . . ." I could barely form the words as the music and the darkness blended with the spiraling passion that built with every touch. And then, just as I thought I couldn't take any more, she nipped me, biting just enough to send me over the edge, and I let out a sharp cry as I floated in the sudden free fall, hovering over the edge of the cliff before I began falling into the darkness of orgasm, the pain of the night sweeping up to surround me with velvet wings as her love cushioned me from the blazing explosion that echoed through my mind.

I came again and once more, and for a moment, everything went black—and I had no clue who or what I was as I hovered between what felt like the gates of life and death. But neither was open to me—I was outside the circle, and so I came back to myself with a shuddering start.

The next moment, I realized I could see. She had removed the blindfold, and now she pressed her lips against mine and kissed me slowly, on my forehead, my cheeks, my lips. I realized I had been crying by the blood that stained her lips.

"Menolly, you and I . . . we have something that nothing can ever sever. You hold my heart in your hands." Nerissa gently untied me, and I sat up, wiping my eyes with the tissues she handed me. "Are you okay?"

I nodded, not knowing how to answer. She had released the fears of the night that had coiled inside me, serpents waiting to strike, but in doing so, she had brought me face to face with the cold truth of who I was. Which was, I supposed, not a bad thing.

"Yes . . . it was just . . . intense." I turned to her, wanting to explain, wondering if I even could begin to. But her expression told me she already knew. Somehow, she knew.

Her smile was slow and sad. "We live in a harsh time, my love. But through it all, we have each other. And we have your family—*our* family."

"I want . . . do you need . . ." I wanted to love her, gently and slowly, but I wasn't sure where she was at. Sometimes my wife needed the blindfolds and bonds as much as I did.

She opened her arms. "Love me however you need. Give me whatever you have to give tonight and I will be happy."

I laid her back, gently, stroking her ripe breasts, lingering over the tawny mound of her pubic hair. "I love you. You know how much I love you." My voice was soft, almost a whisper.

"Yes, I do. Now prove it." She smiled then, through the darkness that surrounded us, and her smile was the ray of hope that I needed.

I loved her, my lips tracing her body, my fingers stroking her until she cried out with passion, my breasts sliding against hers. As fierce as I was with Roman, I was gentle with her. For my Nerissa, I wore my heart on my sleeve, and had finally allowed myself to be as vulnerable as she needed me to be.

After she was satiated, we snuggled under the covers.

"The dragons . . . we owe them a debt." She stroked my forehead.

"No, actually we don't. They were repaying *their* debt to

Camille. I wonder if they will help us against Shadow Wing. How could even *he* stand against a force of dragons? But then, they already gave us a tremendous gift." I described the sights of the night for her—not the blood and death, but the beauty of the dragons as they overshadowed the stars. I told her about Vapor and Vishana, and about seeing Sharah.

By the time I finished, the horrors had pulled back into a soft murmur in the back of my mind. "How was your evening?"

"I played with Maggie. Bruce's mother is one hell of a force. That leprechaun is an alpha bitch, let me tell you. But I was surprised. Do you know how much she admires Iris? She was talking about her all evening. The Duchess was actually telling the twins about how their mother was off riding dragons in a war and how proud she was of her. Of course, they had no clue what she was saying, but I have a feeling this is going to become a family story. A *remember the day Mommy went to fight with the dragons* sort of thing. I think Iris should know that. I know that she thinks the Duchess looks down on her."

I laughed. "Sometimes people surprise you. Sometimes, they come through when you think they're going to let you down." I leaned back on the pillow, starting to feel the pull of the dawn. "The sun will rise soon and I will be sleeping. Please, have a good day, my love. And be safe. Just because we've managed to put a stop to the incursions from Telazhar's side of the tracks, I don't think that's going to stop the hate groups."

"I can handle the haters." She pulled the blanket up around my shoulders, even though I didn't need it. "I love that you let me tuck you in. I don't get much chance to. I'm usually asleep when you come to bed."

We lived in different worlds—she was the daylight, I was the dark, but we shared the space where we met at sunset and somehow it worked. In the darker half of the year, she rose before I went to bed, but summer put a longer distance between us.

I yawned and closed my eyes.

Vampires answered the call of the sun, rising at sunset, falling into the darkness at sunrise. We walked in our dreams, sometimes trapped in nightmares, unable to wake, reliving our own deaths, reliving the past. Other times, we wandered the realms of the Earth, our souls trapped forever in undying bodies, but reaching out with our minds to traverse the ends of the world.

I am what I am, I thought, snuggling deeper under the covers. Whatever I was, whoever I was, it would never be the Menolly who was first born into Otherworld. I had become a hybrid, standing somewhere between who I had been and who I was becoming.

And then I found myself drifting, and I was once again a young girl—joyful and into my maidenhood. I was running through a field, and Camille and Delilah raced at my side. The sun beat down on my face and I suddenly stopped, looking up to reach for it. Blinded, I closed my eyes, but then a flutter on my fingers made me blink. There, a butterfly flickered its wings, perched on the top of my hand. I watched it, breathing slowly, as the painted lady tickled me.

Camille and Delilah stopped, coming over to look at it, cautious not to startle it. And then—as we three stood there—a sudden rush swept up around us, and the air was full of butterflies. They had been resting in their migration on a nearby tree and now the sky was filled with the insects, a blur of beauty and color as they whispered around us.

The butterfly on my fingers rose and joined the lek, and they spiraled around the field, dancing around our heads as we could only stand in wonder, surrounded by the whirlwind of butterflies, watching as they rose into the sky. Camille whispered something—some spell—and we were suddenly floating in the air with them—only a few feet off the ground, but we still were hovering there among the living whirl of color and beauty. The next moment, we tumbled to the ground, but for a brief time, we had flown with the butterflies.

The swarm rose to the top of the tree line and then spiraled off into the distance, as silently and quickly as it had appeared. I raised my hand, waving as they vanished. It had been a moment frozen in beauty, a time when the world had stopped for a moment to let us breathe. We crossed to the stream, but for the longest time, we kept quiet, not speaking, simply marveling in the beauty that could spring out of nowhere, unexpected, and then—in a flash—be gone.

As the sun rose, the vision vanished and I gave in to the pull of sleep. My dreams that day were filled with fire and dragons, and butterflies . . . and beneath everything, a foreboding sense that something bigger was coming—something that would put all our battles to shame.

When I woke and joined the others in the kitchen, I found out that Iris and Bruce had returned to their house and they were over there now, getting resettled after a few weeks in Nerissa's condo. As long as Telazhar was gone, there was no reason for them to worry too much over the rogue portal in our backyard, especially since it still led to the Realm of the Elder Fae.

As I entered the kitchen, Delilah and Shade were at the table, along with Vanzir and Roz. Hanna was humming a tune as she made dinner for the others—she was pummeling a mound of biscuit dough into submission with a rolling pin. Trillian was tearing lettuce for a salad.

"Where are Camille, Smoky, and Morio?" I glanced around.

"Camille and Smoky are still back in the Dragon Reaches. Morio went out to check the land with the guards." Delilah was leaning against Shade, looking relaxed for the first time in weeks. "What do you think about September?"

I stared at her. "I have no clue how to answer that. September is . . . a month?"

She grinned. "I mean for a wedding?"

Shade winked at me and I suddenly understood. "Oh my gods—you mean you're finally going to do it?" Another beat and it sank in. "The autumn equinox!"

"Yes! It seems perfect, and . . . why wait? If there's one thing I've learned lately it's that anything can happen at any time. I want to get married before . . . in case . . ." She quieted down, then shook her head. "No, I refuse to look at it like that. I want to get married because I want to get married, damn it." She brought Shade's hand to her lips and kissed it as he draped his arm around her shoulder.

"I think the autumn equinox is perfect." And it was.

"By the way—Supe Community Council emergency meeting tonight at nine thirty. That's the earliest they could make it in order to notify as many people as they could. Topic is the escalation of hate crimes. We need to go. It's not something we can just blow off." Delilah switched into business mode without a blink of the eye.

"No problem. I'm good with that." It felt odd. We weren't ready to go on patrol, we were just sitting around the table as usual.

Just then, there was a knock on the door. Trillian moved to answer and, a moment later, his voice exploded in an excited flurry of his native language. I wasn't sure what to call the Svartan tongue. The next moment, he strode into the kitchen, dragging another figure behind him. Delilah let out a shout of glee as I jumped to my feet.

"Darynal! You're alive!" Delilah lunged forward, wrapping the Svartan in her arms. "That's for Camille because she's not back from the Dragon Reaches yet." She hugged him again. "And that's from me."

"I opened the door and damned if he wasn't standing right there!" Trillian's smile was a mile wide, relief flooding his voice. Darynal was his blood-oath brother—they were closer than kin—and we had given him up for dead, lost in the Shadow Lands. But here he was, in the flesh, looking safe and unharmed. Trillian turned back to Darynal. "We all thought you were dead."

"There were times I thought all was lost. Taath and I went our separate ways. I have no idea whether he survived, but given what I saw of him on the scouting trip, if anybody could make it through, he could. But . . . then again . . . luck plays a huge factor down there. We got lost in the Fens and that was the last time I saw him. He wanted to keep going. I wanted to turn around and retrace our steps. We argued and he refused to listen to reason."

Darynal was a mercenary like Trillian, one of the best trackers and scouts around. He was good-natured for a Svartan, and we had all come to like the man. And that was saying something because the Svartans weren't all that much of a likable race on the whole. They were an offshoot of the elves who had taken a slightly more sinister bent. But then again, like most of the Fae—hell, like most other races in general—when you really stopped to look at it everything came down to the individual. Society did not always make the man.

"When did you cross over?" Trillian pulled out a chair, and Darynal gratefully slid into it.

"I found my way to Elqaneve . . ." He trailed off, staring at the table. "I can't believe the destruction. So many lives . . ."

"We were there when it all went down." Delilah leaned in. "Camille and I had to fight our way out that night. Menolly was able to escape through the Ionyc Seas, along with Sharah and Chase, thanks to Shade, Rozurial, and Smoky." Her voice caught. "We witnessed Telazhar's storm firsthand."

Darynal shook his head. "Storms will happen, but to create a sentient one, and to use it as a weapon? There is no forgiveness for that. Trenyth told me about the dragons. That you vanquished Telazhar. So we have hope." He leaned forward then, looking battle weary and worn.

Hanna brought over a fresh batch of biscuits, butter, and honey. "There will be dinner soon, but you get a start now. I'll slice you up some cheese, too. You need food."

Darynal nodded. "I haven't had much to eat the past few weeks, true enough. The elves fed me, but I didn't want to accept much from them—they need every scrap they've got." He looked around. "May I wash my hands?"

Hanna led him to the hall bath. Darynal had been over Earthside before; he knew about the technology here.

Trillian let out a long sigh. "We can learn much from him—he's the only one of the scouting party who managed to come through. But does it really matter now, given Telazhar's dead?"

"Don't be so sure." I decided to be polite and take a seat rather than hovering up in the corner like I usually did while the family gathered for meals. "Maybe something he saw or heard can give us some idea of what else Shadow Wing is up to. We know he's trying to create an evil clone of the Keraastar Knights. What else is he up to? And what is he going to do now that his right-hand man is dead and his armies in Otherworld decimated? We need to brainstorm just what we might be facing."

"Give him a night to rest up, though. He's tired. He's been on the move for months. He's been through hell—you can't tell me the Shadow Lands were a piece of cake." Trillian shrugged. "If there were anything vital—that he knew was vital—he would have told us first thing."

"Why don't you make up the parlor for him?" I glanced around. "Is Nerissa home yet?"

"No, she called and said she and Chase were heading out on a call. That was shortly before you got up. I gather that the Freedom's Angels and the Earthborn Brethren are doing their best to become Seattle's major pain in the ass. She said she'll be home as soon as she can and to tell you she loves you."

I must have blushed because Shade grinned at me and added, "I don't mind passing love notes. The world needs as much love as it can get."

As Darynal returned to the table and dove into the biscuits, there was a shimmer in the air. I glanced over at Camille's wards. Nothing was going off—no danger in sight, that we could perceive. The next moment, Smoky appeared in the room, holding Camille in his arms.

"You're back! Is everything okay?" Trillian swung Camille into his arms and kissed her soundly the minute Smoky let go of her. "Look!" He spun her around without taking a breath.

She saw Darynal and let out a squeak that almost pierced my ears. "Darynal! *Lavoyda!*" Even though Camille was not bound by blood to Darynal the way Trillian was, the fact that they were married made the pair brother and sister.

"Camille, beautiful *Ahn shivya*."

I cocked my head. That one I hadn't heard. *"Ahn shivya?"*

Darynal grinned, his smile infectious. "Moon priestess." He returned his gaze to Camille. "I have never been so glad to see a woman's face as now. You . . . you let your husband go hunting me down. Trenyth told me." The smile vanished. "I owe you my life—and don't even try to protest. He may not have been able to track me down, but the intent was there. Loyalty offered is loyalty earned. Whatever you need . . . wherever and whenever, call and I will be there."

Camille blushed, but she reached out and took Darynal's hands in hers. "You are family. You are my husband's brother. You are my brother."

Delilah glanced at the clock. "Hate to break this up—but we need to head to the Community meeting. We should all go. Darynal, you can stay here. Hanna will make sure you eat and are tucked in for the night. You look tired."

"Don't you want to hear our news first?" Camille slumped into a chair. "And I need to change." She grimaced. "I'm still wearing my clothes from the battle."

"Tell us, then go change and shower. We can wait that long." I shook my head at Delilah. "The meeting won't be over by the time we get there. We'll be a little late but not that much."

Camille glanced up at Smoky, but he nodded for her to speak. "The dragons—Vishana said that they are going to send workers from the Northlands to help speed up the rebuilding of Elqaneve. And they have offered, if we need them against Shadow Wing himself . . . they will do what they can."

The thought of a thousand dragons winging their way into the Demon Lord's lair and taking him on with us made the night a whole lot brighter. As Camille and Smoky went up to shower and change, and Darynal ate his weight in Hanna's home cooking, for a little while we were able to sit back and just enjoy a little peace.

Chapter 8

We were almost to the Supe Community Hall when we found ourselves in the traffic jam from hell. I wasn't sure what was going on, but I asked Rozurial and Vanzir—who were riding with me—to check the Seattle Traffic Flow app on my phone.

"Black as a demon's asshole," Vanzir said, snickering. "There's some pretty wicked gridlock going down right now and I have no clue where it starts, but it looks like it all converges on the general vicinity of the Supe Community Council." He frowned. "I don't think we have a hope in hell of navigating through this. Might as well find a place to park and jog over."

"You sure? Maybe it's an accident or . . ." I noticed that Camille had pulled off into a parking lot on the right side of the road. I swerved to follow suit and Delilah did the same. As we all piled out of our various rides—Smoky, Morio, and Trillian were with Camille, Shade was with Delilah—the sound of horns filled the air. Apparently Seattleites weren't all that thrilled about rush-hour traffic during late-evening hours.

"What's going on?" Camille asked, as we gathered between our cars.

Just then, my phone jangled. I glanced at the Caller ID—Nerissa. "I have a feeling we might be about to get an answer." I punched Answer and held the cell up to my ear. "Hey, love. What's going on?"

"You're trying to get to the meeting, I assume?" Her voice was muffled by the sounds of shouting around her.

"Yeah. Where the hell are you? It sounds like you're at some sort of a party."

"Party my ass. Chase and I are over at the Supe Community Hall. Guess what you get when you take a couple of hate groups picketing a couple hundred pissed-off Supes? We've got a potential riot in the works." She sounded more exasperated than anything. "Traffic is deadlocked for blocks and not likely to clear for a while. If you're close enough, I suggest you pick up the pace and hoof it here. Or—say, you have Smoky, Shade, and Rozurial. Tell them to bring you to the hall pronto via the Ionyc Seas. We need you guys here *now*." With that, she hung up.

I turned to the others. "Picketers at the meeting. Nerissa and Chase are there. She said get over there now, through the Ionyc Seas, if possible."

Camille glanced at the guys. "You've all been to the meeting hall. Think you remember it enough to gate in there?"

Smoky nodded. "There's a place out back by the Dumpsters. We helped empty garbage after one meeting—remember, guys?" Rozurial and Shade nodded. "Then aim for that. With a little luck, we won't have to worry about ending up in the middle of a group of Freedom's Angels." He frowned. "I can take Camille and Delilah. Shade—can you take Menolly and Vanzir? Roz can take Morio."

Shade nodded. "I can still travel the Seas, so yes."

We grabbed our gear from the cars and made sure they were locked, and then—in the shadow of the Dumpling Dugout, a local eatery, we vanished into the Ionyc Seas.

* * *

The trip was much shorter than the one we had taken back in Otherworld, and none of us were fazed by it. Or maybe we were all just getting used to the flowing currents of energy. Whatever the case, we were standing in the alley behind the parking lot of the Supe Community Hall. There was a throng of people near the door and spilling out into the street, all waving picket signs.

"You'd think some of these fanatics would learn how to spell." I shook my head. "How hard is it to work a dictionary?"

"Ah, but first you have to *realize* that you can't spell worth a damn." Camille let out a snicker, then sobered. "It's funny, yeah . . . but think about it. This kind of crap leads to hate crimes, and eventually to *final solutions*. And those? Well, both Earthside and Otherworld have seen the results of genocidal maniacs. No different when you're going against someone solely because they're female or Jewish or Muslim or gay or Fae or Were. It all adds up to a massive superiority complex that blinds the senses."

I nodded. "Yeah. So, what next? We need to find Nerissa and Chase." I pulled out my phone and hit Redial.

Nerissa came on the line. "You here yet?"

"We are, in the back parking lot near the Dumpsters. Where are you? There appear to be mobs at both the front and back doors."

"There are, and more marching down the street. I didn't realize that they had so many supporters, though I think that we're seeing some anarchists in the group that join in every freaking protest that happens in this city. *They're* just out to make trouble. And that could make things worse because they like to loot for no good reason, and the hall is smack in the middle of a residential area. We could end up with houses nearby going under fire."

She was right, I thought. And that would be a disaster. "We're heading in. Where should we meet you?"

"We're out front. I think you'll be better off elbowing

your way in from the back—but hurry up. There are more coming and I have a feeling they'll be trying to surround the Hall. Chase has cops headed around the side, but they're having trouble getting through the crowds, too. We may have to call out the riot teams." She hung up.

I quickly filled the others in on what we were facing. "I suggest we head in there pronto."

"Menolly, I think you should fly in. Turn into a bat. You are well known in this town, and it's pretty easy to hide a stake under a coat." Vanzir glanced at the others. "They don't like the Weres and Fae, but this crowd? They have a special hatred for vampires."

"He's right. Do it." Camille motioned for Smoky to go in front. "Delilah, you and I will take the center line. Shade, can you bring up the back? Vanzir, on our left. Roz on our right. You guys are all less vulnerable than Delilah and I are."

I stepped back and closed my eyes. *Think bat . . . think bat . . .* The next moment, my stomach shifted and boom . . . I was in the air. Thanks to Roman re-siring me and then teaching me, my bat shifting was no longer a thing to be ashamed of. I could manage to fly and hold form for quite a while, compared to a year ago. I silently swept up and headed toward the building, at the last minute realizing the windows were going to be closed. But I also knew that the Hall had a fireplace, and this time of year? No fire. I caught an updraft on the breeze and cautiously headed down the chimney, which I realized needed a good cleaning as soot started to fall on me.

By the time I swept out of the fireplace and shimmered back into my natural form, I was covered with grease spots. I managed to startle several Weres nearby, including Frank Willows, a werewolf who was current leader of the Supe Militia. But he smiled broadly when he saw me appear.

"Sorry, but we thought it best I come in the easy way. The others are trying to get through the crowd to the back doors."

"I'll send a group to help in case trouble breaks out. Your wife and Chase are over there." He pointed toward the front doors of the grand hall. The Community Council Hall was a thing of beauty, and had been built after the old one was burned down in another attack.

I glanced around. There must be more than one hundred fifty members of the Supe Community here tonight, and that didn't seem to include any vampires. And then I realized that if Roman caught word of this, he would send reinforcements and that would exacerbate the issue even worse than it already was. I pulled out my phone as I headed over to where Chase and Nerissa were conferring with three humans who looked familiar but I couldn't quite place. One was a pale blond woman—very tall—in a pair of jeans and a white button-down shirt. The second woman was shorter, with dark skin and curly hair. And the man was sturdy and built, and looked like he might be Hispanic. He wore a three-piece suit.

At that moment, I heard Delilah's voice echoing through the milling Supes. "Neely!"

The short, dark woman turned and smiled. "Delilah!"

And right then, my memory clicked and their names flooded back. The three were from the United Worlds Church. They were the founders of the All Worlds United in Peace organization, and they had been attempting to forge inroads on creating a peaceful dialogue between . . . well . . . everybody. The blond was Amanda, the president of the organization, the black woman was Neely Reed who created strategy and policy for the group, and the man was Carlos Rodrigues, the PR frontman.

As Delilah and the others shuffled through the crowd, I tapped Nerissa on the shoulder. She turned around. She was carrying a tablet, her hair was up in a bun, and she was wearing a navy pantsuit and a pale blue blouse. My wife looked so official that I didn't even think of kissing her. I wasn't about to diminish her authority in any way by a show of her personal life, but I still reached out quickly to stroke her arm. She winked at me, then cleared her throat.

"Glad you finally made it. Amanda and her group just got here, too, and they brought counterprotesters. Unfortunately, things have just blown up out there and I'm afraid that we're not going to see the night through without a problem. I've called in leaders from all the various religious organizations and fraternal lodges around here to try to create a common front that can push the fanatics back into the woodwork."

Chase nodded. He waved his left hand, the stump of his little finger suddenly reminding me of how much this man had been through for our family. But the biggest change he had suffered couldn't be seen on the surface. The biggest change was that Chase was no longer human. We had fed him the Nectar of Life to save his life and, barring accidents, he would live a long, long time. In the process, he had discovered that he had a distant ancestor who was an elf. Chase had met him, though we still didn't know much about that story. Perhaps, one day, he would tell us.

"Here's the problem. We have the hate groups picketing—which they are allowed to do. We have the United Worlds Church countering them, which again—allowed. We have nearly two hundred Supes getting pretty damned agitated. Totally understandable. But somebody has to back down before this powder keg explodes." He motioned for Frank to join us.

Frank Willows was a farmer, and he was also head of the Supe Militia. A werewolf, he was a bit more alpha male than I cared for, but it was the tradition of his pack. He sauntered over, joined by Jonas Rigbee, the current alpha of the Blue Road Tribe werebears, and Marion Vespa, owner of the Supe-Urban Café and one of the coyote shifters.

Frank was a sturdy man, not tall but definitely built. "We better take this down a notch. The meeting hasn't even started, and we need something to defuse the mess, by the looks of how things are going."

"I have a suggestion." Neely's voice was neutral and calm, the perfect way to address an alpha Were. "You start your meeting. Our people will do our best to get between the building and the protestors. We won't cause trouble, that's not what we are about—we are a peaceful group who espouse nonviolent protest as the positive way to effect change."

Jonas nodded. "And we value your offer." His voice was gruff, like you'd expect a bear to be, and he looked like a football quarterback. But he was wearing a three-piece suit and carrying a briefcase. "But what happens if they attack your people?"

"We will defend ourselves but we will not lead an attack." She turned to Amanda and Carlos. "Go talk to the group leaders. Ask them to spread out around the building and go into protection mode." As the pair nodded and moved off, Neely frowned. "We organize in group units, and each unit has a leader. Much more functional than just a mass of scattered people."

Chase turned as the door opened and a handful of men and women entered. "Good—they're here . . ." but as he spoke, a groundswell of noise came from outside. We all hurried to the front windows and cautiously opened a couple of them. The crowd had swelled to over a thousand, it looked like, and now we could hear a steady chant rising out of the masses.

"Love not hate! Love not hate!"

The chant gained strength as voice after voice joined in. Apparently, the other churches and organizations had taken to their phone trees, because the swell in crowd size was increasing, and now I was reading signs that directly countered the Earthborn Brethren and their thugs. For every sign reading **GOD HATES FAES** and **DIE WERE DIE**, there were at least ten countering it with **HATE BREEDS HATE** and **SEATTLE STANDS FOR LOVE**. As we watched in silence, overwhelmed by the outpouring of support, someone started singing "Get Together," and the old Youngbloods' anthem of the peace-and-love generation swelled into a massive singalong.

The Earthborn Brethren were being corralled into the center of the incoming protesters, and they were beginning to look nervous. The Freedom's Angels bikers shuffled, glancing at our building, and then at the crowd around them.

"I think now might be the time to show that we stand with the Seattleites who are standing with us." Delilah glanced at Frank, who nodded to Jonas.

The werebear cautiously opened the front doors wide and stepped outside, followed by a handful of the Supes. Neely joined him, slipping her arm through his. After a hastily whispered conference, one by one, the leaders of Seattle's religious orders and lodges followed suit—each one joining together with a Supe and stepping out in front of the building. They joined the singing. My sisters and I followed, spreading out in a line.

I asked Smoky to bring out a lectern and to aim the speakers toward the front of the building. Then I motioned to Camille. "We should say something. You're good at public speaking—you do it. We need to thank everybody for their support."

She frowned but accepted a hand up to stand behind the lectern. As the singing started to die down, she tapped the microphone and cleared her throat. "As you may know—or not know—I am Camille D'Artigo and I'm from Otherworld. I'm half-Fae, as are my sisters—Delilah and Menolly." She paused as scattered cheers went up. We did have a fan base around town.

"We want to thank you all, on behalf of the Supe Community Council, for your support." Then she turned to the protesters, who were effectively roped off by a human shield. "I'm here to tell those who wish us harm that you have no power here. The people of Seattle tell you, you have no power here. Seattle is a diverse and beautiful city, where hatred has no place. Members of this organization have been directly responsible for attacks on Seattle's Supe Community for years, and most recently, they have destroyed a vampire apartment complex and killed over twenty-five vampires in doing so. I know that Vamp Rights has not yet passed legislation, but we consider it murder just as much as if they had killed a werewolf, or a human."

The crowd began to murmur, and unfriendly faces began to turn toward the hate group.

Camille continued. "Every race, every gender, has good and bad members. No group is immune. That is what unites us—we are all individuals, and most of us are looking to coexist as peacefully as we can. Just because my neighbor prays to a different god than I do, just because my neighbor has different color skin, or because they love in a different manner, or because they turn into a wolf under the full moon . . . we can no longer allow these differences to divide us. Division brings hatred. Division brings death. I urge you now to peacefully resist allowing this sort of hate to continue in our city. And I do claim it as my city—I may be from Otherworld, but I have a business, I pay taxes, and I love this town!"

A cheer went up, running through the crowd like a rippling wave.

"Now, we cannot stop people from hating us, but we can make certain it doesn't eat into our hearts. And we can bring into law protection for everyone, regardless of their origin. Protection from hate, protection from assault. Thank you."

As she stepped away from the microphone, the crowd began to clap. Chase took the lectern next. "I am asking the Earthborn Brethren and their followers to leave in peace. And to think twice before staging any more protests. We are watching your organization, and we will find those responsible for the attacks over the past few weeks." He motioned for his men to spread into the crowd.

Apparently, the opposition knew when they were outnumbered, because, with many a glare, they began to push their way out of the throng. The officers made sure that nobody started any scuffles, and by the time the Earthborn Brethren were gone, the meeting had turned into a makeshift meet-and-greet as the crowd dwindled to a few hundred.

"I think we're going to have to shelve our meeting. For now, it would do the members of the Supe Community well to make nice-nice with their supporters and forge some common bonds." I was surprised Roman hadn't sent a contingent over, but right now, I figured it was for the best and I could find out why he hadn't later.

We joined the others, greeting those who had come out to support us, and an hour later, we headed back to our cars to go home. Nerissa was able to slip away. She would meet us at home. Chase had to stay and clear up some work, but he had already called Iris and told her he would be coming home very late.

"Do you think any good came out of it?" I asked as a couple of officers drove us back to our cars.

Delilah frowned. "I think so. For one thing, there's nothing like a common enemy to unite strangers, and while the world as a whole has accepted the presence of Supes, we have reached that odd time when we're trying to integrate into society instead of being the novelty act, you know?"

I nodded. "Yeah, and it's one thing to admire and enjoy the circus, but when the freaks want to set up camp in your town for good, well . . . that can be a whole different ball of wax."

We had reached the parking lot where we had left our cars and were about to split up and drive home when Camille's phone rang. She frowned at the Caller ID. "Trytian?"

Oh, wonderful, I thought as she answered it. Just what we needed. Trytian was a daemon. Unlike demons, daemons were a bit more organized and got along better with everybody else, in general. They still weren't trustworthy and they were dangerous and tended toward the evil side of life, but they could work with others a lot more easily. They were less chaotic, if I was forced to pinpoint the difference. Demons tended to act first, think later. Daemons were smarter. And Trytian's father was leading a covert army, aimed at taking down Shadow Wing.

Trytian was one of our frenemies. He made no bones about his designs on Camille, though he was cautious and kept himself at bay given the force he would face if he tried to do anything about it. But he was also cagey and knew enough to realize that keeping on our good side was better than getting on our bad side. We had a common enemy—Shadow Wing—and while our methods of going against him were different, we did have the united goal of destroying the Demon Lord.

Camille shook her head as she finished the phone call. "We need to head over to Carter's before we go home. Trytian asked us to meet him there in twenty minutes. Something is going down."

The fact that Carter and Trytian hung around together at all was unsettling. Carter was part demon, but he was also part Titan. His father was Hyperion, a major Titan, and Carter was head of the Demonica Vacana Society, working as a records keeper to keep watch over how the Demonkin interacted with humans.

"I don't know which is worse—the chaotic mess we just dealt with, or the prospect of having tea with Trytian." Morio wrinkled his nose.

"The former. Nothing got done, except—I guess—perhaps swinging a strong number of people in favor of enforcing Supe Rights and maybe instituting Vamp Rights. I guess it's worth it if we managed to win over a few influential organizations to our side." I shrugged. "Okay, Vanzir, Roz, hop in and let's head over to Carter's apartment."

Carter lived in a basement apartment. The area was guarded by wards cast by a powerful witch to whom he paid a good deal to in order to ensure protection for himself and his guests, because it wasn't one of the better areas in town. In fact, my Jag—which I missed terribly—had been keyed one night while we were visiting.

The steps leading down to the door—which was below street level—were warded, but we had never had trouble with the magic. Apparently we were not considered a threat. I'd barely raised my hand to knock when the door opened. A tall, lithe woman whom I immediately pegged as some sort of Fae escorted us in. By her demeanor, it looked like Carter had a new girlfriend. He had been dating a dragon named Shimmer for a while, but that hadn't worked out so well, apparently. We had helped him by rescuing her from a vampire that was out to get her employer—another vamp in the area. I hadn't been sure if the pair had gotten back together or not but apparently, they had not.

Carter was sitting at his desk. When he was in his apartment, he didn't bother to cloak up, and so the slender red-haired demigod had horns spiraling from his head, curving back like some magnificent wildebeest. He was handsome and if it weren't for the horns, he wouldn't seem imposing at all. He wore a knee brace on one leg and tended to go for a more genteel look. Right now, he was in a burgundy smoking jacket and a pair of black trousers. But looks were deceiving. If he wanted to, Carter could easily take down everybody in the room.

Trytian was on the sofa. Looking like a dangerously bent Keanu Reeves, he turned a glittering eye our way. Or rather, Camille's way. Smoky noticed, too, and growled just enough to make Trytian flash him a snarky grin.

"Don't worry, draco-beast. I know the rules. But you can't stop me from looking . . . and thinking." He winked at Camille and she bristled, but Carter put a stop to things.

"Down, dog. And Camille, ignore his churlish manners. Daemons are not cultured in proper behavior. Don't let him bait you." He crossed over to the living area from his desk, limping slightly. I was the only one in our family who knew how he had gotten that limp, and I had never mentioned it to the others—it was not my secret to tell. But I knew that it was connected to Trytian and Carter knowing each other, from long, long ago.

Trytian arched an eyebrow. "Take away all my fun, old man."

"Gladly." Carter didn't even glance at him, but his eyes were steady on the packet of papers in front of him. "Please take a seat, and allow me to introduce Liu-an. She's from Otherworld and she works for me, now."

The Fae who had opened the door gave us a quick curtsey. So, maybe not girlfriend. But then Carter tended to employ his paramours as servants, so who knew?

We murmured hellos and Carter motioned to her, whispering in her ear as she passed by him.

"We going to get this show on the road?" Trytian crossed his legs and leaned back against the sofa. He patted the seat next to him but Camille ignored him and took a chair as far away as she could get. Morio sat down next to him, though, giving him a long, feral smile, which made the daemon pull back just a little. I stifled a laugh.

"Please, everyone be seated." Carter waited till we were all sitting down to take his seat. He was truly a gentleman, but from our private conversations, I knew that he was as much into pain as a number of demons were, and he had once warned me that in private, he wore "the ringmaster's hat," as he had put it. Which had told me all I needed to know about his proclivities in the bedroom.

Liu-an returned with a cart laden with drinks and sandwiches, cookies and tea. And, as always, a goblet of fine blood for me. I smiled graciously as she handed it to me with a discreet red napkin. As soon as we were all served—even Trytian—Carter began handing out our dossiers. I had a feeling he kept the office supply stores in business. Every time we came he was busy with reams of paper and file folders to no end. He loved his technology, but it was also obvious that he loved the smell of ink and the feel of paper.

"We have a serious problem. But before we get into that, I need to know what the hell went on over in Otherworld. Whatever you did there has had massive ramifications through the demonic community." Carter adjusted his tablet. "I'm going to record you so I don't have to take notes."

We knew better than to counter him, so we started in on describing what had gone down. When we finished, both Trytian and Carter were staring at us, jaws slightly open.

Trytian spoke first. "You actually convinced the Dragonkin to go to war with you?"

Camille stared at him, hard. "Is that so unlikely? They owed me a debt, daemon. They offered me whatever I chose in repayment. I asked for their help."

Smoky let out another grumble. "Dragonkin may not always be the most congenial, but we do pay our debts without complaint.

Carter cleared his throat. "No wonder the information Trytian brought me seemed extreme, but it makes sense now." He turned off the recorder. "I will let Trytian tell you himself, and then we will discuss the ramifications."

Trytian gave Carter a pointed look. "Extreme? Perhaps. Unlikely? Not at all, given Shadow Wing." He turned toward us, suddenly all business. "My father has spies hidden in the Demon Lord's network. It seems that yesterday, news filtered down to the Subterranean Realms that Telazhar had been killed, and the Otherworld infiltrations were brought to a grinding halt. The messenger also said that, and I quote, 'those three Fae whores stole your spirit seal, Liege.' Needless to say, as soon as Shadow Wing finished grilling him, said messenger was immediately dragged away for torture."

Down in the Sub-Realms, "please don't kill the messenger" was more than a cliché.

"No surprise that Shadow Wing knows it was our doing." Camille set down her tea. "Did he have anything to say about the dragons?"

"Funnily enough, the Demon Lord conveniently ignored the whole dragon angle. Probably because if he didn't, he'd have to include them in his plans for revenge, and I doubt that even Shadow Wing is stupid enough to charge on the Dragon Reaches. Much easier to focus one's rage on targets that are accessible and vulnerable." Trytian shrugged. "According to our source—and he's reliable, so I believe this—the faux Keraastar Knights he's been attempting to create? Aren't working out quite like he hoped. But he's still plotting something with them."

I blinked. "Neither aspect of that sentence bodes well." Trytian gave me a what-do-you-want look. "What can I say? We all know he's unhinged. The Unraveller is pretty much a basket case at this point. He's been tearing through his own armies, killing anybody he thinks might be against him. He's losing it."

"Any chance he just might manage to do himself in?" I was pretty sure of the answer, but we could only hope.

Carter shook his head, though. "No, Shadow Wing is more likely to—as the humans put it—go postal, rather than take himself out. And this defeat seems to have strengthened that mania. If he were just off-kilter, it might play into our advantage, but he's also angry beyond the scope of the word. But that's not the most troublesome piece of news tonight."

I steeled myself. We'd had more than enough bad news lately. "So what is it? Just hit us with it. I hate dragging out the inevitable."

Carter shifted, looking uncomfortable. "A Degath Squad was seen gating out of the Subterranean Realms this morning. As of today, there are three very powerful demons running around here in Seattle. Somebody was strong enough to gate them in, but we have no clue who. I'm betting it's a revenge mission rather than him searching for the last spirit seal. And I'm guessing his targets? The three of you girls."

Chapter 9

It had all started with a Degath Squad. And after we managed to dispatch that trio of demons, we had fought demon generals till they were coming out our ears. We had even fought a god whom Shadow Wing had managed to impress into his service. But every time, they had been looking for the spirit seals and we had just been in the way.

This time? It was personal. And that fact sent a ripple of fear through me. It was easy to see that Camille and Delilah were feeling the same way. Besides the threat to ourselves, personal revenge all too often meant collateral damage, and we had lost enough friends through the years.

As we sat there, soaking up the information, Roxy, one of Carter's cats, came dashing through, then climbed on Delilah's lap and began kneading her jeans. She absently stroked it, then handed the gorgeous Aegean to Camille, who tucked the white cat to her chest and kissed her head. Lara, the other cat—a black-and-white Aegean and Roxy's sister—peeked out from behind the curtain that partitioned off Carter's back rooms from the living room area.

A moment later, Delilah let out a long sigh and leaned

forward. "All right, we have a Degath Squad on our back. Do we know what kind of demons they are?"

"I can field that one." Trytian stretched out in his chair, his legs long, as he shoved his hands in his pockets. He was actually pretty hot, in a dangerous sort of way, but his personality killed the attraction. "Our source who witnessed the gating said that one of them is a Naedaran, one is a Shelakig, and one is a Varcont."

None of them rang any bells. I looked at the others, who shook their heads. "Okay, do you perhaps have a rundown on what they are and what they can do?"

Carter picked up the packet of papers he had set on the table and began handing them around. I glanced over the sheets. There were three, stapled together, and each page held a description of one of the demons. If there was one thing we could count on the demigod for, it was to provide us a detailed dossier on our targets whenever he could possibly do so.

"You can read the details in a bit, but I'll give you a quick rundown. Naedarans are six feet tall. The body's basically a spongy ball of flesh on one leg, with a central eye and a mouth that can devour a human in two bites. They have arms, with three long taloned fingers, and do not let the one-legged status fool you. They can hop faster than most people can run."

"That sounds like a Fachan," Camille said. "Scottish Fae. Nasty sort."

"Perhaps it's an offshoot, but this is far more dangerous, trust me." Carter frowned. "The second demon—the Shelakig—is basically a giant scorpion. Except, rather than the venom only being injected through its aculeus, it's also present in its pincers, which contain a series of serrated edges."

"And how big is the Shelakig?" Trillian sounded as overjoyed as the rest of us looked.

"I'd estimate a good eight feet long, with the tail curving about four feet high. I've never seen one of these; it would be fascinating to dissect one and discover how like their nondemonic lookalikes they are." Carter sounded so matter-of-fact that I felt like smacking him.

"Don't sound so excited about it, okay? This isn't a biology class," I grumbled, but when he flicked a confused look at me, I just gave him a mute shrug.

"I happen to find the study of demonology interesting, so deal with it." I almost missed the playful grin behind the jab, but then he flashed us a smile. "Even I can make a joke now and then."

"So we have a one-legged mouth, a giant scorpion—and I assume the venom is deadly?" Smoky glared at Trytian, who was once again openly staring at Camille's boobs.

"The venom will dissolve flesh on contact, a lot like a hellhound's acidic bite." Carter flipped to the third page. "Trytian, eyes off the woman unless you want me to let her husband take you apart."

Trytian snorted but returned his gaze to the sheaf of papers.

"Now the third demon is the most problematic. The Varcont. This one is most dangerous in the fact that he is humanoid. He'll look like any regular man, except for the red eyes." Carter looked up. "In a sense, he will look like any vampire who might be a little pissed off. In fact, he's very much like a vampire, seeing that vampires are considered, to be blunt, minor demons." He gave me an apologetic look.

"I know what I am, don't sweat it."

"So a Varcont is a vampire?"

"A most dangerous one. Think vampire on steroids. He can walk under the sun, fire does not burn him, and the only thing that can destroy him is a silver stake directly through the heart. He can bring almost any younger vampire under his control, unless their sire is . . . well . . . one such as Roman—or like Dredge was. And the vampire glamour? They have it in spades."

I froze. "He's worse than Dredge was, isn't he?"

Carter caught my gaze and his expression softened. "I'm sorry, Menolly, but yes, he is. Varconts make Dredge look like a rookie."

The silence that followed echoed through the room. I could hear the sounds of everyone breathing, and I knew that my sisters were afraid by the shallow rise and fall of their breath. I had gotten pretty good at reading feelings through breath patterns, and right now I could tell that Smoky and Shade were thinking fast and furious. Trillian was processing. Vanzir and Roz were pissed. And Trytian? Was staring right at me. He shook his head ever so slightly when I met his gaze, and I could see the worry lines crinkling his forehead. Trytian was impulsive, and he was given to an overaggressive ego, so for him to be worried told me that Carter's impassive explanations were, if anything, on the conservative side.

"So what do we do?" I broke the silence.

"Is there any clue as to who gated them over?" Camille studied the packet of information, as if it could magically tell her who was out there playing with a Demon Gate. "I don't think we're going to get lucky and find out that it's some college kid who accidentally stumbled onto the spell this time."

"Yeah, this is no Harold Young situation." I racked my brain, trying to figure out just who Shadow Wing could be using over here. "Van and Jaycee are dead. It can't be them. Wilbur—he might be able to give us some ideas. He's a sorcerer."

Our mountain-man neighbor had bad manners, an even worse attitude, and a penchant for grabbing women's asses, but he was also a powerful sorcerer. And, even with only one leg, he could stand up to one hell of a nasty opponent. We had a love-hate relationship with him, but he always seemed to come through for us.

"Good idea. We'll pay him a visit and find out what he knows."

"We haven't talked to him or seen Martin for a while." I grinned then. Martin had become a running joke, though the origins of the ghoul were less than funny. Wilbur had reanimated his brother's corpse, unable to let him go to cancer, and Martin was like his pet dog. They watched *Jeopardy* together, they hung out together, and sometimes I wondered if Wilbur ever suspected that Martin's spirit was watching over him. Delilah had discovered that a couple of months ago.

"So . . . the fact that two of these three look like monsters means that if they start running around the streets of Seattle, somebody is going to notice them. That probably indicates that whoever gated them over has both a way of hiding them and the transportation to fit them. What would fit an eight-foot-long demonic scorpion?" Morio tossed his dossier on the table. "The Shelakig isn't going to be riding around in the back of a sedan. Or even a van, I think."

"Flatbed truck is out unless the demon held perfectly still, like some giant figurine for an amusement park or some show or something. Maybe a moving van? One of the shorter ones?" It would be ridiculous, though, to expect to track down every short-bed moving van that had been rented out in the past day or two. And we couldn't very well stop every truck we saw on the street and commandeer a look into the cargo hold.

"Another question. Can either the Shelakig or the Naedaran shift into human form?" Camille asked.

Carter shook his head. "No, and even if they were given the illusion, the Shelakig's body is just too massive to fit in that small a space. You can't mask one of those suckers up as Joe Schmoe and expect the illusion to work. Now, the Naedaran, you *could* glamour up and have it work until the thing attacked."

"So the Varcont and the Naedaran can theoretically meander around the streets of Seattle without being noticed, which means trouble." I thought for another moment. "Trytian, do you have any idea where they might be hiding? Even remote theories?"

He shook his head. "Not yet, but I have feelers out in the Demon Underground. Vanzir, you might head down there and ask around. There are factions there who like you, but who can't stand me. No harm in covering the same base twice from different angles. Meanwhile, my father is preparing to make a run on Shadow Wing in the next couple of weeks. He's amassed an army of discontents, and he figures now is as good a time as any to attack, given that the Demon Lord isn't expecting anybody from inside his own realm to take him on."

Once again, silence.

Another beat, and then Carter slowly said, "Is he sure this is the time?"

Trytian shrugged. "My old man does what he does and nobody is going to dissuade him, that I will tell you right now. He's waited a long time for this moment, and he expects me to be in the thick of things with him, which means I have to head down there after we finish talking." Another pause. "It also means I'm likely not to return, given the fury with which Shadow Wing can retaliate. But I am my father's son, and I will march into battle with him."

We stared at the daemon, and for the first time, I felt a measure of respect for him. He had been a pain in our ass for so long that I had gotten quite used to fielding the monkey wrenches he threw into the mix. But when I thought about it, I realized that he would—at the least—listen to reason.

"Are you sure?" Carter seemed to be thinking along the same lines I was. "This could be suicide."

"Well, if I'm going to go out, then I might as well go out in a blaze of glory. We have to stop Shadow Wing—the more insane he gets, the more he's going to try to unravel everything that holds the realms in their place. And while he may or may not be able to accomplish it, the last thing we need is for him to try." And with that, Trytian stood and headed for the door.

Camille shifted in her seat, then jumped up and followed him. "Trytian . . ."

He turned, a look of surprise in his glittering eyes. "Yeah?"

She darted in, planting a quick kiss on his cheek. "For luck."

He grunted softly, then pulled her to him and kissed her long and deep. Smoky and Morio glowered, but Trillian just let out a soft laugh. He knew his wife.

Camille pulled away as Trytian slapped her on the ass.

She smacked him lightly on the arm. "Get out of here. Go join the army. Just don't die. We need daemons we can reason with in the Sub-Realms."

He saluted the room, and then—before we could say another word—the door closed behind him.

"He's going to his death." Vanzir shook his head. "But I admire him for it. He's right, though, there are those in the

Demon Underground who wouldn't take food from him if they were starving, but who will talk to me. I'll head down there now and see what I can find out."

The Demon Underground was an actual place. When I first heard of it, I had thought it was more like the Underground Railroad the humans had formed to secret slaves out of their bondage, but the Demon Underground was exactly what it sounded like. A network of tunnels that shot off from the Underground Seattle area led to a secret passage, which in turn descended into a vast labyrinth of caverns that made up the Demon Underground.

Ever since Shadow Wing had taken over, a number of demons and daemons had fled the Sub-Realms, coming Earthside however they could gain entrance—which wasn't easy. But for those who managed it, they had taken up residence in the Demon Underground and mostly stayed there, minding their own business.

After Vanzir left, the rest of us just stared at one another, unsure of what to say. A Degath Squad on our tails, out for revenge. Shadow Wing was up to something with his faux Knights. Trytian's father was about to wage war on the Demon Lord.

And we? We were poised on what was beginning to feel like a pivotal moment in history.

Camille's phone rang. She frowned, then answered. A moment later, she moved off to one side. I decided to use the time to call Nerissa. She told me she was at home, waiting for us. She and Chase had managed to set up a watch over the Supe Community Hall, just in case some bright nitwit got it into his head to go back and bomb the place.

The others were nibbling on the remains of the tea cakes when Camille returned. "I just put in a call to Vanzir. He'll have to make his trip to the Demon Underground later. Right now both he and I have been summoned out to Talamh Lonrach Oll." She yawned, trying to stifle it but unable to mask how tired she was. "Hell, I don't feel like going out there tonight but I can't say no."

"Do you know what Aeval wants?" Delilah caught my eye, as if she sensed something was wrong.

"No, but she was insistent that I get my ass out there. I'll pick up Vanzir on the way. Morio, you're to come with me. Smoky and Trillian, can you two catch a ride home with Delilah?"

The catch in her voice told me something was up. "Are you *sure* everything's all right?"

Camille shook her head. "I don't know. Aeval just said she has some important news for me, and that Vanzir also needs to be there. I am a little concerned, especially since she wants Morio out there with me. But we won't find out what's up by just standing here. Come on, I can't keep her waiting. She said it won't take all night, so we'll be home as soon as we can."

Both the Fae Queen of Shadow and Night and the Fae Queen of Light and Morning were scary-ass women. And Aeval and Titania had decided, on the suicide of our distant cousin Morgaine—who had been the Queen of Dusk and Twilight—that Camille would succeed her and take the throne. Also the first Earthside High Priestess of the Moon Mother, our sister had a long and arduous road ahead of her.

"Go. Be safe. Call us if you're going to be out there all night so we don't worry." Delilah waved her off.

I let out a sigh. We were done here, it seemed. "I guess we'd all better head out. I think we're just treading water right now." I turned to Carter. "Keep us informed of anything you learn, and we'll do the same."

He stood, walking us to the door. "Be cautious, all of you. Revenge is a lot more personal than just making a grab for the spirit seals. Shadow Wing has you on his personal scope. And mad or not, he's a very powerful and dangerous enemy."

And with that, he shut the door behind us. As we headed to our respective cars—Trillian opted to ride with me, while Smoky went with Delilah and Shade—the night felt filled with prying eyes and unseen dangers. I shivered as I unlocked my car. Unfortunately, I was getting used to the feeling of being terribly, terribly vulnerable.

* * *

By the time we reached home, Delilah was tuckered out.

"I don't want to go to bed yet, though, because I want to know what's happening at Talamh Lonrach Oll." She yawned and poked in the kitchen, looking for a package of Cheetos. Shade found an open bag and handed it to her.

"Then rest on the sofa in the living room. We need some down time, Degath Squad or not. After the assault on Trenyth, we just need a breather. Or rather—you need a breather, given me . . . the vamp thing, you know." It was a lame joke, yes, but she laughed like I'd just won an award on *Stand-Up Central*. Maybe we were all punchier than we wanted to believe.

I followed the others into the living room. Nerissa was there, curled up in one of the chairs, dozing. She woke as I entered the room, giving me a drowsy kiss.

"Chase gave me tomorrow off. So I decided to stay up and wait for you." She scrunched over, making room for me in the oversized chair. I snuggled in with her, leaning my head on her shoulder.

Shade and Delilah curled up in the love seat. Smoky took one of the armchairs, and Trillian settled into the rocker. Rozurial stretched out on the sofa. Another moment and Hanna entered the room with a tray full of goodies. I was about to say that Carter had already handed out snacks, but at the rush for her cookies and tartlets, I shut my mouth. Trillian took the tray from her and set it on the coffee table, and the others, their treasure procured, returned to their seats.

"You want me to bring Maggie in? She's been missing you fiercely, with all the time we've had to spend away due to the goblin insurgents."

"Please do, Hanna. We've missed her, too. Camille and Vanzir will be home . . . well, I guess when they get home. They had to make a trip out to the Fae Sovereign Nation."

"Yes, Miss Menolly. Oh, there was a phone call for you from Lord Roman."

I wondered why he hadn't called my cell phone. Then,

pulling it out and glancing at my missed calls list, I saw that he had and I hadn't heard. By the time stamp on it, I saw that it had been while we were at the meeting. No doubt the throng of protesters and the singing and shouting had drowned out the ring tone.

I listened to his voice message. "My mother wants to see you, and I will expect you tomorrow night here, at ten P.M. sharp. This is a formal-dress occasion. Bring Nerissa with you. I'm going to be exceptionally busy the rest of the evening, so don't bother returning my call. Just make sure you are here."

Frowning, I stared at my phone. What the hell? Wondering if I'd missed something, I replayed it, listening closely. He didn't sound mad—just busy. And given his schedule, I knew he wasn't blowing me off. But Blood Wyne wanted to see me? What the hell was up now?

"Nerissa, love . . . tomorrow night, Roman's mother wants to see both of us." I swallowed, hard. It was one thing taking my wife to meet Roman. But to meet his mother? Blood Wyne was a terrifying figure—beautiful but so far from the human she had once been that she might as well be an alien, for all intents and purposes.

Nerissa paled. "Why does she want me there?"

"I don't know, but we can't refuse. I will protect you, no matter what." But even as I made the promise, the worrisome thought ran through my head that no vampire could stand against the Queen of the Crimson Veil. "There's no use speculating what she wants. It could be anything, given the whims of nobility."

Nerissa nodded, but I could sense her fear. And she was right to be afraid. The Queen of Vampires held an incredible amount of power, and I had no desire to see her wield it—unless it be against a common enemy.

Hanna emerged from the hall, carrying Maggie. Our little calico woodland gargoyle was a baby, about as big as a medium-sized dog at this point. She was a toddler, though, and would remain so for many, many years. Camille had rescued her from a harpy intent on making the baby her lunch, and we had decided to keep her. Maggie was adorable, though dangerous to small animals and children, and I had no clue what we were going to do when she got to her teenaged years. For that matter, I had no idea if gargoyles went through a rebellious phase. Maybe we'd be lucky and she wouldn't. But it would be decades before we had to worry about that.

I reached for her and Hanna settled her in my arms. Nerissa snuggled around both of us. Maggie was covered with a soft, plush layer of fur, and she was just learning to talk. She yawned, her wings opening wide as she stretched her arms, and then she folded them together around her and curled up against me, softly closing her eyes and falling right to sleep. The past few weeks had been hard on her, with so much activity and with only Hanna having enough time to pay attention to her properly. I kissed her forehead and stroked the fur on her back, glancing at Nerissa, who was smiling softly. Maggie snuffled as she slept, and before long, Nerissa had nodded off next to me.

Delilah was playing some game on her phone, and Shade was reading. I stared at him. He had undergone a lot of change—unwelcome changes, at that—yet he was handling it all gracefully. I had no doubt that losing his Stradolan nature to the devil-wraith that had invaded our home had hit him deeply, but he hadn't allowed it to affect how he treated everyone else.

After a little while, Delilah glanced over at me. Maggie was asleep. Nerissa was asleep. Kitten motioned for me to extricate myself and follow her into the kitchen. She gently took Maggie and, just as gently, I slid out from the crook of Nerissa's arm, making sure she was in a comfortable position before following Delilah.

Hanna was still up, sitting in the rocking chair by the stove, dozing lightly. She started as we entered the room. "Let me put her to bed." She rose and—refusing to take no for an answer—carried Maggie into the room they shared to tuck her into her crib.

Delilah wrapped her arms around herself. "Do you ever feel like things are moving too quickly? Like the world has sped up around you and all you can do is hold on for the ride?"

I gave her a soft smile. "Every day since the day I came out of my madness. And yet . . . for me . . . the world feels like it will stretch on forever. It's a solemn thing, knowing that unless somebody stakes me or some accident happens, I'll go on and on until I choose to end it." I usually didn't talk about things like this, but tonight seemed a night for reflection and realizations. "If nobody kills me, someday I'll be forced to make that decision on my own."

Kitten nodded. "I sometimes think about your life and what it must be like." She paused. "Shade and I will be married on the autumn equinox. And then . . ." A flash of fear crossed her face. "I have no idea when the Autumn Lord will want me to bear his child. I don't know if I can do it. I mean, it's one thing to have a baby, but to be the mother to an Elemental? I have no idea how to approach that."

"You'll do fine. Just love your child and . . . teach him or her not to destroy the world in a fit of temper." I repressed a smile, but at least it got a giggle out of her.

"I can just see it. *Go to your room or you can't go out and make the leaves change color!* Or something that seems equally absurd right now." She snagged a couple more cookies off the tray on the counter.

"How's Shade doing?" I opened the fridge, excited to see that Morio had enchanted more blood for me. One label read *chocolate cake* and I eagerly pulled it out. I really did need to figure out a thank-you present for him.

"Shade . . . he's taking everything in stride." She hopped on the counter, eating her cookies and swinging her feet. "That's one thing I've learned about shadow dragons. They tend to be less volatile than the others, from what I gather. He has an even nature. Oh, he can get angry, but he takes things as they come and he deals with them calmly. I know losing the Stradolan genetics hit him deeply—that was an essential part of his nature—but since there doesn't seem to be much he can do about it, he's doing the only thing he can. He's relearning who he is now."

"I know what it's like to have to relearn everything—to be somebody you weren't." I leaned against the granite countertop next to her and sipped the blood. It tasted like a deep dark chocolate cake, rich and thick on my tongue. If it hadn't been liquid, I might have even thought I was really eating something substantial. "If he ever needs to talk, I'm here. I understand what it's like to lose a part of yourself."

As Kitten nodded, the front door opened and Camille, Morio, and Vanzir entered the room. We trailed into the living room after them. Camille looked like the cat who had eaten the canary, and Vanzir had a look on his face that pretty much could be read as sheer terror.

"What happened? What did they want?" I slid back into the chair with Nerissa as she woke up.

Camille and Morio settled down on the sofa with Vanzir next to them.

"I might as well get right to it. In light of all that's happened, Aeval is moving up my coronation. I'm to take the throne at midsummer. And . . . then Smoky, Trillian, Morio, and I will move out to the Sovereign Nation. It's settled—" She held up her hand, looking teary. "I don't really have a choice. The Moon Mother concurs. Derisa was there. I'm going to have to learn on the job, it seems. Titania and Aeval created a new balance when they abandoned the summer and winter courts and moved to one based on the time of day. When they allowed Morgaine to join with them, it forever shifted matters. And now, Morgaine's death has thrown everything off and the balance needs to be set right."

So . . . we had only a few short weeks of being all together instead of until Samhain. I hung my head, not sure what to say. Delilah let out a soft mew, but then pressed her lips together and stared at the coffee table.

"I knew the future was coming, I just didn't realize it was going to come so quickly." Camille sounded incredulous. "But I'm not the only one with news. Vanzir's news is directly impacted by Aeval's decision. But I'll let him tell you about that himself."

I looked over at the dream-chaser demon. He had been recently outed in his relationship with the Queen of Shadow and Night, though only to Camille, Delilah, and me. And I had no clue if he even knew that *we* knew.

Vanzir let out a long breath and cleared his throat. "I suppose the best way to say this is just to come out with it. When Camille moves out to Talamh Lonrach Oll, I'll be going, too. I found out something last month. Aeval . . . I don't know if you realize she and I have been . . . we're . . ."

"Together?" Delilah prompted him, grinning. "We know you're an item. I saw you and Aeval with your tongues down each other's throat."

Vanzir arched an eyebrow. "Well, then. Yeah, we're together. And apparently we have put it to the proof that dream-chaser demons can interbreed with the Fae. Because Aeval is pregnant and she's going to have my child. So I will be moving out to her Barrow as her consort."

That was a piece of news nobody expected.

Camille and Morio sat nonplussed. They must have found out while they were out there. But Vanzir rushed on, heedless of the stunned silence. Or perhaps, because of it.

"The healers tell her the child will be an interesting mix, but her—*our* daughter is healthy and growing just fine, and while there's no chance she'll ever take the crown, Aeval wants me to be with her so the baby will know her father. I decided to follow Chase's example and be there for my child. I've never had a family," he added, his voice softening. "I never had anything remotely resembling a childhood. Even demons need . . . well . . ." He trailed off, looking lost for words.

I sat there, unsure of what to say. Then Delilah jumped up and wrapped her arms around Vanzir's neck. He looked mildly alarmed, but she just wrinkled her nose and smiled.

"Congratulations, Vanzir. You're in for one heck of a ride, I think."

And then congratulations and conversation filled the room.

Chapter 10

Nerissa was rummaging through the closet when I woke up. As usual, my first response was to lurch forward, swiping at her, but she was far enough away to avoid me. Always honed to a fine edge, my reaction upon waking was to attack first, ask questions later. Long ago, I had left a scar on Camille and now everybody knew to be at least ten feet away from the bed. That gave me a split second before attacking to realize where I was and who I was. As long as we had the *over-arm's-length* rule in place, everybody was generally safe.

"What are you doing?" I blinked. The sudden awareness of consciousness always threw me for a loop for just a few moments. Sunset eliminated subtle waking for me, flipping the light switch on with a sudden clarity.

"I have no clue what to wear. What the hell should I wear to meet Roman's mother? And tell me again, why do I have to go?" Nerissa, usually calm and collected, was sounding absolutely frantic. The look in her eyes vied for the time when I suggested she might not need to dress up to go clubbing.

Petrified, along with a side of *what the fuck are you talking about?*

I stared at my feet, not believing what I was about to say. "You have to go because she's the Queen of Vampires and because Roman's my sire, and because . . . because . . . I don't want to have to tell her no." Glancing up at her through my eyelashes, I tried for a grin.

She narrowed her brow, tilting her head. "You have got to be kidding." Then, with a long breath, she dropped the half-dozen outfits that were in her hands. "Fine. Okay, just fine. But you, my love, are going to be responsible for picking out an outfit for me."

I was about to protest when she shook her head. "Don't even try to get out of this."

Meekly, I acquiesced, shuffling over. I had to figure out my own outfit, as well. Roman had specified that the meeting was a formal affair. I wasn't about to stint Blood Wyne her due. I glanced through our closets. We couldn't share clothes—I was far smaller and shorter than Nerissa, so we never had the option to borrow outfits. Clubbing clothes were out, as were professional suits. Jeans? Not in a million years.

Finally, in the back of her closet, I spied a gown. It had a halter top and was a vivid shade of cobalt blue. The skirt flowed out into a gossamer swirl of layers varying from the same cobalt to a pale ice blue. Faint threads of gold wound through the different hues, with just enough sparkle to transform the gown from pretty to exquisite.

"This is gorgeous. When did you get this?" I hung it on a hook on the closet door and began to rummage through her shoes. Her peep-toe gold metallic slingbacks would match perfectly.

She stared at the gown, a soft, sad smile crossing her face. "I wore that to the last party my great-aunt Lucy threw before she died. The aunt who left me the money that I bought the condo with. I loved her, you know. She was a good woman, and for a human to be able to integrate with the Pride is rare.

They never fully accepted her, but she won over more than a few of them."

"She must have cared a great deal for you." I hadn't asked Nerissa all that much about her family. We'd had a few long conversations, but overall, Nerissa had been reticent on her affiliations with the Puma Pride. For one thing, they hated vampires and had all but pushed her out because of her relationship with me.

Nerissa laid out the dress on the bed, then rummaged through her dresser for a strapless, low-back bra and matching thong. "My family . . ." She carried her underwear over to her dressing table and stripped off her shirt. I watched, drinking in the sight of her.

"My father died when I was young. He was shot by a hunter and we found his body the next day. Mom . . . her name is Lana . . . had a young child and no job. She did one of the only things women in our Pride can do. She remarried. Her new husband treated me all right, but he's very alpha. When I showed signs of being interested in learning from Venus, he was seriously annoyed and refused to allow a daughter of his—even a stepdaughter—to follow that path under his roof. He wanted me to marry in the Pride and have babies. And he was even less tolerant when he found out I preferred women to men. I left home early but thought I could manage to stay part of the Pride. When I went back to tell my mother I was getting married to you, she kissed me, told me she loved me, and then asked me never to return."

I stood rock still. Nerissa had never once mentioned this to me. Her family had refused to come to the wedding but, given that the Puma Pride didn't like vamps, I hadn't expected them to. But I had never known any of this. "You have got to be fucking kidding me. She kicked you out of her house for marrying a woman?" And then I stopped. "No, she kicked you out for marrying a vampire."

Nerissa glanced over at me as she lowered herself to the vanity bench, her expression cautiously neutral. "Right."

And then I understood why Nerissa needed to know that

I was truly here for her. Now, my sisters and I were the only family she had left. Venus was off in the Dragon Reaches, and that left very few in the Puma Pride who would accept Nerissa's marriage with me. They didn't even like my sisters, though we had saved their butts once, quite some time ago. No, the Puma Pride worked with us through the Supe Community Council, but that was as far as it went.

Just as suddenly, it dawned on me that my lack of communication skills must have hurt my wife precisely because she had no family to go home to. She had sacrificed her Pride's support to follow her own path, and had lost their acceptance when she threw her lot in with mine. I leaned down, kissing her gently on the lips.

"I'm sorry. They are the ones losing out, my love. And I almost joined them. I promise you, from now on, I'm here for you. Whatever we face—either of us—we face it together."

She smiled then, breathing softly. "Thank you. That's why I'm going with you tonight. We face whatever comes together."

"So, if you're wearing that, what should I wear?" I opened my wardrobe and began sorting through the mass of jeans and sweaters that were my usual garb.

"What about your black gown? It would offset mine really well." She fastened her bra, then slid into clean panties. I still was amazed by her figure. Voluptuous, smart, and strong, that summed up my wife.

"You think?" I rummaged in the back where I kept my dresses. The gown, one my aunt had bought for me many years ago, was black as ink, shimmering with faint silver threads. I wore it at Yule, and now—as I brought it out—I realized that Nerissa was right. In its simplicity, it was elegant and perfect for a meeting with Blood Wyne.

I fingered my braids. My cornrows were my signature mark, but tonight, it felt like I should take them out—let my hair curl around my shoulders. "Will you help me?"

She grinned, then slipped a robe over her underwear. "Sit down. Let me make you up. I don't know what tonight's about, but if I'm to be there, too, it's obviously important and you need to look your best." She unbraided my hair, brushing it gently so that the curls didn't frizz but, instead, hung like a cloud of waves around my shoulders. Then she carefully applied my makeup. I couldn't see myself in the mirror, so I usually settled for a swipe of lip gloss. But tonight? Everything needed to be spot-on perfect.

"There. Refined, elegant, and a little bit deadly." Nerissa stood back, eyeing me. "Now change into your dress. Wear the silver heels with it."

We both dressed, adjusting each other as needed—a tuck here, a cinch there—and finally, we were ready to go. I chose a simple black woven shawl. Nerissa, a pale blue chiffon one. Taking a deep breath, I stood back.

"What do you think? Do I look ready to meet the Queen of Vampires?" I hadn't realized just exactly how nervous I had been until now. And that realization didn't sit particularly comfortably with me. But there was nothing I could do. It was fact, and I wasn't one to ignore what was in front of my face. Blood Wyne made me nervous.

"What about me? I'm not even a vampire and I get to meet this elusive member of royalty." Nerissa giggled, and then her smile fell away. "I'm afraid, Menolly. What if . . . what if she wants to turn me or something like that?"

The thought had actually crossed my mind, but I had written it off. "If she wanted to do that, both she and Roman know that I'd fight to the death. And given that we just destroyed an army with dragons, I have a feeling she might have some new respect for me. I don't think that's it. But I'll do whatever I need to in order to protect you."

And with that, we headed upstairs.

Of course, the others made a brouhaha about our looks, but Camille and Delilah—who I thought would be the loudest—were oddly reticent.

Camille motioned me aside. "I don't like this. Something's up."

"I know, but there's not much I can do about whatever it is. I think we'll be okay. I trust Roman—I have to, after all we've gone through." I glanced back at Nerissa. "Do me a favor? Lend her something silver she can wear inside her dress. Some charm or something that might help if . . . if something happens to me."

"Wait here." Camille raced upstairs and when she returned, she took Nerissa aside. Nerissa glanced over at me, then nodded as she accepted something from Camille. She went in the bathroom and when she came out, I leaned to kiss her but the silver on her body stopped me short. Satisfied, we made our good-byes and headed out.

"I hate driving in a gown like this." I hiked it up so that my legs were free to move as needed.

Nerissa laughed. "You just don't like dresses, period."

"Well, that's true. What did Camille lend you?"

"She gave me a silver pin that I fastened inside my bra. She said it belonged to your mother and that it was mine now. It's shaped like a grapevine." A soft smile played over Nerissa's face. "You asked her to, didn't you?"

"Yeah, I did. And yes, that pin belonged to our mother." Even softer, "It also belonged to me, before I was turned. After that, since I could no longer touch it, I gave it to Camille. I'm glad she chose that—it feels like a good omen." I wasn't much for omens, but sometimes, something just hit right and I knew there was significance to it.

"I love it, and I love having something that belonged to you before . . . well . . . and to your family." Nerissa paused. As I shifted gears and maneuvered onto the street that would lead us to Roman's mansion, she let out a long sigh. "I wish we could just go about our lives. I want the war to be over. I want to settle down with you and just live life."

"I've been thinking about that." I flashed her a grin. "Yes, I've actually been thinking over the future. What do you think . . . when—not if, but when—we defeat Shadow Wing, what if we buy a house of our own? Camille and her men will be moving soon enough, along with Vanzir. Delilah loves our house, so she could live there with Shade and Rozurial. After all, at some point the Autumn Lord is going to decide it's time for her to have his child." It hurt me to say it . . . I loved the house as much as Delilah, but I wanted

Nerissa to know I was all in. That I was looking forward to life with just her.

But she turned around and surprised me as well. "I like the idea, but you know what? What about if we stay there? Delilah's never been that great with running a household, and I don't think she particularly enjoys the responsibility. You and I are good at that sort of thing. There's room enough for all of us, and once Camille leaves, we could fix up the second floor to be an office for me, and a guest room. If you don't think Kitten would mind."

I pulled to a stop in front of Roman's mansion, a crazy grin spreading across my face. "That makes tonight almost bearable. I love that house, to be honest, and that you love it as well makes me very happy." As I glanced up at the four-story mansion that loomed over us, I shivered. "Let's get this over with. Probably nothing to worry about, but you know . . ."

"I know," she murmured. And as the valet took my keys, we approached the fortress of vampire nobility.

The house, four stories high, was surrounded by a long porch that encircled the entire mansion. Gleaming columns lined the porch, Corinthian in nature, and the steps leading up were marble. We rang the bell and a maid answered, curtseying deeply. She was a vampire, dressed very crisp, and the moment she saw me, she knelt in a low bow. By now, Roman's staff knew who I was, and I'd made the effort to learn as many of their names as possible.

"Good evening, Elthea." I smiled at her. She was a young vampire and very nervous.

"Lady Menolly, good evening." She turned to Nerissa. "Madame Nerissa, if I may presume?"

So Roman had told them we were both on the way.

Nerissa looked a little out of her element but nodded graciously. "Yes, I'm Nerissa."

"Please come in. The Master has asked me to escort you to the Grand Parlor."

The Grand Parlor? That was what Roman called a small

ballroom-slash-parlor that he held soirees in. And I do mean *soirees*. Roman didn't throw just any run-of-the-mill parties. He produced *events*. Balls. Soirees. Evenings of symphony or small theatrical parties. The smaller events were held in the Grand Parlor. The larger ones were in the Grand Ballroom.

Nerissa's eyes widened as we followed Elthea through the house. Roman was also a collector, and—much like Carter—his house was overflowing with exquisite objets d'art. He almost crossed the line into excess, but it never quite bordered on gaudy. I found it rather claustrophobic, but he loved it and given his nature, it seemed natural for him to live in what was essentially an art gallery.

"I can't imagine what his insurance rates run to cover all this." Her whisper was light, but Elthea heard it and she glanced back at us, a faint smile on her face. Nerissa blushed, and I reached for her hand, but the moment I stepped near her, a burning sensation repelled me. *The silver.* Well, at least it was doing its job.

We came to a set of double doors and Elthea opened them, giving Nerissa a wide berth as we entered the room. The massive room had a marble floor, highly polished, with tapestries on the walls. Crimson drapes were held back by gold tasseled pulls. The art on the walls was original—I knew that much—and harked back to an age long before either my time or Nerissa's. Divans and fainting couches; elegant, ornate tables that held vases with a single flower, or fruit bowls, or statuary—all were scattered about the room in a deliberate and yet effortless fashion. A massive fireplace with a hearth that had to have been at least six feet wide and at least as tall rose along the back wall. The mantel was polished ebony, like most of the wood.

"Lady Menolly and Madame Nerissa," the maid announced.

Roman was waiting at the opposite end, near the fireplace. He turned, and—seeing us—blurred very faintly and the next second was at our side.

"Thank you, Elthea. You may go." He was casually dismissive, but Elthea gave him a radiant smile and dropped in a low curtsey.

"Yes, Sire."

So, Roman was her sire. That made sense. And she was obviously enraptured with him. Although he was my sire, and I understood the desire to please, it occurred to me that having been sired once before had taken the edge off that hunger.

"Menolly, Nerissa . . . you are both lovely tonight. Absolutely stunning." He lifted my hand to his lips, kissing it gently. But as Nerissa reluctantly handed him her hand when he held out his own, he jerked back, eyes flaring crimson. The blood calmed, but he cocked his head. "You dare to wear silver in my house?"

I realized what a faux pas I had made. "It's my fault. I asked her to." I paused as he turned to me, looking perplexed. "I . . . I was afraid you and your mother might want to turn her." The moment I said it, I realized we had been way off the mark in our fears because Roman gave me a *what-the-fuck* look and started to laugh.

"Oh, my love. If I wanted to turn your wife, I would have done so long ago and without all this pomp and circumstance. Mother has no such intentions either, I give you my word of honor. But if you are wise, Nerissa, you will remove your charm or whatever you have and leave it in the guest bathroom until you leave. We will not touch it, I guarantee you that." He snorted then, shaking his head. "Hurry now. I have a good sense of humor. My mother . . . does not."

Nerissa glanced at me, eyes wide.

"I think you'd better do as he says. This wasn't the brightest idea I ever came up with."

"I think you're right." Nerissa turned and, heading in the direction Roman pointed her, ran as quickly as she could, her skirts swirling around her long legs in a flurry of blues.

When she had vanished through the door, I turned back to Roman. "All right. What's this about? I don't like being in the dark, and I don't like that my wife is terrified because she was called here, too." *I* didn't like being afraid either. There had been far too much to fear lately. "We've had a rough week."

"So I heard through the grapevine. So, you like riding dragons, my love?" He smiled again, a toothy grin, but then quickly sobered. "I cannot tell you what my mother asks. I know what it is, but Blood Wyne swore me to silence until she gets here. But please believe me, neither you nor Nerissa are in danger. Quite the opposite." He pressed my hand to his lips once again, then crossed to a table with a bottle of wine on it. A bottle of blood sat there, too, and he poured three goblets of that, then a goblet of wine.

Curious now, I was still apprehensive, but Roman had never lied to me and I had no reason to believe he would start now. I accepted the goblet of blood and sipped delicately. It was good, very good, and I cocked my head, looking at him.

"You might say, a rare vintage."

I hesitated, staring into the chalice of blood. "That could mean a lot of things."

"It could, but please, don't worry. The blood was given voluntarily. It's from a succubus, so it will be sweeter than wine." He winked. "Their blood is always a delicate mix."

I nodded. Blood did vary, depending on species, depending on the race. Fae blood was sweeter than human, human far more appealing than goblin. Demon blood could have an odd effect on vampires. The blood of a drunk wouldn't get a vampire drunk, but it wasn't as tasty as the blood of someone who was healthy and not under the influence.

Nerissa reappeared. She held out her hand to Roman and he took her fingers in his, bowing as he kissed the top of her hand. He flickered his gaze up to her and winked at her.

"Much better, my dear. You taste far sweeter without the silver. And I give you my word, you do not need it in my house. If anyone were to even attempt to attack you, I would garrote them myself. There would be no forgiveness for such an act." His eyes grew cold as ice—they were pale as frost, anyway, and now the irises almost vanished. "You are my consort's wife. You will never be abused in this house."

Nerissa stared at him straight on, usually a no-no when it comes to vampires. "I believe you, regardless of the weirdness that has happened between us at times."

"I need you to believe me, and I want you to remember this when my mother gets here."

And once again, we were back to nerves. We made small talk, mostly me talking about the dragons and Telazhar, for another few minutes before a soft bell sounded—tinkling like glass. Roman held up his hand.

"Please, come into my office. Bring your goblets. My mother is here." He turned to Nerissa. "I know you must be nervous. Curtsey low when you meet her, and address her as *Your Majesty*. Her full title is *Her Majesty Blood Wyne, Queen of the Crimson Veil and the Vampire Nation*. Take her lead. If she decides to play it informal, she will tell us."

And with that, he led us into a private office that was off one side of the Grand Parlor. Just as lavish, the ornate furniture was white with gold trim. It was rococo, late baroque in style, embellished with flourishes and engravings. The end tables were marble-topped, the sofa and love seat upholstered in white. The desk was especially large, fit for a dandy, with gold trim on every drawer. Plants flourished around the room, and the carpeting was white, which led me to believe that either Roman never fed in this room or he had an impeccable carpet cleaner and maid. Most likely the latter.

And in the center of the room, as we entered, stood Blood Wyne, waiting.

The Queen of the Crimson Veil was like a statue, carved from the whitest bar of Ivory soap. She was colorless, soft, ivory white in skin and with eyes the same frost color that Roman had, with almost no delineation marking the separation of iris to the whites of her eyes. She had been alive for so long that all pigment had faded from her body. Her hair, black that was streaked with white, coiled in a towering braid atop her head. She was wearing a gold tiara, inset with rubies and diamonds.

Her dress was woven gold, beaded with crimson. The neckline was low and straight, and her cleavage swelled gently over the top. The waist cinched in tight, and the skirts flowed out over a mass of crinolines, or a hoop—I wasn't sure which—to trail along the ground. The sleeves of the dress puffed out on top, fitting snugly around her forearms.

Roman immediately swept into a deep kneel in front of

her, and Nerissa and I curtsied low to the ground, holding the pose until she examined us for a moment.

"Rise." The single word resonated through the room. Her voice was low and throaty, rich with power and years of command.

As we straightened up, she held out her hand and Roman quickly moved to kiss it. "Your Majesty, we are honored by your presence."

Blood Wyne looked past him to me. "Menolly, you are looking well." Her eyes flickered over to Nerissa and her nostrils flared for just a second. "Introduce me?"

I almost tripped over my tongue in my haste to obey. "Your Majesty, may I introduce my wife, Nerissa Shale? Nerissa, this is Her Majesty, Blood Wyne, Queen of the Crimson Veil and the Vampire Nation."

I wasn't sure if my protocol was correct—I could never remember who you were supposed to introduce to whom, in terms of importance. I knew there was some rule about it, but I had never paid much attention to Miss Manners or Emily Post, and I hoped that Blood Wyne hadn't either.

If I screwed up, the Queen didn't mention it. She turned to Nerissa, who again curtsied. "So, this is the wife of my son's consort. You are a pretty thing, that I will say." She ran her gaze up and down Nerissa like she was judging a beauty contest. "What are you again, girl?"

If she was offended, Nerissa was cautious not to show it. "I'm a werepuma, Your Majesty. I come from the Rainier Puma Pride." She flashed me a look that said, *You owe me so big.* I gave her the slightest of nods. I'd be paying for this one for a long time, and rightly so.

"A werepuma. Well, now. What does your family think of your marriage to a vampire? I had thought—perhaps my knowledge is out of date—that Weres were not all that fond of vampires." Blood Wyne began to circle Nerissa, nodding to herself.

I glanced at Roman, who simply stared at the ceiling. Yeah, he didn't want to get into it either and as much as I owed Nerissa for tonight, he was going to owe us ever so much more. I planned to make him pay and pay good. He must have felt my stare because he shuffled and glanced at me, then back to his mother.

Nerissa looked like Bambi caught in the headlights. "My family . . . we aren't on speaking terms. They didn't approve of my choice, so I walked away and joined my wife's family instead." Her voice was a little higher than usual, but she was managing to hold her composure under Blood Wyne's scrutiny.

But I was beginning to get irritated. "Your Majesty, my wife is nervous. I would ask of you . . ." I paused. How could I best ask the Queen of Vampires to back off from upsetting my wife without causing a ruckus?

Blood Wyne's lips curled into a smile as she turned to me. "You are protective of your mate. This is a good thing." And then she laughed—not gently, but with a sincere touch of mirth. "I will relent. Nerissa, you are a credit to your wife, and to your loyalties. It must be difficult when forced to choose between one's heart and one's familial duty. Which is precisely the reason I invited you here, today. I know all about your background—don't look so surprised," the Queen added when Nerissa bristled. "Of course I would check into anyone who has access to my son's personal affairs. As his consort's wife, you have precisely that access."

Nerissa glanced over at me, glowering a little, but she shrugged. "You have a point." And then added hastily, "Your Majesty."

"Formalities are for first impressions and throne rooms. You need not add my title every time you speak to me. I won't have your head—or your throat—if you forget." And with that, the strange little soiree relaxed a bit. "I asked you both here for a reason. I doubt either of you will like it, but I hope you understand. And perhaps, in time, you will come to appreciate the value of what I am about to request of you."

Annnnd . . . here it came. Blood Wyne never did anything without a reason—it was beyond her at this point in her existence. So we were about to get a firsthand show in the way she manipulated events. I had seen it in the past, and I had the feeling we were about to get the full monty, so to speak.

"Be seated." She herself took a seat behind Roman's desk. He sat with us, on my right side, with Nerissa on my left, on the sofa.

I reached for Nerissa's hand. She was shaking and I didn't blame her. While I no longer feared they would try to turn Nerissa or dissolve our marriage, whatever she was about to ask wouldn't be something as simple as, *Could you take my dog for a walk?*

"So . . . as you know, the recent spate of hate crimes has increased our need to press for vampire rights in this nation. Worldwide, actually, but for the purposes of this conversation, we will limit our discussion to this country." Blood Wyne paused, and we waited. "Menolly, you have a great deal of pull in this city. And, I suspect, the capacity for influence far beyond the confines of Seattle. Your Otherworld ties are invaluable."

"I suppose . . . yes." I wasn't sure at all where this was going. The sudden talk of vampire rights and politics had thrown me.

"Well, then. What I want you to do is simple. I could phrase it as a request, but as my son's sireling—and therefore directly aligned to me in terms of lineage—you may consider this a direct order. We need you, Menolly, firmly ensconced in the Court of the Vampire Nation. I intend to make you an official member of the family. Consort is all well and good, but because of the nuances the breathers—" She paused, glancing at Nerissa. "Pardon me, I do not mean offense. Mortals, shall we say? Humans, especially, put a great importance on alliances. Therefore, we need to officially induct you into the court life."

"Okay . . ." There was something coming that I hadn't quite grasped yet.

"I am decreeing that you and your wife will both marry my son. You will both take on the title of princess. This is not up for debate."

And with that, the bricks tumbled down, and Nerissa and I were left slack-jawed and silent.

Chapter 11

Nerissa found her tongue before I did. "You want *me* to marry Roman, too? What the hell? Menolly and I are already married."

I winced, but Blood Wyne didn't seem upset. In fact, her voice softened. "I know this is a shock, but trust me, I have good reason. Menolly, you are related to me because he has re-sired you. But I want your succession in the monarchy assured."

That was a new one. "But . . . you are the Queen—and Roman will be the King after you, right? And what about your other children? Wouldn't they resent me?"

All I knew was that Roman had seven brothers and sisters, and Blood Wyne had turned them all. The youngest two had been turned when they were twelve, before they hit puberty, and from what Roman had told me, they ran off and had never been heard from since.

His brother Caleb, until recently the Vampire Nation's regent in western Europe, was a strikingly handsome, and equally violent, man. In a brief meeting a short time back, he had attempted to woo me away from Roman with the intention that we institute a return to the old days when vampires sought to be the scourges of the world. He had broken with Blood Wyne, and last we heard, he had resigned as regent and struck out on his own. But that still left four other siblings, including two who were total mama's boys from what Roman told me.

Blood Wyne laughed softly, leaning forward. "What has Roman told you about his siblings?"

I glanced at Roman, who nodded for me to answer. "Only that two ran off long ago, and I met Caleb—we did not get along."

"Yes, well, Caleb is no longer regent. He seeks to move against me, but I intend for him to be long dead before that happens. My twins, they were staked, long ago. A mother knows these things, and so does a sire, and I was both to them. Viktor and Encee are sweet boys who tag after my skirts. But they know perfectly well they are not fit to rule, and they are content to remain at home. In this monarchy, intelligence matters. The pair are loving, but they have no capacity for leadership. Anastasia might have taken the throne, but she prefers to play her part from behind the scenes. She told me once that she would do anything to help except to wear the crown. As she put it, 'A crown brings with it attempts at assassination.' And she is correct."

That made six, and Roman was seven. "What about your eighth child?"

Blood Wyne glanced over at Roman, whose expression turned dour. He hung his head and shrugged. The Queen returned her gaze to me. "Our dark Paulette. To be honest, she remains imprisoned in my castle. A beautiful captive, as mad as she is immortal. I cannot bring myself to stake her, and yet she is thoroughly an animal. Her mind could not handle the years of life my blood gave to her and she slowly slipped into her predator. We feed her, make sure she has comfort, but she must never be allowed to escape or she would terrorize the land—a dark queen caught by the feral madness of her soul."

Images of Sassy Branson flashed through my mind; she

had lost the battle to her inner predator. She had begged me to stake her, and when the time came, I did. Even as I staked her heart, I was hating myself for it, but afterward, I saw her spirit walking free from her body, at peace once more, and I knew I had done the right thing.

"You should let her go. I don't care how much you love someone. Keeping them alive in that state? It's cruel." If Blood Wyne wanted to be honest with me, she'd get honesty in return.

"I have told Mother the same many times." Roman stood and paced around the room. "I will do it, if need be, but you know we should set Paulette free."

Blood Wyne lingered on my face, searching my eyes. "I will consider your words. But if someone sets her free, it must be me. I both brought her into this world and birthed her into her life as a vampire." A veil of exhaustion seemed to sweep over her face, but then she shook it away and cleared her throat.

"Back to the matter at hand. You see why we need someone who can claim the throne if something happens to me, or to Roman. Menolly, you are my choice. I trust you will not have the desire to claim it too soon. Yet, should you be forced to ascend, you would rule wisely and well."

As the information began to soak in, I found my mind churning with questions and reasons why this wouldn't work. And yet . . . and yet . . . there was a part of me that understood her reasoning. I was already considered the official consort, but that gave me no real authority when push came to shove.

Blood Wyne seemed to sense my ambivalence. "Be assured, this is a political match. Roman will not usurp Nerissa's place as your spouse, except in the Vampire Nation." She turned to Nerissa. "And this is of benefit to you as well. Since you will be considered Second Wife, you will be given the same respect and guarantees of safety as Menolly will. This will cement Menolly's powers within the Vampire Nation. Those who are hesitant now will have no choice but to accede to her authority. Remember, because Menolly killed her original sire, a horrific sin in the vampire community, she has been ostracized by those who value tradition at all costs."

Nerissa frowned, and I could see the gears clicking in her head.

I turned back to Roman, who was once again seated by my side. Everything made sense, given the nature of everything going on. I didn't want to admit it, I didn't even want to *think* about it, but having me as an official part of the court might help. The status of consort was basically that of a glorified mistress.

Nerissa finally found her voice. "What do you expect this to be, then? What would that do to my marriage with Menolly? I really don't want to live here."

Blood Wyne laughed. "Think, girl. How many matches have been made for the throne that are based on love? Queens and kings have been living separate lives since the beginning of time. I do not expect Menolly to cling to Roman and ignore you. While, yes, you *would* be required to live here after the coronation, I have no expectations that the two of you stay here every moment, or that you give up your jobs. Nor will your marriage to Menolly take a backseat."

"How can we be sure?" I finally spoke up. "What assurance do we have that you won't try to edge out our marriage in favor of my alliance to Roman?"

With a soft smile, Blood Wyne shook her head. "Roman may not wish to admit it, but I can tell very well where your heart—and Nerissa's heart—rests. And, as much as my son may wish, I think it's best to call a trump a trump. The two of you love each other in a way that transcends logic. And neither Roman nor I will ever seek to break that bond. If you live here, you will have your own suite together, and you may come and go as you please."

"We couldn't possibly move here until after Shadow Wing is taken care of, even if I were to agree now." I cocked my head. "You know that's out of the question."

Blood Wyne remained impassive. "We will decide that in time."

Nerissa stared mutely at the vampire queen. After a

moment, she turned to Roman. "If we agree—if Menolly does this, will you swear by your life, by your fangs, by whatever is sacred to you, that this isn't your way of trying to take Menolly away from me?"

I started to interrupt, but she held up her hand.

"You see, I get it," Nerissa continued. "I really do. Her Majesty makes sense. What we've seen the past few days . . . what I saw when I went out on those calls with Chase . . . was horrendous. The hatred, the anger, and the destruction aimed at not only vampires but the entire Supe Community? It's terrifying. What's worse is that I know it's just the tip of the iceberg. And having Menolly in a position of unquestioned power would help a great deal."

"How so?" I still didn't quite see why I was the front runner.

"You never think you're important. Not you, not your sisters. But Roman and his mother are right. You don't understand what rock stars you *D'Artigo Sisters* have become in the area. The Fae will listen. Other Supes, who might not take kindly to vampires—like my Pride—will listen. Humans will listen because you are from Otherworld and you still wear that glamour like a cloak. This would help because you could also be a liaison between the Vampire Nation and the United Worlds Church."

I frowned, beginning to understand what she was saying. I hated thinking of myself in any self-important way, but false modesty was as annoying as false pride. My sisters and I *did* stand out in the community, and because of our interactions, people paid attention to what we had to say.

Nerissa turned to Blood Wyne. "Pardon me for saying this, Your Majesty, but both you and Roman are inaccessible. And you're fucking *scary*. Hell, I'm terrified to be here. I'm scared I'll say something that will set you off and boom, *no more Nerissa*. My wife is scary, too, but she is a part of the community. The Wayfarer saw to that. So I understand what you are saying, and I agree that this may be a wise move for you. For the Vampire Nation. But I want guarantees. I want proof . . . I want to have something concrete that I can hold in my hand to calm my fears that you won't try to take Menolly away from me."

"What assurances can we give you?" Blood Wyne leaned forward, her elbows resting on the desk. "I want your cooperation. You are not only beloved by Menolly, but also by those who favor her. The last thing we want to do is to be seen as taking her away from you. Not if we seek to further our acceptance with the world of mortals. Tell us what you want in return."

Well, this was a fine thing. My wife and my consort's mother were bargaining as if I weren't in the room. I was about to say something when I realized that, no—this was a *good* thing. They were coming to terms on their own, without my interference. Which meant a great deal for Nerissa. I sat back and kept my mouth shut.

Nerissa pointed to Roman. "You. I need *you* to seal the deal. Become my blood-oath brother. If you go back on your word after that, I'll have the right to stake you without any repercussions. You agree to that, then we have a deal. I'll marry you, along with Menolly, and we'll move in here after her coronation."

"*Your* coronation, too, my sweet." Roman's lips turned up in a wicked smile. He was enjoying playing cat and mouse with Nerissa. "You marry me, you're both my princesses, although you could never ascend to the throne without becoming a vampire."

"So not interested in becoming a vamp, let alone ruling them." Nerissa's gaze never left his. "Then we have a deal?"

"You have my word and yes, we have a deal. But . . . we exchange blood vows *my* way. I drink—a very little—from you. And you, my dear, drink a few drops of my blood. Are you game?" His gaze was totally fixated on my wife.

I felt like we had reached a line that—once crossed—would forever change the nature of our lives. And it all hinged on Nerissa's answer. I didn't have a say in this. She needed to fight this battle on her own. She was establishing *her* line, *her* boundaries, *her* rules.

Nerissa stood up and walked over to the desk. Blood Wyne sat very still, staring at the pair with an expression that mirrored my own incredulity. But she seemed inclined to the same course of action I was taking: Leave well enough alone.

Roman and my wife were jousting for position in my life. Nerissa would win if she went through with it, even though she would be giving in to Roman in terms of the blood sports. Because anybody who could claim Roman's *life* if he broke an honor code held a dagger over his head, and nothing in his position could refute that. Especially when witnessed by the Queen of Vampires herself. She might be his mother, but I had the feeling Blood Wyne was all about the letter of her law.

Nerissa leaned across the desk to stare Blood Wyne in the face—an act so foolhardy and brave that even I recoiled from the idea. My wife had plenty of courage, that was for sure. "You heard him? He agrees to my terms?"

Blood Wyne nodded, her fangs coming down. But she did not lunge, did not react in any other fashion. "I did. But you'll need a blade, my dear, unless you choose to cut flesh with your own fangs."

Nerissa arched her eyebrows. "Now there is an interesting idea. Roman pierces my neck with his fangs. I pierce his flesh with mine." She turned back to him. "I agree to your terms. Fang for fang, my Prince?"

He laughed, a little too harshly, in a way that made me realize she had turned him on and he was ready to play.

I stepped in. "Remember—she doesn't get hurt."

He waved off my concerns. "Always part of the bargain, my love. All right then, werepuma. Fang for fang. You and me. Let's go." And, in a quick stride forward, he was by her side. "You might not want your dress to get bloody, and if we do this right, it will."

"The same with your fancypants outfit, Liege."

She circled him. Puma was flaring. I could feel it. I had seen her transform so many times I'd lost count. Right before she changed to go running through the forest, Puma would rise and I would always feel a leap of fear in my heart. Nerissa in her Were form was a wild creature, free and passionate, and able to kill with a well-placed blow to the heart or head.

The pair moved to where they were in front of the desk, unencumbered by furniture. They stripped off their clothes and for a moment, I cringed. His *mother* was in the room. But then common sense took hold of me. Blood Wyne was an ancient vampire. Somehow the rules of mother-son modesty pretty much flew out the window when you really thought about the nature of the beast and what we had been discussing.

Both Nerissa and Roman were magnificent when naked, and I wanted nothing more right then than to slide between them for a bit of three-way action. But (a) Blood Wyne. I really didn't feel like fucking my wife and my lover in front of her. And (b) the one time we had tried it, Nerissa and I ended up pushing Roman to the side and his ego had been sorely bruised. So I stayed right where I was.

Roman slaked his gaze over Nerissa's body. "You're absolutely lovely. Menolly knows her beauties." He bared his throat. "You can't kill me unless you stake my heart. I'm going to trust you to hold to our deal. Blood brother, blood sister. Fang for fang. Do your worst, my beautiful Were, princess-to-be."

Nerissa stood back and then, in a transformation that I knew so well by the sight of it, shimmered. Her spine lengthened as arms and legs shifted, face contorting into the silken, sleek muzzle that marked her as one of the big cats. As the beautiful tawny beast emerged, Nerissa let out a long, low growl of satisfaction. She was beautiful, strong, and muscled. *Puma, cougar, mountain lion,* call her what you will, my Nerissa was deadly and brilliant.

Roman's nostrils flared as she neared him. *He's afraid*, I thought. *He's really afraid of her.*

But he held his ground, standing stock-still as she approached. She padded toward him, pausing when she reached his side. Then, with one massive movement, she rose on her hind feet, standing taller than he was. She leaned against him, her huge front paws draping around his neck. He glanced at me but kept his composure, waiting, his neck fully exposed.

Nerissa licked him, from neck to face, then stared directly into his eyes, her muzzle inches from his lips. She let out a loud grunt, then a rumbling purr as she bared her fangs and scraped them across his throat. The blood welled and began to run down his alabaster skin.

With a huff, she leaned in and licked, as another cloud of shimmering light cloaked them. I blinked, startled, and when I opened my eyes, she was there in her human form, her arms wrapped around his neck, her lips pressed to the cut, lapping softly. The sight of them together, along with the energy filling the room, was driving me nuts now. I wanted to be with them, to fuck them both, to take them down in a mad orgy of tongue and breast and pussy and cock.

Roman let out a long groan as she sucked up his blood, then stood back.

She wiped the blood off her face onto her fingers and held them up in a salute. "I pledge never to harm you or your mother. I will be your wife, along with my wife. I will do my best to help your cause as long as it does not conflict with my other oaths, and as long as you swear oath back to me." She bared her neck to him.

I tensed as he neared her.

Wrapping his arms around her body, he slid his fangs deep into her flesh, moaning and shifting as the blood sprang up and he coaxed it into his mouth. Nerissa gasped, letting out a little cry that I knew meant she was enjoying it. A sudden spurt of jealousy crossed my thoughts. She usually saved that cry for *me*—we played with men, but our hearts belonged to each other. Roman laved her neck with his tongue, cupping her waist with one hand and her ass with another as she rubbed against him. He was hard, erect, and firm, and she wrapped one leg around his waist, sliding down on his cock, driving herself onto him, sealing the deal with her body as well. But they didn't move, didn't take it further.

After a moment, he pulled away, his voice so husky that I expected him to come right there in front of us. "I pledge never to interfere with your relationship with Menolly. I pledge never to upstage you, never to step in where I am not welcome. I pledge my protection and whatever I can do to help you in your cause, in your life, in your path."

Blood Wyne stood, looking quite bored. "So, it is sealed. Nerissa, you and my son Roman are blood kin, and this makes you my own blood kin. Should either of you dishonor your vows, the other may claim life as payment, or any other reparations such as you see fit." She glanced over at me and a slow smile crossed her face. "Your wedding will be tomorrow night. Menolly, Nerissa, you may bring your family to witness. Nerissa, you will be the only nonvampire ever allowed into this sacred and honored fraternity. Do not fail us."

Nerissa shivered. "I promise you my honor, Your Majesty."

"Then I will take my leave. Be here shortly after sunset tomorrow night. Roman will tell you what to wear. Prepare for a crowd." And then—like a ghost—she vanished.

After Blood Wyne was gone, Roman and Nerissa turned to me. They were still touching, and the looks on their faces told me they wanted to go on touching. I removed my gown, laying it across the sofa. I wasn't about to step out of the room now.

Nerissa's lips crooked into a smile; she reached out her hand and I took it as she drew me between them. I closed my eyes as Roman pressed against me, his lips on my neck, as his left hand reached around to trail over Nerissa's breast. She gasped, entwining one foot around my leg next to her. The silky smoothness of her skin felt like heaven against my own, and I closed my eyes as her breasts pressed against me.

Roman's arm brushed my nipples, and I reached down to wrap my fingers around his cock. He let out a small sound, and then we were on the floor. One body, one motion, a rhythm of arms and legs and hands. Everywhere I turned, there was skin. I pressed my lips to Nerissa's as she rolled over on top of me, straddling me. I closed my eyes as she moaned into my mouth. The next moment, she shimmied down till her lips were on my clit. She tongued me, swirling around my sex, sucking and nibbling until I let out a sharp cry, my eyes opening wide.

Roman appeared, kneeling in back of her. And then his hands were on her hips, and she let out a long cry as he began fucking her. The sight of him pounding into my wife drove me even higher, and I let out another cry. Nerissa slid three fingers inside me, driving them hard, probing me.

Just then, Roman pulled away, a soft smile on his face. Nerissa and I turned to him and I worried that—once again—he was feeling pushed to the side.

But he just shook his head. "I enjoy both of you, and Nerissa, you are lovely . . . so lovely. But I am content to experience Menolly when we need to ease out the hunger. I just want to watch now, if you would be all right with that."

And right then, I saw that this was his way of showing her that he would keep to his word and bow out of trying to become part of our relationship instead of an auxiliary part of my life. I think Nerissa saw it, too, because she gently disengaged from me.

"I think . . . I was going to suggest we go out for coffee—all three of us, but then I remembered you two can't drink coffee." She laughed, her throaty voice rich and full. She pushed herself to her feet and reached up to kiss Roman's cheek. "Do you like movies, my . . . brother?" And that one word shifted their relationship and the tension in the room drained away.

Roman stared at her like she'd just asked him if he could grow a second head. But then he laughed. "I haven't watched television or a movie in years, but if you like, we can do that." As Nerissa reached for her dress, he stopped her. "I suggest you take a quick wash-off first. You have blood on your chin and some of it has dribbled down to your body. I imagine you wouldn't want to get your dress dirty?"

She laughed. "That would be wonderful. Do you have a restroom near?"

While vamps didn't need to use toilets, we did—indeed—shower. But most vampires kept full bathrooms for their human visitors.

Roman pointed to a side door off the office. "Right there. There's also a mirror, for my human stable members. Use whatever you need as far as towels and soaps. You will find a selection."

As she took her dress and disappeared into the restroom, both Roman and I began to dress.

Roman crossed to his desk and then, pausing, turned back around. "I will keep my promise to her, you know. I will honor my word, and my mother will honor hers. Should you have any doubts."

I held his gaze. Roman was many things. He wasn't a good man; he wasn't nice, per se. But he was a man of honor, that much I knew. Vampire or not, he would back up his word and keep his oaths.

"I don't doubt you." I paused, not sure it was my place to say anything, but then again, I was going to be his wife soon enough. "Your sister Paulette . . ."

"I have been telling Mother for years we need to free her. To let her go. I think . . . I told you my mother turned all of us shortly after she became a vampire. I think the deed weighs on her mind. She took our lives once. Paulette was terrified. I remember that, as much as I've forgotten so many things through the centuries. I remember Paulette screaming as Mother came after her, trying to beat her off. Paulette kept saying, 'Where is my mother? You can't be my mother. Mother would protect me!' But . . . so fresh from turning, my mother wasn't fully in control of herself. She fell on Paulette and held her down, forcing her blood down Paulette's throat right before my sister died. I believe that is quite possibly my mother's biggest, greatest regret. Paulette adored her."

I quietly settled myself on the sofa. How horrible it would have been if my father had done the same to us. Or my mother. At least with Dredge, it had been a stranger, a monster come out of the dark after me. Not someone I loved or respected.

"You need to convince her to stake Paulette. It will free her soul to move on. I know. I saw Sassy after I staked her. She was walking arm in arm with her friend Janet, and with her daughter who had died so many years before. Sassy was happy to be free. Please, if there's anything I can do, let me know." I wasn't sure why, out of everything we had heard that evening, Paulette's story hit the hardest, but it did.

Roman nodded. "I will do my best." At that moment, Nerissa returned, fresh and clean in her beautiful gown again.

"So . . . tomorrow night we get married. As I told your mother, it will be difficult to move in before Shadow Wing is taken care of." I picked up my purse and shawl. "I'm afraid we don't have time to stay for that movie, but there will be plenty of time in the future." It was time to go home and tell the others. I wasn't looking forward to their reaction, but then again, it was no different than Camille's duty to the Fae sovereign nation.

Roman shrugged. "No matter. But listen, I will choose a suite for you and, during the time before you move in, we can redecorate to whatever you like. You and Nerissa shall have the apartment of your dreams. Let that be my wedding present to you both."

Nerissa grinned. "Talk to me, then. I'm the designer in this marriage. By the way, I hope you don't expect me to quit my job."

He shook his head. "We are not so old-fashioned as that. Nor Menolly, either. No, unless you choose to quit—and you both have the option—you may do as you like professionally as long as you don't take up vampire slaying." He said the last so matter-of-factly that it took a moment before we realized he was joking.

That broke the tension for the evening. Laughing, we headed to the door. Elthea was waiting to show us to the front door, and as we drove away, I thought about how much change could happen in the space of one single evening.

Nerissa sat quietly for a moment, then said, "So, we're to be princesses? That sounds ludicrous to me, but I know it's a serious matter. But I always think Disney when I hear the word, and now all I can think of is Vampire Cinderella, or some such mash-up."

I snorted. "No Cinderella, please. She was a drudge." But then I sobered. "You're right in that this is a serious matter. The Vampire Nation is a large and old institution, and this is going to have a ripple-through effect all the way around. No matter how you look at it, Blood Wyne is defying tradition. Not by having Roman marry me, per se, but by including you."

"Oh, I think the fact that you staked Dredge will also play into the matter. She was correct when she said some old-school vamps aren't going to be too thrilled about this. But unless they want to lead a rebellion, there won't be anything they can do about it." She settled back in her seat, staring out the window.

"Don't ever forget, Caleb is out there and until he is found and staked, he might very well try such a thing. He hates everything his mother stands for and wants a dark rule in a world run on fear." I pressed my lips together as I skirted a slow-moving car and zipped through the late-night streets. It was nearing midnight now, and I was concerned about what might be happening at home. Suddenly not wanting to talk about tonight anymore—not till the realization of what we were doing settled—I cleared my throat.

"So, what do you think about the whole Vanzir-Aeval situation?"

Nerissa caught my mood. She snickered. "Vanzir's going to be a daddy. That just seems so bizarre to me that I can't imagine what the hell their kid's going to be like. Confused, for one thing. But . . ." She paused. "Camille will have to move a lot quicker than if she were going at Samhain, like originally planned."

I winced. "I know, and one simply does not say no to one's goddess." I stared into the night, watching the houses flicker past. Some had lights, others were dark. Seattle was a city of late-night techies, yet it wasn't that much of a party town after dark. It was a beautiful place, though, and my sisters and I had fully adopted it as our home. Now everything was shifting. With a pang, I realized this whole thing with Roman meant I wouldn't be moving back to Otherworld. Which was precisely enough to make me long to do so.

As I pulled into the driveway and cut the motor, Nerissa turned to me.

"Well, here we are. I guess it's time we go in and drop the bombshell on them."

I laughed. "Well, I suppose there are worse things than hearing that your sister and her wife are about to become members of the nobility. Okay, let's go deliver yet another buttload of news guaranteed to make their jaws drop."

And so, we headed inside, dressed to kill and with news that would . . . probably not thrill.

Chapter 12

Our news went over like a lead balloon. But there had been so many lead balloons lately that this was just one more on the pile of sinking slag.

"You have got to be kidding." Delilah looked horrified. "What guarantee do you have that Roman and his mother aren't out to get rid of Nerissa from your life?"

Nerissa dropped into the nearest vacant chair. "Because I made him swear blood allegiance with me and that gives me the right to kill him if he tries." She went on to explain—in a much more sanitized version—about them becoming blood-oath kin. I kept my mouth shut. She was doing a better job than I would have of making it sound like the necessary thing to do.

"Think about it," she added. "The vampires will be on our side. The Supes and vamps united means a lot more force to counter the groups like the Earthborn Brethren and Freedom's Angels. Divided, we are only so strong. But if we put up a united front, and if we work with the groups like the United Worlds Church, we can drive the hate groups out of town. I'm a great liaison between the vampire world and the Supe world, given that I'm married to a vampire, but being married to the Prince of Vampires? Together, Menolly and I will have so much power."

"True. Being married to the son of the vampire queen *would* be a coup, even though you aren't in line for the throne. Because you're married to the woman who will be in line to become vampire queen." Camille nodded thoughtfully. "It might work, at that. And, you have to admit, if you're married to Roman, you're a lot safer from the vampires who might be out to get Menolly. Wearing a crown invites assassination attempts from the outsiders, but if I know anything about vampire culture, once you're both actually married to him, it should shut down the whining about Menolly being his consort."

"Yeah." Roz smirked. "They'll be too damned afraid to bitch."

"Point." I edged my way onto the arm of the chair, draping an arm around Nerissa's shoulders. "Vampires don't work on a reward basis as much as other creatures. Fear and respect are much more effective than coaxing them to play nice."

But all that didn't matter. The fact was, we had agreed to do it, and I really didn't have that much of a choice. Blood Wyne was the Queen. I was a vampire, even though I was half-Fae, and as long as I lived Earthside, I would have to listen to her if I expected to be part of the Vampire Nation. Being on the outside? Not the best option.

Smoky unexpectedly took my side. "She and Nerissa make valid points. Consider this: Camille, did you consult all of us before agreeing to take the throne of Dusk and Twilight?"

She shook her head. "True that. What the Moon Mother asks of me, I have to do, regardless of what anybody else thinks."

"And Delilah, you are following the path set out for you by the Autumn Lord. Do we have a right to stop you from that?" Smoky turned his impassive gaze to Kitten, who gave him a tight shake of the head.

"I get your point. I get it. But that doesn't mean I have to like it." She let out a long sigh. "I just . . . I don't know why it bothers me. It's not like I have a premonition and I really do like Roman. At first I thought he might be up to something, but he's come through more than once. It's just . . . so much is changing, so fast." She sounded a little lost.

And then I knew. I knew why she was upset. "I know why it bothers you, Kitten. We're all beginning to go our separate ways. Camille will be moving out to Talamh Lonrach Oll next month. Nerissa and I will be moving in with Roman. After all these years, we'll be leading separate lives."

Delilah pressed her lips together, but a tear began to trickle down from one eye. Shade caught sight of it, and he gently wrapped her in his arms and kissed her forehead.

Camille slipped over to kneel at Delilah's feet. She reached up and took Kitten's hands. "I know this is frightening. I guess . . . we never thought about this day coming. We never thought about when we'd be . . . truly grown up, I guess." Hanging her head, she murmured, "I'm nervous, too. And I wish we could all just live here together, forever. But I don't think the Hags of Fate have that in store for us, you know? I think we're all bound for bigger things."

Delilah sniffled, and Nerissa handed her a box of tissues.

"But who's going to live here? This is our home. We can't just all wander off and leave it." Delilah glanced around. "So much has happened here."

"So much will *continue* to happen here. You and Shade can stay here, as long as the Autumn Lord doesn't mind. Iris and Bruce will still be living here. Rozurial—you'll be around, right?" I gave him a look that basically said, *Say yes even if you don't mean it.*

"Of course I will. I don't plan on going anywhere. And with Vanzir out at Talamh Lonrach Oll, being busy being a daddy, I'm going to need someone to pal around with." Roz shot me a wink.

Kitten let out another soft sigh and wiped her eyes. "I guess I'm just trying to take in everything that's happened over the past months. When Elqaneve fell, it feels like the entire world went to hell." She paused, then said, "At least we took care of Telazhar. I'm grateful for that. And even if things change, we'll all still be Earthside. I miss being home, but I guess . . . I guess this has become our home, hasn't it?"

Camille kissed Delilah's hand and then returned to where she had been cuddling with Morio. "I think we have truly become Windwalkers, in a positive sense. We have two homes. We'll always be torn between the two. Earthside and Otherworld both gave us our roots. But isn't that better than having only one place where you feel at home? Like having an extended family, kind of."

The doorbell rang, saving us from any more arguing about Nerissa's and my impending nuptials. I was closest, so I answered. It was a driver, and I caught a glimpse of a limousine out in the driveway.

"Yes?"

"Lord Roman sent me." He handed me a vellum envelope. "I'll be waiting at the car."

Curious, I turned the envelope over. Sure enough, it was sealed with wax and Roman's signature impression. I opened the letter and withdrew a stiff card, and the next moment burst into laughter. Hurrying back to the others, I poked Nerissa in the arm.

"Get up. We need to change clothes, and then we're off on a shopping trip."

She cocked her head. "What are you talking about?"

"Roman just sent us a note, and there's a limo and driver out front. We—and Camille and Delilah—are to head down to Down the Aisle boutique, where he's arranged for it to open specifically for us. We're all to pick out suitable gowns, because we need wedding dresses suitable for a court wedding, and he indicates that he assumes Delilah and Camille will be our bridesmaids. He notes they should wear black, and we're to wear red." I handed her the note card.

Nerissa snorted. "He assumes a lot, but what the hell. He's paying for the dresses, so we might as well take advantage of it. Besides, I have a feeling that—because this is a political marriage, in a way—we don't have a lot of say in the décor. Which is fine with me. It makes our own wedding that much more special." She wrinkled her nose. "Let's go."

Camille and Delilah glanced at each other, then shrugged.

"A new dress is a new dress, but they'd better not have poufy sleeves." Camille laughed. "You two change. Come on, Kitten. Let's grab our jackets and head out."

"Are you sure it's safe?" Morio stood. "We can go along."

"Listen, if Roman sent the limo, you know the driver will be armed to the teeth. And he'll most likely be a vampire himself. I think we'll be just as safe as if we drove there ourselves. Probably safer." And with that, Nerissa and I headed downstairs to change.

The store was upscale, so much so that the saleswomen looked like models and the clothing was in the back, with only a few high-end pieces leisurely draped over the mannequins that looked way too lifelike. The salon—it was far too pricey to be called a simple store—had overstuffed sofas and chairs for its patrons, and the salesclerk offered Nerissa and the others champagne, and a goblet of blood for me. We all turned her down, and I think she was relieved. The thought of spilling blood on a dress that was obviously costing Roman thousands of dollars made me queasy.

There were four sales associates—Nerissa whispered to me that was what they were called—one assigned to each of us, and a woman who seemed to be directing them all. Her name was Hilde.

All of the women looked tired but were forcing bright smiles and a perkiness that belied their fatigue. I felt bad for them. They had probably worked all day and would have to work tomorrow, and Roman had made sure they weren't going to have an early night of it. But money talked, and they were here to make what would no doubt be a tidy commission.

"What style of wedding will it be? The . . . gentleman . . . who arranged your fitting said that it's to be a formal affair. We've brought in every red gown we could find, and black . . . for the bridesmaids. I suppose that we should get the brides taken care of first, so we can match the bridesmaids' dresses." Hilde looked a little frightened, come to think of it.

"Please relax. We hate putting you to this trouble." I smiled at her, trying to ease the tension.

"No problem at all, miss. We've done vampire weddings before. But thank you. It was rather last minute and I hope we can fix everything to your liking. We have all our seamstresses on hand to fix whatever we can if the dresses need to be altered. Since we don't sell the same dress twice—all our dresses are original—these won't be samples so we should be able to find something in your sizes. While they won't be custom, Lord Roman assured me that would be fine as long as they look elegant."

I nodded. Roman had, once again, thought of everything. But given how quickly this was being pulled together—especially for a court event—I wondered what else was going on behind the scenes. "The dresses *do* need to be formal, but to be honest, I'm not particularly that picky. I would prefer my dress to have sleeves, though, and lace up around the neck, if possible. I have . . . scars." I hated showing others my scars but bit the bullet.

Hilde nodded. "Karen, please take Miss—Menolly, right?—Menolly's measurements and start pulling dresses. Linda—you take . . ."

"Nerissa. And I just want to make certain I don't look like a frilly cupcake." Nerissa smirked. "I honestly don't look good in orange red, so if you could find a gown with bluish undertones, that would be fantastic."

"Well, we should be able to find you something that will look stunning. Linda, please take Nerissa's measurements." She moved over, directing the other associates to measure Delilah and Camille while we were waiting. A few minutes later, after a bustle and flurry of tape measures, Linda and Karen vanished through an archway.

"I feel like I'm in some surreal movie . . . *Night of the Living Brides*, or something." I whispered, keeping my voice low, not wanting to offend Hilde. After all, it wasn't her fault we were shopping for wedding dresses at one in the morning.

Nerissa stifled a snort. "*Brides of the Living Dead*?"

Camille and Delilah looked a little dazed, and I realized they were tired. "I'm sorry you had to come. I guess Roman just assumed . . ."

"Roman assumes a lot, but he's right. We're going with you to that wedding, and if anybody gets to be your bridesmaids, it's us. Just promise me that we don't have to give blood to the groom or anything like that." Camille leaned back, crossing one leg over the other, and closed her eyes while we waited.

A few minutes later, the associates returned, each trailing a garment rack behind them. Each rack contained several red gowns. The majority were a deep crimson, a few were burgundy, and a few—a fire engine red that almost made my eyes hurt.

Karen pulled one of the dresses off the rack. "This should be your size." She held it up.

I fell in love with it at first sight. The burgundy would go better with my hair. The dress wasn't overwhelming—no huge hoop skirts, no Cinderella ball gown. It was a mermaid-style wedding gown, in a rich burgundy brocade, form-fitting over the bust and hips to sweep out as it came to the knees. The train was embellished with detailed tone-on-tone embroidery. The high-necked mandarin collar and cap sleeves were lace—the same burgundy—and the floral patterns embroidered on the train also adorned the gown from the waist up. While it wasn't long sleeved, it was absolutely exquisite in its simple elegance.

"I didn't know I could fall in love with a dress." I hesitantly reached out to run my fingers over the material. "I love this. I could wear this as a ball gown, too." Because to me, my actual wedding dress would always be the dress my mother wore when she married my father—the one Camille and Delilah had secretly altered for me when I married Nerissa. This dress? While it signified an important event, this dress was one I'd wear a second time, that I wouldn't want to put in a showcase and keep forever as a memory.

Nerissa nodded her approval. "Mine should match yours in color and a similar style."

Karen sorted through her dresses, then came out with one. "What about this?"

The dress was another mermaid gown, though one-shouldered, and heavily beaded across the bodice. It was sparkly, where my dress was a satinlike finish, and while it had more bling, Nerissa could pull it off. The floral beaded accents would play off the embroidery on my own, and the colors were close enough not to be jarring. The hem trailed to about the same length mine did, and together, the two looked good.

"I think that will work." Nerissa stood and examined it. "What do you think?" She turned to me, holding it up to her.

"You'll look great in it. Okay, we'll try these on. Meanwhile, go ahead and start finding bridesmaids' dresses that will work for Delilah and Camille, please."

Karen and Linda led us back to a large dressing room. As we undressed, I saw them both stare at me for a moment and I knew they were looking at my scars, but neither said a word. They quickly fitted us into the dresses. The only problem was that mine was too long on me.

"That may be a problem given the embroidery on the train. It's about three inches too long for you. Can you handle heels?" Linda frowned, scrunching up her face.

"I can handle them." Truth was, I never wore heels that high, but I figured if worse came to worst, I could ask for Camille's help. And, from my sister's expertise, I knew that if I found a pair of platform pumps, I could go to four inches without a problem.

"Then you're sure?" Linda got a playful look on her face. "Are you two saying—"

"Stop! Don't even ask it." Nerissa stopped her before I could. "We'll take them."

When we were done and back in our clothes, we returned to find that Camille and Delilah had been fitted in simple deep black, A-line mermaid dresses with plunging halter top necklines. With the addition of thin gold belts and simple gold necklaces, the dresses looked elegant; they mimicked the wedding gowns' styles and yet didn't overpower either of my sisters. Camille had the cleavage and Delilah had the height to handle the gowns.

"Looks good to me," I said.

"This has been one of the easiest dress searches I think I've ever overseen." Hilde grinned. "Usually somebody in the wedding party is having histrionics over this dress or that. And we almost always go through a half-dozen gowns, if not more."

I could hear the underlying curiosity beneath the words. I decided to give her some gossip for the trouble of pulling her out of her bed in the middle of the night.

"This is going to be a very unusual wedding, Hilde." I tried to suppress a laugh. "Given that Nerissa here, and I, are already married, and we're marrying into a royal vampire clan."

Her eyes lit up. "Really? So you are marrying . . ."

"We're marrying a vampire prince. Together." I winked at her. Beside me, I could hear Nerissa stifle a snort.

"A prince . . . wait—*a* prince? Just one?"

I nodded. "Yes, we're both to be his wives." And with that, we took our purchases—thoroughly protected by garment bag covers—and returned to the limousine. We kept quiet till we got home and the driver dropped us off. I didn't want to say anything that could be reported back to Roman and his mother, quite possibly to be taken the wrong way.

"You're bad, Menolly." Camille laughed as we trudged up the steps of the front porch. "But you made her night. She'll have something to talk about, for sure. Did you see the prices on those dresses?"

I shook my head. "I have to admit, I didn't."

"I was standing by the woman who was writing up the invoice. Yours was ten thousand, Nerissa's was twelve . . . and Delilah and I—our gowns were five thousand each."

Thirty-two thousand dollars' worth of dresses for one political evening. I didn't even want to think about what the cost would be if we'd had more time before the wedding. Roman would have insisted on custom work, if that were the case.

"Hey, what about shoes? I need platform heels." I had nothing of the sort in my closet at home, and Nerissa's feet were far larger than mine. Camille might have a pair I could wear, but they'd still be big. "I need four-inch heels to manage that dress."

"I can pick them out for you tomorrow. I know your size and I can find something that will work for one evening." Camille shrugged. "Underwear?"

"I've got underwear, and I'm not buying special panties just for Roman. This is a political assignation, not a love-based union. We're not spending the night with him in the honeymoon suite." I drew the line there. Besides, the wedding itself would involve a blood bond, I knew that much, and that was considered more binding than sex among vampires.

As we entered the living room, it was apparent the guys weren't about to go to bed without us. They were all there, fueling up on cookies and chips.

"What's this about panties and honeymoons?" Roz winked at me.

"Oh, go buy a pair of panties for yourself. None of your business." I held up the hanger that my dress was on. "We just bought thirty-two thousand dollars' worth of dresses. Is Hanna still awake? I want to put these someplace safe from Maggie and anything else that might mess them up."

Trillian shook his head. "No, she went to bed an hour ago. I'd say put them in the parlor, but Darynal is fast asleep in there. He's exhausted."

"Here, I'll take them for you." Before any of us could say a word, Smoky was up and collecting the garment bags. "I'll put them up in the spare closet in the hallway on the second floor. There's nothing much in there, I believe."

As he headed up the stairs, dresses in hand, I turned back to Trillian. "How is Darynal doing?"

"He went through a lot of hell down there in the Southern Wastes. He's sleeping a lot, eating a lot, and not too talkative yet. I've tried to find out what happened while he was down there, and he's fine for a while but then just lapses into silence. I'm not certain, but I think he was captured by a goblin group and quite possibly tortured. They have a way of playing rough with their victims." His eyes clouded over, but then he shook his head. "I told him he's welcome to stay here as long as possible. He doesn't seem in a hurry to return to Otherworld."

"That's fine." Camille glanced at the parlor door. "I know what PTSD is like. I still have nightmares of Hyto, and sometimes . . . flashbacks." She bit her lip but then shrugged it away. "But I'm working on it."

"I think we all have nightmares of when Hyto kidnapped you," I said, my voice soft. "I know that—even though he's dead—I still dream of Dredge now and again. I think we'll always carry this crap with us, even when we have dealt with it. There's no way you can unmake a part of your life."

Camille sighed. "No, there isn't. And you can let go of trauma, but the wound it leaves—there's always going to be some sort of scar tissue there to remind you."

The clock chimed. It was four A.M.

"You guys go to bed. I'll be headed there in a little over an hour. But you all need to sleep. Hell, Nerissa, you have to work tomorrow. Can you get off early to get ready for the wedding? You could have all my stuff laid out so that all I have to do is dress." I wheedled her, leaning up to kiss her cheek.

"Oh stop it, of course I'll do that for you. And I'll just call in early, tell Chase I need the day off. I've built up enough of them over the past few months, that's for certain." As everybody else started to traipse off to bed, Vanzir opted to stay with me in the living room.

When we were alone, he sprawled on the sofa. "So, I'm going to be a father." His voice was shaky and I suddenly realized how little attention any of us had really paid to the effect the announcement was having on him.

"How do you feel about that?" I could see he was nervous, and maybe—maybe even a little scared.

"What kind of father am I going to make? I'm a daemon. I was a slave, several times over. I have very few morals other than knowing that the biggest bad is the one we don't want." He shrugged. "What am I supposed to think? Aeval is choosing to have the child and I don't know how to feel about it."

"Has she told you why she decided to have the child? I would think it's a big deal for a Fae queen to . . ." I almost said *breed* but then thought I might offend Vanzir.

But he caught my nuance. "*Breed* with a demon? Yah, a fucking big deal. And even bigger once they find out I'm no demon prince or prize catch. I haven't got anything to offer a kid. I don't have anything to offer Aeval, really. I don't know why . . ." He paused, then cocked his head, flashing me a sly look. "What made you choose someone so different from you? Someone who really doesn't share your nature?"

"You mean Nerissa? Maybe . . . maybe just because I fell in love. Maybe because something about her . . . I couldn't stop thinking about her. And when I finally admitted it to myself, I realized that I had opened my heart up. Who knows why Aeval chose you, but choose you she did and now you're going to be parents together. I'd get used to the idea, if I were you, and quit trying to reason out why."

He let out a long sigh and leaned back, covering his eyes with his arm. "I don't want to be in love. And damn it, why did I have to fall for a queen? This is ridiculous. I don't deserve . . ."

His little slip caught my attention immediately. I pushed his feet off the sofa, forcing him to sit up, and then sat down beside him.

"Listen to me, Vanzir. You are no longer a slave. To *anyone*. You're no one's possession." I hesitated but then decided what the hell, and pressed my hand to his chest. I could feel his heart beat. Could sense it, really, even though it beat at a different rhythm than humans or Fae.

"What's in there . . . what's in your soul . . . it isn't dictated by your birth. It's not dictated by how you were treated when you were growing up. Oh, we always carry things around with us, but you've come so far since we first met you. You matter to my sisters and me. So don't you ever let me hear you say you don't deserve love. Or happiness. Because, dude, you do."

He took my hand in his, holding it tightly as he stared at the floor. "I don't know if I can do this. I'm afraid I won't know how to love a child or treat my kid the way she . . . deserves. I'm afraid of failing."

"Look at Chase. He was terrified. His father abandoned him. He's spent his life trying to make bad things better, and I think that part of that's due to his childhood. But when Sharah had to return to Otherworld, you know how frightened he was."

Chase had been furious over being shunted into single parenthood. Finally, we managed to help him understand that Sharah's duty to her race was stronger than her duty to family. And we helped him step up to the gate and take the reins.

"Yeah, I know that. But . . . I guess . . . what if I drop the kid? Or hurt it somehow?"

I laughed, letting go of his hand and clapping him on the shoulder. "I think all parents are probably afraid they're going to kill their children. It's an innate fear. I'm sure Aeval will have nannies and governesses or whatever they call babysitters out there. And you'll make mistakes—so will she. Every parent makes mistakes. But most kids live to adulthood. And no matter how bad you screw them up, trust me . . . I'm pretty sure you'll do your best to make sure their childhood is nothing like yours was. Am I right?"

He smiled at that, then shrugged. "Yeah. But I draw the line at wearing knee breeches or whatever the Fae nobility wear."

"You'll teach your child to listen to punk rock and wear ripped jeans." I glanced at the clock. "I'd better get downstairs. Sunrise will be along in an hour."

He nodded. "I'm heading back to the studio for the night. Menolly . . . thanks." And before I realized what he was doing, he darted in for a quick hug, then dashed away. As the door closed, I stared at it, thinking that Delilah was right. Everything was changing. Nothing would ever be the same. And right now, that felt like a good thing, even if it was a little sad.

I wandered into the kitchen and saw that Hanna had left

a bit of washing up to do for morning. I still had about an hour, so I scrubbed a few pots and pans, then dried the dishes and put them away. I glanced around the empty room. Before long, this house would be a whole lot emptier. The giant oak table Smoky had bought would be far too big except for holidays.

Feeling heavy of heart, I slid through the secret door that led to my lair. As I quietly descended, listening to Nerissa's snores, another thought hit me. Maggie would have to stay with Delilah. I couldn't take her into a lair of vampires. Camille couldn't take her out to Talamh Lonrach Oll. And the thought that I'd have to leave the little gargoyle behind hit me like a sledgehammer. By the time I reached my lair, bloody tears were racing down my cheeks.

I crept into the bathroom and cried as softly as I could. I cried for the loved ones we'd lost. I cried because our lives were all changing and it was just hitting me how much I was going to miss the way things had been. I cried because I didn't really want to be a vampire princess, even though I recognized just how much I would be useful in that position.

And, after I was all cried out, I washed up and then quietly crept into bed beside Nerissa. My love, my rock, the woman who made my life joyous instead of just bearable. She had changed me. She had rocked my world and turned it upside down. As had Smoky, Morio, and Trillian for Camille. And Shade and the Autumn Lord for Delilah.

Maybe some things were worth letting go of the past for. Maybe some changes could be good, even when they were scary. As the rising sun crept over the house, I felt its pull and—as I slid into a deep slumber—a soft, resigned peace filled my heart. Tomorrow night would be a busy evening. I hoped for easy rest and I got it. No dreams or nightmares crossed my path.

Chapter 13

The entire vampire community of Seattle seemed to be seated in the gallery below. As Nerissa and I peeked out the curtain on one of the side balconies, I realized that if the Fellowship of the Earthborn Brethren wanted to damage the vamp population, they should have attended with flamethrowers and stakes. Luckily, my guess was they didn't know squat about what was going on.

Roman hadn't skimped on the decorations. A thousand flowers must have filled the hall, wound round every post, formed into garlands that draped leisurely across the stage, and the smell of gardenias and lilacs filled the air. An entire symphony was positioned in the orchestra pit, playing something I didn't recognize—it was light, airy music, oddly out of keeping with the more gothic elements of the wedding, but it was pretty. A small choir stood behind them, waiting.

The guests filled the room—there must have been at least five hundred vamps out there in the audience. I knew full well they weren't all from around here. They must have come on the run, summoned from different areas of the world, because Blood Wyne was the one officiating, and wherever you found a queen, you found members of her court. But where nobility walked, so did the requisite security, and they were lining the aisle and the edges of the stage. Except the ones on stage were actually hovering in the air, a circle of vampires ready to drop down on any enemy at the first sign of trouble.

I pulled back and closed the balcony's curtain. The old theatre had once been grand, but now she was fading like an aging glamour girl. The brocade on the seats was still lovely, if a little threadbare, and the curtains on the stage were crimson to honor Blood Wyne. All in all, aged but still refined and elegant.

Nerissa and I were dressed and ready. Camille had fixed our hair and taken care of my makeup. The dresses fit perfectly, and she had found me a pair of shoes that would work fine—faux crocodile peep-toe pumps with four-inch heels and a one-inch platform. I was able to walk in them just fine. Delilah and Camille both looked gorgeous in their bridesmaids' dresses, but Nerissa—she took my breath away. The beaded gown fit smoothly but snugly over her figure, and her hair was swept up into a chignon, with wispy tendrils curling down around her ears. Camille had found us jewelry, too—a sparkling Swarovski crystal tiara for Nerissa, and for me, gold combs to sweep my curls back into a cascading tangle down my back. I wore no necklace, but I did wear the wedding band Nerissa had given me. Nerissa was wearing a tiered necklace—ever-descending loops of sparkling crystal on a floating necklace. She, too, wore her wedding ring.

As she looked at me, tears formed in her eyes. "I know this isn't our wedding day . . . not really . . . but you are so beautiful." She leaned down and lightly brushed my cheek with her petal pink lips. "I hope we're doing the right thing."

"Well, make up your mind now because if you think we aren't, we'd better get the hell out of town in the next twenty minutes. If we play the part of runaway brides, I guarantee we won't be coming back to Seattle." I gave her a toothy grin, then sobered. "Seriously, if you want to go, we will. I'll leave with you. I won't make you go through with this—ever. But make up your mind now."

She paused, thinking it over for a moment, then shook her head. "No. We gave our word. And Roman gave his. I trust him to stick to our deal. And really, I do see the logic behind it. No, we'll honor our end of the bargain." And so we rejoined the others in the staging room. A dozen assistants were running around, making certain everything was ready.

Smoky, Morio, Trillian, and Shade were out in the audience. I wasn't really worried about them. If any vamp even got the hint of an idea to put the fang to one of them, I figured the vamp would come out on the worst end of it. All Smoky and Shade would have to do was to turn into dragons and that would put a stop to any such idea. I wondered if Roman's brothers and sisters were here—at least the ones who were capable of traveling and not out for his blood—but decided not to ask.

Roman entered the room, followed by an entourage of security officers. His warlord's body cut a gorgeous figure, dressed in a pair of black leather pants, and a crimson shirt, open at the neck, and his hair was out of the ponytail, hanging long around his shoulders, silken and shining. He wore a golden crown—a circlet that fit snugly around his head. As he glanced at me, the smile that crept around the corner of his lips would have made me catch my breath, if I still breathed. He was captivating, his glamour out in full force, and the fact that he was my sire only made it have more impact. But I knew I wasn't the only one. Beside me, Nerissa gasped as I nudged her with my elbow and she turned around.

"Roman . . ." My voice trailed off. I wasn't sure what to say.

"You're gorgeous." Nerissa said it for me.

He laughed, his voice rich and pleased. "And you, my brides-to-be, you are both exquisite." His gaze slaked over us and he bowed low. "Radiance embodied."

Feeling oddly out of place, I kept my mouth shut. At times, Roman could slather on the charm way too thick, but he meant every word. And tonight was more his than ours. A sudden wave of sadness swept over me, though. I wished he could be marrying someone who truly loved him the way he deserved. But a little voice inside whispered, *In time, love may grow. For all three of you.*

Camille and Delilah looked slightly uncomfortable as Roman turned to them. "My dear sisters-in-law. You both are quite beautiful tonight. I thank you for being here. I know you may not particularly approve, but trust me, my mother and I wish no deceit or worry to fall on your family. Menolly and Nerissa have my blood-promise that I will not intrude any more than necessary, and they hold my heart in their hands to stake if I do."

Camille cleared her throat. "Well, that's not quite the most charming entry into our family, but you've helped us in the past, and we do appreciate everything. If this is the way we can give back, and Menolly and Nerissa feel it's the right thing to do, we abide by their wishes."

I felt oddly comforted that she wasn't acting like everything was perfectly normal. I knew they had reservations, but I also knew that what she had said was their way of acknowledging our choice, even if they had misgivings about it.

One of the ushers from the main hall peeked in and gave us a two-minute warning.

I quickly turned to Roman. "Fill us in—you haven't told us what to expect."

"It's simple enough. We walk down the aisle like in any wedding and go up on stage. Your sisters go first and stand to the side. My mother will be on stage waiting for us. She will marry us, and seal the union by feeding each of us a drop of her blood." Before Nerissa could ask, he turned to her. "You, too, yes. She'll ask us our pledges, and we simply say yes. It will be nothing you don't already expect from our discussion last night."

"And after?" I was hoping he wouldn't demand we stick around and party.

"We—the wedding party and your guests in the audience—will retire and we'll leave. There will be a party overseen by our advisors, which will include all of the regents, for all of the guests. Blood Wyne will receive them in a private hall afterward, with full security, but we're not expected to attend. She'll be taking care of more court business than anything else during that time."

I nodded, running through it in my mind. "Then I guess we're as ready as we'll ever be."

"Right on schedule, then. Shall we? First I will go, then Camille and Delilah, then Nerissa and you, my love. And trust that you'll be watched over by the tightest security force in this nation. Even the president's Secret Service can't match our squads."

And so we got in a line, and as the door opened, I could hear the music swell from the hall below. We headed down the stairs and then, positioned in front of the doors leading into the theater, waited for the music to announce our entry. A sudden blast of whirling notes shot out and I cocked my head. Even I recognized the *Carmina Burana*.

Roman leaned around Camille to quickly whisper, "Music fit for a prince and his brides. My mother loves this piece. It reminds her of our days when we ruled the countryside."

And then—before I could answer—the doors opened and he began striding down the aisle. I watched his gait—it was measured and deliberate, neither fast nor slow. Everyone in the audience stood, bowing or curtseying as he passed by. By the looks on their faces, I suddenly realized this was a deadly serious event. We weren't playing Cinderella and Prince Charming here. The vampires in this room, and more like them all over the world, viewed Roman as their liege. Blood Wyne was their queen and they knelt to her rule and decree.

And then he was on stage, waiting by the altar that was in the center, and it was our turn.

The music swept into a frenzy as Camille and Delilah neared the stage and Nerissa and I began walking down the aisle. The sight of five hundred vampires positioned on either side of us, bowing in a silent wave as we walked by, was a terrifying sight, and I realized just how much damage we could do if we went postal on the city. Beside me, Nerissa's heart was beating fast and furious, and I realized that my sisters and my wife were probably driving every vampire in here a little bit crazy. Suddenly feeling insecure, even though

I knew that Roman's security was incredibly tight, I put myself on high alert as we made our way to the end of the aisle and up the stairs.

As we took our places, the music died down and then swelled up again—this time with a heavy, deep tone—resounding with restrained power. The back curtains opened and Blood Wyne—in full regalia—glided out to the stage. She wore a heavy dress of crimson, with skirts as wide as I was tall. Gold threads sparkled through the weave, and her robe trailed behind her, the train a good ten feet long. Her diadem of rubies and diamonds sparkled against the upsweep of her hair, and I realized she was floating about three feet off the floor, even though her feet were hidden by her skirts. It gave her an imperial look—larger than life.

To one side of her, a few steps behind, was a vampire in an elegant but simple black suit. To the other, another in a simple black dress. Both had eyes as pale as Blood Wyne's, and I realized they were old—very old. They both had white hair, and their skin looked almost like alabaster under the lights. I had the feeling that they were just about as powerful as she was, but they trailed her with respect. The next moment, the woman was staring straight at me, her cool eyes aloof, and yet there was wisdom there, and cunning. She tilted her head just the slightest bit and I locked gazes with her, trying to fathom what it was she did. The other vamp looked at Nerissa, then at me, then returned to staring straight at Blood Wyne as if he were feeding her energy.

Blood Wyne raised her hands and the crowd cheered, thundering the halls of the theater. As she lowered her arms, a dead silence swept through. They moved to her beck and call.

"Citizens of the Vampire Nation, sons and daughters of the Crimson Veil, I, your queen, come before you tonight to witness the marriage of my son and heir, Roman, Lord of the Vampire Nation."

Again, a thundering applause that died off abruptly as she raised one hand.

"By the laws of the Covenant of the Crimson Veil, under the watchful eyes of Kesana, the Great Mother of the

Vampire Nation, I do bind and legitimize these ceremonies. Let the proceedings begin, and they will hold as my word and will as Queen of the Crimson Veil."

The vampires to either side of her echoed in a refrain, very monotone, "So it is and so it will be. Recorded into the History of the Vampire Nation, this ninth evening of May in the twenty-fourth cycle of the reign of Blood Wyne the Magnificent."

I glanced at them again and realized they were record keepers. I'd heard rumors of them among some of the demonic races, and among the vampires. They were creatures whose sole duty it was to record into memory every important thing that happened. They were walking encyclopedias.

As the ceremony proceeded I began to tune out her words. With all the pomp and pageantry, I was bored. I let my consciousness filter toward the audience, listening. There were the sounds of a very few people breathing. The sounds of their breath stood out as odd in an auditorium filled with over five hundred bodies.

I wondered how many stories were here . . . how each person had been turned. Vampires lived a solitary existence by nature, but put us together and we could create a massively powerful force, if we didn't do each other in first. Could Blood Wyne accomplish what she hoped to do? Could she create a unified Vampire Nation that could integrate with the other communities on the planet? And perhaps find a way to coexist without having the hatred and fear between the living dead and those still breathing? I hoped so. Because I was tired of the fighting.

"Menolly?"

The sound of my name jolted me out of my thoughts. I jerked, realizing she was talking to me.

"Do you pledge your life and your troth in the service of the Crimson Veil? Do you pledge your loyalty to Roman, Lord and Heir to the Throne, within the keeping of your other sacred oaths? Will you wear the title and crown as Princess Consort, with honor, with loyalty, on threat of your life?"

The oath went on and on. I was now listening carefully,

because pledging oath? A serious business and one I would never take lightly. I listened to every word, every nuance, to make certain I wasn't agreeing to something I couldn't uphold, but Blood Wyne and Roman had worded it carefully. It would neither compromise my oaths to my sisters, nor to Nerissa.

So when Blood Wyne finally paused, then asked, "Do you, Menolly Rosabelle te Maria D'Artigo, accept and pledge to these vows, upon your life and limb and the sacred blood?" I was able to answer honestly.

"I give you my word, my pledge, and my oath."

Blood Wyne waited, as the historians intoned, "Menolly Rosabelle te Maria D'Artigo accepts and pledges to these vows upon her life and limb and the sacred blood." She then turned to Nerissa and basically ran through a similarly long and complex vow. Nerissa was looking half dazed and I had the feeling she'd rather be just about anywhere else right now.

"Do you, Nerissa June Allison Shale, accept and pledge to these vows, upon your life and limb and the sacred blood?"

Nerissa coughed, as if Blood Wyne had caught her off guard. "I give you my word, my pledge, and my oath."

The historians once again echoed her oath.

Blood Wyne turned to Roman, who straightened his shoulders. "Roman, Lord and Heir to the throne of the Vampire Nation, do you pledge . . ." And she was off. His oath was as long as ours, and just as serious. Roman listened intently, his eyes focused on his mother, nodding quietly as she spoke. When she finished, he made his pledge—which included a vow to keep Nerissa, me, and our family safe and protected, and to come to our aid whenever we needed—and the historians finalized it into history.

Then Blood Wyne held up one arm. In her opposite hand she held a long, thin blade, with which she sliced to one side of her vein. As the blood welled up, she held out her wrist, first to Roman, who gracefully bowed, then leaned forward to lick the blood that was bubbling up. Then she turned to me. I followed suit and the blood hit me like champagne—effervescent and unnervingly tingly. Nerissa shivered just enough to tell me she was nervous, but she accepted Blood Wyne's proffered arm and licked the blood.

Then, one by one, we followed suit—each slicing our arms, though Nerissa was far more cautious than Roman or I because she could die from bleeding out—and offering them to Blood Wyne, and then to each other. When everybody had traded a drink, Blood Wyne raised her arm again and the audience roared its approval. The deal was done, and we were bound by blood.

"I present to you Lord Roman, Heir to the Throne, and his Princess-Consorts Menolly Rosabelle and Nerissa June Allison." Blood Wyne's voice echoed through the theater, and once again a roar of approval thundered through the room.

The rest of the ceremony was mostly formal procedure, wrapping it up. Nerissa and I would go through our coronations at a later date, though our status was official as of now. Then Blood Wyne turned to leave the stage, the historians following her. Next, Roman, with Nerissa on one arm and me on his other, exited behind the Queen. Camille and Delilah followed behind us, guarded closely by the security forces. When we were backstage, we saw Shade, Smoky, Trillian, and Morio there waiting for us. They had been hustled out of the audience before the end, apparently.

Nerissa let out a long breath and leaned against a wall. Even though she had the courtesy not to say it, I could hear the *Thank gods that's over* that I knew she was thinking.

Roman turned to us. "I would love to take you and your family out for a magnificent dinner, if you would allow me. Just because you and I cannot eat, doesn't mean they shouldn't." He smiled so charmingly that once again, I felt a little like a fraud.

But as if he sensed what I was thinking, he took me aside. "Menolly, I want you to know that I am content. Marriage was not always struck as a love match. All through history, it has been an institution of politics and convenience. I grew up in a time when marriage was a way of cementing allies. And that is precisely what we have done here. We have struck a match that will ensure the strength of the Vampire Nation. And that is what matters to me."

I gazed into his eyes. I knew he had fallen for me, even though I had warned him many times to guard his heart. But his intentions were clear. He meant every word he said. And that was when I realized that Roman was as much a creature of duty as my sisters and I were. He was playing his part, like Sharah was hers, like Camille would when she took the throne of Dusk and Twilight. He wasn't mewling like a heartsick lover over the fact that I wasn't his true match. Roman was taking it in stride and doing what his position called him to do.

That wiped away my worry. He had given his oath not to interfere with Nerissa and me and—for perhaps the first time since we had met—I truly believed he understood and accepted where we all stood.

"Thank you," though, was all I said.

He inclined his head softly. "We all have our parts to play, and I have been around far too long to let such a thing as love sway me away from my duties. Now, please, allow me to be a gracious husband and take my new family out for a grand dinner. Mother, of course, will not be joining us. She will be at the cotillion but we are not expected to make an appearance."

Curiosity won over. "Why not? We are the bride and groom . . . brides . . ."

"Because just like the honeymoon, they expect we'll be at our stable, feeding madly because of the passion and buildup of the moment."

My stomach lurched at the thought. It wasn't that I didn't enjoy a good drink, but the thought of wading into a room full of willing bloodwhores and letting loose on them spoiled my appetite. "I think dinner's a much better option."

And so we went out, and Roman and I drank a goblet of blood while the others plundered the menu at a local seafood house. I grinned, because before long Roman was joking with the men as if he were one of them, and I began to see a side of him he rarely showed—the side that needed and longed for friends. For buddies. He couldn't have them with his subjects, and I doubted he trusted anyone in the Court well enough to fraternize like this. But he was spot-on having fun, from what I could tell, with Smoky and the others.

By the time we finished and left the restaurant, it was closing time—midnight—and we were all much more relaxed.

Nerissa yawned. "I need to sleep. I have my workout with Jason tomorrow and since it's a weekend, he's training me twice as hard."

Roman insisted on escorting us to our cars and asking her about what she was learning. He slipped into the backseat of my Mustang, saying he'd just fly home from our land. Nerissa repressed a laugh, though I caught a faint snicker, and proceeded to tell him all about her martial arts training.

"I could hire you the finest trainers, dear wife."

The minute it came out of his lips all three of us suddenly fell silent, and then first Nerissa cracked up, and then Roman and I joined her.

"That sounds so freaking weird. I can't believe I'm married to a vampire. And a prince at that. This is just the final straw. After word gets out, I'll never be able to go back to the Puma Pride. Do you realize what they're going to say about me? I'll be officially excommunicated. Pariah." She was laughing, but I could hear the hurt beneath the surface.

Apparently, Roman could, too. He gently placed his hand on her shoulder. "I am truly sorry that your love for Menolly—and now this—has put you in such a position. And I'm sorry that your Pride mates can't see beyond the surface to honor the love you hold in your heart. You will always be part of Menolly's family and—now—mine."

Nerissa glanced into the backseat at him. She placed her hand on his. "Thank you, Roman. Thank you for understanding."

"You're my second wife, and my first wife's true love. What kind of monster would I be if I didn't acknowledge your pain and the hurt it causes you in your heart?"

And then we went back to discussing her training, but the shift in mood had firmly set in. Not the awkward oddness of the situation, but the feeling that we were now truly bound together by something greater than words.

As we pulled into the yard, Roman leaned over the backseat and planted a kiss on both our cheeks. "You have a good evening, and start looking at what kind of suite you want. I think . . . we have five rooms, along with a bath, that are not being used on one of the upper floors. The windows for your bedroom can be removed, so the sunlight will never reach you. So, five rooms—a bedroom, dressing room, sitting room, workout room, office, and bath."

And with that, he slipped out of the car. Leaning back in through the passenger window, he added, "The rooms are quite large. I'll have someone measure them and send the information over tomorrow. Start planning now so I can hire decorators." And then, with that, he was off in a blur and vanished into the sky, in bat form.

Nerissa stared after him. "I'm guessing this isn't going to be a DIY project with visits to Home Depot, is it?"

I snorted. "With Roman involved? Not likely. I doubt we'll be donning painter's pants and climbing stepladders. He means it, by the way, about the planning. So I guess we'd better spend a few evenings going over designs. I'm not picky, though I do like green." In fact, I loved green. Nerissa loved pink. I had the feeling we were going to end up in Christmas Town by the time we were done—either that or a dated Laura Ashley ad for cabbage rose print dresses from the shabby chic era. But as long as we were together, it didn't matter.

Inside, we found the others giving Vanzir, Roz, Iris, and everybody else a rundown of the wedding. When they invited us to join in, I shook my head.

"No, I think I'm about weddinged out. What about you, Nerissa?"

She snorted. "No, just no. As much as I love this dress, I want to get out of it, wash the blood off my arm, and then take a long, hot bubble bath."

We left the others to tell them about the night and headed downstairs. When we were in our cozy nest, Nerissa and I helped each other out of our clothes. We were both too unsettled and tired for sex, so she filled the tub with Warm Vanilla Sugar, her favorite fragrance, and climbed in, easing back to rest her head on a bath pillow.

I wrapped myself in a long T-shirt that I slept in sometimes and then pulled a satin robe around me. I wasn't cold, but the feel of the material was comforting. Before long, Camille and Delilah had joined me. Nerissa was still in the tub.

"Will you braid my hair up again? It's pretty like this, but I'm . . . it's not me." I seldom took it down from the long cornrows, and by now they had become as much a part of me as my scars were, as being a vampire was.

Camille took one side, Delilah the other, and as they braided away, interspersing the colorful beads Nerissa had bought me for a present some time back, I flipped on the television. We got surprisingly good reception down here, thanks to cable, and I found an episode of *Jerry Springer*, delighting Kitten. She had the weirdest crush on the talk-show host, and how she could sit through hours of the drivel escaped me, but it made her happy and so we watched with her, not talking, but just enjoying being together.

When Nerissa padded in, wearing her pink camisole and boy shorts, they automatically made room on the bed for her. Camille left Delilah to finish my braids, and she took the brush and began to glide it through Nerissa's hair. Nerissa closed her eyes, almost purring.

After a while, during a commercial, Camille finally spoke. "This is the weirdest wedding night ever." She sounded a little worried, as if she were afraid of offending us, but I let out a bark of laughter, as did Nerissa. Delilah joined in.

"I dunno about this. Politics suck, but you know, this could be the saving grace that binds the regular Supe Community together with the Vampire Nation. Think if we were united, how much more clout we'd have." I shook my head, happy to have my braids back. "Think . . . about what we might be able to accomplish."

"I'd rather think about that than the Degath Squad." Delilah rummaged through her pockets until she found the candy bar she was looking for. "I dread going out for them, but I guess tomorrow we'd better start making inquiries. We have to find them before they find us."

"What I'd like to know is what exactly Shadow Wing means to accomplish by creating the faux Keraastar Knights. I need to know more about their history, and the only one who knew much about it was Queen Asteria. And she's dead and all their written history pretty much bit the dust." Camille frowned. "I guess I'll ask Aeval. She might know, but this has to do directly with the spirit seals and since she was on the opposing force in that battle . . ."

Delilah suddenly straightened up and, mouth full of candy, asked, "What about Pentangle?"

Camille tilted her head to one side, considering. "She would know—she would have to know. And it's not like I've never met her. She came to me when I was trapped in Gulakah's mind. I wonder how I can get in touch with her."

Summoning an Elemental Lord or Lady seemed incredibly risky, but for something of this nature, Camille was right. She should go directly to the source who could tell her details she might otherwise never find. The Keraastar Knights were bound to the spirit seals that we found, and when enough of them gathered, they would be instrumental in repelling Demonkin and holding the realms apart. The Maharata-Verdi, an ancient scroll that was created when the spirit seal was first broken into nine pieces and scattered, predicted the force of nine knights rising. Each would be a magical warrior to fight against the demon hordes. A Fae Queen would ride at their helm, bringing them together. That Fae Queen, we now knew, would be Camille. But we needed as many of the spirit seals as we could find, preferably all nine of them, and we also needed to find the Keraastar Diamond, a gem that the Fae Queen needed to wear to bind the knights and unite their power.

If the demons did break through into this realm, if they were able to reunite the worlds, as Shadow Wing was attempting, there was a good chance that everything would go boom. Not as in *nuclear explosion* boom, but the magical chaos unleashed would change the face of the planet and all civilizations living in all three of the realms—Otherworld, Earthside, and the Sub-Realms.

Sobering, I turned off the TV. "I guess you guys should get to bed. I'll spend what time I have left before sunrise seeing if I can find out anything on the Degath Squad. I've got several vamps I can e-mail to ask if they know about anything. And I think I'll e-mail Neely from the United Worlds Church and start moving ahead on forging a relationship between them and the Vampire Nation."

And with that, Nerissa crawled into bed as I went into the sitting room and fired up her laptop. Camille and Delilah kissed me good night and headed upstairs to their loves.

The wedding had been an odd diversion, but now our minds were back on the demons. Because while we had taken out Telazhar, there was a Demon Lord on the horizon, waiting to meet us in battle. And he wouldn't wait forever.

Chapter 14

As the light of the room startled me, I rose from my sleep to see Camille sitting on the opposite side of the room, waiting for me to wake up. I was on the edge of the bed, about to lurch across the room when the reality of where and who I was once again crashed down on me. As I shook the cobwebs from my head, it suddenly dawned on me that her face was wet, her eyes luminous with tears, and she looked like she wanted to be anywhere but sitting there.

"What's going on?" I looked around for my clothes. But something made me hesitate.

Tears streamed down Camille's face and she didn't answer.

My stomach lurched as I realized that something had gone horribly, drastically awry. Then—oh shit, *the demons!* It had to be the demons.

"Did the Degath Squad put in an appearance?"

She slowly stood. "Menolly, I have to tell you something. I asked the others to let me be the one to do it. They're ready to go out hunting. You need to get dressed so you can come with us. But first we have to stop by the FH-CSI. We need to go to the hospital."

Hospital? Hunting? The butterflies churning in my stomach turned into metal-jawed leeches. I eased myself down on the vanity bench. "What happened, Camille? Did something happen to Nerissa?"

She handed me a pair of jeans and a sweater that was hanging over my clothes tree at the end of the bed. "Get dressed."

I grabbed them out of her hands and yanked off my sleep shirt, hustling the jeans up over my hips. "Please, just tell me. How bad is she hurt?"

"There's no good way to say this." Camille shook her head. "Menolly, Nerissa isn't the one in the hospital. It's Chase. He was trying to protect her. The Degath Squad kidnapped her, and he tried to fight them off. We don't know where they took her. Chase is in serious condition. He'll live, but he got hit by a nasty dose of the Shelakig's poison. Without the Nectar of Life in his veins, he would have died."

As the impact of her words hit me, a creeping panic began to rise. *Nerissa had been kidnapped. My wife had been abducted.*

I yanked on my boots, my hands shaking so badly that I couldn't zip them. Camille knelt by my side, brushing my hand away.

"You can't panic, Menolly. You can't let your fear take over. You know that's only going to complicate matters. You have to stick with me, hon. You have to get a grip. We'll find her and we'll save her, but we need you in control of yourself."

"What if we don't find her, though? What if they kill her first?" Every instinct in my body urged me to let out my predator, to run wild until I found them, but Camille was right. I had to get a grip on myself. I counted to ten, then counted again, slowly, whispering each number until I managed to bring myself back from the edge.

She zipped up my boots, then stood and brushed my braids back from my face. "First off, we've dealt with this before. Remember Karvanak and Chase? We have something they want, and we know what it is. They want the spirit seals. They won't kill her—they'll keep her alive. She's their hostage, their ticket to power and they know if they hurt her, we'll do everything in the world we can to destroy them. They realize that if they harm her, they'll never see the spirit seals." Pressing her lips to my forehead, she whispered, "I promise you, we will find her."

"Can you do a Locate spell?" I was grasping at straws. Sometimes her Moon magic worked, sometimes it didn't, but I was willing to chance any possible backlash.

She took my hand. "Already on it. Come upstairs with me. We've been working on this since we found out what happened. Delilah's over at the hospital. She called about ten minutes ago to say Chase was coming around. He might be able to tell us something. Meanwhile, I've been doing my best to locate her via a spell, but I can't get a read on her. Not her, and most importantly, not her body. With Morio's help, I should be able to tell if she's dead, but nothing's showing up, so the good news is she's most likely alive. Vanzir took off to the Demon Underground, and he phoned a few minutes ago that he's on his way home. Roz is over at Carter's. We're doing everything we can think of."

Her words hit like tiny little sledgehammers, pounding into me one after another.

I stood, motioning to the stairs. "I think I'm ready. When did this happen?"

"Around two thirty, Chase called Nerissa. He said there was some sort of altercation and he needed her for victim support. He dropped by to pick her up—he was already on the way—and they headed off together. The next thing we know, forty-five minutes later, Yugi called us to say that Chase was in the hospital, violently ill."

"Where were they going?" My rage-meter was simmering on high to explosive, but I finally managed to scale back the threat of detonation. Camille was right. I needed to be in control and focused if I was to help rather than hinder.

"We aren't sure. Delilah will have more info when we

get to the hospital. I've set the home phone to be forwarded to my cell in case the . . . the demons call about her."

Damn it. If I weren't a vampire, I could wake up at any time, just like normal people. Once again, for the first time in a while, I cursed my nature. "I can't stand this, Camille. I'm going to panic and if I panic, I'll lose it."

We entered the kitchen. Smoky was there, and Morio and Shade, and they turned to me, their faces a show of sadness and support. Trillian came in from the back porch, shaking his head.

"Nothing on the property. I looked everywhere, just in case." He stopped when he saw me and automatically opened his arms. The gesture hit me, and I started to cry. I leaned into his hug, and he patted my back.

"Come on, girl, we need you strong. Cry later. Revenge and rescue, now," he whispered in my ear, and slapped me on the back.

I sniffled, and he handed me a tissue. As I wiped away the blood streaming from my eyes and blew my nose, I forced the panic and guilt to subside.

"There now," Smoky said. "Let's get going. Hanna, you take Maggie and stay down in Menolly's lair. I don't want either of you in danger. Iris and Bruce will be up here with the babies in a few minutes and they will join you. Vanzir and Rozurial will meet us at the hospital."

Darynal popped in from the living room. He was dressed for hunting, it looked like, at least—Otherworld style. "I'm going to help. I don't know your streets, but I'm useful in a fight."

I started to protest but stopped. We needed all the help we could get. And that meant I was calling Roman as soon as we were in the cars.

"Fine. Shade and Darynal can ride with me. Camille, are we ready?"

She nodded. "Let's get a move on."

As Hanna opened the kitchen door to usher in Iris, Bruce, and the three babies, we headed for the front door, and all

I could think about was how long I could stretch out the demons' deaths, as soon as we had Nerissa home safe again.

The medical wing of the FH-CSI had grown over the past couple of years to encompass everything a hospital could do, only it was geared toward Fae and Supes. The front door to the building led to a long hall, with the police headquarters to the left, then we passed an elevator leading to the floors belowground, and then on into the medical wing.

Mallen, an elf and the chief resident in charge ever since Sharah had been called home, was waiting for us. He held up his hand and picked up the phone.

"Yugi? They're here." As he hung up, he motioned for us to follow him. "Chase was hurt badly, but he should make a full recovery, I think. The Shelakig's poison hit deep, and he got it from both pincers and from the sting. Those creatures are like a fully loaded armored tank."

"How did you know what it was that attacked him?" Camille glanced over at me, her face lined with worry. We had almost lost Chase once before when he was helping us fight the demons. The man had proved his courage far more than once.

"He managed to give us a description before he passed out. He was conscious when we got to him." Mallen paused. "Menolly, you should know now that—before he fainted—Chase told us that they hadn't hurt Nerissa."

My heart leaped and I could have kissed the elf right there. I nodded, trying to summon the courage to believe that she was still unharmed, wherever they had taken her.

As he stopped in front of Room 200 and pushed open the door, the sound of machines jolted me back to the last time we had visited anyone here. I had said my good-byes to Chrysandra, a waitress who had become my friend as well as my employee, when she was killed during the burning of my bar. Wincing from the memories, I followed Mallen, and the others entered after me.

Chase was in a bed, under sheets so white they blinded me.

His face was pale and he was sweating. Four IVs fed into his arms, an oxygen mask was strapped to his face, and he had electrodes plastered on his chest. I noticed restraints on his wrists. A nurse watched over him closely. All of this told me our detective wasn't out of the woods just yet, not with that close supervision. But his eyes were open and he struggled to sit up as we entered the room. The nurse put a stop to it by simply pushing him back against the bed with a stern look.

"You stay put. The last thing you want to do is encourage that venom to move farther through your body. Until we have neutralized all of it, you're not going anywhere." Mallen pulled out a pen and glanced over his chart, then moved to examine the IVs.

"What are you giving him?" I slowly eased closer to the bed. The beads of sweat on his forehead gave him a clammy look, and I realized he was far too pale for normal. Camille moved to where she was beside me, and as we stood there, the door opened and Delilah came in.

"You're here. I was getting something to drink." She joined us, watching as Chase struggled with his breathing. He wheezed from beneath the oxygen mask.

Mallen turned back to us. "A powerful cocktail of antivenins—we had to synthesize something that would work because the Shelakig's venom doesn't quite match anything we have available. But lucky for Chase here, one of our residents is skilled in magical alchemy and she was able to blend the antivenins against rattlesnake bite and a funnel web spider bite into a cocktail that seems to be working. But he's had several convulsions and every time that happens, the venom spreads a little farther. We've got him on restraints so that when he does seize, he doesn't hurt himself or thrash around too much."

The elf was calm as he spoke, but the look in his eyes told me that Chase was still in danger, and that Mallen wasn't altogether certain of the treatment plan.

"If he hadn't taken the Nectar of Life and if it hadn't had so much time to work through his body and effect the cellular changes that it has, I'm afraid we would be out one detective." The elf paused. "You can talk to him, but only for a few minutes. I don't want him excited, nor do I want him tired out any more than he already is."

I nodded. "We hear you."

Yugi scurried in at that point. "Before you talk to him, talk to me. That way you can conserve your questions and he won't have to go over anything he already told us." He motioned for us to follow him out the door and down the hall to a break room. I glanced back, reluctant to leave Chase alone, but the nurse and Mallen were there, and we could trust them.

As we gathered around the long table, Yugi took the head chair. He motioned for us to sit down. "I know you're in a hurry to get out there, to find Nerissa, but you need to know what happened before running off."

As much as my heart was screaming *Get on with it*, I forced myself to sit down and listen.

"At two-twenty-five a call came in for Chase. The person said he had been attacked by a group of bikers and that he was sure it was a hate crime. He said his girlfriend had been with him and that she had been sexually accosted and needed help, but they didn't feel comfortable going to the hospital—not even here. Chase asked him if it had been the Freedom's Angels who attacked them, and the man said yes. So he wrote down their location and called Nerissa, since she's our victim's advocate, and told me he'd drop by to pick her up. He said that the FAs were up to their tricks again and that we may have to run a sting on them to get rid of them. He left here right after that."

Camille cleared her throat. "He got to our house at a little before three, because I happened to glance at the clock when Nerissa ran out the door. She said she had to go out with Chase on a call and that he was picking her up."

"That's what Delilah told us. Chase called me at three twenty to tell me they were en route to . . ." Yugi consulted the file. "316 Chamber Hall Drive, which is a small private lane off California Way SW, out in West Seattle near Discovery Park."

The wheels were turning in Camille's head; I could see

it on her face. "Let me guess, there are no houses on Chamber Hall Drive?"

"Right. It's a relatively new street so there are no houses, yet. Developers are preparing to tear out the greenbelt, but they haven't yet. They got there at three fifty—there was a lot of traffic. Chase radioed in that there weren't any houses, and they were going to poke around a little in the wooded thatch. I called his cell twenty minutes later, worried when he hadn't checked in. I sensed something was off. He managed to answer, but he sounded terrible. He said a giant scorpion had attacked him, and that some freak show one-legged creature had grabbed Nerissa. We immediately headed out there. By the time we arrived, Chase was going into convulsions. He managed to tell us she was alive and unharmed the last he saw of her, and that he had tried to stop them but the giant scorpion hit him hard with the stinger. Then he had a seizure and passed out."

"How did you know it was a Shelakig?" I leaned forward, trying not to picture the Naedaran manhandling my wife. She would have fought back. Had they hurt her after dragging her off?

"There aren't that many giant scorpions in the world who can deliver this load of venom. Besides, Shelakigs are known in Otherworld. I did some work down in the Southern Wastes while I was living there, learning about toxins and magically induced illnesses, and they had a few of them there." Mallen shook his head. "I knew that—over here—the only way to fight the toxin would be to mix antivenins. Luckily, there's a medic I know at the local dispensary who was able to get his hands on both types and send me a few vials of each. We've got them on a fast drip into Chase's body, but we can't just overload him. I also have a countervenom spell going, but that can only handle so much of the toxin."

"Where did it sting him?"

"That's another stroke of luck. It managed to sting him in the leg. If it had been near his heart, he'd be dead. If it had been near his spine, he might be paralyzed."

And with that sobering thought, we quickly told Mallen

about the Naedaran and the Varcont. "This was planned, it wasn't happenstance."

"Like I said when I woke you up, they took her as a hostage. What better way to get what they want? And we know what they want."

Camille looked so pale I thought she was going to faint, and at first I wondered what was going on, but then the full scope hit me. *The spirit seals.* We knew they were going to demand the spirit seals—what else could they want? And if that was the case . . . there was no way in hell we could give them up. If Shadow Wing managed to collect all of them—and with the ones we had, he'd be terribly close—he could begin to reassemble them and bring the worlds back together, and that would not only devastate all three realms but give him and his demonic army full access to take over Earthside and Otherworld.

Which meant we absolutely could not accede to his demands. And that meant . . . I forced myself to stop. I didn't dare allow my thoughts to wander into dangerous territory. I choked back the panic that had begun to rise once more and brought my attention back to Yugi.

"Is there anything else we should know before we go talk to Chase?" I caught Mallen's gaze straight on. He looked at me, and in that moment, I realized that he knew exactly what we were facing—what I was facing.

"No, I don't think so. Except he's a very lucky man. I think we can stem the flow of venom before it does any permanent damage. He's had a rough go of it and he's not fully out of the woods yet, but I believe we've reached a turning point. Please, don't wear him out. Ask your questions judiciously." And with that, he led us back to the hospital room.

As we entered the room, Chase was sitting up—or rather, his bed was propping him up. He looked weak, utterly exhausted. The nurse was checking his leg, Sharpie in hand. The thigh was horribly swollen, purple with streaks of blue and black radiating out from a very large puncture wound in the lower thigh. A thick black circle surrounded the wound, and Chase grimaced, watching as she drew another, larger circle around the first.

"The venom has radiated out again, but the rate appears to be slowing." Mallen examined the wound. He pressed one side of the puncture wound and a stream of steaming yellow pus ejected from the puncture point, fountaining up and out. It smelled rancid, as though it had been festering for days instead of hours. Beside me, Camille and Delilah both let out a small groan and turned away.

"I know, I'm a prize cow, aren't I?" Chase's voice was raspy and weak, but he tried to smile.

"Shut up, Johnson. You just focus on getting better." Even though I wanted to run over, to shake him and make him cough up any little clue that might lead us to Nerissa, my gratitude that he had tried to save her at risk of his own life outweighed my instinct.

"I'm sorry," he wheezed. "I tried so damned hard to make them let her go."

"You did what you could. Just tell us anything you can think of, that you didn't tell Yugi, that might help us. Did they say anything? Did you hear anything—see anything at all?" Delilah pulled a stool over to sit by the bed. She and Chase had been an item for a while, and now they were blood-oath brother and sister.

Chase struggled to catch his breath, then closed his eyes as the IVs silently dripped into his veins. After a moment, he said, "The one who caught hold of her—the one-eyed creature . . ."

"The Naedaran?"

At that point, Vanzir entered the room. He shook his head and slipped up to stand beside Camille and Smoky.

"Yes, he said something in crude English. I know I heard him say something . . ." As he floated between waking and sleeping consciousness, it took everything I had not to urge him on in a frenzy of unhelpful cheerleading. A moment later, he opened his eyes again. "I remember. He said . . . *Get her ready. The gate's waiting, and the Saraktanas are going to guard her.*"

"Saraktanas? Are you sure?"

"Yeah, that was it, because I thought it sounded so odd."

Vanzir let out a slow breath. "I know exactly what he's talking about and it's bad news, I'm afraid."

We all turned to him. "What does it mean?"

"In the common demonic tongue, Saraktanas translates to 'seal wearers.' That verifies—with what I've learned in the Demon Underground—that they've taken her back to the Subterranean Realms."

And with that news, I lost it.

Red as blood, a crimson haze, was all I could see around me. The freaks had Nerissa and they were going to die. Period. Die in a bath of blood and fire and frenzied mauling. I wanted to rip out their throats, drink them down to the ground, and then grind them under my feet once they were drained. The hunger to hurt them grew as I swung around, grabbing the nearest chair and sending it against the far wall, where it landed in a tangle with a metal cart that currently stood empty. The clatter was enough to raise the dead, but it did nothing to soothe my anger, and I was about to send my fist through the wall when Chase moaned as he tried to sit straight up.

But before he could manage it, Camille put all her force into her voice as her words reverberated through the room. *"MENOLLY, STOP!"*

I froze, unable to continue as the fury began to diffuse and I shook my head, my ears still ringing with her voice. As I glanced over at the bed, Chase groaned, his face clammy. Instantly chagrined, I reined in my anger and retracted my fangs.

There are very few ways to calm down a vampire who is in a frenzy, but Camille possessed what was known as *the voice of control*, a rare force able to yank a vampire out of bloodlust. Somehow, Chase had developed the ability after consuming the Nectar of Life, which seemed to have awakened his own gifts. Both of them had managed to stop me cold a couple of times in the past.

Camille walked over to me. "Let's go outside the room

for a minute." She wrapped her arms around my shoulders and led me out of the room, leaving Mallen to attend to Chase, and the others silent and pensive.

She walked me to the waiting room. "Sit down. I'd say take a deep breath but that's moot, so do whatever it is you do in place of it now."

I closed my eyes, searching for that sparkling light deep in my memories that I used for an anchor. When I had been turned, the OIA—or rather, the YIA; we had moved over to the OIA later on but the latter was a child agency of the former—had spent a year rehabilitating me rather than face the scandal that my father threatened them with. They had sent me into severe danger without backup, and they knew the risks but didn't fully disclose them to me. The only thing that saved them from being brought up on charges was that my father held a lot of public respect, and he demanded they do what they could to fix the damage in return for not pursuing the matter. The fact that I was half-human also helped them. The Court would have been lackluster on their charges, given my heritage. But scandals breed even more scandals, and the YIA wanted to avoid any more publicity than they already got from me being turned.

One of the tricks they had taught me was to hold on to an inner light—to use that as the touchstone and anchor for all that I once was, and all that I had now become. And the visualization worked. If I could find my way to that light and hold tight to it, I was able to keep my inner predator under control. It acted as a stronger anchor than just about anything I had ever tried.

As I leaned forward, my elbows on my knees, Camille gracefully sat down beside me. She didn't try to stroke my back, or take my hand, for which I was grateful. I wasn't a touchy-feely person—even before I had become a vampire I had been a little bit put off by people reaching out before I invited them to. But she just sat there, waiting.

Finally, I was able to speak again. "They took her to the Sub-Realms, Camille. What the hell are we going to do? I know we can't give them the spirit seals. I know that, but I want to kill them, drive them to dust. I want to hand over anything they want in order to set her free."

Camille cleared her throat, and I could tell she was choosing her words carefully. "Even if you gave them what they wanted, you know they wouldn't keep their end of the bargain. And say . . . say they did keep their word. They're demons, bent on taking over this world. Do you and Nerissa really want to be sitting at their side when they raze through in a mass of destruction? Because you know that if you give them the seals, you might as well just hand them the keys to the kingdom and say, *Come on in, boys. The water's fine.*"

I stared at my hands. I knew she was right. I didn't want to know, I didn't want to do anything but rush off to try to save her, but in the end—Camille was correct. How could I hand over two worlds in exchange for one life? It wasn't in my nature to mass-sacrifice others, and Nerissa would hate me if I did that.

"I hate them. I want them dead. Painfully, slowly, executed."

Camille let out a long sigh. "I know, but we don't even know how to reach them at this point. And maybe we should focus on just getting her out of there instead of on what we're going to do to them. We aren't monsters, Menolly, even though sometimes it feels like we're forced to be. Once we free her, clean quick kills and out. Torturing them won't do anything but take us down to their level."

I shook my head. "No, but be real. There's a little sadist in all of us. Try as we might to deny it, you can't tell me that there isn't the smallest bit of satisfaction when you crush the spider you're afraid of, or when your neighbor who has it so easy gets a speeding ticket. You've gloated over victory enough to know the feeling. And if you're honest, you'll be truthful about feeling just a little joy when Hyto was destroyed due to your command.

She bit her lip, then shrugged. "You're right. I was relieved . . . and I was glad. I was grateful he was dead and that he had been forced to watch me stand there, commanding his death. After what he put me through, after his attitude in front of the Dragon Council, I just wanted him gone."

I nodded. "You see? And don't think for a moment I am saying he didn't deserve it. But you felt satisfaction over his death. No, schadenfreude is alive and well in all of us, if we just look deep enough."

She considered this. "You're right. I can't deny that. I really can't."

"Then don't deny me my desire for vengeance, because regardless of whether I get it, the feelings are there and they are real. I won't be a hypocrite and try to suppress them with a lot of self-righteous drivel." With that, I felt strong enough to stand again. "We'd better get back in there and decide what to do next."

"I think I know what comes next." Camille quietly swung in behind me. "And I really don't want to think about what it means."

Chapter 15

"Vanzir, did you find out anything while you were in the Demon Underground—and Roz, you put in a visit to Carter. What did he have to say?" I straddled a chair, trying desperately to remain calm. I kept hold of that inner light like a drowning man might clutch a life vest.

We were gathered around a table in the conference room. Chase had been agitated about being left out of the loop, but Mallen did what he could to soothe the detective and told us to take our business out of the hospital room. Yugi had graciously offered us the use of a conference room and had coffee and donuts sent in to fuel our brainstorming session.

Vanzir frowned, taking a donut and biting into it. "I asked everywhere. Nobody knows what's up. The fake Keraastar Knights? The anti-knights that Shadow Wing tried to develop? They were a miserable failure, I gather, but nobody knows where the hell they are. And nobody seems to know the reason for them vanishing. Yes, Shadow Wing threw a major hissy fit, but he's not stupid and he wouldn't just kick them out with their spirit seals in tow. None of my usual sources could come up with anything else. Now, of course, we know they're going to be guarding Nerissa by what Chase remembered."

"Carter told me just about the same thing," Roz said. "Except for one major difference. He did . . . well . . . whatever it is Carter does, and he assured me that two of the demons from the Degath Squad are still around. The Varcont and the Shelakig. I'm not sure just what kind of scrying Carter can do, but he told me the Naedaran returned to the Sub-Realms. He probably took Nerissa with him."

"Then we find the pair of them. And I get information out of them. But that means taking them down alive. And *that* means finding them first." And then I paused, a thought cropping up. "I can get us extra manpower. I'll be back. All of you, wait for me."

And, like lightning, I raced out the door, heading for my car. There was one place I could go—one person I could turn to who would vastly increase our odds of finding the Demonkin. And he had to agree, given that he was Nerissa's blood-oath brother.

Roman was in his study. As I entered, a look of surprise stole over his face. "I didn't realize you were coming over tonight, love." He stood, smiling, but the smile dropped away as I rushed up to him, shaking my head.

"This is no social call. Roman, we need you. We need you, we need your men. *I* need you."

He motioned for me to bring a chair closer to him. "What's going on?"

"They got my Nerissa. They took her, damn it."

"They? They who?" His forehead creased and his eyes grew even more pale. That was never a good sign, if you were on the opposite side of the fence from him.

I quickly outlined everything that had happened. "They took her down to the Sub-Realms, and I can't . . ." I paused as my cell phone rang. "Hold on." I glanced at the Caller ID. Blocked. Frowning, I punched the Talk button and held it to my ear. "Yes?"

"Menolly D'Artigo. You know who we are, and you know what we want. You have seventy-two hours to collect all of the spirit seals that you own and bring them to us. We will contact you shortly before the deadline with directions on where to take them. You must have them by then, or the Were will die, and it will be a slow, lingering death at the hands of our Master."

"How do I know she's alive—" I started to say, then stopped myself. Chase had lost part of a finger when a demon general sought to prove that he had really captured the detective. I couldn't put my Nerissa to that chance. But the opportunity to say anything was cut off when the line fell silent and I realized they had hung up.

"It's come. The ransom demand. I have seventy-two hours to hand over all the spirit seals we have. But . . ." I glanced over at Roman.

"You can't do that." His voice was soft, but firm. "You can't give them that much power, even for her life."

I shook my head, tears forming. As they began to race down my face, Roman leaned forward to kiss them away. I crumbled into his arms and he held me as I sobbed in a way I couldn't around anybody else. He would keep my predator at bay while I caved in to the despair and the aching hole that had seared itself into my heart.

After a time, he handed me a tissue and called for a maid. "Bring Lady Menolly a new shirt, please. Something . . . black."

I wiped my eyes. "Will you help us? I need to find the two demons that are still over here so I can interrogate them. We need them alive. I need to find where in the Sub-Realms they took Nerissa. I have to know if they're hurting her." I felt desperate. I slid down on my knees in front of him. "Please, Sire . . ." I had never begged for anything except death from Dredge. Now, I would beg for Roman to help me with Nerissa, if that was what it took.

He gently took me by the shoulders and lifted me to my feet. "You need not beg me, nor grovel in my presence. Nerissa is my blood-oath sister, she is my wife, and she is—most importantly—your wife and your love. We will find her and bring her back safely." And then he picked up the phone and called for the head of security.

Roman drew me down on his lap and, there, he silently held me until Trent, his chief guard and the one who monitored all scouting parties, entered the room a few minutes later. He saluted, then bowed. During life he had been a bouncer in a bar, and he was a big burly dude.

"I want you to gather as many men as you can possibly spare, and go out in pairs through the city. Menolly, tell him what we're searching for."

I outlined what the demons were like.

Roman waited till I was finished, then said, "We *must* take these demons alive, so be prepared. Silver shackles will hold them, so wear gloves. Silver chains will help to bind them, so again, gloves and heavy gear for all concerned. I want you to find them and bring them back here. And any guard that sloths off? Will be tossed in the feeding pit."

I had never heard him use the term before, and I wasn't sure I wanted to know what the "feeding pit" was, so I ignored it for now. As Trent took down all the information from us and then left, I felt oddly calm—almost numb. I mentioned it to Roman.

"You are entering a state where you'll be able to be of more help than harm. I know how much you love her, but you will do Nerissa no good if you can't control your emotions while we search for her. The men will report in every hour. I will call you immediately if we find anything, see anything, or catch anyone. Now go back to your family—you need them with you more than you need me right now, and that's perfectly all right."

"I don't want to live without her, Roman. She . . . she brought me out of a pain that I never thought I'd be able to leave. I was just existing when I met her, you know? She gave me a reason to really, truly live again." I felt so empty, so hollow that the entire world seemed to vanish around me, and once again, I felt like I was in a dark, deep hole, looking for the single star whose light had drawn me out of that inner abyss.

"I know." He kissed me softly on the forehead. "Nerissa . . . I could grow very fond of her. She is a spark of life and brightness in the eternal night that both you and I inhabit. She's unafraid, uninhibited . . . We will bring her home safely. I promise you, on the moon and stars, we will do all that is in our power."

I wanted to go out on the hunt with everybody else, but Camille and Delilah encouraged me to stay at home instead. I begged them to stay with me while the men all went out hunting the demons, along with the massive legion of vampires Roman had managed to drum up. There were at least one hundred vamps roaming the back roads of the city, looking for the demons.

Pacing, I felt like I was wearing a hole in the carpet. Camille fretted, doing the dishes for Hanna and tidying up, while Delilah sat, polishing Lysanthra—her dagger—and honing the edge of it with a sharpening stone.

After a moment, she said, "You wouldn't believe how many ghosts I saw at your wedding."

That brought me out of my thoughts. I turned. "What are you talking about?"

"The wedding . . . with Roman. I saw so many ghosts hanging around that theater it felt like a convention." She shrugged. "I debated whether to mention it, but it was just odd. I didn't let them notice that I could see them, but it was disconcerting to say the least."

Delilah had recently developed the ability to see—and interact with—ghosts. She had returned to Haseofon, the temple of the Death Maidens, to learn how to harness the power and to avoid being overrun by panicking ghosts who wanted her help. Apparently, it came at a certain level of being in the service of the Autumn Lord, and it meant she was progressing in her training. Sometimes I wondered just where she would end up. She was destined to have the Elemental Lord's child, via Shade as a proxy father, but what would that mean? And what would the child be like?

"Where do you think they all came from? Do you think they are attached to the theater?" The last thing I wanted to do right now was go ghost hunting, but at least this gave me something to focus on other than letting my mind run crazy over what was going on with Nerissa.

"I don't think so. See, I think the vampires brought them in." She frowned, adjusting her stance so she could work the stone around the slight curve in the blade. "They were all in the audience, some standing two or three deep behind some of the vamps."

And then I knew what they were. "They're spirits of people who were killed but not turned by the vampires, don't you think? Do . . . do I have any with me?" I wasn't sure I wanted to know, but then again, maybe knowing was a good thing.

Delilah gazed up at me, her eyes soft-focusing. After a moment, she shook her head. "No, you don't. I would tell you if I saw any, but you seem to be free of them. Either they deserved what they got, or they moved on already."

Relieved, I dropped onto the sofa beside her. Camille moved past, sorting through the magazines on the side table and carrying an armful away to put in the recycling barrel.

"I feel like I'm becoming unglued. I wish I could just fall asleep, but I can't. I want to go railing off into the Sub-Realms but until we know more, I can't. Come sunrise, I'll go to my bed freaking out because I won't be able to wake up if something happens, not until night falls once more. Some days I hate what I am, Kitten."

She put down her dagger and the stone. "Sometimes we don't have a choice. So we do what we can and try to do it in the best way we can." She reached out, stroked my braids back. "I've had to learn to accept living in a path I never could have imagined for myself."

Camille finished straightening up. She walked over and turned on the television, finding an old black-and-white science fiction movie. It looked archaic, considering the technology abounding around us, but it was interesting enough to keep my focus diverted from my thoughts. We had watched through about seventy minutes of it when my phone rang. I jumped, grabbing the cell from the table where I had set it for easy access. *Roman.*

"Yes? Did you find them?" I didn't even bother with a hello. I knew he'd understand.

"Yes, we helped Smoky and Trillian take down the pair. Smoky suggested taking them to the safe room at your bar."

"Good idea. We'll meet you there." I wanted to ask if there was any sign of Nerissa but decided to wait. If it was bad news, better to hear it in person. As I jammed my arms into my jacket, Camille and Delilah followed suit. "They have the Shelakig and the Varcont. They're headed for the Wayfarer—to the safe room. Let's go." As we headed out the door, I called Derrick to warn him. "Close early. Get everybody out of there. These are very dangerous demons and I don't want any customers hurt."

"Will do, boss." He hung up without further ado.

The drive was murder on my patience, but I forced myself to drive the speed limit. If I had learned one thing over the years, it was that collateral damage was a hard thing to have on your conscience. The streets were mostly empty around the bar, and parking was easy to find at this time of night. Camille and Delilah pulled in right after I got there, and we all headed into the bar.

Derrick had done a good job of emptying the place.

"I gave out coupons for half off their next purchase to get them to leave without grumbling." He wiped his hands on a bar towel. The werebadger had been the most loyal employee I had had, and he had proved himself time and again as both competent and helpful. His T-shirt stretched over his wide shoulders and tight stomach, and he cut a good-looking figure, which—I hated to admit—was an added draw to bring women into the bar.

"Are they here yet?"

"No, but I got a call from Smoky shortly after your call. They're on the way. Roman is having the demons transported in an unmarked armored truck. He said to tell you, he thinks you're going to have trouble fitting one of them down the stairs."

"That's because it's a freaking giant scorpion." Camille frowned. "You widened the staircase, though. They have to have them bound, so maybe you can somehow navigate it through the door well. Or maybe Smoky can carry it downstairs through the Ionyc Seas." She shivered. "Though I hate to think what might happen if it got loose out there. I don't know exactly what it could do to him, but . . ."

But the danger was a very real possibility. "We'll wait and see what he says. Meanwhile, will you two go down and prep the safe room? Take out anything the creatures might destroy. Derrick, can you help them?"

He nodded, escorting them to the door leading to the basement. "Tavah and Johann are downstairs, guarding the portal. They can help out, too."

The basement of my bar contained a portal that led directly to Y'Elestrial, in Otherworld. I had kept a constant guard on it since the day I took over as bartender, and when I actually took over as owner of the Wayfarer, I had increased security. After the fire that had devastated the bar, I had beefed it up even more. At night, I used exclusively vampires to guard. During the day, I had moved our bouncer Pieder—a giant—to guard duty, along with a Fae warrior. Pieder was the brawn, but definitely not the brains. But his size made him an excellent deterrent.

A moment later, the front door opened and Morio strode through. "We have them out in the truck." He glanced around. "You emptied the place?"

"Yeah, Derrick, Camille, and Delilah are downstairs clearing out the safe room. What's the situation with the Shelakig? Will we be able to get it downstairs? That's not a very wide opening. Camille was thinking that Smoky might have to take it down through the Ionyc Seas."

Morio snorted. "The Shelakig is no longer a concern. The Varcont is out in the truck, but the Shelakig—its body is stuffed in the back. The thing went crazy and we had no choice but to kill it. They are dangerous, unpredictable creatures, and I'm surprised Shadow Wing even bothers using them because there's no way they can be seen as tractable."

My stomach lurched. "You killed one of them?"

"Wouldn't have helped us in any case. The creature doesn't speak English or Calouk or any form of language we can think about. We couldn't communicate with it, and the Varcont wasn't helping us any." Morio shrugged. "The thing came at me, and Smoky and Shade managed to catch it before it connected, or I'd be in the hospital with Chase right now. After seeing the sheer size and strength of that thing, I think it's a miracle he managed to survive the attack."

At that point, Smoky and Shade entered, carrying the Varcont. He looked like any old vampire, except he exuded a flaming energy that hit me in the gut just by standing near him. His eyes were brilliant crimson, and his fangs—horribly long compared to most vampires'—were showing as he hissed at me. But he was bound in silver chains. Those would burn him doubly so, given he was both vampire and a major demon. I caught my breath as he fixed his gaze on me. There was something mesmerizing about him. It drew me in, and I found myself moving toward him.

The next moment, Roman appeared and I snapped out of it when he barked my name. Shaking my head, I blinked and looked at him.

"What just happened?"

"Apparently the Varcont is a Greater vampire."

"Like Dracula. That must be why Otherworld consigns them to the Sub-Realms." Dredge had been on his way to being a Greater vampire, but he hadn't quite made it. Which led me to wonder about Roman and Blood Wyne. Were they still considered minor vampires? My confusion must have shown on my face.

"Greater vampires possess something the rest of us don't—a demonic spark. We're all considered demons by the majority of people, but these creatures . . . they inherited more of the demonic energy passed down from when the Great Mother Kesana was turned. Remember the tale—she gave herself up to the demons in return for immortal life, and so she was born into vampirism. Most vampires never inherit much of the demonic side, but a few . . . a few do.

And their powers far outstrip ours—even my mother's." Roman frowned. "The sooner we get him into the safe room, the better I'll feel."

"Bring him down, along with the remains of the Shelakig." I motioned to the door and headed downstairs.

As I passed by the Varcont, he laughed. "We have her, you know. We have your pretty, pretty little werepuma, and can you imagine the things our Master might do to her? She is a delightful play toy."

I froze, then slowly turned around to face him. Every instinct in me screamed to throttle him. "You're going to tell us all about where you took her. You can make this easy, or you can make this rough. Your choice."

"I'd rather tell you how loud she screamed when we caught hold of her." He grinned, insolent and sneering, and leaned forward as much as his chains would allow. "You may have me, but I can withstand your tortures much easier than she can withstand our pleasures."

That did it. I leaped forward, but Roman—who was standing right behind me—caught hold of me and yanked me back.

"Stop."

"Let me at him. *Please.* Let me question him." I knew exactly what I'd do to him, and it wasn't pretty and it wouldn't be something I'd ever tell my sisters. My predator was near the edge and if I let her out, the Varcont wouldn't stand a chance against me. Not at my full rage. The energy seethed around me in a haze of red and I wanted to bathe in his blood, to rip him apart a little piece at a time until he gave up every single piece of information we needed.

"No, Menolly." Roman glanced around, then motioned to Vanzir. "I will question him. Vanzir, you will come with me."

Smoky cleared his throat. "I will go, too. We will find out everything we need to know."

"Go where?" Camille stood on the edge of the staircase. She gave a quick look at the Varcont and backed away to the side. Delilah joined her. By now the other vamps had brought in the body of the Shelakig, in pieces.

"We're going to have a little talk with the Varcont here," Roman said. "And the three of you? Are not invited. I will not have you taking part in this . . . any of you. Smoky, you and Vanzir can help me. You are strong enough to withstand what we must do." His voice was steel-cold, and his eyes were pale as frost.

I recognized the warning signals. Roman was about to go full throttle on the Greater vampire and he was going to pull out all the stops. I wanted to be there, but one look at his face told me he wouldn't allow it—and he would pull rank as my sire if I insisted.

"But . . . Nerissa . . ."

"Nerissa is your love. He'll use that to force you into a situation that—my love—you truly do not wish to be in. I will not have you becoming a monster just to defeat one. As much as Smoky and Vanzir and I care about Nerissa, we don't love her the way you do. And that works to our benefit." And with that, they hustled him down the staircase, Roman's guards following as they carried pieces of the broken scorpion demon with them.

"Typical man. I'm strong enough to do this. How dare they push me out of the loop?"

"He's right," Delilah said, as the door slammed behind them. "You're too close to the situation and the demon would use that to hurt you even more. It's not because you're a woman, it's because you are vulnerable because of your connection to her. So deal with it and let them take care of the dirty work."

I wanted to protest, but there was nothing I could say. I mutely jumped up to sit on the counter, staring at the door to the basement.

Derrick leaped over the counter and pulled two drinks for Delilah and Camille—simple shots of a spiced blackberry brandy. He handed me a bottle of our best blood.

"You all need a little fortification, I think." He leaned on the counter, flipping a peanut into his mouth.

Camille pulled her glass to her. "Delilah's right. It's not because you're a woman, you know. That's not why Roman won't let you down there. The three of them . . . they've dealt in torture before. Smoky's got the physical strength to handle the demon and the emotional makeup. So does Vanzir. And Roman . . . he's probably tortured more people in his life than we can count." She said it simply, but her words still chilled me to the core.

Roman and torture . . . the two went hand in hand, really. He had been a warlord. He was son of the vampire queen. While he had his good side, and while I did not doubt he was a fair man, I couldn't ignore the fact that he had been a scourge to his enemies. And the word *enemy* was fraught with meanings. *One man's enemy is another man's savior*, as the old Y'Elestrial saying went.

Camille frowned. "Bring me a punch bowl, Derrick, and the clearest spring water you have."

He shrugged, but acquiesced. Camille settled at a nearby table, motioning for him to put the bowl in front of her and to fill it with water. As he did so, she shook her head as Morio frowned and started to say something.

"I need you to help me, damn it. So just do it."

Morio shrugged. "All right, but I think it's a mistake."

"Then if it is, we'll know soon enough."

Trillian repressed a grin and sidled over to where Delilah and I were standing. "And that's how our marriage works, my dear sisters-in-law. In case you ever wondered who runs things, it's your sister. Camille's word is our command."

I tried to smile but was too deep in my own dark thoughts to manage it. "What's she doing?"

"I believe she's going to attempt to scry."

Delilah let out a little gasp. "I hope to hell she's not trying to see into the safe room. I just have a very bad feeling about what's going down in there—not for our guys, but for the other side. It's not going to be pretty at all."

"I'm not, so don't sweat that." Camille glanced up at us. "I'm doing my best to pick up whatever I can about Nerissa. There's no way my magic could reach into the safe room anyway—it was built to keep the strongest magic at bay. I'm not going to waste time trying to eavesdrop on them. Like you said, I really don't think I want to know what's going on down there right now, you know?"

Delilah nodded. I wished I could agree with them, but I desperately wanted to be there, to make the Varcont eat his words.

Another moment and Camille dropped into a deep trance as she stared into the water. Morio was standing behind her, his hands on her shoulders, feeding her extra energy. You could practically see it wrap around the pair, weaving like a silver trail of mist, or silver plumes from the tail of a peacock as it zipped this way and that around them.

Camille closed her eyes, her voice lilting over a simple chant.

Moon Mother, grant me the sight.
We need your help this night.
Please hear my call, hear my plea,
And bring the gift of vision to me.

There was a brilliant flash in the room as the silver mist plunged into the bowl and spread through the water. Camille opened her eyes and leaned forward, gazing at the surface of the now-churning liquid. She let out a long breath on it, and the water immediately calmed into a placid pool, sparkling with silver light.

A moment later, she let out a little cry. "I see her. I can see Nerissa. She's . . . she's chained in a stark room. Red rock, red brick? The walls are red and they're made of some sort of stone. She's clothed, though she looks pretty banged up. And she's just sitting there, staring—there's a window in the room, with bars on it. Not glass, but an open window. She's staring up at the window. I can't see much else, but it looks like there's a plate of some sort on the ground next to her and what looks like the remains of a meal. She . . . she's crying."

I was at her side in a flash, trying desperately to see what Camille was seeing, but all that I saw in the bowl was the water with a mist across the surface of it. "Can you speak to her?"

"I don't know . . . let me try. Nerissa . . . Nerissa, can you hear me? This is Camille . . ."

She waited for a moment, then glanced back at me. "I think she might have heard me in the back of her mind. She jerked around and looked at the ceiling."

"Tell her we're going to come save her. Tell her I love her!" I was desperate to make contact, to feel like somehow she would know that I was on the way.

"Nerissa, Menolly is here. She loves you. We're doing everything we can to save you. Hang on. Just hang on." Camille paused another moment, then let out a sigh. "The scene faded. I think she may have heard me, but I can't be certain."

I wanted to cry. I wanted to scream for Camille to get her back, but I knew magic didn't work that way—it wasn't a telephone. Magic was far from exact, and with Camille, for it to work without backfiring when it wasn't death magic was a minor miracle in itself.

"Thank you," I whispered, unable to say anything more.

At that point, the door to the basement opened and the men reentered the room. I glanced at their faces. They looked grim, but there was a satisfied smirk on Vanzir's face that gave me hope.

"What happened?"

"We know where she is. We just have to figure out how to get there." Smoky flashed an impassive look my way. "She's being held in a small outpost in the Sub-Realms. And we ascertained that as of yet, she hasn't been hurt in any lasting way. Shadow Wing's busy with his anti-knights and while he sent a demand for ransom to you via the Varcont, he hasn't had time to inspect Nerissa himself."

"How do we get there? Where's the outpost?" I jumped up, running over to Roman, who opened his arms to welcome me in.

"We have to find someone who can create a Demon Gate, then go through to the Subterranean Realms to find her. We have the coordinates needed to do so." Vanzir paused, then added, "The Varcont won't be causing any more problems."

I shuddered slightly. I could smell the blood on Roman's lips, and his eyes were bright, like they always were after he fed. He felt twitchy to me, and I realized that feeding on a Greater vampire had to have had an effect on him. I had drunk demon's blood several times, and it always charged me up in a way that was hard to describe. Think of it as putting high-octane fuel in a car that was used to regular.

"That leaves us the question of how we find someone who can create a Demon Gate for us, someone we can trust?" I glanced around at Delilah and Camille.

"That's simple enough," Delilah said. "Wilbur can do it."

And just like that, I realized that we were actually going to head deep into the Sub-Realms to rescue my wife.

Chapter 16

Wilbur's house was close to ours. By the time we arrived, it was two in the morning and Martin opened the door. Wilbur had been in the Special Forces, stationed down in South America where he first learned necromancy. Now he was a one-legged mountain man stuck in the city, and I had the feeling he was lonelier than hell. Hanging with a ghoul—even when it had been your brother—didn't provide much interaction. And Wilbur's social skills were dreadfully lacking.

Martin recognized us. He was kind of like a dog who had been trained that certain people were safe not to bark at, or attack. He let us in, then shuffled toward a room off the living room. Camille crossed the doorway and turned to Roman. "Enter and be welcome."

And just like that, Roman was able to enter the house. It occurred to me that it might be a good idea for people to have a talk with their friends about inviting strangers into the house. In general, it was a dangerous idea, but even more so if the stranger turned out to be a vampire.

Wilbur used to sleep upstairs but now, probably because

of his leg, he seemed to find it easier to use the downstairs bedroom. A few minutes later, one very grumpy mountain man appeared. Wilbur resembled the boys of ZZ Top, only a bit bigger and burlier, and he didn't dress nearly as nice. He was wearing a pair of sweatpants and a baggy top and his hair was all shades of messy, including the massive beard.

He rubbed his eyes, staring at us blurrily. "What the hell do you want at this time of night?"

"We need you to create a Demon Gate that will allow us to travel to the Subterranean Realms so I can rescue Nerissa." The words came streaming out of me as though I had just lost my supper and vomited all over the floor.

Wilbur blinked and scratched his balls. He was not one for niceties or manners. "I think you'd better sit down and start making some sense." As he headed back into the living room, we followed. I wanted him to just get on with it, but I also understood just how delicate a spell it was, and how much energy was required. One did not just gate open a doorway to hell, so to speak. At least, not unless one had a good reason, craziness notwithstanding.

We settled in the living room. Wilbur cleared his throat and blinked, squinting at Roman. "Do we know each other?"

"I don't believe so, and I'd prefer to keep it that way," Roman said, grinning at Wilbur. "But this is not the likely outcome; therefore, allow me to—"

"Just give me your fucking name, dude, and stop prancing like a pony." Yeah, that was our Wilbur. Blunt as always and more than a little bit rude.

"Roman, Lord of the Vampire Nation."

That seemed to make an impact. Wilbur subtly shifted, his eyes widening. "I think I need some coffee." He turned to Camille. "Sweet cheeks, would you and your gorgeous bouncing boobs make me some?" His eyes were glued to her cleavage. Again, Wilbur to the core.

She just gave him a disgusted look, then laughed and pushed herself to her feet. "Trust me, you don't want to mess with my boobs. They're dangerous in the wrong hands." And with that cryptic remark, she vanished into the kitchen.

I let out a grunt. "Dude, this is serious. We need you to be serious with us."

Wilbur gave me a long look. He was usually a lecher, and he could be a real son-of-a-bitch misogynist, but the fact was, he had always come through for us in the past. He had lost his leg because of his friendship with us, as well.

"What's going on, Dead Girl?" That was as close to an endearment as he ever got with me.

"Demons have kidnapped Nerissa and they're holding her hostage. We absolutely cannot pay the ransom they're asking. It isn't a matter of money, but of . . . saving the world, basically. So we need to sneak into the Sub-Realms, track her down, and rescue her." I held his gaze, not working my glamour. If he did this, I wanted him doing so willingly because creating a Demon Gate could backfire on him, and in the worst scenario, it could put his life in jeopardy.

"And to get into the Sub-Realms, you have to have a Demon Gate. I take it you can't go through the Ionyc Seas?" Wilbur knew a great deal about our abilities. He never had ratted us out, not once.

"Right, because the only one who's been in the Sub-Realms is Vanzir, and he can't travel through the Seas. He can go via the astral plane, but that's a highly dangerous trek when you're talking about leading a group into the demonic realms." I folded my arms across my chest and leaned back. "Wilbur, I know you don't have a stake in this . . ."

"But you need my help." He stared at me so intently that for a moment, I feared he was going to ask something from me that I really didn't want to give him. But after a moment, he shrugged. "What's a little Demon Gate among friends? All right, I'm in. But you listen to what I say, do what I tell you, and don't mess up. Got it?"

I nodded. "Got it."

"How many people do you need to transport?"

Camille returned from the kitchen and handed a mug of coffee to Wilbur.

Roman straightened up. "Menolly will be taking a group of five vampires with her. I'd rather send more, but the smaller the party, the easier it will be to escape notice. By the laws of the Vampire Nation, I'm not allowed to go—only one crown may be away at war at any given time unless the war comes to us."

Wilbur stared at him for a moment, then shrugged. "And who else?"

"Before I answer, does anyone know about the day?" I licked my lips, a thought occurring to me. "Is there . . . does the sun shine in the Sub-Realms? Will I have to worry about it?"

Trillian shook his head. "I've lived there, remember? When Svartalfheim was located there. You will have no sun to worry about, nor moon to rise over the night. There is a constant glow of fire and smoke, but you will never find the source of it. It's warm—too warm, and the air is bone dry. Water can be found, but much of it is stagnant and filled with bracken or algae. The vegetation that grows in the Subterranean Realms is twisted and windswept, and dry as dust. A constant wind blows across the land and it never stops. After a while, you begin to hear voices in it and if you try to listen, they can drive you mad. I will go with you. I know my way around to some degree."

I gulped. It sounded so alien and strange, and so far away. "I don't want everybody with me. Some of you have to stay here, to guard the portals and our family. Smoky, I think you would stand out far too much."

"He would, he would positively shine, but I will go." Shade moved to stand beside me.

Delilah started to stand, but I shook my head. "I will not take you to the Sub-Realms, Kitten. Not if I had to go there alone. I refuse—don't ask and don't argue." She had lost so much of her naïveté over the years, but I would not strip away what remained, and I had the feeling that a visit to the Sub-Realms would wipe the slate clean and leave her without the joyous optimism that helped hold our family together.

Camille started to say something, but I shook my head again. "Neither will I take you. You're slated to be Queen of Dusk and Shadow. I won't jeopardize your life. Vanzir—will you come?"

He unfolded his arms and grinned at me. "Thought you'd never ask. Of course."

"We will go in light. Vanzir, Shade, Trillian, and I will go, along with the vampires Roman assigns me. Better we keep the party light, to escape notice. That makes nine of us."

Nine, to walk into the darkness. I thought of *The Lord of the Rings* and was vaguely comforted that the Fellowship had contained nine members. But they had Gandalf and we didn't. And they, at least, knew where they were going. Although we had coordinates, that wasn't quite the same. Or at least it didn't seem so to me.

I turned to Wilbur. "When do we leave?"

"I need at least three hours to prep a Demon Gate. Come back at five A.M. Not a moment sooner or you may distract me and that could disrupt the spell or cause it to fuck up in a way that would make Witchy-Boobs proud." He leered at Camille, but even I could tell his heart wasn't in it. He seemed downright depressed.

"Wilbur, is something wrong?" I glanced at the clock. We'd be cutting it close before sunrise, but we'd make it if everything went right.

He frowned, staring at the floor. "I'm just pissed. Your old lady, she's always been nice to me. Even when I copped a feel, she just smacked my hand and told me to fuck myself. But . . . she always had a smile for me, and a civil word. It's just wrong that they took her from you."

As he looked up into my eyes, I understood that he really did understand what it was to lose someone you loved. I glanced over at Martin.

Delilah shifted, then blurted out. "Wilbur . . . Martin . . . he's still—"

Camille broke into a coughing fit, so loud she startled Delilah into silence. Delilah glanced at her, then at me. I gave her a subtle shake of the head. Who knew what finding out the truth would do to Wilbur? It might flood him with guilt over animating his brother's body. It might send him over the edge.

Wilbur's nostrils flared. "What were you saying, Puss-Puss?"

Delilah let out a long sigh. "Just that . . . Martin . . . he's still . . . his suit needs cleaning, I think. It kind of smells."

The necromancer gazed at her, as if trying to fathom her leap in logic. He shrugged. "I'll take care of it in the morning. Martin cares about his appearance; he wouldn't want to think he had a bad case of B.O." And with that, he shooed us out of the house.

As we left the house, Roman drew me off to one side. "I will leave you here. I have business I cannot ignore, my love. But . . . if you need me, I will do my best to rearrange my meetings." He took my hands, kissing the palms softly but with so much restrained passion that I wanted to propel myself into his arms and just stay there, safe and hoping that everything would work out for the best.

I let out a soft murmur, then said, "No. You go take care of your business. Roman . . . if I don't . . ."

"I will not listen to defeatist talk. You will return and you will rescue your love and my second wife. I have more faith in you than I think you do." His gaze never left me as he leaned down and gently brushed my lips with his. "Menolly, you were not my choice for princess based on looks nor on your name, nor on how sexy you are. You were made for the throne. You have the heart of a warrior and the brilliance to lead. And you have one trait I lost long ago. Compassion. These things make you fit to wear the crown. I'll send the vampires to you. Now, go get our Nerissa and bring her home."

And with that, he clicked his heels together, then bowed and—in a blur—was gone.

I joined my sisters as we headed across the street to our property. Vanzir had vanished ahead of us. Delilah, Camille, and I were walking arm in arm up the driveway. We had paved it because it had become a perpetual mud hole every time we got heavy rain.

The night sky looked like we might be headed into clear

weather. The temps were running in the low sixties, but it felt almost balmy. On either side, brambles reached out to snag our clothes as we passed by, and huge trees shadowed over the drive. There were crystals and wards hidden in those trees, and they surrounded the entire acreage. It had taken days for Camille and Morio to supervise setting them up and then another couple of days for them to enchant the grid. For the most part it held and worked, though there were always exceptions that slipped through.

As we strolled along, it occurred to me that—if things went south—this could be the last time we'd be together. I stopped as the house came into view. The three-story Victorian was home, now. It was home, and the basement was my lair, and the thought of moving into Roman's mansion left skid marks in my stomach. But we couldn't freeze our lives as if nothing were changing. The world thrived on change, and without it, stagnation would rot anything from the core out.

I motioned for them to join me on one of the benches that we'd placed along the walk.

"Listen . . . I've been thinking. If things don't work out—if something happens and I get stuck down there, or worse . . ."

"Don't even say it." Kitten was in full denial, but then she paused and a dark look washed over her face. "What do you need if that happens? What should we do?"

"Don't come after me. Don't try to save Nerissa or me if anything happens. Somebody has to be here to fight against Shadow Wing. Somebody has to carry on the family. I want to know that you two will be safe—following your destinies, if I meet the final death. I've already died once. If it has to happen again, I want to know that you're both still alive and safe."

I hated saying the words. They felt like an invitation to Fate. But then again, Fate had never played kindly with me. The Hags of Fate had spun me a difficult path, and the threads of my life couldn't go on forever, no matter how long I lived. At some point, even vampires faded, stretched too thin by the days and years and millennia.

Camille took my hand, and Delilah's. "We promise. Menolly, when you died, when you were turned and sent back, for a long time you remembered things differently than how they happened. You broke my arm, you almost killed me—and you blanked that out. But I'd do everything again, if I had to. I'd do it all over. We want to go with you, but we'll respect your wishes." Her voice was throaty, as if a wellspring of emotion were struggling to break free.

Kitten nodded, tears slipping down her cheeks. "I hate this. It feels like we're saying good-bye."

I kissed both of their hands and then stood, pacing across the drive to stare at a rowan tree that was blossoming up and over the road. The leaves were young but they would grow, and the berries would turn brilliant red. They were protective, rowan were—keeping away the lightning. *Mountain ash* . . . that was another name for them. I plucked a branch and played with it before turning back.

"We are, at least until I rescue Nerissa. But so many people never get to say good-bye to their loved ones. So many times, someone walks out the door and they're gone forever—hit by a car, or their heart gives out, or a random bullet from a maniac's gun finds them. And their families are left without ever having the chance to say good-bye. Let's face it, I'm headed on a very dangerous mission. I'm going to the Subterranean Realms. Maybe we'll be graced by the gods for once, maybe we'll find Nerissa and rescue her without a struggle. I'd love that. But . . . maybe we won't. I just want to make certain I've said everything I need to before I leave."

As I handed Camille the branch, she stared at it softly. "Then I guess I'll say what's on my mind. I love you, Menolly, and I want Nerissa back. But a part of me wishes you'd just let her go—chalk it up to the horrid collateral damage that we seem to leave in our wake."

She held up her hand before I could speak. "I know you can't. And I wouldn't respect you if you actually did. But the selfish part of me doesn't want to worry . . . doesn't want to wait and watch for someone to come through the door who might not make it home. The selfish part of me is the one who's talking right now. And I need to be honest, and get it outside of me."

She shrugged. "But I also know that if it were one of my husbands, I wouldn't hesitate to go hunting him down. Which brings me to another thing. I lied when I made my promise. Because if something happens to you, then something will have happened to Trillian, and I'll have to come after you, if only to save him."

"Same for me and Shade." Delilah took the branch. She played with the leaves. "But . . . I mostly want to say that you'd just damned well better come home. Because Camille won't watch *Jerry Springer* with me, and she won't watch the old sci-fi movies I love, not without protesting. And if you don't get your ass back here, then I'm going to come looking for you in my Death Maiden guise. Because *nobody* can stop a Death Maiden. Not even a demon."

And that was it. We stared at one another, and then I began to laugh and threw my arms around their waists as we started back to the house. We had said all we could. I just wanted to spend the rest of the night listening to them chatter and playing with Maggie, before I walked into the gates of hell.

Vanzir had news for us—good news, actually. "I managed to connect with Trytian's contact who is still over Earthside. He finally answered his cell. I told him what was up. Don't even bitch at me about it because you're going to thank me."

"All right, as long as Trytian doesn't hand us over to Shadow Wing."

"Trytian will meet us at the coordinates and help us from there. He and one or two other trusted guards." Vanzir's eyes flared, and he gave me a cockeyed grin. I realized he was trying to help in the best way he knew how.

"How did his contact get in touch with him so quickly?" I still wasn't buying it, not all the way at least. But if it *was* true, then we had another leg up and every bit of help we got counted.

"They're soul-bound, like Camille and her men. Only

they can trade thoughts. It's not all it's cracked up to be. I've known some other demons who have that ability and unless you're very careful, it leads to somebody eventually killing somebody else for a stray thought."

I wanted to believe it, but I was afraid to. Instead, I decided on a wait-and-see approach. "Thank you, Vanzir. It will be good to have help on the other end."

"I know you aren't sure about this . . . but trust me. It will work out." And with that, he vanished into the kitchen.

At five, we were standing at Wilbur's door again: Trillian, Shade, Vanzir, the vampires—who were named Ron, Jacob, Sandra, Tico, and Jorge (who were twins)—and me. The faint hints of dawn were creeping over the horizon, and in half an hour, the sun would rise from its journey across the other side of the world. Of course, it was the Earth that had done the traveling, I thought, not the sun, but either way . . . morning would arrive.

I knocked on the door. Martin answered and led us to the basement, where Wilbur always did his work. After his house had been torched and he had lost his leg to the arsonists, he had the staircase revamped so it was much easier to descend. He'd added in one of those motorized chairs that would carry you up and down the stairs, and he used it on days when he just wasn't feeling up to snuff.

We descended to the newly renovated basement. It was finished now, spotless in a way that I never would associate with Wilbur, and well lit. As we stopped in front of one of the three doors leading off the small central chamber, Martin clumsily raised one hand and tapped at the door. A moment later, it opened.

Wilbur stood there in a brightly colored robe that looked straight out of the South American jungles. None of us were sure if the runes emblazoned on both his robe and headband were Aztec or Mayan, or maybe something more obscure, but they were obviously from that region. The headband was woven, blue and yellow, with runes beaded on it. The central point over his forehead—his third eye—contained a brilliant sapphire, the size of a half dollar. A necklace of bone—snake vertebrae—embraced his neck, with polished spikes from what must have been a massive smoky quartz geode.

As he silently led us into the room, I was taken aback. The chamber was massive, not a particularly high ceiling, but it must have taken up half the space of the first floor. Tables and chests lined the room, and a chair and sofa were next to a bookcase that was overflowing with books. The pervasive smell of musty roots and herbs filled the air, even though the walls and all surfaces were a bright, shiny white. But what caught my eye more than anything was the brilliant flaming archway in the center of the room. The flames gave off no heat, and they flickered but did not spark or hiss. Magical fire—a fire that did not burn. *The Demon Gate.*

Runes floated in the air, inscribed within the transparent flickering flames. I shivered, and beside me, Vanzir let out an appreciative whistle.

"Nice, very nice. I can feel the power emanating off it, and it's extremely clear. Wilbur, you do good work." Vanzir shook his head. "I never thought I'd be going back. I swore I would never again cross worlds to that place, but I guess once you say *'Never'* the gods say, *'Game on!'* They like to fuck with us, don't they?"

"That they do." I glanced over at Trillian. "How about you? Are you ready to head back into the Sub-Realms?"

"No, but I've been there many times and always managed to keep myself out of trouble. We're a resilient lot. If we have to face down the demons, I'd rather put my lot with you than anybody else. So, are we ready to head out?" He was wearing black jeans, a black turtleneck, and a motorcycle jacket. He had brought his sword with him. Vanzir had armed himself with a set of nasty-looking daggers.

I, on the other hand, was wielding the battle-ax I'd taken off a cave troll when we rescued a dragon-shifter named Shimmer. I had opted for a pair of black leather pants, a gray turtleneck, and a crimson leather jacket. The crimson was a nod to my status as vampire princess. Even as the words crossed my thoughts, I let out a snort.

"What's so funny, Dead Girl?" Wilbur had picked up the nickname for me from Ivana—the Maiden of Karask. She was a deadly and freaky Elder Fae, and we had made all too many deals with her. I had the feeling the pair had been spending far too much time in each other's company.

"I'm a princess. I'm a princess and I'm off to rescue my . . . other princess. Just call me Princess Charming."

"I think you'd make a better Leia than Cinderella. Leia had guts and could shoot like a son of a bitch." Wilbur snorted. "Unless you want a pink palace, and then we can call you Snow White when you fall asleep each morning."

"Please, no. I like dwarves but I've never slept with one, and I'm not cut out to be anybody's housekeeper." I stared at the Demon Gate, realizing that my laughter was covering up one hell of a deep-seated fear. Walking into the Sub-Realms was an insane thing to do. What I'd told my sisters about if we didn't come back . . . that wasn't just hyperbole. No, there was a very real chance this was a head-on suicide mission and I knew it. But I couldn't leave Nerissa there, and we couldn't give Shadow Wing the spirit seals. So, there was nothing else to do.

"I'm ready." I shivered, a goose walking over my grave.

Trillian rested a hand on my shoulder. "We've got this. We'll bring her home. Just pay attention to Vanzir and me—we've both been in the Sub-Realms. If we say duck, duck. If we say jump, jump. Got it, girl?"

I nodded. "I understand. I just hope to hell Vanzir's right about Trytian and that he's waiting there for us."

"There's only one way to find out." Vanzir nodded to Wilbur. "We're ready. How do we get back?"

"I'll leave the Demon Gate up as long as I can—as long as nothing else comes through. But you have to be aware that any sorcerer or necromancer with enough power can destroy it from the other side. That's one thing I can't control." Wilbur's expression was solemn. "I've taken strides to combat that possibility, however." He handed each of us a bone charm on a leather thong. "I made these. Consider them . . . a magical GPS signal. I'll have a chance to track your signature with them. They aren't guaranteed, but there's a chance I can pull you through, if something does happen to the Demon Gate. I made one for Nerissa, too." He handed me the extra. "When you go through the gate, it's not quite the same as walking through one of your Fae portals. It's going to hurt, so be prepared."

I stared at the flaming maw, tucking Nerissa's charm into my pocket and zipping it closed. "I guess . . . the only way to find out is to go. What do we do?"

"I set it for the coordinates that Vanzir gave me. So you just . . . step through."

I realized we were stalling. With a glance at Vanzir and Trillian, I moved toward the gate. Shade swung in behind me, silent in his support. Wilbur stood beside the portal and, as I met his gaze, he gave me a solemn nod. I silently leaned up and planted a faint kiss on his cheek.

"Thank you," I whispered.

"Thank me when you get back with her. Now go, Dead Girl, and stay safe. But . . . when you get back, if it's still during the day, you'll pass out immediately, I assume. There are no windows in this room, so the sun won't be able to harm you, but if that's the case, whoever is with you can just lift you onto one of the tables and let you sleep out the rest of the day." He looked at the other vamps. "That goes for your friends, too. But you might want to warn Nerissa so she doesn't panic."

"Got it." With a deep shudder, I turned back toward the gate. There was nothing left to say. Anything more and I might lose my nerve. I glanced up at Shade and he nodded. Without further ado, I steeled my shoulders and stepped through.

The flash of runes startled me as I passed beneath the magical gate, and then—a deep searing pain wrenched through my body. Hot like a blade off the forge, it pierced through my soul, burning deep to my very core. Bathed in fire, I froze, unable to move.

This must be what it's like to step into the sun. So bright, so hot, so brilliant and transcendent in its pain. Like the phoenix, burning to ashes before being reborn into the dark of the night. I danced with the flames as the runic symbols coiled around me, shifting me body and soul into a realm where I did not belong. Every fiber of my being resisted the energy. The very air was acrid, filled with desire and hatred, with a power so deep that it coiled at the base of a mountain, greedy and ancient, older than the wyrms of the earth, older than Kesana, the Mother of the Crimson Veil. Here, evil ran free and easy, and base emotions were elevated.

And then, as the psychic river of a power so ancient and so corrupt flowed freely around me, I opened my eyes to find myself standing in a valley of rock formations—crumbling and roughly weathered, and striated with reddish streaks. The sky was illuminated by a pale light, but it was neither the moon nor the sun. Roiling clouds, rust colored and dusty, filled the air, churning through the sky.

As the others appeared through the Demon Gate to join me, I gazed out over the landscape, realizing that we were actually here. We were in the Sub-Realms.

Chapter 17

As soon as we were all there, I tried to shake the cobwebs out of my head. "Wilbur was right, that hurt like a son of a bitch."

Shade nodded. "Yeah, Demon Gates aren't noted for their pleasure trips. They're created to handle creatures of immense power and stamina. What hurt you would tickle them. It didn't bother me because of my dragon heritage, and I'm guessing Vanzir was fine, but I'll bet Trillian and the other vamps weren't too happy."

Trillian rubbed his head. "You can say that again."

Vanzir was glancing around. "Shut up until we know if we were spotted." He motioned for us to hide behind the nearest outcropping of rocks and I immediately obeyed, motioning for Roman's vamps to follow me. Trillian and Vanzir began to scout around, and I realized they fit here—Vanzir more than Trillian—but they had gone into a mode that felt perfectly suited for this place. Cautious and edgy, on high alert.

As we waited, I began to feel like we were being watched. Nervously, I glanced over my shoulder, up to the high rock shelf above us. The clouds and the illumination made everything appear in silhouette—dim and hard to see the details, but I had the feeling there was something moving around up there. I crouched down and began to work my way toward Vanzir. Before I could go farther than a few feet, however, there was a noise as figures leaped down, falling a good twenty feet to land at our backs.

Immediately, I was on my feet, battle-ax raised. Vanzir and Trillian had turned and Shade and the vamps had weapons poised. But a guttural laugh stopped us, as Trytian slid out from the shadows with a group of four daemons behind him.

Trytian was dressed in camo—red and rust and brown and black, which worked like a charm. He looked terribly harsh here, in his native element, and his buddies, while they could pass for human, obviously weren't. There was an edge to them that whispered *Do Not Fuck With.*

"You're lucky it was us." Trytian glanced over at the Demon Gate. "You found somebody who knows what he's doing, though. I'll give you that. That gate won't be easy to take down, if anybody manages to find it."

Vanzir crossed to him and the two, arms raised, clasped hands in the air as if they were about to arm-wrestle. After a solid shake, they let go.

"Were you able to find out anything else?" Vanzir asked.

Trytian gave us a brief nod, his gaze focusing on me. "I found out where they're keeping the werepuma. There's a detention center about seven miles from here by foot. She's there. I would have given you coordinates that were closer, but once you get a few miles in, the place is swarming with Shadow Wing's soldiers. It's not a full encampment, but there's enough coming and going that I think they might have a good chance of noticing the Demon Gate. We'll go in via a roundabout way. I know a back path that leads up to the detention center. There will still be a few guards, but I have a feeling we're going to face far fewer that way."

A wave of relief washed over me. "You're going with us?"

"Hell yes. Anything to muck up Shadow Wing's plans. My father knows nothing about this little operation, but he put me in charge of causing as much mayhem as possible to trip up the enemy."

I laughed then, softly so my voice wouldn't carry. *"The Great Escape."*

"What?" The daemon looked clueless.

"Movie. Steve McQueen starred in it. One of the characters—Bartlett—said, 'What my personal feelings are is of no importance. You appointed me Big X. And it's my duty to harass, confound, and confuse the enemy to the best of my ability.' It reminds me of that."

A spark flickered in Trytian's eyes. "Exactly. You understand. Rescuing your wife will do just that. So I'm taking on the job."

"Then you lead." I found a sudden faith in the daemon. He hated Shadow Wing, and so did we. Common enemy, common goals.

Trytian arranged us so that he and one of his party—Lokail—were at the front. After them, came Vanzir and me, then Shade and Trillian, then Roman's vamps. After that were the other three daemons. Which made our party fourteen strong. We were all dressed in clothing that was essentially camouflage. Vanzir had a red baseball hat on, which covered the shock of blond hair. Trillian had braided his hair and he, too, now slipped on a black bandanna, tying it below the braid, to hide the shining silvery-blue highlights. Shade reached down, caught up a handful of the red sandy soil beneath our feet, and streaked it through his amber hair. My own hair was camo enough, and the daemons had dark or reddish-dark hair. None of Roman's vamps were light-haired, so we were good to go.

We started out, Trytian cautiously leading us through the maze of rocks that jutted upward from the floor of the Sub-Realms. A surreal desert, it made me think of the deep Southern Wastes of Otherworld, where rogue magic mingled into the dust clouds, wandering the vast dunes. The hoodoos towered into the air, harsh, jutting fingers of rock spreading out like a forest of stone trees. Rough and running brown to deep rust, their tops jaggedly slashed the sky above us.

Two rows behind me, Ron whispered, "This reminds me of Bryce Canyon in the Moab desert. You can get lost in there and never find your way out."

I glanced around, wondering if the Sub-Realms looked this way all the way through. Finally, I tapped Vanzir on the shoulder. "Is every place here like this?" My voice, even though I kept it low, felt like it echoed around me, ricocheting from rock to rock.

"No, there are oceans and lakes, but they are more tropical. There are mountains, also . . . snow demons come from there. The seasons do change, but it's not quite like Earthside or Otherworld. It's an environment all its own." Vanzir looked preoccupied. "We are far from any cities, at least I know that."

I frowned. "Cities? I know there are cities here, but . . ."

"I was born in Quantell, a city on the edge of a vast desert. Not a desert like this, but rolling dunes that go on and on without end. I remember very little of it, though, because shortly after I was born, my mother sold me to a trader, who took me with him to a fortress in the mountains. There, he trained me to use my powers as a weapon, and then he traded me to a demon general. I don't know what he got in return, but from then on, I was both a weapon and a sex slave. Karvanak won me in a poker game."

A look passed through those kaleidoscope eyes, the ones we could never settle on a color for, and his voice was gruff and harsh. I could sense the memories behind the words—just as my own voice sounded when I talked about Dredge.

"I understand. You know I do. At least, to some extent." I had been tortured and abused for a night before being turned. Vanzir had spent a good share of his life as a slave.

"You more than most. And Camille, as well." And that part of the subject was closed. After another pause, he said, "Shadow Wing was born and came to power in Vaikish. It's a vast city—spread throughout the dunes like a mystical Ceredream that rises out of the sand. Efreet live there, and Salamanders, and other fire spirits. And Soul Eaters, like Shadow Wing, congregate there. He climbed on the backs of others, assassinating his way to claim the throne. At least in this area."

"I don't fully understand, I think. Nor my sisters. So Shadow Wing is not the Demon Lord of all of the Sub-Realms?" We had never fully managed to come to grips with how the hierarchies worked here. There wasn't much written on the subject, and those who knew best—the Demonkin—didn't go parading the knowledge around.

"There are other lords, in other lands. The Sub-Realms are as vast as Otherworld, perhaps even more so. There are levels to the realms, worlds within worlds. Some are far less fearsome, others total pandemonium. Some would drive you mad if you even set foot in them. Their energy there is not meant for the likes of mortals, even if they are vampire or Fae." Vanzir shrugged. "I might manage it, but I wouldn't want to try."

Trytian turned around. "Shush, you two. We need to move in silence." Then, "What he says is correct. Never go waltzing around unescorted down here. If you go through the wrong door, you will be lost forever."

As we moved onward, the landscape became a labyrinth of twists and turns through the rocky terrain. I began to realize that I would easily be lost if it weren't for Trytian guiding us—there were no landmarks that I could see, no identifying markers or structures. The light overhead held steady, never growing, never darkening, and I wondered if there was any change to the endless half light.

"Does it ever get dark?" I finally asked, when the sea of reds and rusts started to blur into a haze of murk.

Vanzir shook his head. "No, never. And never brighter than this. At least not in this layer of the Sub-Realms. In some places, it's black as pitch, blacker than any darkness you've ever encountered. Darker than the grave, in fact. Any light is absorbed. Ancient monsters sleep coiled in that realm, and they shift and stir, causing great quakes with their turning. Once in a long while, one wakes and blazes out into the other realms, taking with it death and destruction and anguish."

I shuddered, thinking of the wyrm we had recently fought.

These creatures sounded worse than the ancestors of dragons, and they were terrifying enough. "They sound primordial."

"They are, and in their rage, they know no boundaries."

Trytian glanced back. "We're coming to the end of this part of Stone Rock Fields."

"Is that what you call this area?"

"Yes, but be wary. When we emerge, we'll be facing a far greater danger, and you must be very cautious when crossing the river."

I was about to say that I didn't drown all that easily when Trytian led us out of the maze of hoodoos. Even from this distance, the heat was tangible from the rush of lava racing through a very large channel. An overpass arched over the riverbed, rising at least fifty feet away from the surface, and it started a good twenty feet back from the edge of the river of molten rock. But the arch was old and looked like the rock had crumbled away in places, and the thought of crossing over the lake of burning fire scared the hell out of me. I could tell Trillian and Vanzir weren't all that thrilled either. Even Shade looked askance.

"I'd fly over, but that would likely attract attention," he mumbled.

"Yeah, but if you do, I'm going on your back." I flashed him a faint grin. I thought about turning into a bat, but I really didn't want to be in a form that was more vulnerable while we were here—not if I could help it. "Seriously, is that overpass safe? I seem to see pebbles and rocks falling into the lava."

Trytian shrugged. "What's safe and what isn't? Safety is an illusion, anyway. But to calm your fears, yes, it should hold us up as we pass—it's been there for thousands of years. And whether or not it does, the fact remains it's the only way across unless, as your friend says, he turns into a dragon and flies. But that will surely attract some unwelcome attention and I highly recommend you think twice about it."

The sound of the coiling strands of flowing rock hissed and popped, sending cinders up onto the edge of the bank. I shivered, again thinking of how far we were from home, and how much I'd hate to be stuck down here.

"Then let's get over it and get done. The more we stand here, the more I really don't want to go." I moved forward, but Trytian stopped me.

"Let me go first. And when you go, don't run, be cautious with your footing, but keep a quick pace. That will prevent you from being burned. If somebody attacks while we're up there, I don't care what you want to do. You get to the other side before you return the attack. Fighting up on top of the arch is suicide."

"What's the river called?" I followed as he neared the start of the overpass, trying to keep my mind from thinking about just what we were about to do.

"We call it Xilan Ki, but the closest translation would be *Fiery Mother's Milk*." Trytian was setting a good pace and I followed, watching where he put his feet. Several places along the overpass had been broken through, so that there were a scant few inches of stone on either side, which left a gaping hole in the center of the overpass. The lava boiled below us, hissing on its frantic journey through the heavily fortified channel, where years of buildup had produced a smooth half pipe of hardened obsidian stone.

As I watched, Trytian edged along the left side, testing each step, clinging to the stone rail that rose up to keep us from falling over the edge. I followed suit.

"Do you have any rivers here that have actual water in them?" I shuddered as a few rocks the size of my fist broke away and fell into the seething river below.

"Yes, we do. Some of them are quite beautiful, too. There is beauty in all places, even this gods-forsaken wasteland." He was edging over another dicey area, but once we were beyond that, it was relatively easy going to the other side of the bank.

When we were all on solid ground again, well away from the heat of the flowing lava, I leaned back against a nearby boulder and tried to regroup. I was eminently grateful I had refused Camille and Delilah's offer to come with me. They were tough, but this was really rough going.

"Where to from here?" I glanced around. Now that we were over the river, all I could see in either direction was barren, red dunes. The rust of the jagged outcroppings had weathered away here, I thought, leaving only worn sand behind.

Trytian shaded his eyes, gazing around at the plains. "We cross the Plain of Winds, and then we will go through a petrified forest, and after that, we come to the detention camp where they are holding your wife. The plains only go on for a couple of miles, but they will not be easy. The gusts are constant and stiff—between that and the shifting sand, it takes time to pass through. Watch your footing; there are creatures that hide in burrows waiting for people to pass by, much like trapdoor spiders. They will eat anything that moves. And there are dunes that are very much like quicksand, easy to sink down into and not so easy to pull yourself out from. Follow in each other's footsteps, stay in your lines, and try to keep up."

He started off. I wanted to ask when the winds would pick up, but it was like stepping from night to day. The moment we started out onto the rolling hills of sand, the winds swept in, shrieking past with a fury that was reserved for the strongest windstorms back Earthside. I estimated the gusts to be running close to fifty or sixty miles an hour, enough to knock a person off their feet if they weren't prepared for it. Combined with the blowing sand and the difficulty of gaining even footing, our progress slowed tremendously.

One foot in front of the other. That was what I focused on. Keeping in Trytian's path, following him as we trudged along. It was useless to speak here—a waste of breath for those who actually breathed, and a waste of energy for those of us who didn't. The sand was blowing in my face and eyes, and the granules stung as they blasted past me.

A glance told me Trillian and Vanzir had thought along the same lines. They brought out eye protection—goggles, of all things. I found myself a little irritated they hadn't thought to warn Shade and me about it, so we could have picked up a couple of pair, but then Trillian reached forward to hand a pair to me, and he gave one to Shade. Gratefully, I slid them over my face, finding an instant relief from fighting to see through the constant barrage of sand.

As we pushed our way through the dunes, I began to slide further and further into my thoughts. Talking was useless, and it took every ounce of energy to keep upright against the howling winds that seemed to grow stronger with each step. The plains might only be a few miles wide, but those miles seemed to take forever as we trudged along.

As we continued, a wall of sand rose beside us, sloping up to form a tall hill directly to our left. It made me nervous—what if the winds shifted and it came cascading down on us? But we were nearly to the other side. In the distance I could barely see jutting shapes of something I assumed were the petrified trees, and I just held hope that we'd make it out before being covered by the cascading drifts.

A scream cut through the wind. I turned, forcing my body to shift against the steady gale, and saw that the vampires I had brought with me had moved out of formation. Ron had vanished, and to the side of where he had been standing, there was a gaping hole in the wall of sand.

"Ron!" I tried to struggle back to him as the soles of his boots slowly vanished inside the sudden tunnel.

Jacob and Sandra were closest to him, and they pushed forward, trying to get to him, but the sand closed over the hole and it was as if he had never been there. I turned, frantic, to Trytian, but he shook his head and resolutely turned forward, beginning to move again. Torn between wanting to help Ron, to find him, and realizing that we were going to have to leave him behind, I bit my lip till it was bloody but returned to the trail and tried not to think about what it was that had reached out to drag him into its lair.

Another half hour and we stumbled out of the plains. The wind died to a slow *whoosh*, as the dunes once again faded into hard rock beneath our feet. We were staring at the petrified forest that sprawled in front of us. The trees had once been real trees—that much I could tell—but now their trunks had hardened to stone, and they were surreal sculptures rising from this barren land.

My ears hurt, and my throat felt raw. I turned to Trytian. "What happened to Ron?"

"Sand beast got him. Once they have hold of you, you're dead. He was dead by the time they got him in there, vampire or not. They cut you into pieces and eat you." His bluntness hit hard, but I realized that he was doing me a favor by taking away any hope that I had for rescuing Ron, and also by reassuring me that his death had been quick.

I pressed my lips together and nodded.

"Come, let's get into the forest, where we can rest a bit. The going will be much easier than either the rock sculptures or the Plain of Winds were. There is no undergrowth, no living thing in the forest save for a creature or two who might be hiding in there. The trees turned to stone long ago, and there is nothing to impede our way." Trytian motioned for us to follow him into the woods.

The stone trees were eerie, and while the wind still blew stiffly here, it was nothing like what it had been out in the plains. But it whistled through the trees, and where knotholes had been, the gusts created mournful notes, like blowing through hollow reeds. The plains had been rough and tiring. The forest was downright eerie.

Trytian led us to a fallen log. Even without foliage on the trees, the trunks were big enough and thick enough to hide us from sight. "Rest here for a bit. If you have food, I suggest eating now. If you need water, we brought some that is safe to drink. Any water you might find in the forest, avoid—it will be heavy with ores and minerals that might injure you."

Trillian and Shade found a log to sit on. Vanzir headed over to talk to Trytian. Sandra, Jorge, Tico, and Jacob huddled together on another fallen log. I wandered over to them.

"I'm sorry about Ron. I want you to know that I appreciate your efforts—you're doing great." I wasn't sure what to say. They had been ordered to come with me, so it wasn't exactly like they had volunteered for this mission. But then again, this was their job. There was a fine line to walk when discussing the death of a guard member with his companions.

Sandra and the others immediately were on their feet, bowing to me.

"Thank you, Your Highness."

I realized then that they were not my friends. I was their princess, and I couldn't just sit down and mourn Ron's death with them. That was their place, and they needed me to leave them alone to do so. "I just wanted you to know, Ron's death won't be forgotten." And then, before they could answer, I returned to Trillian and Shade, settling down beside them.

"You can't hang with the boys now, Menolly." Trillian spoke softly, making sure his words did not carry. "You belong to royalty. You can't go out there and be just a regular guy . . . woman . . . vampire, again. Even in your bar, you're going to have to pull back a bit. I hate to break it to you, but everything changed the moment you put on that crown."

"I'm just beginning to understand how much." My mood fell as the weight of what I had taken on began to hit home. But nothing mattered so much as finding my wife, safe and alive. "As long as we can find Nerissa, I can handle anything. Even if it means I have to hand over running the bar to Derrick." I paused, then asked, "And you . . . how will you feel living out at Talamh Lonrach Oll, when your wife becomes the new Queen of Dusk and Twilight?"

Trillian shrugged. "I've lived many places in my life. I enjoy living in the house with everyone else, but truth be told, the thought of moving? As long as I'm with Camille? I don't care whether we go back to Otherworld, or stay Earthside. Houses come and go. Love is what lasts."

Shade frowned. "Delilah's having a hard time, but I'm hoping to be able to help her move through the fear of change. Because change will come as it will, and there's nothing we can do to prevent it. In fact, try to stop it and you trip over the turning wheels."

"Ain't that the truth." I flashed him a weary grin. "I discovered that one the hard way. Kitten has never had an easy time with change. She's a cat—and cats like their routines. I remember once, when we were little girls—it was shortly after Mother died—Camille decided that we were going to change what we usually ate for breakfast. We had been having porridge since we were babies. But Camille said that Father had ordered her to switch us over to 'grown-up' breakfasts. So we moved to eggs and ham and crusty bread. Delilah threw a fit. She went on a hunger strike."

"I'll bet that lasted a good hour." Shade laughed.

I nodded. "All of one day, actually. But every morning for a week she cried. She wanted her porridge. We finally figured out that it reminded her of Mother giving us breakfast. She was terrified Mother's spirit would be angry with her for 'forgetting' her. Once we calmed her down and helped her understand that she wasn't betraying Mother's memory by eating her eggs and ham, she was fine with it. Sometimes it just takes a change of perspective to be able to accept life's vagaries."

And even as I spoke, I realized that I needed to pay attention to my own words. And perhaps bring the thought up that everything was going to be all right—that we needed to move on with our lives, and that nothing could tear us apart.

"I'll have a talk with Kitten when we get home. She'll listen to me, and to Camille. We can set her mind at ease. Plus, when she marries you, I imagine things will change for her. She'll see that she's moving on, too. Once she realizes that she's not being left behind, that we're not running away from each other but rather to the next stage in our lives, I think she'll be okay."

Shade reached out and took my hand. "Thank you, Menolly. I'm grateful to have you and Camille as sisters-in-laws. I love Delilah, in a way I never expected to love anybody. When the Autumn Lord assigned me to her . . . I was a dutiful servant, yes, but not sure what to expect. Then I saw her—long before she ever knew me—and was struck by how strong she was even through the vulnerability."

"She's always had a certain naïveté." I shrugged. "It's her Achilles heel, as well as a charm."

"That's not what drew me in. I'm not fond of weak women, but I saw what your sister could become. I see what she *will* become, and I'm grateful she's able to keep her essential self while she evolves. She's good, and kind, and loving. And she'll put her life on the line for those she cares about. Those qualities . . . those are why I love her. Not her looks—though she is beautiful to me. Not the little girl. I love the woman who can calmly fight off a horde of zombies, and then turn around and coo over a bunny rabbit."

Trytian and Vanzir joined us at that moment.

"I'm sorry about your man—Ron, was it?" Trytian shrugged. "There's never a good way to lose someone. But I couldn't let you try to rescue him. It would have been far too dangerous, and vampire or not, he was already dead."

"I'm grateful you made that clear. It allowed his companions peace of mind. And here, I think that is something that is hard fought for, and hard won." I shivered. The starkness of this realm—the harshness—was burning itself into my psyche with every move we made. There would be no joy here, not the joy that felt clear and pure. The Sub-Realms were as tainted a place as I'd ever experienced, and I had no desire to ever come back.

"Stay here too long, and you lose your soul," Vanzir whispered. "I am still trying to regain mine."

"I think Aeval will help you with that." Trillian pushed himself to his feet and stretched.

"I hope you're right."

Trytian cleared his throat. "We should move onward, if you've had enough chance to rest."

We were all good to go, so we began the march deeper into the forest. The trees were dark here; they had taken on the sheen of granite, though I realized they were actually fossilized wood. But they were misshapen, bent and twisted, and without any greenery, they appeared like creatures out of some nightmare realm, ancient beings that perhaps moved so slowly no one ever noticed until one day, they had crept out of the forest to right below the window and were brushing against the glass.

I wondered—the trees over Earthside, and in Otherworld all had sentience of some sort; they had a form of consciousness that witches like Camille could sense and sometimes tap into. Did the petrified trees still retain what consciousness they had once had? And if so, did they have any conscience to go along with it? Or did they seethe, slowly festering anger at the demons who wandered this realm, destroying the land and blighting everything they touched?

The walk through the forest was easy going, comparatively, but we would have been lost without Trytian to pave the way. He seemed to have an instinctive knowledge of which way and where to turn, though I could see no noticeable landmarks. I had no idea how much time was passing. I wasn't tired; there was no pull of the sunrise to drag me down into sleep. Which raised the question: Did the vampires here walk the world day and night, unending, never resting? And if so, was that how they grew so terribly strong?

These thoughts, and others, flitted through my mind as we hiked through the petrified forest. We were silent, because who knew what ears might be hiding behind the stone trees? But after a while, Trytian held up his hand. He motioned up ahead, and I noticed that the wood seemed to be thinning out. We were near the opening.

He motioned for everyone to huddle close. "We are near the exit to the forest. When we come out, a short quarter mile to the left will take us to one of Shadow Wing's encampments. He is not there, but the place is overrun with his demons. The path to the right leads to the detention center, and that is where they took Nerissa. I can't be sure she's still there, but I would guess she is. We'll have to be cautious from here on out, to avoid attention. We do not want to take on the encampment. There are far too many demons for us to handle. I will lead us a roundabout way and we will skirt the path, keeping to the outcroppings of stone and scrub that border the area. Follow my orders. Do not diverge from them, or you will bring the entire encampment down on us and we might as well slit our throats before they catch us. Do you understand?"

Everyone nodded.

"What happens when we get to the detention center?" I prayed that my wife was all right and that she was still there.

"We break in, however we see best, and hope we manage through. Then we run like hell back to the stone forest. There, we keep a move on until we make it back to the Demon Gate. I hope you aren't tired because there will be no rest until we manage through. We don't have that luxury. So . . . are you ready?" He glanced at each of us, and we nodded in turn.

"Then let's go rescue your wife." And with that, we headed out of the frying pan into the heart of the fire.

Chapter 18

As we came out of the forest, I wasn't sure what to expect, but I was surprised to see some actual living vegetation, though it was scrub brush like that found in a lot of desert places. The soil was hard, and the stone outcroppings were back, but they were even more weathered down, to the size of giant red boulders rather than true hoodoos.

A sense of activity filled the air, compared to the dead silence of the forest. There were creatures here, Demonkin, and even though we could neither see nor hear them, I knew they were out there. Part of me wanted to charge ahead, to race on and find Nerissa regardless of the cost. But I reined myself in. I would only hurt our chances if I ran off half-cocked. I had promised Trytian that I would follow his orders and I was intent on keeping that promise.

Trytian paused, as if listening, then nodded for us to follow him. We hunched, racing low to the ground, from the edge of the petrified forest over to the first big boulder. Part of me felt like we were in some oddball sci-fi action movie, on an alien planet, trying to keep hidden from the terrifying inhabitants of the new world. But I wasn't laughing. Because if the Demonkin caught us, we were dead meat.

The boulder was a good ten feet in diameter, and smooth, as if it had been worn down over the years by a million footsteps crossing its path. We crouched behind it for a moment as Trytian edged out, gauging whether the way was clear. And then on to the next one, which wasn't *on* the path, but next to it. We darted from rock to rock, ringing the outside of the path, and I began to notice more dry clumps of long, spiky grasses as we went. The bushes were frequent, and I could smell the foliage now. The lack of greenery made what little was around stand out. The scent wasn't unpleasant, a slightly pungent, dusky smell, like old bitter herbs.

I wondered what the scrub brush was, but my alarm bells were ringing and I knew better than to ask any unnecessary questions. We were four boulders over from the first, and Trytian suddenly froze, motioning for us to get down. We crouched in the shadow of the rock, waiting, as the sound of marching feet echoed toward us. I wanted to see what was coming along the path, but kept still—freezing into position. Demonkin had senses very different than ours, and some of them were all too astute when it came to nuances in sound or motion.

The marching grew louder, dozens of feet stomping in unison, as a cloud of dust rose up from their passing. It filtered through the air to us, and Trillian and Shade very quietly covered their noses and eyes. I realized they were trying to prevent any sneezes from happening. Another few minutes, and the marching began to fade, and then, in a little while, it vanished into the petrified forest.

Trytian slumped against the rock, Lokail beside him. He caught my gaze and—for one of the first times since we'd met him here—smiled at me. With a weary shrug, he motioned for us to follow him into the thicket of scrub brush, and before long, we were around the back side of a hill, away from the path, skirting the area.

* * *

We threaded our way through the scrub, stopping more often than we wanted. The detention center wasn't that far away from the petrified forest, but going the long way around was tedious and every moment we had to freeze, thinking some sound was coming our way, was another moment that I found it harder not to just rush in like some fool.

Finally, we reached a point where Trytian motioned for me to come up beside Lokail and him. He nodded ahead, and I saw it. There, about three hundred feet away, beyond a patch of yellowed, spiky grass, was a building. It was carved from red stone and reminded me of an adobe structure, squat, with a flat roof. It wasn't altogether large, so unless it had an underground section, it shouldn't take us long to search. The main problem that I could see from here was the three guards standing atop the roof, holding bows and arrows.

Trytian waved me silent when I started to open my mouth. He motioned to two of his buddies from the back, who moved up beside him, and pointed to the guards on top of the building. They nodded and—as they moved out from behind the scrub brush—they shimmered and all I could see was a faint wave in the air where they were. The ripples in the air began to move, and I realized the daemons were on the move.

A blur, a ripple, a wave . . . that was all we could see as they moved ahead toward the building. Trillian and Shade watched over my shoulder, both looking fascinated. Whatever race of daemons they were, I had never heard of them before, and I had the feeling neither had either of my companions. Vanzir, however, just shrugged when I glanced his way.

There was a faint ripple against the side of the structure and the next moment, the daemons scaled the wall and appeared on the roof of the building, immediately attacking the guards. The moment they attacked, they appeared in full form again. But they were unevenly matched—whatever demons were atop that structure were strong as hell.

Our men managed to bring down one of them, and then a second, but then it was one-on-one as the remaining demon skewered one of our guys and he fell. The guard was shouting something when—the next moment—he had no head. The head rolled off as the daemon brought his short sword straight across in a blow that looked strong enough to slice wood.

Trytian shrugged. "We're in for a pound . . . that cry was bound to alert others." And he was off and running.

I leaped to my feet, fast on his heels, and the others were only seconds behind me. We sprinted the stretch, then were suddenly at the building. The door was nearest me and I didn't wait but yanked it open, too worried they would kill Nerissa if they knew we were coming.

The inner chamber was dim, lit by a couple of lanterns. I darted in, followed by Trytian and Shade. The others were only seconds behind us.

Inside, I was surprised that there wasn't a contingent waiting. But then I stopped, skidding to a quick halt. Four demons stood there—I wasn't sure what kind but one was a Tregart. The other three were also human-looking, but I knew better than to let that fool me. And around their necks, they each wore a pendant. *The spirit seals.* Four of them.

Trillian skidded to a halt behind me. He must have noticed right off, because he let out a slow whisper. "The spirit seals."

I glanced around, frantic.

In the corner, in a cage behind iron bars, sat Nerissa, staring at the floor. She jerked her head up at the commotion and when she saw me, she let out a strangled note and rushed forward to the bars, grabbing hold of them and shaking them. Her eyes were wild and I realized that her inner puma was feeling trapped, captive in a way that a non-Were would never understand. Her hair was stringy, hanging down in mats, and she looked like she'd been dragged through the mud and back again.

At that moment, Jorge screamed and I whirled around, startled out of my fixation. I was just in time to see him turn to dust in front of my eyes, at the end of a stake wielded by one of the demons. Another scream, and Sandra vanished.

I sprang toward them, but Shade grabbed my arm. "Be cautious, they have stakes. Let us go in first. You work on that cage." His eyes were blazing and he let out a roar and moved toward the demons, along with Vanzir and Trillian.

Trytian was busy blocking the door, and the two remaining daemons with him were joining the guys. I raced toward the cage, leaning my ax against the side of it. The sight of my wife, trapped and wild-eyed, triggered me, and I grabbed the bars and began to bend them, slowly working the metal with as much force as I could. My hands were burning—the part of me that was Fae still reacted to iron, but I would heal. Nerissa began to calm down, though she hadn't said anything yet. But another scream chilled me to the bone. I glanced over my shoulder. Tico was gone. That left Jacob. And one of Trytian's comrades had also fallen, which left Lokail, one other daemon, the guys, and me. We were rapidly losing our forces.

"Go, help them!" Nerissa finally found her tongue.

Grabbing up my ax, I let go of the cage and headed over to the nearest demon.

He was wearing a brilliant ruby—the spirit seal that I recognized from our fight with Karvanak, the Rāksasa. And he *wasn't* carrying a stake. He was fighting Trillian, wielding a nasty-looking sword against Trillian's slim but lethal silver blade. The demon was winning, driving Trillian back toward the wall, the spirit seal giving him a tremendous amount of skill. But there was something off about his movements, even though his strength seemed greater, and I realized he wasn't quite in alignment—almost as though he was blurred, out of sync.

The spirit seal isn't meshing with his energy—that has to be it!

As I swung in behind him, he suddenly realized I was taking aim, but it was too late. I raised my ax high over my head and brought it down to bear right on his back, cleaving the blade in between his shoulders. He let out an unholy scream and almost yanked the ax out of my hand as he turned, blood spraying Trillian. I managed to keep hold of the hilt, dislodging it from his flesh and swinging it again.

He lunged forward, all semblance of skill vanishing as a look of panic spread on his face. I still had no idea of what kind of demon he was, but he let out a garbled screech—I had no doubt it was some sort of curse—and swung his sword hard. I danced to the side as my ax met his blade, cleaving the sword in two. But I had been so vigorous in my attack that my battle-ax—not meeting flesh or something more solid to dig into—continued its motion, lodging firmly in the stone floor.

The demon stabbed at me with the broken sword, clipping my arm, hard. It couldn't really penetrate the way it would have with the tip, but it sliced through the jacket, gashing my arm deep. Thankfully, it didn't sever it, and so I yanked the ax out of the stone and, one-handedly, brought it sideways, biting deep into my opponent's side.

At that moment, Trillian attacked from the back, the thin tip of his sword skewering through the demon's chest to spit him like a chicken over a rotisserie. Between our combined attacks, the demon wavered, tried to clutch at the spirit seal but failed, and then toppled forward.

I glanced over to see Shade and Vanzir working on the guard next to us, so I darted forward, grabbed up the spirit seal from the fallen demon, and thrust it into my pocket. A surge of energy raced through me and I was startled to see the wound on my arm begin to heal up. I healed fast—vampires always did—but this was definitely quicker than usual.

Jacob and Lokail were fighting the third guard. Trillian had moved on to help Trytian, who—with the remaining daemon—was working on the fourth guard. I decided that Jacob and Lokail needed my help the most, and I was right, because at that moment, the demon skewered Jacob through the heart and he vanished.

"That does it . . . I'm done with this shit."

I slid in beside Lokail, who was grimly hacking away with his sword, and began to repeatedly batter the demon with one quick blow after another. That gave Lokail the chance to slip around behind him and slice him between the ribs.

The demon—this was the Tregart—blinked in surprise, right before I brought the ax down on his head. Wincing—brain matter is ugly no matter who you are, unless you're a zombie and then it's lunch—I jumped back out of the way as the Tregart face-planted in front of me. I motioned for Lokail to go help the others while I retrieved the spirit seal from the dead demon's neck. *Emerald. The first seal we had found.* Shadow Wing had stolen it from us when he killed Tom Lane. Somberly thinking about Titania's fallen lover, I quietly slipped the seal in my pocket with the other and zipped it shut.

Shade and Vanzir had taken down their opponent and tossed me the smoky quartz necklace. But Trytian and Trillian were having a hard time with theirs. We couldn't all fight him at once, there wasn't room, so I went back to breaking Nerissa out of the cell. I had just managed to bend the bars far enough apart for her to climb through when there was a short, harsh scream, and a roar. I whirled around just in time to see Lokail go flying across the room—without a head.

The demon was no longer in human form, but where he had stood, there was now a massive hydra with four heads. The chain holding the spirit seal had snapped as he transformed, apparently, because I saw the amethyst pendant fly through the air to fall next to me. I snatched it up, stuffing it in my pocket with the others.

"Let's get the fuck out of here!" Trytian shoved Trillian toward the door. "We can't fight a hydra."

"I can." Shade moved back and the next moment was transforming into his dragon self. The rest of us ran for the door.

As we burst out of the complex, I frantically looked around for any more demons, but the rest seemed to have marched off with the contingent we had seen leave. Frantic, I grabbed Nerissa's wrist and we made for the cover of the scrub. As we reached the first massive, sprawling tree, we turned to see the two monsters breaking through the roof, locked in combat.

"Damn Shade, we could be off and going now if he hadn't decided to stay and duke it out." I was furious. We needed to get the hell out of Dodge, and there wasn't room to play hero here. It wasn't like they wouldn't figure out who had gutted the complex.

"Get moving." Trytian pushed me forward.

"But Shade—"

"Move. You remember the route, I'll bring up the rear."

Trillian gave me a grim jerk of the head. "He's right. Get a move on. Vanzir, go with them. I'll fall back with Trytian."

I realized Nerissa was barefoot. I wanted to give her my shoes, but that wasn't possible—she couldn't fit in my boots and that would hurt worse than the desert floor. But I motioned to Vanzir. "Your shirt. Tear it so she can tie the rags around her feet and have some protection."

"No, I've got a better solution." Nerissa stepped back and—in a shimmer—changed into her puma self. She started loping along beside me, sleek and confident.

We headed out. I didn't want to leave Shade, but then a moment later there was a great shaking of the ground and we turned to see Shade swooping in behind us. The hydra had fallen. Shade landed beside us and I realized what he was up to.

"Climb on his back. We can make better time back to the gate this way. Nerissa—change back."

"We'll be noticed by everyone and everything in the area." Trytian frowned.

"Like word isn't going to get out about what just went down? This way they may not have time to catch us. Hurry up!"

I hoisted Nerissa up onto Shade's back, then climbed astride the skeletal dragon's vertebrae. Within seconds, Trillian, Vanzir, and Trytian joined us. Shade took off, a bumpy takeoff for sure, but we were airborne and aimed directly for the forest. We swept overhead and from the air, I realized just how dangerous a labyrinth the forest was—even as clear of undergrowth as the petrified trees were, the chances of getting lost were incredibly high. The forest stretched on east and west for miles.

We flew over the soldiers below and, without being asked, Shade dove lower and strafed them with dragonfire. Screams rose as we passed by, and I didn't see how deadly the attack had been, but that pretty much guaranteed Shadow Wing would remember us with none too fond a thought.

We came to the Plain of Winds and the ride grew very bumpy. Nerissa leaned forward, and I pressed against her, trying to keep our balance as the gusts landed like walloping fists, ever-shifting. The next moment, we were in the Ionyc Seas. Dizzy from the ride and the winds, and now the currents of the sea, I let out a groan, but within moments, it seemed, we were out again, and we were over the hoodoos. There was one place near the Demon Gate that seemed big enough for Shade to land, and so he did. As we staggered off his back, stumbling around like we were all drunk, Shade shifted back into his natural form.

"Damn, that was one hell of a ride." Even Trytian was reeling.

"Let's get through that damned gate. Remember, if I immediately fall asleep, just arrange me on the table until nightfall." And with that, I grabbed Nerissa, who looked dazed and exhausted, and headed over to the Demon Gate, never so happy to see a portal in my life.

One by one, we stepped through. And as the burning pain hit, I welcomed it in. Because I had Nerissa with me, she was alive, and we had managed to survive the Sub-Realms.

As I opened my eyes, after the first fury of waking subsided, I realized I was, indeed, lying on the table in Wilbur's workroom. But Trytian, Trillian, Nerissa, Shade, and Vanzir were there—along with Wilbur, and none of them looked like they'd bothered to clean up. None of them were near enough for me to attack them, either.

Wilbur snorted. "Good aim, Dead Girl. You picked three minutes before sunset to return. So you've had the shortest nap in vampire history."

I blinked. I actually did feel exhausted, and the weight of the trip hit me full force. "I kind of wish we had returned at sunrise so I could sleep it off."

"You want I should create another Demon Gate for you to go through so you can come back in a while?" But the mountain man necromancer was laughing, and his eyes crinkled as he smiled softly. "I destroyed the other the moment I realized you were all back . . . well, those who made it."

He paused, and I realized that he was talking about the five vamps I had taken with me. "We lost our men and Trytian lost his forces, too." I turned to the daemon. "I owe you one. A big one."

Trytian, for once, just shrugged. "No, you don't. We're in this together, and because of your mission, you managed to deal a heavy blow to Shadow Wing—one that will help us tremendously. I have to return to my father and tell him."

And then I realized what he was talking about. I had a pocket full of spirit seals. Shadow Wing was left with *none* of them. The swirling energy suddenly surged through my body, even though I wasn't wearing them, and my fatigue dropped away.

I sat up, cautiously. "Yeah, you're right. Come on over to our house. We need to talk about this—all of us—and what it means. And Camille needs to . . . put these into hiding."

Wilbur came with us; it only seemed right, given we had yanked him into our service again, and we headed across the street to our house. As we walked, I pulled Nerissa off to the side a little.

"How are you? Did they do . . . did they hurt you?"

She shook her head. "Not really. Oh, I'm terribly hungry and thirsty. But they were definitely using me for bait. And as far as I could tell, the demons wearing the spirit seals were there, waiting to take possession of the ones they expected you guys to bring to them. Shadow Wing must truly be off his nut if he thinks you'd trade them for me."

I wasn't sure what to say. How do you tell your loved one that you wouldn't have bargained for her life because the price was too high? But Nerissa said it for me.

"I'm . . . listen. I'm so grateful to be alive, and back with you. But thank you for not doing as they asked. I had prepared myself to die. There's no way we could ever give Shadow Wing the spirit seals and hope to keep him from destroying everything. I guess what I'm saying is that I didn't expect you to come for me, and I would have understood if you hadn't.

I thought . . . I thought I heard Camille calling, but I guess that was my imagination."

I smiled softly. "No, she was searching for you. We had to do something. But you're right—in a war, you don't hand over the ultimate weapon to your enemy to save a life." I kissed her then, softly, on the cheek. We'd have our time later, but for now, we still had work to do.

Trytian left us by the door. "I need to get to the Demon Underground. I have to get back to the Sub-Realms and let my father know I'm alive and tell him of our victory. This is a huge blow to Shadow Wing, but you know he's going to go ballistic. Be cautious. I'll be in touch as soon as I know anything more about what he's planning. I think now is a good time for my father's army to strike."

He took off into the night. I found myself hoping we'd see him again, hoping he would make it through the war. If he and his father could take over in the Sub-Realms, maybe we'd have some chance of forging a treaty with them—some possibility of peace.

The moment we opened the door, the household was in an uproar. Camille and Delilah dragged us into the living room, and Hanna immediately began clanging the pots and pans in the kitchen. We were probably going to be facing a feast—or rather the others would.

Shade let out a long whistle. "We're exhausted, dirty, hungry, and thirsty. Let us have a chance to wash up first, please, before we go into details. Nerissa's all right, given the circumstances, so give us a little breathing room." He laughed, but I had the feeling he was one step short of barking orders. The fight with the hydra seemed to have set him on edge. But then again, the whole experience had set me on edge.

They backed off, and I sent Nerissa down to bathe, while I motioned for Delilah, Camille, and Smoky to follow me into the parlor. I closed the door behind me and turned to them.

"While we're cleaning up, you have to get these to the Dragon Reaches. Smoky, you and Camille need to travel there tonight. *Now.* We can't chance losing them again. Even now, Shadow Wing will be raging, trying to plan his next move against us."

As I spoke, I unzipped my pocket and withdrew the four spirit seals. They hummed in my hands, their proximity to one another making them practically vibrate. As I laid them in Camille's hands, she gasped. Delilah let out a shout and so did Smoky.

"Shadow Wing had his faux knights guarding Nerissa. We had one hell of a battle, and we lost all five of my vamps, and all of Trytian's comrades. It was touch and go there at the end." I softly stepped back. "Take these now—please. Don't wait. We've dealt Shadow Wing two horrible blows in the past few days and he's already unhinged. The Unraveller is going to be after us now with everything he's got."

"But now that we have all the spirit seals—well, except for the final one that still remains hidden—can't we just assume he's locked up for good again?" Delilah frowned, staring at the seals like they were ticking time bombs.

I shook my head. "No, because the portals are still breaking down, and because now he'll have revenge in his heart. We can't let down our guard."

"Our next step is to find the final seal and the Keraastar Diamond. Then I can create the Keraastar Knights and bring them together to fully destroy Shadow Wing. But I have to take the throne first—and that will happen next month, during Litha. The Summer Solstice is going to be one hell of a show, that's for sure." Camille glanced up at Smoky. "She's right. We need to get these to the Dragon Reaches now. Your mother is a secure guardian."

He nodded. "True. Get changed for the climate, while we guard these. I don't want to take any chances, not even here in the heart of our home. Not with four spirit seals in our hands."

Camille headed off, stopping to give me a kiss on the cheek. "I'm so happy Nerissa is home, love. Take care of her. Even if they didn't hurt her, the Sub-Realms . . . I can see it in your eyes. There are places our kind should never go, places that scald the soul."

I nodded. "Too true."

As she closed the door behind her, I gazed over at Delilah, remembering what Shade and I had talked about. "Kitten, come over with me by the fireplace. Smoky, can you . . . well . . . just give us a minute."

He nodded, moving to the corner of the room where he sat in one of the overstuffed armchairs, staring at the pendants in his hand.

Delilah frowned. "What's wrong?"

"Nothing . . . not really. I just . . . I wanted to talk to you about something that I thought of when I was in the Sub-Realms."

"What's it like there?"

I shivered. "Harsher than you could dream. Harsher than any place has a right to be. There is no softness there, no gentleness. Kitten, just being there reminded me of why we fight against Shadow Wing." I drew her down on the sofa. "Listen, I was thinking . . . while we were trudging through a forest of stone, about when we were kids. About when you thought you would be dishonoring Mother's memory if you ate eggs and ham instead of porridge for breakfast."

She tilted her head to one side. "What a curious memory to crop up while you were there."

"I know." I didn't want to tell her what Shade had said to me. She might think he didn't have faith in her. "But it made me think . . . it's going to be hard when Nerissa and I move in with Roman. And then, Camille moves to Talamh Lonrach Oll next month. You realize this will be the first time we've ever lived apart? I guess it just hit me while I was over there, how we're all going our separate ways."

She smiled softly. "Shade's worried about me, isn't he? He asked you to talk to me?"

I sputtered, but she shook her head and took my hand. "I know him—this has *concerned fiancé* written all over it. And it's okay. *Really.* I'm glad he cares enough about me to worry. But I think . . . I think the little kitten who, when we first came Earthside, would have been terrified to face this day, has grown up now. I'm ready to face what life has to offer. This last bout of training, to gain a handle over seeing the dead and talking to them? Has made me aware of how many stages of life there are. And it made me see how fear can trap us. I don't want to be like one of those ghosts—trapped because I'm afraid to face the fact that life is moving on."

Relieved, and yet a little bit surprised, I squeezed her hand. "Yeah, I guess, me, too. I think it's time we grew up. We need each other—we always will. Yet it's like we woke up one day, looked around, and life stood there saying, *Are you ready? Are you ready to face the next phase?* We have to say yes, or we get stuck—like your ghosts."

"Exactly. And Camille needs to know we're okay with this. She's been mother to us for so many years now, but it's time we helped her realize she can let that job go now. She's becoming a queen. She'll have bigger things to worry about than us. So I'll tell Shade that he doesn't have to worry about me. Yes, I'm sad the three of us won't be living together, but I'm ready to get married. I'm ready for whatever my destiny has in store for me. And you—you're a princess now." She grinned. "Are you going to wear pink, and a diamond tiara all the time?"

I smacked her playfully. "Dork." Then, planting a kiss on her cheek, I shook my head. "Queens. Princesses. And a Death Maiden? Who would have thought it would come to this?"

At that moment, Camille entered the room, dressed for the journey to the Dragon Reaches. "I'm ready. Let's head out and get those babies to safety."

She kissed us, and then, tucking the spirit seals safely into her pocket, she stepped into Smoky's embrace, and they shimmered out of sight, into the Ionyc Seas.

Chapter 19

Nothing ever seems to get back to normal after a major shift. You find the new normal and go from there. After Camille and Smoky headed to the Dragon Reaches, I took a long, well-deserved shower, and then we gathered in the living room and told everybody else what had happened. I called Roman to tell him the news, and by the time the evening was in full swing, Nerissa had crashed, asleep in the rocking chair, and Trillian and Vanzir were dozing in the parlor. Nobody wanted to leave, though. We all seemed to want to stick together for the moment, enjoying the sensation of safety.

Over the next few days, we were still sorting out the aftermath. Tanne and Iris shut down every rogue portal they could find. The dragons sent their Builders to Elqaneve and the rebuilding began in earnest. Y'Elestrial contacted us, stating that—in no uncertain terms—we were expected to come home for a celebration where we, along with the dragons, would be honored for defeating Telazhar. Camille was out at Talamh Lonrach Oll a lot, deciding on how to decorate the Barrow she would be living in. And Nerissa and I toured the suite we would be living in over at Roman's and began making decisions on décor.

About a week after we had rescued Nerissa, Trytian reappeared and the three of us met him at Carter's in the evening. The weather was starting to turn toward true spring, and the temperature was balmy. After the barrenness of the Sub-Realms, I would never again fail to appreciate how much I loved both Otherworld and Earthside.

Carter welcomed us in, with the usual array of refreshments. Trytian was wearing some bright shiny new medal, and this time he didn't glom onto Camille. At least, not quite so much.

"My father sends you all his best. To be honest, he was put out with me for not latching onto the spirit seals myself, but I think even he realizes they're far too dangerous in the hands of the likes of us. He's grateful that Shadow Wing no longer has them, however, and not only did I get a promotion, but he sends you this." He handed us a thin sheet of paper.

I stared at it. Spells could have a way of triggering if they were written on paper and then opened by the target. But Camille reached out and took it, opening it without hesitation. She scanned the paper, then let out a gentle sigh.

"Thank your father for us. We will keep this with gratitude." She handed the paper to me.

I scanned it. Trytian's father had put into writing that he owed us a debt and we could call on him at any time, and he would be bound to help us. It was kind of like someone handing you a blank check. You don't cash it until you really need it.

"How is Shadow Wing doing? Any news on that front?" We hadn't heard a word in the past week, and I almost didn't want to know. But better to face your enemy head on and know what they're up to than to find them creeping around your back in the middle of the night.

"He's gone over the edge. We drove our forces in and cut down a huge swath of demons, but we couldn't find him. When he found out you reclaimed the spirit seals and destroyed his faux knights, he lost it. There are deserters right and left signing up with us. Hell, if he keeps this up, maybe his own men will do the trick and destroy him for us, but I wouldn't bet on it. Shadow Wing is smart and he's also in a full-on rage, never a good combination. But we're still pushing on, taking out as many of his demons as we can find."

"Shadow Wing won't let it rest—not as long as we're alive. At some point, we have to face him and take him down, or we'll live the rest of our lives in fear." Camille leaned back, crossing her legs. "We can't be looking over our shoulders the rest of our lives, wondering if he's going to pop up like the bogeyman." She paused, then said, "Do you think we should take the fight to him? To the Sub-Realms?"

Trytian and I shook our heads at the same time.

"No, you don't want to go down there. We have to find another way to dispatch him. I've been thinking about that, by the way. If we could find some sorcerer powerful enough, maybe he could directly gate Shadow Wing here, and we could destroy him when he showed up?" It sounded insane, but then again, we'd seen enough things that would be considered nuts that I decided to throw the idea out there.

Everybody stared at me like I had lost my mind, but then Delilah cocked her head. "Well, it might work. We could bring everybody and everything we have to bear on him."

"What do you think?" I turned to Camille.

"You're fucking nuts. But even if it might work, there's no way we are ready for that. For one thing, the Keraastar Knights play a big role in his demise according to the prophecy, so I need to find that last spirit seal and then train them. Put the idea on the back burner. If Trytian and his father's army can keep Shadow Wing occupied till then, your idea just might have a chance." She looked over at Carter. "What do you think?"

"I think that if you plan it out, you may succeed." The demigod shrugged, his horns gleaming in the dim light. "It's something to work toward. And it's a better idea than going to his home turf to attack him. Meanwhile, I'll put out feelers for any sorcerer I can find who could handle gating over a Demon Lord."

"You do know that if things go wrong, you'll have

unleashed a horrendous force Earthside." Trytian's voice was soft but firm.

I held his gaze. "Yes, but he won't have his armies with him, and if we destroy the Demon Gate the moment he comes through, then they won't have a chance to follow him. I have to ask, though, that you don't tell your father or *anybody* about this plan. If somehow the demons find out about it, they might be able to plan ahead and find a way to wrest the advantage away from us."

Trytian shrugged. "I'll give you that one free and not even force you to call in your favor."

"So, we have a plan of sorts . . . I guess, the next thing, we find that last spirit seal. Carter, keep your ears peeled for its whereabouts." I gazed at my goblet of blood. We had a plan all right, and maybe—just maybe—for once we had a leg up on the Demon Lord.

The trip to Otherworld was coming up, and Chase was a bundle of nerves.

"I can't believe I'm finally going to see Sharah." He had Astrid with him, and for the first time in a long time, the detective seemed truly happy. We were all going, for a change, leaving a strong contingent of guards from Talamh Lonrach Oll to guard the house. Hanna would stay home with Maggie, and the Duchess was here to watch the twins, but everybody else was going with us.

The woodland near our house—about five minutes away by car—crackled with magic. The trail through the undergrowth and trees had at first been difficult to navigate, but over the years, Grandmother Coyote had given us permission to create a path, narrow but accessible. We wound through cedar and fir, through bracken and huckleberry and the stinging nettles that grew like tenacious warriors, barbed and ready to welt their adversaries.

The forest was alive here—awake. Even I could feel that, and as we exited the trees and entered the circular grove where Grandmother Coyote made her home, the grass seemed to let out a long sigh. The lea that nestled in the circle of cedar and fir and oak shimmered, even though we were near the dark moon, and Grandmother Coyote stepped out from the other side of the glade. Her robes were gray-green, shrouding her body and head, but her hair peeked out from the sides of her hood, brilliant white in the evening dusk.

As Grandmother Coyote stared at our group, she let out a cackle.

"How far you have come since that first meeting, girl." She turned to Camille. "How far you have all come." Cloaked in gray, the Hag of Fate was old as the hills, old as the planet and beyond. Her face was a map of the roads she had followed, her eyes mirrored the eons she had seen, and her teeth were steel sharp in her mouth. The Hags of Fate lived outside of time, and they were bound to all realms. Immortal—only the Hags of Fate, the Harvestmen, and the Elemental Lords could claim true immortality—they were beyond the reach of all charm, all magic, every transition the planet watched go by. They were unchanging in a world of change, weaving the threads of fate and destiny without care, without opinion, without judgment.

Camille nodded. "It seems like so long ago and yet . . . and yet . . . we still have so far to go. I hope you don't mind us traipsing through your portal."

"That's what it's here for." As the old woman stepped back, we filed through toward the portal in between the tree trunks. I glanced back at the group.

Chase was here with Astrid, and Iris and Bruce. Trillian, Morio, Smoky, and Shade stood behind them. Nerissa was by their side. And Rozurial and Vanzir were also with us. We neared the portal, and then, with me leading the way, Delilah and Camille and I walked through together, back home, back to where we had started our journey.

The Barrow Mounds of Elqaneve were busy with activity. Gone were the massive number of armed guards, and the reason was obvious when we saw a couple of dragons circling the skies. Carriages were there to take us into the city, and as we climbed in, everywhere were signs of activity. Men, though we had no idea if they really were men or dragons, were thick along the roads, rebuilding the cottages and houses that had been destroyed. Signs of life were springing up, and gone were the straggling nomads who had been displaced. I squinted; in the late-evening dusk, I could see what looked like a refugee camp, but it looked neat and tidy and people were sitting around eating dinner rather than staring forlornly at the road.

One of our escorts turned to me, his eyes bright. The elf had a look in his eyes that I had not seen for some time from a member of the Elfin race. *Hope.*

"The dragons sent the Builders, as they call them. I'm not sure what race they are—and we do not ask. But they have taken over and are quickly rebuilding across the land. I don't know how many of them there are, but they seem to be everywhere, and the dragons themselves are guarding our lands from the skies while our capital city is being restored. I think a new age of alliance has been formed between the Elfin race and the Dragonkin."

There was a lot to rebuild, and a lot of lives had been lost, but now they had some semblance of a future. We rode in silence the rest of the way until we reached Elqaneve. The grounds around the palace were in the same state of busy-ness, and all the rubble had been cleared and marble walls were once again beginning to rise from the foundation of the palace. Off to one side, a temporary courtyard had been erected, and as we clambered out of the carriages, Chase let out a cry and raced forward, Iris following behind him carrying Astrid. Sharah was standing there and she forgot her crown, forgot her royal dignity, and launched herself into his arms. As they held one another, Trenyth approached, but then he stopped and walked away, giving them the moment they so needed.

Trenyth listened to our story, then settled back. "So, we have hope once again. Just make certain when you find the last spirit seal, do not fit all of them together or you will rip open the realms, and that would be just what Shadow Wing wants. Keep them separate in their pendants, and find the Knights who can wield them. Camille is right. She must seek out the Keraastar Diamond. Without that, you cannot hope to command the Knights to the full extent you need to."

She nodded. "I understand. Do you have any clue where to find the Diamond?"

"Pentangle would know; you are correct in that assumption. Go in search of her." He paused. "You do realize that when you are one of the Fae Queens, you will have to give over to duty more than you might wish."

"What do you mean?" Camille looked confused.

Trenyth started to say something, then just shook his head. "You will find out in due time." He looked at the three of us. "Go now, your carriages are waiting to take you to the Barrows so you can travel to Y'Elestrial. Elqaneve will send a delegation to the parade and celebration tomorrow. And I have no doubt you will find old friends waiting there for you." With that, he stood and then, in an uncharacteristic move, he quickly leaned in and kissed our foreheads, one after another. "Go in peace, girls. I wish your father could be here to see this day. You would have made him proud."

And with tears threatening all of us, we headed out the door, leaving Chase and Astrid in Elqaneve, where they would stay with Sharah for a few days.

Tanaquar—the Court and Crown of Y'Elestrial—personally oversaw the ceremonies. We had come through hell for her, for our city-state, for both our worlds. And that hell was not over, but for now, we could breathe and take a few moments to relax.

The citywide celebration was to be held at night, so I could attend.

But for now, we dodged the unofficial ceremonies and rode out to the outskirts of the city, to a house that we knew so well. As we stepped out of the carriage, our lovers by our sides, a sense of melancholy and memory swept over me.

Here, we took our first breath. Here, we grew up, fighting the prejudices against us. Here, we loved our mother and lost her. And here, we now returned.

Aunt Rythwar was waiting, looking so much like Father that Camille let out a soft cry, and Delilah burst into tears. She bundled us in and fed us—Morio had brought enchanted blood for me—and seemed to know that we needed silence more than anything. After making sure we were all settled, she vanished into her room with a flurry of kisses and promises that if we needed anything, we need only tap on her door. Our dear old cook, Leethe, was gone, of course, but Auntie's cook and housekeeper were kindly enough.

The house had been repaired from the damage it took during the civil war, and other than losing our father and Leethe, time had stood still here.

Smoky nudged Shade. "I think the girls need some time." Nerissa nodded and guided the men toward our rooms, leaving the three of us alone in the living room.

Camille swept her hand over the clock. Father had brought it from Earthside for Mother, to give her some sense of home. So many trinkets, so many memories. A crystal vase, blown by a glass smith in town, that I had bought for my mother one Yule long ago. A hand-carved whistle a relative had given to Delilah. An embroidered scarf that Camille had struggled to make, before everybody realized she had no skill with the needle and thread. Everywhere we looked, our history followed us. Everywhere we looked, we were reminded of our past.

After a moment, Camille headed for the doors to the garden and we followed her, dressed in gowns that we had long ago put away when we traveled Earthside. Camille was in a sparkling purple gown, low cut, shimmering with beads that mirrored the stars overhead. Delilah had changed into a green gown, simple and straight, with a soft gold belt tied around the waist. And I was wearing an indigo gown, velvet soft and draping like a Grecian toga.

We linked arms, strolling through the garden. The last time we had done this was the night before we went Earthside for the first time. We had come out here and talked about what our new life would hold for us. We had pictured a vacation of sorts, or perhaps exile, but we hadn't known what was in store for us. All our illusions and expectations from then had been shattered, some for the better.

"So." Camille finally spoke. "When we go back, you and Nerissa will be moving into Roman's house?"

I nodded. "He's decorating now. I let Nerissa have full rein. We both know she's better at that than I am, and as long as one of the rooms is done in green, I'll be happy."

Delilah smiled softly. "I have a wedding to plan. Shade and I want a big affair, I think. Nothing simple. Now, if I could just get Jerry Springer to preside, I'd be thrilled." She laughed. "And I promise, no Cheetos for the wedding cake."

Camille broke away and sat down on the garden bench. We joined her, the scent of roses wafting over us. Birdsong filled the evening, and the ivy along the gate row rustled with a sudden influx of moonglow moths that swept down to rest themselves under the dark moon.

"I'm scared of becoming queen. Of taking the crown. I have no idea what to expect."

"We didn't know what to expect when we moved Earthside either. You'll do fine. Aeval dotes on you, you know." I turned to her. "Did you ever dream . . ." I drifted off. The question was ridiculous, of course. None of us had ever dreamed that we'd be where we were right now.

She stared up at the sky, at the stars shimmering overhead. "Tomorrow night, they will cheer us on and hail us as heroines for bringing the dragons. I kind of wish we could duck out, ignore it and tell them just to go be good to each other and stop fighting."

"We can't, though. We're grown-ups. Princesses and queens and Death Maidens, oh my. And with all of that, we have to put up with the pomp and circumstance, and the annoying ceremonies." Even as I said the words, the weight of what we were facing hit home. I could tell they were both feeling it, because Camille leaped to her feet.

"Yes, we do. But tonight, we can just be us. Come on." And she raced out the gate, kicking off her shoes. We followed, as we had when we were children, as she led us into the meadow beyond our garden gate. As we ran through the dusk, under the silent moon, the scent of wildflowers rose to greet us and I flashed back to when we were children. But the memory vanished as Delilah took my hand, and Camille grabbed hers, and we formed a ring like we used to, careening madly through the grass, shouting and laughing like we were children.

And then, as she stood back, Delilah and I continued to dance, while Camille concentrated. The next moment, we were all hovering in the air—a few feet above the ground, laughing wildly. Of course, she couldn't hold it for long, and we went tumbling to the ground. Dizzy from the sudden burst of activity, we lay there, watching the stars as they shimmered in their vast panorama. Without the traffic and millions of lights to drown them out, they blazed overhead, gleaming like a thousand diamonds showering us with their light.

A few minutes later, we propped ourselves up on our elbows.

"I guess . . . this is really it. We aren't coming home to Otherworld to stay. Any of us." Kitten's voice quivered, and she sounded ready to cry.

"You never know what the future brings." Camille pushed herself to a sitting position and crossed her legs. "Look at where we're at now."

"She's right." I wrapped my arms around my knees, drawing them to my chest. "Unless we have some horrid accident . . . our lives have so much farther to go. How can we predict what's going to happen beyond this year or next? The Hags of Fate have a way of dipping in and changing things when you least expect it. But for now . . . we go on with our lives. I go to Roman's, Camille heads out to Talamh Lonrach Oll, and you and Shade get married. And we find Shadow Wing and defeat him for good."

And so we sat, holding hands, under the brilliant stars. Because sometimes we needed to take life one day at a time. Sometimes, we needed to slow down and dance in the meadow and watch for shooting stars with our best friends.

We needed to savor the victories, because the final battle against Shadow Wing was coming. And we needed all our reserves to face the rising storm.

CAST OF MAJOR CHARACTERS

The D'Artigo Family

Arial Lianan te Maria: Delilah's twin who died at birth. Half-Fae, half-human.

Camille Sepharial te Maria, aka Camille D'Artigo: The oldest sister; a Moon Witch and Priestess. Half-Fae, half-human.

Daniel George Fredericks: The D'Artigo Sisters' half cousin; FBH.

Delilah Maria te Maria, aka Delilah D'Artigo: The middle sister; a werecat.

Hester Lou Fredericks: The D'Artigo Sisters' half cousin; FBH.

Maria D'Artigo: The D'Artigo Sisters' mother. Human. Deceased.

Menolly Rosabelle te Maria, aka Menolly D'Artigo: The youngest sister; a vampire and *jian-tu*: extraordinary acrobat. Half-Fae, half-human.

Sephreh ob Tanu: The D'Artigo Sisters' father. Full Fae. Deceased.

Shamas ob Olanda: The D'Artigo Sisters' cousin. Full Fae. Deceased.

The D'Artigo Sisters' Lovers and Close Friends

Astrid (Johnson): Chase and Sharah's baby daughter.

Bruce O'Shea: Iris's husband. Leprechaun.

Carter: Leader of the Demonica Vacana Society, a group that watches and records the interactions of Demonkin and human through the ages. Carter is half demon and half Titan—his father was Hyperion, one of the Greek Titans.

Chase Garden Johnson: Detective, director of the Faerie-Human Crime Scene Investigation (FH-CSI) team. Human who has taken the Nectar of Life, which extends his life span beyond any ordinary mortal and has opened up his psychic abilities.

Chrysandra: Waitress at the Wayfarer Bar & Grill. Human. Deceased.

Derrick Means: Bartender at the Wayfarer Bar & Grill. Werebadger.

Erin Mathews: Former president of the Faerie Watchers Club and former owner of the Scarlet Harlot Boutique. Turned into a vampire by Menolly, her sire, moments before her death. Human.

Greta: Leader of the Death Maidens; Delilah's tutor.

Iris (Kuusi) O'Shea: Friend and companion of the girls. Priestess of Undutar. Talon-haltija (Finnish house sprite).

Lindsey Katharine Cartridge: Director of the Green Goddess Women's Shelter. Pagan and witch. Human.

Maria O'Shea: Iris and Bruce's baby daughter.

Marion Vespa: Coyote shifter; owner of the Supe-Urban Café.

Morio Kuroyama: One of Camille's lovers and husbands. Essentially the grandson of Grandmother Coyote. Youkai-kitsune (roughly translated: Japanese fox demon).

Nerissa Shale: Menolly's wife. Worked for DSHS. Now working for Chase Johnson as a victims-rights counselor for the FH-CSI. Werepuma and member of the Rainier Puma Pride.

Roman: Ancient vampire; son of Blood Wyne, Queen of the Crimson Veil. Menolly's official consort in the Vampire Nation and her new sire.

Queen Asteria: The former Elfin Queen. Deceased.

Queen Sharah: Was an elfin medic, now the new Elfin Queen; Chase's girlfriend.

Rozurial, aka Roz: Mercenary. Menolly's secondary lover. Incubus who used to be Fae before Zeus and Hera destroyed his marriage.

Shade: Delilah's fiancé. Part Stradolan, part black (shadow) dragon.

Siobhan Morgan: One of the girls' friends. Selkie (wereseal); member of the Puget Sound Harbor Seal Pod.

Smoky: One of Camille's lovers and husbands. Half-white, half-silver dragon.

Tanne Baum: One of the Black Forest Woodland Fae. A member of the Hunter's Glen Clan.
Tavah: Guardian of the portal at the Wayfarer Bar & Grill. Vampire (full Fae).
Tim Winthrop, aka Cleo Blanco: Computer student/genius, female impersonator. FBH. Now owns the Scarlet Harlot.
Trillian: Mercenary. Camille's alpha lover and one of her three husbands. Svartan (one of the Charming Fae).
Ukkonen O'Shea: Iris and Bruce's baby son.
Vanzir: Was indentured slave to the Sisters, by his own choice. Dream-chaser demon who lost his powers and now is regaining new ones.
Venus the Moon Child: Former shaman of the Rainier Puma Pride. Werepuma. One of the Keraastar Knights.
Wade Stevens: President of Vampires Anonymous. Vampire (human).
Zachary Lyonnesse: Former member of the Rainier Puma Pride Council of Elders. Werepuma living in Otherworld.

GLOSSARY

Black Unicorn/Black Beast: Father of the Dahns unicorns, a magical unicorn that is reborn like the phoenix and lives in Darkynwyrd and Thistlewyd Deep. Raven Mother is his consort, and he is more a force of nature than a unicorn.

Calouk: The rough, common dialect used by a number of Otherworld inhabitants.

Court and Crown: "Crown" refers to the Queen of Y'Elestrial. "Court" refers to the nobility and military personnel that surround the Queen. "Court and Crown" together refer to the entire government of Y'Elestrial.

Court of the Three Queens: The newly risen Court of the three Earthside Fae Queens: Titania, the Fae Queen of Light and Morning; Morgaine, the half-Fae Queen of Dusk and Twilight; and Aeval, the Fae Queen of Shadow and Night.

Crypto: One of the Cryptozoid races. Cryptos include creatures out of legend that are not technically of the Fae races: gargoyles, unicorns, gryphons, chimeras, and so on. Most primarily inhabit Otherworld, but some have Earthside cousins.

Demon Gate: A gate through which demons may be summoned by a powerful sorcerer or necromancer.

Demonica Vacana Society: A society run by a number of ancient entities, including Carter, who study and record the history of demonic activity over Earthside. The archives of the society are found in the Demonica Catacombs, deep within an uninhabited island of the Cyclades, a group of Grecian islands in the Aegean Sea.

Dreyerie: A dragon lair.

Earthside: Everything that exists on the Earth side of the portals.

Elemental Lords: The elemental beings—both male and female—who, along with the Hags of Fate and the Harvestmen, are the only true Immortals. They are avatars of various elements and energies, and they inhabit all realms. They do as they will and seldom concern themselves with humankind or Fae unless summoned. If asked for help, they often exact steep prices in return. The Elemental Lords are not concerned with balance like the Hags of Fate.

Elqaneve: The Elfin city in Otherworld, located in Kelvashan—the Elfin lands.

FBH: Full-Blooded Human (usually refers to Earthside humans).

FH-CSI: The Faerie-Human Crime Scene Investigation team. The brainchild of Detective Chase Johnson, it was first formed as a collaboration between the OIA and the Seattle police department. Other FH-CSI units have been created around the country, based on the Seattle prototype. The FH-CSI takes care of both medical and criminal emergencies involving visitors from Otherworld.

Great Divide: A time of immense turmoil when the Elemental Lords and some of the High Court of Fae decided to rip apart the worlds. Until then, the Fae existed primarily on Earth, their lives and worlds mingling with those of humans. The Great Divide tore everything asunder, splitting off another dimension, which became Otherworld. At that time, the Twin Courts of Fae were disbanded and their queens and Merlin were stripped of power. This was the time during which the Spirit Seal was formed and broken in order to seal off the realms from each other. Some Fae chose to stay Earthside, others moved to the realm of Otherworld, and the demons were—for the most part—sealed in the Subterranean Realms.

Guard Des'Estar: The military of Y'Elestrial.

Hags of Fates: The women of destiny who keep the balance righted. Neither good nor evil, they observe the flow of destiny.

When events get too far out of balance, they step in and take action, usually using humans, Fae, Supes, and other creatures as pawns to bring the path of destiny back into line.

Harvestmen: The lords of death—a few cross over and are also Elemental Lords. The Harvestmen, along with their followers (the Valkyries and the Death Maidens, for example), reap the souls of the dead.

Haseofon: The abode of the Death Maidens—where they stay and where they train.

Ionyc Lands: The astral, etheric, and spirit realms, along with several other lesser-known noncorporeal dimensions, form the Ionyc Lands. These realms are separated by the Ionyc Seas, a current of energy that prevents the Ionyc Lands from colliding, thereby sparking off an explosion of universal proportions.

Ionyc Seas: The currents of energy that separate the Ionyc Lands. Certain creatures, especially those connected with the elemental energies of ice, snow, and wind, can travel through the Ionyc Seas without protection.

Kelvashan: The lands of the elves.

Koyanni: The coyote shifters who took an evil path away from the Great Coyote; followers of Nukpana.

Melosealfôr: A rare Crypto dialect learned by powerful Cryptos and all Moon Witches.

The Nectar of Life: An elixir that can extend the life span of humans to nearly the length of a Fae's years. Highly prized and cautiously used. Can drive someone insane if he or she doesn't have the emotional capacity to handle the changes incurred.

Oblition: The act of a Death Maiden sucking the soul out of one of her targets.

OIA: The Otherworld Intelligence Agency; the "brains" behind the Guard Des'Estar. Earthside Division now run by Camille, Menolly, and Delilah.

Otherworld/OW: The human term for the "United Nations" of Faerie Land. A dimension apart from ours that contains creatures from legend and lore, pathways to the gods, and various other places, such as Olympus. Otherworld's actual name varies among the differing dialects of the many races of Cryptos and Fae.

Portal, Portals: The interdimensional gates that connect the different realms. Some were created during the Great Divide; others open up randomly.

Seelie Court: The Earthside Fae Court of Light and Summer, disbanded during the Great Divide. Titania was the Seelie Queen.

Soul Statues: In Otherworld, small figurines created for the Fae of certain races and magically linked with the baby. These figurines reside in family shrines and when one of the Fae dies, their soul statue shatters. In Menolly's case, when she was reborn as a vampire, her soul statue re-formed, although twisted. If a family member disappears, his or her family can always tell if their loved one is alive or dead if they have access to the soul statue.

Spirit Seals: A magical crystal artifact, the Spirit Seal was created during the Great Divide. When the portals were sealed, the Spirit Seal was broken into nine gems and each piece was given to an Elemental Lord or Lady. These gems each have varying powers. Even possessing one of the spirit seals can allow the wielder to weaken the portals that divide Otherworld, Earthside, and the Subterranean Realms. If all of the seals are joined together again, then all of the portals will open.

Stradolan: A being who can walk between worlds, who can walk through the shadows, using them as a method of transportation.

Supe/Supes: Short for Supernaturals. Refers to Earthside supernatural beings who are not of Fae nature. Refers to Weres, especially.

Talamh Lonrach Oll: The name for the Earthside Sovereign Fae Nation.

Triple Threat: Camille's nickname for the newly risen three Earthside Queens of Fae.

Unseelie Court: The Earthside Fae Court of Shadow and Winter, disbanded during the Great Divide. Aeval was the Unseelie Queen.

VA/Vampires Anonymous: The Earthside group started by Wade Stevens, a vampire who was a psychiatrist during life. The group is focused on helping newly born vampires adjust to their new state of existence, and to encourage vampires to avoid harming the innocent as much as possible. The VA is vying for control. Their goal is to rule the vampires of the United States and to set up an internal policing agency.

Whispering Mirror: A magical communications device that links Otherworld and Earth. Think magical video phone.

Y'Eírialiastar: The Sidhe/Fae name for Otherworld.

Y'Elestrial: The city-state in Otherworld where the D'Artigo girls were born and raised. A Fae city, recently embroiled in a civil war between the drug-crazed tyrannical Queen Lethesanar and her more level-headed sister Tanaquar, who managed to claim the throne for herself. The civil war has ended and Tanaquar is restoring order to the land.

Youkai: Loosely (very loosely) translated as Japanese demon/nature spirit. For the purposes of this series, the youkai have three shapes: the animal, the human form, and the true demon form. Unlike the demons of the Subterranean Realms, youkai are not necessarily evil by nature.

PLAYLIST FOR *DARKNESS RAGING*

I write to music a good share of the time, and so I always put my playlists in the back of each book so you can see which artists/songs I listened to during the writing. Here's the playlist for *Darkness Raging*:

3 Doors Down: "Kryptonite"

A. J. Roach: "Devil May Dance"

AC/DC: "Hells Bells"; "Back in Black"

Adam Lambert: "Mad World"

Adele: "Rumour Has It"

Air: "Playground Love"

Alice Cooper: "Welcome to My Nightmare"; "Wish You Were Here"

Android Lust: "Here and Now"; "Saint Over"; "Dragonfly"; "Stained"

Beck: "Farewell Ride"; "Emergency Exit"

Black Angels, The: "Evil Things"; "Holland"; "Broken Soldier"; "Young Men Dead"; "You're Mine"

Black Mountain: "Queens Will Play"

Black Rebel Motorcycle Club: "Feel It Now"

Bob Seger: "Turn the Page"

Bon Jovi: "Wanted Dead or Alive"

Bravery, The: "Believe"

Broken Bells: "The Ghost Inside"

Bryan Adams: "Run to You"

Buffalo Springfield: "For What It's Worth"

Cat Power: "I Don't Blame You"

Celtic Woman: "Scarborough Fair"

Chris Isaak: "Wicked Game"

David Bowie: "I'm Afraid of Americans"

Depeche Mode: "Blasphemous Rumors"

Eastern Sun: "Beautiful Being (Original Edit)"

Eels: "Souljacker Part I"

FC Kahuna: "Hayling"

Feeling, The: "Sewn"

Fluke: "Absurd"

Garbage: "Queer"; "#1 Crush"; "Bleed Like Me"

Gary Numan: "When the Sky Bleeds, He Will Come"; "Dominion Day"; "The Angel Wars"; "Hybrid"; "Melt"; "My Shadow in Vain"; "Petals"; "Walking with Shadows"; "Down in the Park"; "I Am Dust"; "Here in the Black"; "Everything Comes Down to This"; "My Breathing"

Gorillaz: "Demon Days"; "Kids with Guns"; "Clint Eastwood"; "Stylo"

Jessica Bates: "The Hanging Tree"

Lorde: "Yellow Flicker Beat"

M.I.A.: "Bad Girls"

Marilyn Manson: "Personal Jesus"; "Tainted Love"; "Arma-Goddamn-Motherfuckin-Geddon"

Mark Lanegan: "The Gravedigger's Song"; "Phantasmagoria Blues"; "Methamphetamine Blues"

Matt Corby: "Breathe"

Motherdrum: "Big Stomp"

Nine Inch Nails: "Head Like a Hole"; "Deep"; "Down in It"

Nirvana: "You Know You're Right"; "Rape Me"; "Heart Shaped Box"

Orgy: "Blue Monday"; "Social Enemies"

A Pale Horse Named Death: "As Black as My Heart"; "Bathe in My Blood"; "When Crows Descend upon You"

People in Planes: "Vampire"

Puddle of Mudd: "Famous"; "Psycho"

R.E.M.: "Drive"

Rachel Diggs: "Hands of Time"

Rammstein: "Wollt Ihr das Bett in Flammen Sehen"; "Rammstein"; "Ich Will"; "Sensucht"

Rob Zombie: "Living Dead Girl"; "Never Gonna Stop"; "Mars Needs Women"

Screaming Trees: "Where the Twain Shall Meet"; "Dime Western"; "Gospel Plow"

Simple Minds: "Don't You (Forget about Me)"

Soundgarden: "Fell on Black Days"; "Superunknown"; "Black Hole Sun"

Stone Temple Pilots: "Atlanta"; "Sour Girl"

Sweet Talk Radio: "We All Fall Down"

Tamaryn: "While You're Sleeping, I'm Dreaming"

Tina Turner: "One of the Living"

Toadies: "Possum Kingdom"

Tom Petty: "Mary Jane's Last Dance"

Verve, The: "Bitter Sweet Symphony"

Voxhaul Broadcast: "You Are the Wilderness"

Warchild: "Ash"

Wumpscut: "The March of the Dead"

Zero 7: "In the Waiting Line"

Dear Reader:

I hope you have enjoyed Darkness Raging. *Please be aware: This series will continue, but you* will *need to check my website for more information on when, where, and how to find the next three Otherworld books.*

Up next in my release schedule from Berkley will be Flight from Mayhem*—the second Fly by Night book! Alex and Shimmer are taking on a serial killer with a very special power, one that lands Bette in deep trouble and the Fly by Night Magical Investigations Agency in a panic! Look for* Flight from Mayhem *in August. You'll find a special excerpt that follows on the next page.*

Then in September, I invite you to meet me in Whisper Hollow once again, with Dreaming Death*—the second Whisper Hollow book!*

Thank you so much for your support, and I will see you in the next book. For information on all my upcoming releases, and all my books, please visit my website at Galenorn.com.

Bright Blessings,
The Painted Panther
Yasmine Galenorn

The wind blew through my hair, streaming it back under the helmet as the massive engine purred between my legs, vibrating through my entire body. I gripped Alex's waist with my hands, my breasts pressing against his back as we leaned into the turn. His body was icy even through his butt-hugging jeans and snug leather jacket. He smelled like Bay Rum, and by now, I knew that scent all too well. I knew every curve of his body—six weeks of steady sex had ensured that.

We were headed toward the 520 Bridge, and as we neared the floating bridge that stretched out for over a mile over the lake separating Seattle from the Greater Eastside, I could feel the call of the water—a deep, sensual recognition that washed through my core, making me ache for its depths. The water and I had a special connection, seeing that I was a blue dragon and my very nature was connected to the life-affirming liquid. But tonight we weren't headed to the beach so I could swim. No, it was party time.

I wasn't sure exactly where we were going, but apparently

Bette was in charge of it, and that was all Alex would tell me. "Unless you've been to one of Bette's parties, you've never been to a party."

With that less-than-comforting thought ringing in my head, I swung onto the back of his Suzuki Hayabusa and held on as we swung out into the April night, under a heavy cloud cover. As we wove through the silent city streets, Alex deftly maneuvered the rumbling machine through the labyrinth of roads. Seattle had to have been planned out by some drug-crazed cartographer who randomly decided to have one-way streets change direction at major intersections.

As we gobbled up the miles, the streets grinding beneath the bike's wheels, I glanced up at the pale shadow of the moon. She was gleaming from behind the cloud cover, two days past full. We were on the bridge now, and the wind was churning the water to splash up and over the edge. To our left, the specter of the new bridge they were building rose into the air, a dark silhouette of a bigger, wider passage, a reminder of how outdated and potentially dangerous the current bridge had become. There was a one in twenty chance it would go down, floundering to the bottom, if the area had another major earthquake. And the chances of a major earthquake in Seattle? Were *when*, not if.

We passed a car that had stalled out, and then we were over Lake Washington and coming up on Bellevue. But we were headed to a private residence on Lake Sammamish in Redmond. Not Bette's—she lived on a houseboat at the Gasworks Marina—but her current beau's house. Apparently he was some software engineer at a startup that had firmly put down roots in the area. High tech was king here, and this was the land of Microsoft, Starbucks, and money.

I inhaled another breath of Alex's cologne. It was comforting—familiar in a world that was so alien to me. In my world, I had nothing like this. In my world, I was an outcast, pariah. Here, I mattered. At least in some small way.

We leaned into the gentle curve of the exit as we swung off of 520 and onto West Lake Sammamish Parkway NE. As we passed through the suburbs and past Marymoor Park, we came to a fork in the road, where the parkway split off into Bel-Red Road. We veered left, keeping on the parkway, as we curved toward Lake Sammamish. A few minutes later we swung onto NE 38th Street and down to the end next to Idylwood Park. To the left were a string of houses and we pulled into the driveway of the last one before the lakeshore. There were a string of cars already here. I gazed up at the house. It was huge—one of what were commonly called McMansions around these parts, and it had its own private beach access.

As Alex idled the motor, then switched it off, I unbuckled my helmet and slipped it off, shaking my hair free. I swung off the bike, hopping aside, as Alex put down the kickstand and then joined me. We hung the helmets over the handles of the bike and—as I ordered my hair to straighten itself and smooth out the frizz—we headed for the beach.

Alex wrapped his arm around my waist. One thing I'd say for him—he made an attentive boyfriend. I wondered for the umpteenth time why Glenda had let him get away. He was a handful when it came to stubbornness, but in the six weeks we had been going out, I had never once felt neglected. In fact, in some ways, the attention was overwhelming.

I was six feet tall, and Alex had me beat by an inch or so. His wheat-colored hair was tousled and shoulder length, and his eyes were pale—frosty. Handsome in a scruffy, rugged way, he also happened to be a vampire, and he also happened to be my boss and parole officer, so to speak.

"Where is everybody?" I glanced around, looking for the party site.

"Down at the edge of the water. Bette said they had a bonfire going." His arm still encircling my waist, we headed down the sloped road leading to the shore. There was a gate—of course. Around here, it seemed like everything fun was gated off for private amusement, but this one was open and the sounds of laughter filtered up from behind the foliage-thick hedges barring our view.

We wandered through the gate and within a couple of minutes, found ourselves on the lakeshore. Sure enough,

Bette was there, manning the massive grill. Covered with dogs and burgers, the smell set my stomach to grumbling. Now that I couldn't shift and eat myself a horse or a cow every now and then, I found that I had to eat every day, several times, just like humans, and it wasn't more than a couple hours and I was hungry again. That had been one of the most surprising discoveries when I came Earthside.

"I'm going to find Ralph. Go say hello to Bette for us." Alex gave me a slap on the ass and meandered off into the crowd.

I was slowly getting used to being around crowds—I'd been a loner most of my life, and in the Dragon Reaches, where the population was nowhere near the size of the human population, being a loner meant truly being alone. I glanced around, finally steeling myself to wander through the crowd of strangers over to Bette. But the next moment, a familiar voice intruded into my thoughts.

"Hey, Shimmer!"

I turned to find Ralph standing there, his Flying Horse energy drink in his hand. The man consumed caffeine like there was no end to it. He smiled, but I could tell something was unsettling him. The longer I was around others, the more I realized that I was somewhat of an emotional barometer. It was a blue dragon thing, though I hadn't realized it extended beyond my fellow dragons, and I wasn't sure just how comfortable I was with the fact that I could walk into a room and sense that Ralph was irritated at his family, or that Bette was hungering to jump her current boy-toy of the month.

Ralph nodded me off to the side. He was around five-eight and lanky, with brownish-black hair and John Lennon glasses, tinted dark. Good looking in a geek-chic way, Ralph was also a certified computer genius and a werewolf. Over the past few weeks, his crush on me had abated, especially since Alex and I had gotten together, and now the awkwardness had passed.

"Shimmer, I'm worried about Bette. Where's Alex?" He strained his neck, looking around. "I thought I saw you come in together."

"We did, but he took off toward . . . Hell, I don't know where he went. Is Chai here yet?" Chai was my best friend—a djinn—who had followed me when I got exiled from the Dragon Reaches to keep an eye on me. He was a good sort, though unpredictable like all djinns, and he had settled in as my roommate and did a great job at keeping the place spotless. He also significantly cut down on the heating bill by radiating enough heat when it got chilly to create a comfortable temperature.

Ralph shook his head. "Not that I know of. Anyway, Bette's putting on a good show but I caught her crying earlier, and you know how often *that* happens. When I asked her what was wrong, she pretended she had an eyelash in her eye, but those were real tears, all right."

The tone of his voice told me enough that he wasn't exaggerating. I glanced over at the Melusine, wondering how to approach her. She was flipping burgers onto a plate that Dent, her current beau, was holding. He was a software genius, and had made enough to afford a house on the lake. Ralph had told me in private that Dent was just a poser—that he really wasn't all that good at his job, but was able to fake his way through. But poser or not, he made Bette happy and that's all that mattered.

"I'll corner her and see if I can find out what's going on." But at that moment, my attention was violently yanked away when Alex's voice thundered over the murmuring of the crowd.

"I swear if you don't get your ass away from me, woman, I'm going to put the fang to you!"

What the hell? I glanced at Ralph, who shook his head. We headed in the direction of the outburst and as we threaded our way through the crowd, I suddenly realized that someone was standing next to Alex who I really didn't want to see.

"Oh crap." I face-palmed, shaking my head. "I don't want to deal with this right now."

"You and every other sane person on this planet," Ralph muttered.

There, standing in front of Alex, one hand on her hip, the

other shaking a finger in Alex's face, was the pleather-clad, red-haired succubus who I had hoped might have just fallen off the face of the Earth. Alex's ex-girlfriend, Glenda sure didn't live up to her namesake. She was a harpy-tongued bitch, rather than an enchanting witch, all right.

"You're pond scum, Alex Radcliffe. You bottom-feeder. Cocksucker! Motherfucker!"

Alex stared at her, a look of partial amusement and partial irritation on his face. "To think, I used to kiss that mouth. Glenda, what did you expect? You're the one who broke up with me, but it was far too long in coming. Face it, we're done. We were done years ago but neither one of us had the courage to let go. It was time. You weren't happy, and neither was I."

He shifted, darting away from her shaking finger. But his casual tone seemed to just fuel her fire.

"I should have drained you—I should have sucked your chi down to the core." Her voice kept rising, and now everybody was staring at them.

I tried to sidle out of the way, not wanting to draw her attention, but that was a hope gone to hell in a handbasket. As I stepped back, I accidentally bumped against one of the guests, and in trying to keep from knocking him over, I shifted too far the other way and promptly ended up losing my footing. I wavered, teetering on one foot, and then—in slow motion, like in the movies—I went careening into the pool, gasping as I was submerged into the chlorinated brine that masqueraded as water. As I bobbed to the surface, shaking my head and sputtering, I saw that every head had turned to stare at me.

Alex was staring at me with an incredulous look on his face. Then, before I could make a move to get out of the pool, he began to laugh, slapping his thigh. "Oh, Shimmer, bless you for breaking up this little tête-à-tête. I needed that laugh. Get out of there, woman, and dry off."

Glenda gave him a seething look. "How dare you ignore me?" The clap of her hand against his face echoed through the air.

Alex stopped laughing. His eyes turned a dangerous shade of crimson and he let out a low hiss. "Don't you ever strike me again, Glenda. Not if you value your life. I put up with your tantrums for too long, but no more. Hit me again at risk of your life. *Do you understand?*"

Ten seconds flat to turn him from an easygoing ex-pat Aussie to a deadly predator.

Glenda's eyes widened as she took a step back. "This isn't over, Radcliffe." Then, she suddenly turned my way as I swung myself out of the pool and began to wring out my hair, the scent and taste of chlorine making me queasy. "And you . . . you'd better hope we never cross paths. I blame you for this—you got your hooks into him. I knew from the start that's what you were out to do."

I stared at her, a cold rush washing through me—and it wasn't the fact that I was soaked through and the wind had picked up. "You need to rethink that little threat, Glenda. You may be a succubus, but let me remind you that *I* am a dragon."

She locked my gaze for a moment, then snorted. "Yeah, a neutered one. You can't even change shape when you're out of water."

I was about to make a retort when Chai showed up. Over seven feet of gorgeous, muscled golden body, with a high ponytail—jet black—and seafoam-colored eyes, the djinn cut a formidable figure in his formfitting V-neck tee, and the jeans that he had assumed as his clothing for the day. I envied him his ability to create a wardrobe out of wishes—he could wear anything he wanted without worrying about the cost. But right now, clothes were the last thing on his mind.

He leaned over Glenda, and she actually cowered back. "If you ever threaten my little sister again, I will personally stuff you in a bottle, seal it shut, and toss you out on the Ocean of Agony. Do you understand?"

Glenda let out an audible gulp, fear washing across her face. "I was just about to leave."

"Then, may I suggest you go *now*?" Chai's voice, which could boom so loud, was barely above a whisper but somehow it seemed a far worse threat than if he had been yelling.

Glenda whirled on her stiletto heels and marched off, not saying another word. Alex and Chai watched her, both with grim expressions on their faces. I shivered as Ralph handed me a towel. Bette was hurrying her way over with Dent by her side.

"Are you okay, Shimmer? I'm sorry you took an unexpected dip." Dent seemed perfectly amiable, if a little bland. "I don't know if I have anything that will fit you, except a terrycloth robe, but if you want to change into that, we can wash and dry your clothes while you wait."

I ran the towel over my hair, squeezing out as much water as possible. "Thanks, I'd appreciate that."

Alex touched my elbow. "I'm so sorry about Glenda. She's a real . . . well, she's got a temper on her and it looks like she's decided to blame me for the breakup. But why now?"

"I know why. She found out we're together. She doesn't want you, but she doesn't want anybody else to have you, either." I shook my head. "She's a real winner, that's for sure."

Bette cocked her head. "Follow me. Dent, take over the burgers, would you? I'll show Shimmer to the bathroom where she can shower and dry her hair while I find her a robe. Chlorine leaves a nasty residue." She linked her arm through mine and began to steer me toward the path leading up to the house, leaving Ralph, Alex, and Chai to discuss Glenda's inopportune appearance.

"You okay, sugar?" Bette was the chain-smoking, leather-clad, curse-like-a-sailor grandmother I never had. Clad in leopard print jeggings, a chartreuse V-neck body suit, and a black leather jacket, she was loud and nasal, with a bouffant so high it rivaled Marge Simpson's hair. How she managed to navigate on the platform CMPs she wore confounded me. But Bette was also, by now, a good friend, and had introduced me to several delightful Earthside delicacies, like Sees Candies—though I didn't have much of a sweet tooth—and dripping, oozy fast-food cheeseburgers.

I nodded. "Yeah, I am. Glenda had better watch out, though, or Alex will take her down. He's a gentleman, but not when threatened and she crossed a line tonight."

"You aren't spoiling for a catfight, are you? Because honey, I know you're a dragon, but Glenda's mean as a junkyard dog, and she's got a lot of tricks up her sleeve. She wouldn't hesitate to fight dirty." Bette sounded so concerned that I wanted to hug her.

"Nope, not spoiling for a fight at all. I'd be happier if she just disappeared. But you . . . Bette—Ralph said he thought something was wrong, and I sense it, too. What's going on? Your smile is pretty much skin deep right now." Now that I was next to her, I could tell that she was upset over something. The emotion radiated off of her in waves. "Are you upset at Dent?"

She blinked. "Dent? Why would I be? No, he's just a little bit of fun right now, and both he and I know that. But now that you mention it, I am worried, but it's not about me—it's about a friend."

"Ralph? Alex?"

"No, no one you know." She led me into a large bedroom that was decked out in black and white, with potted palms. The floors were hardwood, thank goodness, so I wasn't saturating the carpet with the water that trickled off my clothing. She held up one hand, while darting into an enormous walk-in closet, then returned with a thick, plush terrycloth robe. It was a pale shade of blue, and I smiled. My favorite.

"There's a bathroom through that door. Take a shower and warm up, get the chlorine off you. And on the vanity, you'll find a blow dryer so you can dry your hair. If you need anything, let me know. There are clean towels on the side of the vanity."

I wanted to ask more about who she was worried about, and why, but decided that could wait till I got the chlorine off me. I hated the stuff, and it didn't like me much, either. I seemed to get a reaction to it, and that had put a dent in my swimming in pools for a while, until I'd managed to find a saline pool nearby and signed up for a membership there.

Slipping out of my wet clothes, I stepped into the shower, the warm water streaming over my body. Dent probably wasn't the one who used honeysuckle body wash—I had smelled it on Bette before—so I figured the bottle was hers. I lathered up, soaping away the stink of the chlorine. It didn't exactly burn me, but I noticed a pale rash that rose up when I went too long without washing after it touched any significant portion of my body.

Glenda's arrival nagged at me. I wasn't seriously worried she would hurt me—regardless of my temporary limit on powers, I could still beat the crap out of her, though I had doubts my water magic would affect her in any significant way. But the fact that she had decided to interfere meant something was up. She hadn't moved on, and considering the way she ill-used Alex, I had the feeling that she was finding it difficult to dig up somebody else who would put up with not only her violent temper, but her inborn need to fuck every man she saw. Succubi weren't cut out for relationships. Neither were incubi. And yet, some of them—against all odds—kept trying.

After I finished, I stepped out of the shower and wrapped my towel around me, then another around my hair. As I padded over to the vanity, I saw that Bette had taken away my wet clothes, and had laid out the blow dryer and the robe. I toweled the water away, then slid into the robe and tied it tight.

I stared at myself in the mirror. Six months ago, I had been sent Earthside. Exiled for a crime that I fully admitted to. The alternative was to stay in the Dragon Reaches and let Greanfyr—the white dragon I had stolen from—hunt me down and execute me. And if he did, nobody would raise a wing to stop him, given my persona non grata status.

As I softly ordered my hair to untangle itself, the shimmering streaks of blue and purple gleamed among the dark strands. They were natural. They indicated who—or rather, what—I was and were as much a part of me as was my tattoo. My ink was a reminder to me that I belonged, when everybody else said I didn't. A blue dragon, the tattoo coiled up from my waist with the tail curling near my hip. The dragon slinked up my right side, surrounded by waves, curling up so that the neck and head coiled over my right shoulder and down my arm, with more ocean waves along the side.

I flipped on the blow dryer, the heat warming me as I instructed my hair to section out, holding itself away from my head while I aimed the blowing air at it. That was one lovely thing about being a dragon—my hair had a mind of its own and I could make it behave however I wanted. Which was why—when the Wing-Liege cut it—it had hurt me so much, and been so painful. Our hair was part of our body, a part of our mane when we were in dragon form, and unlike humans and Fae, it had nerve endings and could register pain and pleasure. Touching Alex's skin with my hair gave me a thrill, even as having someone yank on it could hurt like a son of a bitch.

As the hair fell into place, smoothing softly against my head in clean, gleaming lines, I began to shake off the evening so far. Earlier in the afternoon, I had been uneasy about coming here. I thought it was just because I would have to face a bunch of strangers and pretend to be Fae—my cover was that of a water Fae, a nymph, to be exact. Humans didn't really know about dragons, and we aimed to keep it that way as much as possible. But something had set me on edge, and now I wondered if I had been anticipating Glenda showing up.

When my hair was dry and smooth, I slid my feet into the plush terry slippers Bette had left next to the robe and headed into the bedroom to find her sitting there, checking her phone, with a worried frown on her face. She glanced up as I sat down beside her.

"All washed up and clean?"

"Yeah, the chlorine is off my skin, so I should be fine. You get some bad news?" I leaned back in the chair, thoroughly enjoying the soft sinking feeling of the cushions.

Bette looked about ready to say "no" but then she paused. "I'm not sure if it's bad news or not. That's the problem. I told you I'm worried about a friend, right?"

She seemed reluctant to say anything, which meant she wasn't at all sure on what she was chewing on. I knew Bette and she wasn't reticent with her opinions unless she really wasn't clear on what she thought about something.

I nodded. "Right. Why don't you tell me and we can decide if it's bad news together?" I motioned to the robe. "I really don't feel like wandering around in a group of strangers wearing nothing but a bathrobe. Plus it will give them time to change the subject to something other than Glenda,

Alex, and me." Grinning, I stuck my feet up on the ottoman and settled back, thinking that if Dent had this kind of furniture, I'd consider hanging out with him, too.

Bette lit up a cigarette and, as usual, let it dangle off her lip. I was about to ask if Dent let her smoke inside, but then saw a few ashtrays scattered around, which meant he probably smoked, too. Bette was no fool—she never got involved with nonsmokers or teetotalers who might try to curb her habits. But she was also gracious enough to refrain from lighting up in my house, or over at Ralph's, and she kept her smoke downwind.

As she inhaled deeply, then blew out a ring to make even a dragon jealous, she gave me a little shrug and put her own feet up. "All right. I hate telling secrets—it sounds so ridiculous at times, but, fuck a duck, this has been eating me up. I don't know if you realized that I go down to volunteer at the Supe Community Council once a week. I teach an art class."

I stared at her. It was hard to imagine Bette doing anything of the sort. But I kept quiet and nodded.

"So, a lot of my students tend to be elderly Fae—mostly Earthside. They're . . . think of them like the great-aunt in the upstairs attic. They've lost just enough strength and vitality to lack confidence, but they're still in fairly good health. Which means another few hundred years to go before they die, but they aren't ready to die just yet."

I knew very little about the Fae when they aged—my kind tended to keep to themselves for the most part. It was mostly due to arrogance, but regardless of the cause, there were few dragons who took an interest in the outside world, or outsiders for that matter. We tended to be an insular race.

Bette puffed on her cigarette. "So, the problem is this: I have a student there, a friend really. Her name is Marlene, and she's one of the Woodland Fae. She's a lovely woman, but she's drifting, really. When the Fae get as old as she is, especially the nature Fae, they tend to get a bit . . ." She looked like she was trying to find a polite word for what she was thinking.

Ever helpful, I said, "Balmy?"

A nod, then—"Yeah, balmy sums it up. Marlene and I get together and play poker, and we watch movies, and take walks in her garden because she's too old to go out in the wild anymore, but I keep an eye on her, you know? Make certain that she's eaten lately and isn't just sitting in the garden, dozing during the rain."

I sighed. In my realm, when dragons reached that age, they slept in their dreyeries until they never woke up again. They were treated by their families as sleeping gods, venerated and waited on. But among humans—and some of the Fae—the aging ones were treated with less respect, and often just left on their own, discarded like used tissue.

"I understand. You make sure she's okay, and that's a good thing, Bette. But what's the problem?"

"Marlene told me a few days ago that she's dating a young man. I was surprised—she's no Melusine, and she's never mentioned wanting to explore that side of her life again. In fact, I thought she was pretty much over any interest in anything but pottering around. But she told me he makes her feel young, and that he romances her." A dark look flashed through her eyes. "I don't trust him, Shimmer. Marlene's a lovely woman but she's not a cougar, and she's very, very wealthy."

I blinked at that. Vampires tended to accumulate wealth. The Fae? Some of them did, but Woodland Fae weren't that interested in material goods, especially the Earthside ones.

"You think he's out for a sugar mama?"

Bette croaked out a laugh. "Pumpkin, I think he's out to get what he can. I can't come out and tell Marlene what I think, though—it would hurt her feelings terribly. So I'm going to just have to bite the bullet and find out what I can behind the scenes. I'm going to ask Alex if he minds if I use Ralph's know-how to see what we can find out about the guy. I need his last name, though, and she hasn't given it to me. I'm supposed to meet her for lunch tomorrow, and thought I'd be able to pick up a few more tidbits then. Would you mind joining us? I know you can read emotion, even though you try to hide it."

I stared down my nose at her. "Oh, really?" Even though

she was spot-on, it surprised the hell out of me to hear that she knew. I hadn't mentioned it to anybody but Alex. But then, he and Bette were thick as thieves and for all I knew, she was privy to our entire relationship.

"Shimmer, you've been working with us for almost seven months. By now, you should know that there aren't any secrets in the office." She cackled, then, and puffed on her cigarette again before tamping it out in one of the ashtrays. "Which is why I can tell you this. Glenda? She's not done with the pair of you. I'd expect trouble from that little bitch, because honey, you cross a succubus? You've got a mess of worms on your plate."

And with that lovely thought filling my head, I agreed to have lunch with Bette and Marlene the next day, but even as she brought me my clothes—now clean and dry—all I could think of was Glenda, the bad and brazen, and what revenge she might be planning.

New York Times bestselling author **Yasmine Galenorn** writes urban fantasy, mystery, and metaphysical nonfiction. A graduate of Evergreen State College, she majored in theater and creative writing. Yasmine has been in the Craft for more than thirty-four years and is a shamanic witch. She describes her life as a blend of teacups and tattoos, and she lives in the Seattle area with her husband, Samwise, and their cats. Yasmine can be reached at her website at galenorn.com, via Twitter at twitter.com/yasminegalenorn, and via her publisher. If you send her snail mail, please enclose a self-addressed stamped envelope if you want a reply.